Praise for Susan King and her novels

"HISTORICAL ROMANCE AT ITS BEST."
—Rexanne Becnel

"A consummate storyteller."—*Publishers Weekly*

The Sword Maiden

"King deftly spins a mystical Highland romance between the daughter of a Scottish clan leader and a humble blacksmith. . . . A keen ear for dialogue and the ability to create multifaceted characters who capture the reader's sympathy." —*Publishers Weekly*

"Magic, myth, and history blend to perfection as master storyteller Susan King lifts readers to new heights, enchanting them with tales of valor, magic, and passion. . . . Allow yourself to be awed by Ms. King's wizardry and swept away by her three-dimensional characters in a story to rival the greatest legends."
—*Romantic Times* (Top Pick)

"The bewitching fairy tale . . . creates a vivid, masterful setting that swept this reader away. . . . [It] kept me on the edge of my seat until the very last page. . . . *The Sword Maiden* is a story that historical romance fans will not want to miss, and if you have never tried a historical romance before, I highly recommend that you pick up a copy of *The Sword Maiden*, and let it sweep you off your feet!"
—The Romance Readers Connection

continued . . .

The Swan Maiden

"With its well-conceived plot, fast pacing, and strong visual elements . . . this feisty historical romance will enchant."
—*Publishers Weekly*

"Enchanting . . . Ms. King pulls the readers into the period, involves them in the action, and stirs their hearts."
—*Rendezvous*

The Stone Maiden

"Susan King—whose research into the territory of time and period is evident—strongly draws readers into the plot and her characters' lives."
—*Publishers Weekly*

"Filled with excitement. Susan King shows why she is considered by fans and critics to be one of the monarchs of the genre."
—*Midwest Book Review*

The Heather Moon

"Passion, adventure, and history abound in *The Heather Moon* . . . an excellent escape into the days of yore."
—*Affaire de Coeur*

"A must for fans of Scottish romances."
—*Romantic Times*

Laird of the Wind

"King spins a complex, mesmerizing story . . . lyrical, compelling, exquisitely vivid."
—*Library Journal*

"A treasure."
—*Bell, Book & Candle*

Lady Miracle

"Masterful plotting, compelling love story—and more. . . . Extraordinary . . . mythically lovely . . . brilliant storytelling."
—*Publishers Weekly* (starred review)

"Marvelous and superb . . . truly a treat, like savoring a fine Belgian chocolate, reading her work is almost sinfully delicious."
—Painted Rock Reviews

The Raven's Moon

"A marvelous Scottish tale . . . absolutely wonderful characters, breakneck pacing, and a great setting. A real page-turner. I couldn't put it down."

—Patricia Potter

"King keeps the tension high. Nonstop outlaw raids, bone-chilling storms, bonds of kinship, feuds, spies, betrayals . . . all lead inexorably to an explosive resolution." —*Publishers Weekly*

The Angel Knight

"Magnificent . . . richly textured with passion and a touch of magic." —Mary Jo Putney

"Susan King has written a romance of tremendous beauty and heart. Her books will stand the test of time." —*Affaire de Coeur*

The Raven's Wish

"Powerful, magical, and delightful . . . will keep readers on the edge of their seats." —*Romantic Times*

"Susan King [has] the heart of a romantic, the deft touch of a poet, and a historian's eye for detail."

—Rexanne Becnel

The Black Thorne's Rose

"Magnificent." —Virginia Henley

"Excellent . . . filled with mythical legends and deep-rooted superstitions that add mystery and mayhem to an extremely powerful story." —*Rendezvous*

"Fantastic. . . . A medieval tapestry that will enchant the reader." —*Affaire de Coeur*

ALSO BY SUSAN KING

Kissing the Countess

Waking the Princess

Taming the Heiress

The Sword Maiden

The Swan Maiden

The Stone Maiden

The Heather Moon

Laird of the Wind

Lady Miracle

The Raven's Moon

The Angel Knight

The Raven's Wish

The Black Thorne's Rose

"The Snow Rose" in *A Stockingful of Joy*

TAMING THE HEIRESS

Susan King

A SIGNET BOOK

SIGNET
Published by New American Library, a division of
Penguin Group (USA) Inc., 375 Hudson Street,
New York, New York 10014, U.S.A.
Penguin Books Ltd, 80 Strand,
London WC2R 0RL, England
Penguin Books Australia Ltd, 250 Camberwell Road,
Camberwell, Victoria 3124, Australia
Penguin Books Canada Ltd, 10 Alcorn Avenue,
Toronto, Ontario, Canada M4V 3B2
Penguin Books (N.Z.) Ltd, Cnr Rosedale and Airborne Roads,
Albany, Auckland 1310, New Zealand

Penguin Books Ltd, Registered Offices:
80 Strand, London WC2R 0RL, England

First published by Signet, an imprint of New American Library,
a division of Penguin Group (USA) Inc.

First Printing, July 2003
10 9 8 7 6 5 4 3 2 1

Printed in the United States of America

To David,
for his endless patience,
with love

Acknowledgments

Many thanks to many friends for support and some valuable plotstorming—especially to Mary Jo Putney, Patricia Rice, Pat Gagne, Jaclyn Reding, and Julie Booth. I'm very grateful to Victorian costume expert Meredith Bean McMath for dressing my characters from the inside out, and for suggesting that gorgeous Worth gown. Thanks are due also to ex–diving instructor and dear friend Linda Lawhorne for inspiring the diving scenes. And lastly, thanks go to Matt Jachowski—who knows why.

Prologue

Scotland, the Inner Hebrides
Summer, 1850

He washed out of a cold sea in darkness, finding a desperate grip on a huge rock that soared upward through crashing waves. As he lay motionless on the bulwark of rough stone, the water swept over him, withdrew, and surged high again.

Lungs burning, he crawled higher on the sloping rock and collapsed, shivering and naked. Peering through darkness and lashing rain, he gradually recognized the unique profile of his sanctuary: Sgeir Caran, the largest rock in the notorious Caran Reef that lay west of the Inner Hebridean islands. The half-mile crescent of black basalt rocks, many of them entirely submerged, formed a wicked lure of eddies and whirlpools, trapping countless boats and ships over the centuries. He had found safety in an unlikely place.

For now, it was enough to lie on the still, solid breast of the rock; enough just to breathe. He knew this reef, had studied and measured its jagged points in his capacity as a lighthouse engineer. He had listed the ships wrecked upon these rocks, had numbered the lives lost. A few of the names were known to him, for they were his own kin.

The reef had taken his parents, wrecking their ship and sinking it while they sailed on a holiday journey, having left their thirteen-year-old son and his sisters in the care of a relative. The devastating loss had forever changed the course of his life and had altered him heart and soul. He wondered, now, if he was destined to join them here.

Perhaps he had done so already, but with his usual obstinacy, he simply had not yet recognized death. He sank his head down and closed his eyes, clinging to the rock.

Pelting rain brought him back to awareness, and his shivers confirmed that he was indeed alive. The gale still raged, its black storm clouds swallowing the half-light of the Hebridean night sky. Daylight had been a warm glow when he sailed out, with no hint of a storm.

He had been a fool to come out alone, sodden drunk, on a dare. But Dougal Robertson Stewart, heir to the estates of Kinnaird and Balmossie, never turned down a challenge, never quailed at physical danger. He welcomed risk—but perhaps it was time to reconsider that, he told himself wryly, as he crawled naked up the black and slippery incline of the rock.

A high, fierce wave rose and crashed down over him while he scuttled out of the water's reach toward the long upper plateau of black basalt. Two hundred feet away, a stack rock soared in an eerie natural tower. Caves permeated the far end of Sgeir Caran, but Dougal was too exhausted to seek them out yet. He lay supine, summoning his strength while he watched the writhing, turbulent sea and felt the cold sting of rain on his bare back.

They had vanished, the beautiful ones who had carried him here through the storm. Graceful yet frightening, the creatures had appeared just as he was drowning in the deep. They had pulled him onto their backs and galloped forward with the waves, their manes pale froth, their hooves whipping the sea to wildness.

He had heard of the legendary sea kelpies, the water horses who raced through the foam. Tonight he had seen them himself, had twisted his fingers in their white manes and placed his feet on their magnificent backs while they carried him forward like the steeds of Neptune.

Or had he dreamed it?

My God, he thought, shoving a hand through his wet hair, *I am drunk, indeed, and in a sorry state.*

Concussed as well, for he had taken a blow to the head when his borrowed fishing boat had overturned in a high swell brought on by the sudden storm. Fighting to stay conscious, caught in restless waves, he had clung to the boat's underplanking. When his wet clothing dragged him under, he had stripped bare to save himself. As the boat sank, it sucked him downward—until a legion of pale horses had swept him onto the shoulder of the great rock.

As he got to his feet, an arching wave slammed over him. He grabbed a stony ridge to keep from washing into the water, but the force of the wave knocked his head against the rock. Helpless, he sank into a black void.

When he opened his eyes, he saw a perfect pair of bare feet.

Pale and delicate, perched mere inches from his face, the small toes and slender ankles showed beneath the hem of a white gown. Rain splashed the rock all around her, soaking the fabric of her garment.

A sea fairy, Dougal thought dimly. No mermaid, for she had lovely lower limbs.

As she sank to her knees, he saw the sweet blur of her face and simple chemise. Drenched hair spilled down in fine, small curls. She wore a blanket over her shoulders, which she slipped off to wrap around him, murmuring as she did so. The thick, warm wool felt divine, and her touch felt like heaven's own.

He began to thank her, but his hoarse voice failed.

"*Ach Dhia,* you are alive, then, and a man come out of the sea," she said, sounding calm despite the hellish storm. "I have waited here for you."

Gaelic. He understood some, spoke less than that. Had she said she had waited for him? He nodded uncertainly.

"Ach, you are cold and shivering. Not yet used to your human form, I think." She tucked the shawl higher. "When I waited here to keep our ancient promise, I thought I would be very afraid of you—but you are as weak as a babe just now. You may be a king in your world, but you need care in ours."

Ancient promise? He stared at her, uncomprehending. "I came out of the sea," he managed in awkward Gaelic. His mind was so muddled he could hardly think.

She smiled, and he heard the silver-bell sound of a fairy's laughter. A gust of wind took the rest of her reply. She took his arm and urged him to his feet. Rising on shaking legs, he felt like a babe, indeed. She tucked her shoulder under his arm and he leaned gratefully on her. Despite her elfin appearance, she felt solid, strong, and offered capable support.

"Who are you—" he croaked out, but the wind snatched words away, making any exchange nearly impossible. He set out over the rock with her, their heads bent against the gale, her gown and the blanket whipping and soaked.

Was she human and shipwrecked, too, in this wild place? Or had his nightmare transformed into a wondrous dream? Whoever—or whatever—she was, he was not alone here, and that made him deeply glad for her company. She seemed utterly magical, a spark of dancing light in the blackness, a fey creature made of gossamer and seafoam.

He knew some islanders still believed that the ocean was inhabited by kelpies, selkies, mermaids, sea fairies, blue men, and the like. Having witnessed the water horses of the Otherworld himself that night, he could easily believe that the girl might be made of magic in human form. Whatever she was, he thought of her as a sea fairy, for they were said to be beautiful and delicate and very kind creatures.

In an onslaught of wind and rain, he stopped and gathered her close under the plaid, shielding her slighter form with his tall, solid bulk. Waves slammed the rock, arching, drenching. Under the plaid, the girl clung to him, her arms around his waist as they withstood wind and lashing rain.

Again he wondered if he were dreaming. Either he was stranded naked on a Hebridean rock with a sea fairy—or had he made it back to shore and lay sleeping off the effects of Mrs. MacDonald's whisky, consumed during Mr. MacDonald's wake.

Vaguely he remembered a night of drinking, mourning, music, and fond stories of the deceased. He had swallowed too many drams out of politeness and camaraderie during a fine wake for a good man. When his companions had dared him and a friend to row a complete circuit of the reef, he had not turned down the challenge. The fellow who raced him had paused to retch over the side, and Dougal had rowed onward, into the mouth of the gale.

The girl cried out as the wind shoved and whipped. Dougal held her securely and kissed her brow to reassure her. Gazing over her head at the haze of rain, he wondered if he would die here on this rock, with this strange and beautiful sea fairy in his arms.

Seeing the black crease of a cave opening, he tugged her toward it. She stumbled and fell, and Dougal bent to sweep her into his arms, fighting the winds as he carried her inside the crevice. The niche was just large enough for them to huddle inside. He set her on her feet and she went again into his arms, a natural seeking of comfort and protection. They watched the storm, her cheek upon his chest, his arms wrapped around her.

Sheeting rain and shrieking winds broke large stones loose from the slope and sent them skating effortlessly into the sea. Waves loomed and crashed down over the rock, deluging the plateau, sliding away only to arch upward again.

Water swirled around their ankles in the little cave, and the spray stretched wraithlike toward them. Dougal turned his back to the opening to protect the girl from the sting of spray and the biting winds. Clasped in a shivery embrace, he remembered that he was nude and she nearly so, yet it did not seem to matter. Her curving form pressed against his harder planes generated a little blessed heat between them. That, and the solace of the other's presence, were far more important. He wondered, oddly, if fairies even cared about proprieties.

He sensed the moment when she relaxed against him rather than clung, when she conquered her fears and discovered her strength and confidence. Her breath fell into rhythm with his own, and she calmed and grew lush in his arms.

Desire, raw and sudden, rushed through him like a flame. As if she felt it, too, she pressed closer, nestled her brow against his cheek, wrapped her arms around his neck. Her thin, soaked chemise was no barrier between them, and her breasts were soft globes against his chest. The curve of her hip fit his hand, and the whole of her seemed to meld to him.

He did not know how the kiss began, the tilt of a cheek, the nudge of a chin. Lips touched, caressed. Her mouth was soft and willing, his exploring. Thunder boomed and the sea slammed the rocks below, and the next kiss was deep, wild, and desperate. One hungry kiss followed another like rushing waves. A fierce urgency blazed in him, something he could not seem to stop, something he had no words to question. He slanted his mouth over hers, wove his fingers into the dampness of her hair to tilt back her head. Her lips were fervent under his, and her immediate, willing passion seared him like a whisky brose, all cream and fire.

The raging storm faded from his awareness, and in its place he felt only this exquisite comfort, craved this offer of salvation at the gates of hell. He encircled her in his arms, his mouth tender on hers as he drank deep of the kiss, edged her lips with his tongue, found her lips inquisitive in return. Her small waist, the flare of her hips, was maddening. He throbbed, heart pounding, and wondered in a vague and dreamlike haze if he should stop.

She answered by taking his face in her hands and flattening her belly against the urgent hard core of him. That touch felt white-hot, charged with a need as desperate as his own. He pulled back, sucking in a breath. Rain and spray pummeled the overhanging arch, and he ducked farther into the little cave with her, leaning his back against slick rock, the plaid a damp curtain around them. She leaned against him, tilted her face upward, and her kiss was feverish and consuming.

Lightning crashed, rain sheeted down, loose stones skated over the plateau, and the great rock seemed to shiver underfoot. His only refuge from fear and death was the fervent, tender sanctuary of her embrace. Touching her, kissing her, he felt alive and invincible. He wanted her to feel that, too, and to take strength from it as well.

Sweeping his hands down her back, he pulled at her hips, snugged her against him, let her know—how could she not?—what he wanted. Desire burned hot enough now to take what was left of his reason. Cupping her breast, he stroked the nipple to vivid life, then turned to the other breast while the girl moaned intimately in his ear. She arched against him as he slid his fingers down her taut belly, tearing aside the damp film of her garment. When his fingers discovered her heated, moistened cleft, she moaned and surged against him, graceful as the sea.

A bright split of lightning flared toward the rock, and the girl whimpered in his arms, then arched and opened for him, wild, luscious, the sweetest rescue he could imagine. Sinking into her with a low groan, he shuddered and felt her shiver out her own release. He leaned heavily against the wall, heart slamming, and held her silently. She kissed him, and he tasted salt tears or the sea.

He still trembled, caught in the aftermath of the exquisite power of two souls poised at the brink of death, raw with fear, desperate for solace. Cradling her head in his hand, he kissed her wild, damp curls. She felt fragile and small, and he wanted to protect her, cherish her. Yet he feared that she might vanish into the mist, leaving him alone with the nightmare.

The onslaught of rain and crashing waves continued while she remained safe and warm and quiet, tucked in his arms. *I am dreaming,* he thought. *Surely I am dreaming.*

You know what you must do.

Margaret MacNeill leaned her back against the stone of the cave and looked out. Veils of fog obscured the sea and the long reef, but she saw that dawn approached. Rough greenish waves frothed over the edge of the great rock. Through the mist, she could not see the Isle of Caransay, her home, but she knew it lay a mile east of Sgeir Caran.

She glanced at the man who lay sleeping in the shallow cave beside her. All the while, her fingers worked the red thread she had plucked from the plaid that covered him.

You know what you must do, her great-grandmother had said. Well, it was done.

She wove the little thread with golden hairs from her head, deep brown from his. She had dreaded staying alone one night on Sgeir Caran, as island tradition demanded of her. Expecting a lonely, fearful night, she had never imagined that a legend would spring to life.

The legend snored as he slept, swathed in the plaid that her great-grandmother had woven. His dark head and one broad shoulder were visible. Shivering with the memory of secret, exciting touches, of soul-stirring kisses, she smiled to herself.

Deftly she plaited the threads and the hairs of two lovers into a love knot, then began to weave another thread and more gold and brown strands. When she had two tiny braids, she tied them into two circlets. Sliding one onto her finger, she crawled forward and slid the second one onto the finger of the sleeping man.

There, she thought. It was done, all as Mother Elga told her. The marriage made last night was fixed now. Touching his silken head for a moment, she sat back again by the entrance.

If the kelpie appears to you, her great-grandmother had instructed her, *you must go to him and ease his loneliness, for such is our ancient agreement. Every hundred years, the lord of the deep claims a maiden from Caransay for his bride. In return, he will protect the island from harm. If he has a child of that maiden, all the better for the islanders, for he will bestow great favor and fortune on them. And you know we need his help now more than ever.*

Meg had been educated in the island village and on the mainland, as well. She considered herself part of the modern world that existed beyond their remote little island, and she had dismissed the old beliefs as she gained womanhood. But her great-grandmother Elga and her grandmother Thora accepted the old legends as truths. The ancient tradition of the kelpie of Sgeir Caran, unique to Caransay, was greatly valued on the island.

She had agreed to sit out one night on the rock. The islanders faced broad eviction at the hands of an owner who preferred sheep and money to proud men and their families. Aware of that inevitable threat, Meg had told herself that one night on Sgeir Caran would do no harm.

She had never counted on gales—or kelpies. Bursting from the sea like a muscled arrow, the man had appeared on the rock while the storm that birthed him raged on. He was hard and beautiful and astonishingly real. She had expected to be frightened, but had felt compassion for him instead, for he was weak from his ordeal and in need of her help.

When he had smiled at her, her heart melted. As he had put his arms around her and kissed her, she had whirled helplessly into his spell, and she lingered there still.

The luscious, strange fog of Elga's potion—whisky and certain herbs—lingered, too. Last night that drink had fired her blood so that she had behaved with shocking freedom, expressing her passionate heart, swept along in a delirium of tenderness and powerful need.

Willingly, madly, she had fulfilled the ancient bargain—had even craved it. In the darkness and the rain, she thought she would die but for the succor of his arms.

In the light of day, she would not be able to live with herself. She ducked her head in hot shame, then reminded herself that he was magic—he was not real. What had happened between them lay outside normal experience. She need not be ashamed of such an extraordinary act.

She glanced at him, yearning to be in his strong, comforting arms again. But she must extricate herself from his spell or lose herself to his power forever. If he saw her in sunlight, if he touched her again, he would capture her and take her down to the deepest part of the sea, where she would be lost to the world always—or so the legend claimed.

That cannot be so, she told herself. But he had appeared. It must be so. She rubbed her eyes, feeling Elga's strong whisky potion still lingering in her blood.

He sighed in sleep, stretched, and the plaid fell away. In the grayish light before dawn Meg saw him clearly. He was long and lean, muscled tight, a powerful, beautiful man. His features had the uncommon symmetry of true beauty, and his hair was deep, shining brown, with straight black brows and black whiskers smudging his jaw. The dark hair on his chest tapered over his flat belly to his taut, nestled sex.

That sight made her belly tighten. She twisted the love knot on her finger, her cheeks blushing hot, and she saw his eyes flutter open. Sea green, as the legend said. But he must not see her now. She leaned back in the shadows, relaxing when he slept again.

In the silvery hour before dawn, she gazed at the man of the Otherworld, her husband by right of loving and ancient agreement. He had roused magic in her life, her body, her heart. An adoring, unquestioning devotion flowed through her.

He shifted again, stirring. Meg's heart pounded. A small voice told her that he must be a real man—that she was foolish to trust in the legend. Yet the voice of generations and the potion swirling through her told her that he was the *each-uisge* himself, the great sea kelpie, the most powerful of magical water creatures.

If he saw her, touched her, she would never again go home.

He stretched, yawned. Moving in sudden fear, Meg stepped out of the cave and fled, running barefoot over the rocky plateau while dawn brightened through the mist.

At the low end of the rock she saw a boat oared by her grandfather. He had kept his promise to come for her at dawn, and he had brought his wife, Thora, with him.

She gave in to impulse and ran down to the boat. Norrie handed her in and pulled away quickly, while Thora threw a thick plaid around her shoulders. The boat plowed through waves and fog toward Caransay.

Meg looked behind her. The man had risen, draping himself with the plaid. He stood in the cave entrance like some ancient warrior, gazing toward the west and the open sea. He did not turn to see their boat slip toward the east.

"He's there," Thora breathed. "He's there!" She clasped Meg in her arms.

"Huh," Norrie grunted, rowing.

Meg felt a deep tug on her heart. She could not leave him alone on the rock, no matter if she risked all that way. Turning to tell Norrie to go back, she glanced over Thora's shoulder—and saw the prow of a second boat glide through the mist toward the western side of the rock. Two men oared the vessel.

Walking down the slope, her lover waved to the approaching boat, then grabbed the rope the men tossed to him. When it drew close, he climbed in and was greeted with backslaps.

Fog slipped into the gap, and they vanished from sight.

Meg turned back. Her grandparents had not seen it, and Meg said nothing. Inside, she felt ill. She had lain not with the great kelpie, but with a man. Just a man.

Many knew of Caransay's ancient legend, but only Meg and her grandparents knew about her planned rendezvous for the previous night. Somehow, word must have gotten out—perhaps Elga had boasted—

and the man had come to the rock intent on sexual mischief, no doubt on a drunken bet. Even now, he was probably gleefully detailing his adventure to his friends.

Gasping, tears starting in her eyes, she bowed her head.

Thora hugged her. "I am sure the kelpie was tender and charming last night, for that is his way and his magic," she whispered. "If a child should come, we would rejoice and give it a loving home. And the kelpie will protect Caransay from harm, blessing us with good fortune for the sake of his family." She smiled.

Oh God, Meg thought. *A child.*

Chapter One

Strathlin Castle, near Edinburgh
July, 1857

"A home," Sir John Shaw said, sniffing as he peered down his bulbous nose, "for young women of questionable morals? Lady Strathlin, as a member of the board of Matheson Bank, once owned by your estimable grandfather, Lord Strathlin, I feel it my duty to advise you against such an unwise investment."

"Matheson House is hardly intended for women of ill repute, Sir John," Meg replied calmly. She folded her hands and faced him over her oak writing desk, which was set in a bright and pleasant corner of the library at Strathlin Castle. Morning sunlight streamed through the tall windows beside her, and the pale blues and golds in the Oriental carpet reminded her of the soothing colors of a Hebridean beach. That carpet, and the beautiful seascape painted in oils and hung over the library mantel, helped ease her bouts of homesickness. Even after seven years, she still missed the Isle of Caransay, though she visited there as often as she could.

A week from now, she would holiday on the island

once again. She drew a deeper, freer breath at the very thought.

Sir John regarded her with bleary eyes through a smudged monocle lens. "You are founding a home for unmarried young women who have borne children. These females have exceedingly poor morals, madam."

Meg frowned. "Sir, I have much sympathy for these women. Sometimes girls of good moral fiber find themselves in difficult circumstances and in need of shelter and medical care. I wish to provide help in such situations. That is all."

"May I remind you that you are the Baroness of Strathlin now, no longer—" He sniffed, leaving the rest unsaid.

"No longer Miss Margaret MacNeill of Caransay, a simple, provincial girl?" She smiled tightly. "Now I am Margaret, Lady Strathlin. My inheritance of my grandfather's title set some of the English lords on their ears, even though it is proper enough in good Scots peerage."

He gave a distinct harrumph and adjusted his monocle. "It was quite a burden for a female of your age, and some of us thought Lord Strathlin had gone mad to leave his fortune to you. Why, you barely spoke English when you first came here. Had no shoes, I think!" He snuffled a laugh.

She smiled, glad to encourage his awkward attempt at humor. "I did not speak good *Edinburgh* English, but I was educated and I learned that what is proper for everyone is also proper for a baroness. We are obligated to show compassion toward our fellows and our sisters, sir, regardless of our—or their—social position."

Nodding, she glanced at the unopened letters piled on a silver tray on her desk. There was much work to be done. Generally each morning she read mail and discussed the replies with her secretary, but Mr. Guy Hamilton had not yet arrived, and Sir John had stayed overlong.

"Madam, your fortune now exceeds that of the queen herself." Sir John sat forward, folding his hands on the head of his cane. "You can afford to support all the charities in Scotland if you wish. I urge you to fund this one anonymously. Sir Frederick advises it, as well, and recently expressed his concern to me."

"Sir Frederick Matheson has no business doing so."

"He is your cousin, madam, and also on the bank's board. I understand from Sir Frederick that he now is your fiancé, as well. May I offer my congratulations? It is an admirable match."

She stared at him. "He told you that?"

Sir John seemed to visibly squirm under her intent gaze. "Pardon me, madam. Sir Frederick is beside himself with happiness and blurted what was obviously a personal secret between you two, at least for now." He smiled stiffly.

"Sir Frederick did ask me to marry him, but I have not accepted. His news to you was . . . quite premature."

"Of course you will want to discuss any marriage arrangement with your advisers. In all fairness, the matter of your marriage is of such interest to the bank's board that it would be nearly impossible for you to enter an engagement without discussion."

"When I decide to marry, sir—if ever," she added, "I would make that decision from my heart, with the advice of only the man involved. I would hope the board would be accepting of it. However, I have no such news to report. Indeed, I may never wed," she murmured, glancing away. "I am grateful for my good fortune, but this inheritance . . . makes a loyal and loving relationship most difficult. It is not easy to trust any man who has affection for me. Surely you understand. And I hope you will discuss this with no one else. I value my privacy so very much."

He cleared his throat. "Well—aye—of course, lass. Madam," he stammered.

Folding her hands, she gave him a dry smile. "Thank you for your concern, Sir John. Please instruct the bank to disperse the funds to the new housekeeper at Matheson House as I require."

"Very well, madam." He stood. "A cheque will be sent."

She felt no sense of victory. "Thank you. Good day, Sir John." He bid her farewell and crossed the carpet to a set of double doors with etched-glass panes.

She sighed. Great wealth, while it had eased some paths in life, created thorny thickets in other parts of her existence. Though she had been able to help many people—including the islanders on Caransay when she had purchased that lease—she still bore a burden, secret and deep, that she would carry for the rest of her life. The gift of the kelpie, as her grandmothers called it, had brought her happiness, tremendous good fortune, and a beautiful son. And more heartsickness than she could imagine enduring.

Without the windfall of her considerable inheritance, she would have found herself in similar circumstances as the young women she wanted to help through her charitable institution.

Unmarried and secretly with child, Meg had been named heiress to Lord Strathlin's estate upon his sudden death. Aided by family and friends, protected by money, her secrets would never be known. Her child was safe on Caransay in the care of others.

Daily, she felt regret and sadness, and she knew she might never recover from the private shame of meeting—and loving—his nameless, unforgettable, despicable father.

Married. She wanted to laugh. According to old Scots law and her insistent grandmothers, she was already married.

Feeling her cheeks heat, she touched the little golden locket concealed beneath the neck of her day dress of dark blue satin brocade. The locket contained a tiny portrait of her blond-haired son and a ring woven of red thread and strands of hair. She wore it always.

Always, for she could not forget the passionate dreams of that night. And she saw her son only four times a year, so that the months without him tore at her heart. Strathlin Castle was a magnificent place to live, its old shell refurbished in grand style a century earlier, but it had never felt like home to her. The castle had too many rooms, too many possessions, and the niceties of existence were legion. She preferred the simplicity of island life, where days were vibrant with immediacy, where tradition created reassuring routine, and where the wondrous beauty and awesome power of Nature did not need to be imitated in pretty paintings or in the colors of an expensive carpet.

She glanced the long length of the library, where her companion and former governess, Mrs. Berry, sat reading in a far corner, her black skirts spilling out of the confines of a green leather wing chair. Meg's other constant companion, Mrs. Shaw, the young, widowed daughter-in-law of Sir John, was downstairs discussing the week's menus with the housekeeper. That duty Meg gratefully entrusted to her quiet, capable friend.

Both ladies had been of invaluable help to her over the past seven years, and one or the other made a concerted effort to be nearby whenever Meg met with male advisers and business acquaintances, as Mrs. Berry had unobtrusively done this morning.

A knock sounded on the door, and then a young maid, small and brown haired, dressed in dark gray with a white apron and cap, looked into the room. "Ma leddy, Mr. Hamilton is here."

"Thank you, Hester. Send him in, please."

Moments later, a tall, lean, dark-haired man crossed the room with a brisk step, his face familiar and welcome, his brown eyes twinkling. Meg smiled in delight to see her secretary.

"Good morning, Lady Strathlin." At her invitation,

Guy Hamilton sat in a blue brocaded chair opposite her desk. His long body was relaxed and agile as he settled himself, and the subtle air of verve that surrounded him somehow made her feel more energetic as well. "I do apologize for being late."

"No matter. I am simply glad to see you. Sir John was here, all in knots over my proposed home for young ladies."

"He can be a sour old screw, but he has your best interests at heart. I stopped by Uncle Edward's law office before coming here, or I would have helped you fend off Sir John. Hello, Mrs. Berry. On loyal duty, I see," he called pleasantly. Mrs. Berry smiled and waved, then went back to her reading.

"Mr. Hamilton, please look through these," Meg said, pushing a pile of letters toward him. "I've added a list of the replies I think necessary."

"Very good. Where is Mrs. Shaw this morning?" He glanced around the library, and Meg was sure that a slight flush spilled through Hamilton's shaven cheeks for a moment.

"Downstairs, making up menus with Mrs. Louden. They are all in a kerfuffle, as Mrs. Berry likes to say, over the soiree, though it's nearly two months away yet."

"It is certain to be an extravaganza." He smiled as he flipped through the letters.

Watching him, Meg saw the subtle etching of sadness in his fine brown eyes. Widowed years earlier, Hamilton had always kept his grief private and his mood calm and positive. He efficiently took care of his duties as Meg's secretary and more, overseeing her correspondence and her travel and social schedules. A new lawyer and new widower when Meg had first employed him as her secretary, Guy's gentle humor, graciousness, and innumerable kindnesses had endeared him to her as a treasured friend.

"Sir John told me that Sir Frederick also disapproves of Matheson House for Young Ladies. And apparently Sir Frederick told him that he and I are engaged to be married."

Hamilton frowned. "How very odd. Perhaps Sir Frederick was wrongly encouraged by your kindness."

She nodded. In the first years of her inheritance, she had valued Sir Frederick's banking counsel and enjoyed his social company, and later, when he was in deep mourning for his wife and his bills began to mount, she had rescued him from a financial deal that had gone sour. "The money was of no consequence to me. Far more important to show loyalty to a friend."

"My dear, you are a very generous friend, as I can attest myself. Years ago you paid my wife's medical expenses when the cost might have broken me. Not only generous, but lovely and good-hearted—and the richest woman in Scotland. Lady Strathlin, as a man, let me say that is a perfectly lethal combination."

"Oh," she said in surprise, feeling her cheeks heat.

"Any number of men are in love with you, and some will certainly scheme to marry you." He smiled mischievously. "Not me, my dear. I adore you, of course, but I have set you firmly on a pedestal, where you belong."

"I shall only topple." Meg laughed a little. "If I have any other suitors, they are better behaved than Sir Frederick. No one else has asked for my hand, or for cash funds, either."

"If any fellow makes unwanted advances toward you, I want to hear about it." Guy fisted a hand on the chair arm. His wide-shouldered capableness and the stalwart gleam in his eye were reassuring. "Let me speak to Matheson."

"Thank you, but I will speak to him. However, it must wait until I return from the Isles."

He nodded, then gestured toward the silver tray. "Quite a few letters this morning, I see."

"There's another basketful on the side table. There

seems to be a good number of acceptances for the soiree for Miss Jenny Lind in early September."

"I expect everyone will attend."

"Oh, there is so much to do beforehand." She felt a moment of panic, wondering how she ever let Angela Shaw convince her to do this, although Meg knew it would be gracious and considerate to host a soiree for the celebrated Swedish Nightingale. "Oh! Did you send an invitation to Mr. Dougal Robertson Stewart?"

"The engineer? Yes, a servant delivered it to his rooms last week. The man was difficult to find, and the invitation simply could not be sent by daily post. Most of the time he's out in some remote place putting up lighthouses, and his family seat is out in Strathclyde. Fortunately, he keeps rooms in town with relatives on Calton Hill. . . . I think you do very well to invite this Mr. Stewart. A gesture of truce, as it were."

"He is arrogant enough to see it as a gesture of surrender."

"When you finally meet him, I hope it will not come to blows," Guy said in a droll tone.

"I will behave if he does," she snapped. "His letters over the past several months have been insistent to the point of rudeness. And his latest action is a little declaration of war, in my opinion. Obtaining parliamentary permission to construct barracks on my island, when we denied him the right repeatedly, was—simply odious!"

"Mr. Stewart does whatsoever he wants, it seems."

"And is impatient, arrogant, and demanding in the process." She softened a little. "I do admire the fact that in his letters he continually shows consideration for the welfare of his men, but he has been simply obstinate in his dealings with my soliciting firm."

"I hear that in person he is the very devil for charm."

"His letters do not reflect a whit of it," she replied.

"Nonetheless, my sister-in-law, who knows him, says

that Mr. Stewart is seldom seen at parties—rather like his nemesis, Lady Strathlin." Guy grinned. "But when he does appear, she says young ladies practically faint cold away."

"Surely he cannot be that terrifying."

"She meant his appeal, madam. You are losing your sense of humor over the strain of this matter," Guy teased gently. "He is a handsome fellow, from what my sister-in-law says, but it is his daring heroics that give him such a romantic aura. Saving the workmen who fell in that bridge disaster in Fife last year was a remarkable feat."

She nodded. "*The Edinburgh Review* reported that he dove into the cold sea to pull each man out of the water before assistance could arrive. It takes an admirable man to do such a thing."

"Your generosity was equally admirable, madam. You paid the medical costs of the injured men and contributed funds to restore the bridge after its collapse. Unfortunately, that did not melt Mr. Stewart's hardened heart toward you."

"Nor was it intended to do so. I wanted only to help."

"Madam, you asked my uncle to send over Stewart's latest letter. I have it." Guy removed an envelope from his pocket. "He included a copy of the queen's order, and also—"

"Do not tell me. More plans," she droned, scanning the pages he handed her. "Well, he is infuriating, but persistent. He sends letters and plans every month, and none of our arguments sway him. Odious man," she muttered, studying the copy of the queen's note of permission for Stewart's project and the meticulous line drawings included on another page. Recognizing the coastline of Caransay and then a sketch showing Sgeir Caran's stark grace fitted with an elegantly proportioned lighthouse, her heart quickened.

"It is a grand thing, that design," Guy murmured.

"It is," she admitted, "but I hope it does not go up."

"Uncle Edward thinks he may be able to halt Mr. Stewart's funding, and thereby delay or prevent the construction, regardless of government writs. The man requires fifty thousand pounds to complete the work, a great deal of it from private sponsors interested in supporting the project. I doubt the queen will fund his lighthouse out of her own purse."

"Nor will I." Meg frowned, reading Stewart's letter again. His neat, black, spiked script gave her an immediate sense of a strong, confident man with a certain edge to his character. "His pleas on behalf of his men are stirring, but he goes too far in forcing this issue."

"That rock is a dangerous place. He should not allow construction to proceed there."

Holding Stewart's letter, Meg felt a strange, hot current surge through her body. The talk of Sgeir Caran brought back emotions and memories that she wanted to forget—but could not.

"He is arrogant," she said quickly, tapping her fingers on Stewart's envelope. "He has invited himself and his project to Caransay."

"When you are on holiday there, perhaps you could meet with him to explain that he risks a legal quagmire if he persists."

"I refuse to meet such an odious man while on my holiday. That would ruin my stay."

"It may prove impossible to avoid him on an island seven miles long."

"I will avoid him," she said bluntly. "And we will rid ourselves of his project somehow. When I purchased the island's lease, I promised my kin and tenants that Caransay would remain a paradise, free from threats and outsiders. I must keep my word. And the thought of a lighthouse on that rock . . . is unbearable." She glanced away. "Please tell Sir Edward that his law firm may deal with Mr. Stewart as seems fit. I believe I will add a personal note to the next letter they send him. It is time I voiced my opinion directly to him."

"A good idea, madam. Perhaps when you are on Caransay you could play spy, rather than general, and see what Mr. Stewart is like from a safe distance."

"If he looks thoroughly wicked, I shall withdraw his invitation to the soiree."

Guy chuckled. "While you are gone on holiday, I shall assist Mrs. Shaw here at Strathlin with the arrangements."

"Excellent." Still holding Dougal Stewart's letter, Meg considered it again. Plain stationery and unadorned black script with an ink smear or two gave her the impression of a practical, wholly masculine man who preferred simplicity and directness. She now knew that he was handsome and well educated, and there was ample evidence that he was a man of courage and integrity. Finding those qualities highly attractive in a man, she wished she could like him.

But he was the most stubborn man she had ever dealt with, and he threatened all that she held dear and had vowed to protect. Only on Caransay could she escape to peace from the demands of a life she had never planned for herself. Stewart stood poised to change that forever. His lighthouse would destroy the privacy of Caransay and the mystery and traditions of Sgeir Caran.

If that lighthouse could be built anywhere else, it would be done, even if she had to pay the costs herself. Mr. Stewart could go with it to Hades for all she cared, so long as he left Sgeir Caran, and Caransay, alone.

Sgeir Caran. Suddenly, vividly, she remembered a beautiful, virile man standing on a black rock in a wild storm. Feeling a hot blush, she crammed the letter back in its envelope.

Mr. Stewart could not be allowed to destroy the sanctity of that place.

Chapter Two

Like a gleam of gold among driftwood, the girl caught Dougal Stewart's attention as he stood on the beach talking with his first foreman. Hands at his waist, he stopped midsentence and glanced at her. Standing a little apart from the other islanders who were working and chatting on the beach, she shone like a candle flame amid their sturdy forms and faces.

"Ah . . . er, the Ordnance Survey map," he resumed, looking at Alan Clarke. "Did you have a chance to go over it yet?"

"I did," Alan replied. "And last evening I walked through the hills at the center of the island. There is good granite to be quarried there. Mackenzie will be the one who can say best, though, with his schooling in such matters. He'll be back at the barracks by now."

Dougal nodded, distracted again by the blond woman. A trick of the amber sunset made her look as if she were formed of light and magic. She reminded him of the girl who still haunted his dreams, but he knew that one did not exist—at least in the earthly realm. Unless fairies were real, he had conjured her years ago, and had been unable to rationalize her or forget her.

He cleared his throat, aware that if his thoughts could be known, Alan would think him utterly daft. Sea fairies, indeed. The young woman standing on the beach was lovely, and for that reason alone she was intriguing.

"Hullo, who's that with Norrie, then?" Alan asked, seeing her himself. "Bonny thing."

"Aye." Dougal turned his head. "She is."

Golden haired and reed slim, she shaded her brow with a hand and watched as the women and children helped the fishermen who had come in from a day's work. Laughing and calling out as they worked, they pulled the boats high on the sands and dragged nets bulging with fish and creels full of lobsters out of the water's reach. A few children paused to speak with the girl. She nodded, smiling at them before they ran off again.

An elderly man strolled over to her, smoking a pipe. Dougal recognized tall, white-haired Norrie MacNeill, a crofter fisherman who sailed twice weekly to the Isle of Mull to fetch mail and supplies for the islanders. He had grudgingly offered to do so for the lighthouse crew as well. When Norrie spoke, the girl smiled and wrapped her arm in his. He patted her hand.

Clearly she was Hebridean, Dougal surmised. She was dressed as plainly and practically as the other women, and everyone seemed familiar with her. A brisk breeze whipped at her dark skirt, revealing bare calves and bare feet, hinting at her slender form. Thick honey-colored hair, wildly curled, was partly tamed by a black ribbon. She wore the plaid arisaid shawl that was common among the other women, but she had dropped it down from her head so that it draped over her shoulders and breasts.

She turned to look in his direction, her hand above her eyes. Sensing her stare, he felt an odd response within, like the turning of a key. Fantasy or not, she reminded him strongly of the exquisite sea fairy he had dreamed of one wild black night, when he had been in a bad way.

Frowning, he looked away. He needed a long night's sleep. The work pace was making him imaginative and maudlin.

Near the water's edge, some members of his crew hauled up the fishing boat they used daily to cross back and forth to Sgeir Caran. Today they had drilled and hacked into black basalt to cut the foundation cavity for the lighthouse. As resident engineer, Dougal supervised every aspect of the work and often lent a hand with the actual physical labor.

Tired and gritty from the day's efforts, he tensed and then relaxed his stiff shoulders. He craved a wash and fresh clothing, a hot supper, and time alone in his hut to study plans by lamplight. The engineering log needed to be filled out each day with a report of progress, and measurements needed to be carefully checked and rechecked before the next phase of work.

He glanced down the crescent of white sand that defined Caransay's small natural harbor. The single quay was tied up with fishing boats, and more boats rested on the sand. Two dark headlands framed the beach like enormous sentinels, the black rock matching the basalt of the reef a mile or so out to sea.

Seagulls called, reeling overhead, and waves swept over the pale, soft sand. Dougal turned, enjoying the salty breezes that fingered his thick brown hair, fluttering his coat and collarless shirt—he rarely wore stiff collars or neckcloths out here, though he made it a practice to wear vests and coats out of deference to the women. Children raced past him, splashing and laughing in the surf. A few of them scrambled up the nearest headland, shouting to one another as they followed a rudimentary path there.

"She must be Norrie MacNeill's granddaughter,"

Alan said. "He said he expected to fetch her from Mull this week for a visit. Apparently she lives off Caransay."

"Ah." Dougal nodded. No wonder he had not seen her before.

"Maybe she'll dance wi' me at the Friday ceilidh," Alan mused. "Last Friday I sat with Norrie's auld mum all night. Mother Elga tells a good tale and sings a fine song, but she isna much for dancing." He chuckled. "We noticed, the lads and I, that Caransay has nae so many young and unmarried lassies. I wish you'd looked into that before you arranged for us to stay here the whole of a year." Alan shook his head.

"You'll work harder without distractions." Dougal grinned.

"Ha! So will you, clever lad, wi' nae fine lassies to charm, flockin' aboot you as they did in Edinburgh and Glasgow. Och, look! There goes my heart." Alan watched as the young blond woman walked toward the headland with long-legged grace, skirt swinging neatly. She waved toward the children climbing the rock, calling for them to come down. "Oh, what a pity for me if she's married and a mother already." Alan sighed dramatically.

"If she's just a sister or cousin to those sprites, you still have a chance."

"I doubt it. See that tall fellow wi' her noo? Och, and the smile she gave him, it breaks my heart. That coulda been for me, that bonny smile."

"Aye, well," Dougal commiserated. A tousle-haired man wearing the baggy jacket, trousers, and boots of a fisherman joined the young woman. She smiled at him even as she snatched the shirttails of the smallest of the bold climbers, plucking the blond boy off the headland slope. The child leaped down beside her and took her hand.

Watching the girl greet what must be her own family, Dougal felt a keen disappointment, as if he had finally found his sea fairy only to lose her again. Alan asked a question about the next day's plans, and Dougal replied, all the while sensing the girl's bright presence.

Glancing out over the sea as he spoke, he narrowed his eyes against the sunset glare on the waves. Breezes stirred his hair as he gazed out toward Sgeir Caran.

A mile from the island, the massive black rock was easily visible, thrusting upward through the waves, silhouetted against the golden sky. Sgeir Caran was the largest formation in a half-mile-long archipelago, the Caran Reef, whose rocks littered the sea like thorns. Many of the points were treacherously hidden below the constant sweep of the Atlantic.

Most of the time, Dougal saw Sgeir Caran in terms of the challenges of the work and in relation to geology, weather, the physics of wind and wave force, and so on. But sometimes, when the light was extraordinary or the mist deep, the rock seemed like an otherworldly portal, an ancient place of legends and magic. He often remembered the night he had nearly died out there, when water horses and a sea fairy had saved him. Years later, the sublime magic lingered in his heart and mind. He would never understand what had happened that night.

Fool, he told himself, turning away. He needed his attention on the here and now. Hard enough to work out on Sgeir Caran every day without dreaming of what could never be.

"She will find you," Alan said.

Dougal turned, startled. "What?"

"The Baroness of Strathlin. When she hears we're about to quarry stone from her island, she'll come after you."

"There's little she can do now. Lady Strathlin will have to accept it."

"At least she's at a safe distance in Edinburgh."

"Aye, but I hear she keeps a manor house on the

other side of the island. She'll come here sooner or later. I mean to meet her when she does."

"She might come to Caransay and whaup yer head for being a great loon and causing her grief."

"I have been invited to a soiree at her home in late September. She can whaup me there at her convenience."

"Fought you every step of the way, she has."

"Well, her solicitors have done the real fighting."

"She canna be bothered wi' a working man who lacks a lofty title, eh? Lady Strathlin has nearly two million pounds, they say—two million!" Alan shook his head in disbelief. "Your own inheritance is fine, but a wee sum compared to that."

"True. Well, she gives freely to charities, and she assisted in the costs after the bridge collapsed last year."

"You're a fair man, Dougal Stewart. Truth is, she canna find it in her heart to be generous wi' the Caran light. We need contributions. Those Fresnel lenses you ordered for the tower will be bright as fire but devilish expensive. 'Twill up the cost to nearly sixty thousand pounds by the time we are done."

"I've heard from interested investors in Edinburgh. If I attend Lady Strathlin's soiree, I can tap those fellows for commitments. As for the lady, she would never invest in this."

"She's hell's own gale. But you've never run from a storm."

"That particular storm is over," Dougal said. "Now all we need is good luck and good weather to finish the job." He turned and saw Norrie MacNeill looking toward him. The old man lifted a hand, and Dougal waved while still speaking to Alan. Moments later, the fisherman and the girl crossed the beach toward them.

Graceful, poised, lovely, she held his attention. All else seemed to fade. He heard the rush of the sea in his ears, and his heart beat hard and fast. He thought of his dreams of the sea fairy, and the sudden longing he felt had crushing strength.

Whoever the girl was, he told himself, she was real—and he had best collect his wits.

He looked like a pirate, dark and wild, hands at his waist and booted foot propped on the edge of a fishing boat. All banked power, casual strength and assurance, he turned his head to see Meg and her grandfather crossing the beach. She felt his gaze ripple through her, though he was still a distance away.

She expected Dougal Stewart to be a handsome, charming man, but she did not understand the strange effect he had on her.

Intrigued, she suddenly wanted to go to him despite their clashes by letter. Then her grandfather caught Stewart's glance, waved, and Meg had no choice but to advance and meet him.

Someone called her name, and she turned, waving to her cousin Fergus MacNeill, who was with his foster son, her child, Iain. They walked along the upper beach, laughing. Earlier, Meg had been glad when Iain had listened to her and had obeyed her in coming down from the headland. Although she saw him only when she was on the island, she wanted a solid and real relationship with her son, and so he believed that she was his cousin. Meg and her family had thought it best that Iain accept Fergus's wife, Anna, as his mother, but Anna had died with the birth of a daughter a year ago. As yet, Iain had not been told the truth about Meg, though someday soon she wanted to tell him.

Fergus was a responsible and doting father, but with two small and energetic children under his care, he had decided to live with his grandparents Norrie and Thora. Together with Mother Elga, they all took a hand in raising Iain and small Anna.

After watching Iain wistfully for a moment, Meg turned back, prepared to face the obstinate engineer.

She wondered what Mrs. Berry might say about meeting the man with her hair loose, her feet bare, and only two petticoats beneath her skirt. Her traveling companion was currently ensconced in what was called the Great House—for it was the largest house on the island—with its luxuries, its privacy, its restful atmosphere and secluded beach. Meg, however, came to Caransay for homecoming as much as holiday. She preferred to stay in her grandparents' croft house, where she could be closer to them and to her son.

She liked the freedom she enjoyed outside of Mrs. Berry's constant eye to abandon stays, crinolines, stockings, and shoes in favor of practical, comfortable clothing and bare feet. On Caransay, Meg savored the freedoms she had lost on the mainland.

"What will you tell the man?" Norrie asked.

"He has reason to loathe me." Meg answered in Gaelic, her natural tongue when she was on Caransay. "How can I introduce myself to him as Lady Strathlin now, dressed like this? I should invite him to tea at the Great House and act the proper baroness."

"He would expect the lady to wear shoes, at least." Norrie huffed a laugh as they strolled down the beach. Her grandfather never hurried, and Meg appreciated his pace now. "I am thinking the man should be made to guess," Norrie said. "The surprise will do him good."

Meg laughed despite her nervousness. "My solicitors are looking for some way of removing him. I wish they had done it before today."

"Look there." Norrie gestured with his pipe. "Those are the houses these men put up. Lowland structures like that will not stand up in a good rain. They do not know what a house needs to be out here in the Isles. We told them the roofs were good, though. Oh, very good, we said, when they were building." He chuckled. "May they all blow out to sea and carry the engineers with them!"

Beyond the bay, she saw the thatched roofs of several cottages with ropes applied as netting, but nothing compared to the solid nets weighted with heavy stones that secured Hebridean thatching. She nodded. "I never agreed to any of this, you know."

"We know." Norrie clamped his teeth over his pipe stem. "We have heard all about the argument between you and this lighthouse engineer. We agree with you—they should be gone from here. The people are wondering what you will do."

She nodded. She must do something, for their sakes, for that of Caransay and Sgeir Caran, and for the legends.

"He is not a bad fellow, this Stewart," Norrie said. "I have nothing against the man or his crew. It is the construction I do not like, for the harm it causes the great rock and the island."

"I am concerned about the colonies of seabirds and wildlife that settle on that rock each year," Meg said. "And, of course, we value our hard-won privacy here—" She stopped suddenly. Dougal Stewart had turned, and she had seen his face clearly for the first time.

Never in her life had she come close to fainting, even when she wore snug stays. Now she gasped and felt the world reel under her feet. Stunned, she placed a hand on Norrie's arm.

"What is it?" he asked.

"I—I nearly tripped." She wanted to hide her astonishment.

She expected a handsome man, a charming, daring, infuriating, and obstinate man. She knew he was heir to a Strathclyde fortune, the builder of lighthouses that withstood awesome forces, a man who dared and did what others could scarcely imagine.

But she never expected that the engineer who was intent on ruining her island was the same cad who had fathered her child and had broken her heart. Her kelpie, returned to her.

His gaze, as he watched them approach, was intense and penetrating. Did he know her? Was she mistaken?

As she drew closer she became sure it was the same man. He had the same lean, tough grace, the same thick, waving hair, the identical face, its balanced features very nearly beautiful.

As she drew closer she saw that he was stunning, astonishingly so, with a rugged, casual beauty, not perfect but fascinating in quality. Rich brown hair fell in sun-streaked waves, framing a face with straight dark brows and lean, symmetrical features. He wore an umber coat, black trousers and vest, and a collarless white shirt. He had shoved hands into pockets, and now righted his posture as she approached.

Her hand went unconsciously to the locket at her throat. She drew her arisaid up over her hair to hide the gold and to shadow her face. She walked over the damp sand near the water's edge, where Dougal Stewart stood with the other man, and her knees quivered. Would he recognize her?

She could hardly tell him in anyone else's presence that she had met him on that rock. Nor could she tell him that she was the baroness. Not now. Not yet.

"Grandfather," she said, plucking at his coat sleeve. The shush of the waves, the call of seagulls, the shouts up and down the busy beach kept her words private. "Please do not tell Mr. Stewart who I am. Tell the others to keep it to themselves, too. Please, Grandfather. The dispute with Mr. Stewart belongs with my lawyers, not here on Caransay."

"True. Then it can wait."

She sighed in relief as they approached Stewart.

"Mr. MacNeill," he said, holding out his hand. "How nice to see you, sir." He smiled at Meg and nodded. His eyes narrowed, but with the natural interest of a man, not a former lover.

Good. He had not recognized her. With her skirts hiked over her bare calves, her sleeves rolled, in the shawl of a native Isleswoman, she would not look as he remembered. And in seven years she had changed—she was a grown woman now, had birthed a child.

He was the same: still striking, with a fine etching of sun and experience around his eyes and slight creases beside his mouth. He had filled out some, not quite the slim, wiry build she recalled. His eyes, edged in sooty black lashes, were the muted gray-green of a stormy sea.

She wondered if he was still capable of playing deceitful tricks. Judging by his letters to Lady Strathlin, he was.

He smiled at her, and she lifted her chin defensively. She could not succumb to his charm and attractiveness. He had hurt her deeply, but she was not sure how to react to him now.

"Good day to you, Dougal Stewart," Norrie said in stilted English. "Alan Clarke. This is my granddaughter, Margaret Fiona MacNeill. Margaret—Mr. Stewart and Mr. Clarke." Meg blessed her grandfather for the simple introductions. She reluctantly offered her hand out of politeness.

"Miss MacNeill," Dougal Stewart said, taking her fingers.

A dreadful mistake, she realized, to allow him to touch her. The contact went through her like a shock. Catching her breath, she saw him watching her, his eyes intense and penetrating. Her heart pounded. Surely he knew her.

Meg shook hands with Clarke in turn, then folded her hands while Dougal Stewart asked Norrie about the mail runs to Mull.

"Miss MacNeill, are you from Mull?" Alan Clarke asked. He was a pleasant fellow, blond and blue eyed, not as tall as Stewart, with a burly frame. He smiled easily and sincerely, and she liked him immediately.

"I came from Mull, yes," she said. That was true—

Norrie had picked her up with Mrs. Berry two days earlier. "I grew up on this island so I come back here as often as I can."

"Caransay is a beautiful place," Stewart said, turning toward her. She sensed something piercing in his gaze, a keen and perceptive intelligence. Suddenly she wished she had turned and fled upon seeing him on the beach.

For seven years she had felt angry at this man even though he filled her dreams at night, keeping her always on the edge of yearning. She could not forget how he had kept her safe in deepest fear, had taken her with him into ecstasy—and then had betrayed her.

Temper rising, she wanted to tell him her identity here and now, both as the girl on the rock and as the baroness he despised. But she could not, for Norrie and the other islanders watched her with covert curiosity. They knew that the baroness was about to speak to the engineer, and later she would ask Norrie to tell them to keep it a secret. In their great loyalty, she knew they would comply. But none of them knew the rest of it.

She would not tell him now and reduce herself to engaging in an emotional brawl with an infuriating, selfish, stubborn man. At all costs, she would retain her dignity. Later she could meet with him privately at the Great House, although she did not yet know how much she should tell him.

"Mr. Stewart," Norrie said. "Angus MacLeod said you went to Mull earlier, and hired his son to take you. But I sail to Tobermory twice a week when weather allows. This week I fetched my granddaughter, too. Next time you wish to go, Dougal Stewart, I will take you, and bring you back. No need to pay a man to go over the waves for you when Norrie MacNeill will do it for free."

"Thank you. I shall remember." He smiled acknowledgement.

Watching him, Meg suddenly felt swamped with panic, grew dizzy where she stood, the water calmly lapping at her feet. He would be on the island for a while, but she could not risk the baroness's reputation by revealing the whole truth to him. Few people knew that Iain was her child.

If Dougal Stewart learned about his son, he could claim the boy as his own, could even take Iain away from her and her family forever. *Oh dear God,* she thought.

She dared another look at him and he seemed to be studying her, his expression perplexed. "Miss MacNeill," he said, "may I ask . . . have we met before?"

Chapter Three

"I do not believe we have been introduced before, Mr. Stewart," Margaret MacNeill replied. Her voice was quiet and melodic, her English perfect, with the soft lilt of the Gael rather than the broader lifts and falls of Scots English. Her words seemed carefully chosen, and she herself seemed cautious and wary, as if protecting herself in some way.

Dougal noted that she was slender and neatly made beneath her plain garments. Her feet were sand dusted, her clasped hands smooth and lovely. If she worked with nets and gutted fish, like many Hebridean women, her hands did not show the wear. Thick golden curls were pulled back and partly covered by a lightweight plaid. Beneath the shadowing of the draped plaid, her features were beautifully symmetrical, the delicate jaw decidedly stubborn.

No wonder he thought he had seen her before. Such fair coloring and elegant bones were typical of many Hebrideans due to Viking ancestry. Norrie had it, too, in his fair complexion, high cheek bones, and vivid blue eyes.

Her eyes were luminous, silvery aqua. Frowning as

he studied her, he remembered a moment when he had opened his eyes from sleep to see the girl sitting at the mouth of the little cave they had shared in the storm. In dawn's light, he had seen her face and her extraordinary eyes clearly, their color the delicate blue-green wash of a sky just before dawn.

Margaret MacNeill had those eyes. In fact, she was so much like the sea fairy he remembered that he felt the shock of recognition all through his body—a prickling along his skin, a deep clutching of certainty in his heart and gut. Could she have been real and he so muddled at the time that he had not known?

If she knew him, she gave no sign, no start. She seemed calm and cool, but he noticed a fine-drawn nervousness, a tight clasping of her hands, a flickering away of those eyes, the clenching of her narrow toes in the sand.

Still frowning, uncertain quite yet, he gave his attention to Norrie MacNeill. "Mr. Stewart is the chief of the lighthouse on the rock," Norrie told his granddaughter.

"Resident engineer," Dougal corrected, smiling. "I was assigned here by the Northern Lighthouse Commission. We have a grant of permission to build on Sgeir Caran and to maintain work buildings here on Caransay."

"I know, Mr. Stewart," the girl said crisply.

If she recognized him, Dougal realized, she was hardly delighted to see him. He could not blame her. What he had done was reprehensible. Disturbed by that thought, he kept an outward calm, yet he knew he must speak with Miss MacNeill alone, and soon.

What he would do about this, he did not yet know. Clearly he owed her an apology and an explanation—providing his behavior that night could be explained. He had been a thousand times a fool, and he must admit that to her.

"I saw you and your men cutting into the hard place today," Norrie said. "I heard your sledges and chisels when I went out over the waves to draw in my nets."

"The hard place?" Alan Clarke asked.

"Sgeir Caran," Margaret MacNeill explained, and Norrie hissed as if to shush her. "My grandfather, like many Hebridean fishermen, will not say the rock's name aloud."

"It is not a good thing," Norrie said.

"I'll remember that," Dougal said. "I will do my best to respect local traditions while I am here."

"Then why do you build on that rock," the girl asked tartly, "when it is legendary among the people of this isle?"

"I was not aware of any legends associated with the rock."

"The hard place belongs to the *each-uisge,*" Norrie said. "The lord of the deep."

"The who?" Alan asked.

"A sea kelpie," Margaret MacNeill told him, "supposedly a creature of great magical power, who sometimes takes the form of a white horse and sometimes the form of a man."

"It is said that he comes to Sgeir Caran now and again, seeking a bride," Norrie went on. "That rock is his, you see. If his bride pleases him, he will quiet the storms that blow over Caransay, summon more fish into our nets, and bestow good fortune upon us all. If he is ever displeased, he will raise heavy storms and the fish will flee our nets. His power could sink that hard rock, and this island, into the waves."

"Your kelpie is no fellow to cross," Dougal said.

"Our traditions make certain that the *each-uisge* is happy," Norrie said, nodding.

"What do you do, leave him baskets of fish?" Alan asked. "I imagine he can catch his own easily enough. If I were the kelpie, I'd want oatcakes and whisky and all the bonny lassies I could get." Norrie began a dry chuckle but stopped when he glanced at his frowning granddaughter, who seemed unamused.

"We have respected our traditions for centuries," she snapped, "even if some do not."

"I beg your pardon, Miss MacNeill." Dougal inclined his head. He knew that a Hebridean day could be ruled by a string of superstitions that covered from one dawn to the next and every situation in between. Traditions, legends, and belief in magic gave the people a sense of security and power in a harsh and unpredictable place. Alan murmured an apology, as well, as the girl looked sternly from one man to the other.

"We have heard about your troubles with the lady," Norrie MacNeill said then.

Dougal nodded grimly. "I assume you refer to my dispute with Lady Strathlin. I understand that the baroness keeps a holiday home on this island. Might she come to Caransay soon? I would like to meet with her, and show her the work we are doing out on Sgeir Caran."

An awkward silence followed. The old man dragged slowly on his pipe and clicked it between his teeth. "I am thinking the lady is not here," Norrie finally said.

"Not now, aye. But if she comes to the island, I hope someone will let me know. I would like to meet with her."

"It could be that when she is here, she will stay at the Great House and not see anyone."

"The Great House?" Dougal asked. The girl said nothing, huddling her hands under her plaid, tipping her head into shadow. He could not read her expression, but he felt her gaze, steady and keen—and not favorable.

"Clachan Mor, her manor house on the other side of the island. It is the biggest stone house on Caransay, and so it is named. If the lady comes here," Norrie said, watching the smoke curl out of his pipe, "perhaps you can send her a note."

"I have written letters to the lady before. If she comes to Caransay, I must speak with her myself and show her our work."

"She does not like visitors here." Norrie cast him a sharp glance. "You do not have her permission to use our beaches and harbor. We know what you did to gain the right." He shook his head as if disappointed in Dougal.

"It was business. I had little choice," Dougal said, surprised by his urge to win the old man's approval.

"Well, the lady does not welcome strangers on Caransay, but if she comes to Clachan Mor, she will be told that you are here." Norrie straightened his shoulders and pointed with his pipe toward the rock in the distance. "If you wish to please the lady and win her good opinion, find another rock for your light tower. She disapproves for the sake of privacy and because the location is dangerous."

"It is very dangerous," Margaret MacNeill said. "There are wild storms there and high waves."

"Aye, Miss MacNeill, I know," Dougal answered quietly, looking down at her. "Great black storms and waves high enough to wash over the rock." Her aqua gaze fastened on him, and he saw a sudden flash of defiance and anger there.

Oh aye, he thought. *You are the one.*

Deep in the night, unable to sleep, Dougal left his barracks hut to walk over the machair, the wildflower meadow that stretched across the island near the dunes. Overhead, the sky had finally darkened—summer skies in the Hebrides sometimes held light until an hour or so before dawn—and the moon was high and pale, reflecting in ripples upon the sea.

Hands shoved in his pockets, Dougal strolled deep in thought as he considered a stubborn engineering problem. Rectangular stone blocks, each weighing several tons, had to be precisely trimmed to fit the circular foundation cavity. He had drawn diagrams and devised measurements, yet each block had to be hand shaped in situ to ensure the tightest fit between the stones. He could rely on his masons, but his figures and his analysis of the problem must be as accurate as possible. A long walk often helped him think.

Pausing, he gazed over the sea. His mind felt as restless as the waves tonight, not because he puzzled over granite blocks but because Margaret MacNeill had invaded his dreams. She had slipped into his arms in some vague setting to comfort him with her lips and a luscious embrace that turned hot and passionate. She had whispered her forgiveness before he could apologize to her. Then she had asked him to forgive her. *My dearest girl, you did nothing wrong. My dearest . . .*

A most disturbing fantasy. He had dozed over his papers, waking in a warm sweat and a wrench of longing, half aroused and unaccountably furious with himself. Grabbing his coat, he had gone out to walk off the haunting power of the dream.

As he watched the sea, waves poured to the shore, rolling, plunging, streaming in a soothing, seductive rhythm. Moonlight shone pale green through arching water, and the lace-edged curls looked like the proud heads and breasts of white stallions.

There are your water horses, he told himself.

Seven years ago, he had been drunk, concussed, and on the verge of drowning when he had seen those creatures. A man might imagine anything under such circumstances, even sea fairies.

So the girl on Sgeir Caran had in fact been a real Hebridean woman, and the pale horses who had saved him had been merely waves, ridden in on luck. He had been daft, with no firm grip on reality. Well, now he would have to make up for that somehow.

He could not live with himself, knowing what he had done to that young and innocent girl and seeing the fire and snap in her accusing eyes now.

Far out, Sgeir Caran was a black silhouette against the lavender sky. Smaller rocks jutted through swirling water, part of the long reef where so many ships had sunk, so many lives had forfeited.

His father and mother had been swallowed near that wicked reef in hell's own storm. Their ship had not gone down on Sgeir Caran, but had wrecked on the numerous points elsewhere in the reef. If a light had existed on the highest of the rocks in the Caran Reef, the ship carrying his parents would have skirted the treacherous archipelago and gone safely to port.

He shoved fingers through his hair, sighed deep. He would continue to fight for the lighthouse on Sgeir Caran with every ounce of will and determination he had. That light would prevent tragedies and save lives, if only the baroness and her league of lawyers would realize it. For Dougal, the light would also serve as a monument to those who had died among those rocks.

Nothing must prevent that silent memorial from going up.

He hardened his mouth and his hands, fighting the memory of their faces, their voices and smiles, their laughter. He could not let himself think about them, about the guidance or the love he had missed so dreadfully, all these years.

Watching the vast water that covered their remains, he knew that he still struggled with the grief and anger he had tried to conquer long ago. Growing to manhood, he had honed his self-control and heightened his daring as a way of fighting his feelings. Death was no matter to him. He had faced it too many times now to fear it. He had been shipwrecked himself, had endured the fury of storms, had dived deep, climbed high on scaffolds, risked much to put up these lighthouses. And he had learned the keen thrill in daring, had further learned that courage was simply a matter of faith over fear.

And of all the lighthouses he had taken a hand in constructing, this one was by far the most important to him.

He was more determined than courageous in this matter. He was known for sheer stubbornness. He would never give this up, despite Lady Strathlin's disapproval or that of the islanders. Besides, the physics and logic of the matter dictated Sgeir Caran as the best site. He had the support of the Northern Lighthouse Commission and the Stevenson firm, who had designed the tower and had sent him out here to execute it.

He must do this. He owed it to the souls who had disappeared out there. He owed it to his father, strong and kind and too vibrant to die so young, and to his mother, slim and quiet, a bookish lady with pretty coppery hair and the sweetest of smiles.

God. He hurt. Disbelieving the intensity of the feeling after eighteen years, he sucked in air as if it were medicine for the excruciating pain, and felt it ease.

"Mr. Stewart." The voice was calm and soft.

He whirled. He had not expected to see anyone out here, least of all her. She stood knee-deep in moonlit flowers and grasses. Wind rippled through her hair, shifted her skirt.

She must be made of magic after all, to appear when he needed her. An urgent desire filled him to take her into his arms and seek comfort in her soothing spirit, as he had once done.

As she looked at him, he sensed tension in her, a vulnerable defensiveness, as if she feared he would shatter her. Feeling a twist of longing and regret, he wanted only to hold her, to ask forgiveness, to bring her into his life again. But he did not think any of that was possible.

She walked closer, the hem of her skirt and her feet

dusted with sand. She must have come over the sand dunes, though he had not noticed, absorbed in his thoughts.

"Miss MacNeill," he said more calmly than he felt. "I am surprised to find anyone out and about at this hour."

"I could not sleep. When I am here on Caransay, I sometimes like to walk out before the dawn. The chance of seeing the northern lights is worth losing a bit of sleep."

He glanced at the sky. "I've seen them a few times, but never here in the Isles."

"Did you come out here to look for them, too?"

"Actually, I came out to puzzle over some engineering problems." And to shake himself free of a dream, yet the dream stood beside him now. He watched the sky to keep from staring at her like a cow-eyed fool.

"It may not be dark enough tonight to see the lights," she said. "Well, good night, Mr. Stewart." As she passed, he caught a waft of a sweet fragrance.

He turned with her. "Let me escort you, Miss MacNeill. It does not do for a young lady to be alone in the darkness."

"I am perfectly safe on my island," she said. "I wish you good luck with your puzzles."

He could not let her go so easily. He strode beside her through the stretch of grasses and blooms. "So this is what they call the machair," he said.

"It is," she said.

"Do you know what all these flowers are?" he asked. He did not particularly care, but he wanted an excuse to talk to her.

"I do," she said, and kept on walking.

"Are those buttercups there?" He pointed. "And harebells?"

"Buttercups, harebells, daisies," she answered. "That tall stuff is yarrow and wild oat grass. That's meadowsweet over there. What you are crushing underfoot are small purple irises past their bloom now. And over there, closer to the hills, are wild strawberries and brambles and clusters of wild roses that spread over the rocks until you can hardly see the stone."

"It's lovely."

"Mmm," she agreed. "If you close your eyes, you can smell them. All throughout the hills here, the heather blooms so thick that the hills look dark pink from far out at sea. Is there anything else you would like to know?"

"Aye," he said, watching her.

"About the machair," she qualified. "No one planted it, no one tends it, but it flourishes. It has always been here. Sometimes the daisies turn the machair to white and gold and the bees tumble drunkenly through a heaven of flowers."

He glanced at her as they walked. "You love this place."

"Of course I do," she answered. Beyond the meadow, beyond the dunes, the sea shushed endlessly to shore. "It is paradise."

"Apparently the baroness agrees."

"You need not walk with me any farther."

"I'd rather you had an escort in the middle of the night."

"Why? Because there are strange men about?" she snapped.

"Where?" He turned, hands in pockets to look, hoping to make her smile. But she remained serious. He drew a breath, felt as if he were about to plunge into some unknown sea. "I think you do not like me much, Miss MacNeill, or do I imagine it?"

"Imagine what you like."

"If I did," he drawled, "you might be very surprised."

"Go back to your barracks, Mr. Stewart."

"I will, when I have seen you safely home."

"I do not need you here. We none of us need you here."

"Ah, I suspect you refer to lighthouses, and not simply a stroll in the moonlight. Are you by any chance acquainted with Lady Strathlin?"

Her steps faltered, but she kept walking. "Why do you ask?"

"She shares your good opinion of me. Her passel of lawyers would agree with you, too."

"We cannot all be wrong," she said.

He huffed grudging admittance and smiled in the darkness when she laughed softly. They trudged side by side through the grasses and flowers. Glimpsing the shadow of a rock among the grasses, he took her elbow to guide her around it.

A simple touch, but the contact went through him like a lightning bolt, a crackling awareness that tingled like a spark. Stunned, he let her go, telling himself it was only the romantic moonlight, the lush sound of the sea, the strange magic of the hour before dawn. In daylight, he would not have felt so vivid a sensation, nor would he entertain such astonishing thoughts.

They walked ahead until he saw a croft house tucked against a hill. He could make out the whitewashed contour, a heavily thatched roof, and small, darkened windows. The house faced a small bay, sparkling and peaceful in the moonlight. "I assume that is where we are headed?" he asked.

"It is. You can leave me now."

"No need to bristle so, Miss MacNeill."

She turned to stare up at him. A fresh breeze fluttered her skirt and the plaid shawl that was wrapped around her shoulders. Strands of her hair sifted loose to frame her face. "I am not bristling. I do not bristle."

"You," he said quietly, "are like a porcupine whenever I am near." He reached out to brush back the hair from her brow. She leaned away her head. *See?* he wanted to say.

"Tell me, do you know Lady Strathlin well?" He was curious.

"Well enough. Everyone on Caransay knows her."

They stood on a rise above the croft house and its little bay, where the machair dropped away into a long sandy bank that led down to the shore. Looking at the croft house in moonlight, Dougal saw that it was larger than he thought at first, with two wings attached to the main body of the house, whitewashed and topped by thick thatch and roof ropes. The whole formed a pretty picture with the sparkling bay while pink dawn billowed at the lowest edge of the horizon over the sea.

"Is that the Great House?"

She laughed, soft and low. "That is Camus nan Fraoch—Heather Bay, we call it. My grandparents live there."

"So you stay there when you are on the island." She nodded in answer. "Tell me, do you live on Mull with your husband?"

"My husband? I am not married—and I live on the mainland."

"Forgive me. On the beach, I saw you with a man and a small boy, so I assumed they were your husband and son."

"That was my cousin Fergus MacNeill and . . . small Iain."

He nodded, relieved. Her name had revealed little, since Scotswomen frequently kept their maiden names after marriage. Not wanting to pry with too many questions, he assumed that she lived with her parents or other relatives on the mainland. Many Islesmen had sought livelihoods in the Highlands and Lowlands, sometimes settling along the coastal areas. Since Norrie had fetched her from Mull, Dougal assumed she lived along the coast in Ardnamurchan or Moidart.

"Where is Clachan Mor, the baroness's estate?" he asked.

"Hardly an estate," she said. "Just a manor house. Look that way." She pointed, taking his sleeve when he looked the wrong way. "The Great House sits at the foot of those hills."

He dimly saw a stone manor house, boxy in shape with a flat façade and several windows, nestled near a dark hill. A sandy peninsula stretched below the house into the water.

"Do you know when the baroness might be there again?"

"I do not really know."

"Are you privy to her plans?"

"Sometimes." Her eyes sparked, and he felt that she knew more than she would reveal. "She values her privacy on Caransay and conducts no business when she is here."

"I hear she keeps to herself, both here and on the mainland. We have corresponded for several months, yet have not met."

"I'm aware of your correspondence, sir. It is not amiable."

"True. Well, if I cannot meet her, perhaps I can persuade you to convey a message to her, since you know her personally. Although I will wager that Lady Strathlin is heartily sick of messages from me," he added wryly.

She was looking up. The moonlight caught the curve of her cheek, and a strange pinkish light spread over her face in a beautiful, eerie glow. Her eyes grew wide as the moonlight brightened oddly.

"Oh, look!" she cried, pointing out to sea. Dougal turned.

A pale green arc bloomed on the horizon and expanded, exploding in sudden swaths of light and color. Pink and green swirled overhead, flinging out like silken veils. Dougal watched, entranced. Without thinking, he lifted a hand to take her elbow again, a gentlemanly gesture, yet he wanted simply to touch her, to feel a bond with her in that moment, when the sky flared so joyfully, miraculously, overhead.

"Oh, so beautiful," she breathed.

"Beautiful," he agreed. "The aurora borealis."

"The Merry Men, we call the northern lights here."

"In the old days, I hear, the lights were believed to be gigantic supernatural warriors—especially when the sky flowed red as if from blood." He had read that somewhere.

"When I was a child, I thought they were angels rejoicing in heaven," she mused, looking up while the sinuous dance of colored lights continued.

He smiled. "I have seen them a few times elsewhere," he said, "but they never seemed so beautiful as they do tonight."

As she tipped back her head to watch the display, he watched her. Lambent color suffused her skin and hair, and her long throat and the clean line of her jaw were graceful. He was deeply tempted to slide his fingertips over her creamy skin, through her silken curls. She seemed familiar and dear to him, reunited after so long, all her secrets still his, her passions one with his. He craved a joyful welcoming, such as whirled overhead, but she was cool, distant, and somber.

"The colors are pale tonight," she said. "They are usually more brilliant when the Merry Men go dancing."

"The sky is not as dark as it will be in fall or spring."

"Will you still be on Caransay then?" she asked.

"Most likely," he said. "Perhaps we can walk out to look for the lights another time, when it is darker."

She stared up at the magical glow, and Dougal remembered how beautiful she was in the glow of a lightning strike, in rainy darkness, in the clear pink of dawn. He knew how alluring she was in the rainy shadow of a cave, how she felt, drenched and shivering, in his arms. His body pulsed.

He stepped closer, motion following thought, and she tilted her head to look at him. "Tell me," he said gruffly, "that we have met before." He wanted her to know that he was not a madman.

"I—" She paused, still watching the mystical brightness.

"Tell me," he insisted. "Were you there that night? Or did I dream it?"

She knew what he meant. He saw the keen perception in her eyes, in her expression. She did not answer, but only watched the sky. Her silence was clear admission.

"My God," he breathed. "How could this be possible?" Taking her shoulder, he pulled her closer, leaned toward her, afraid to trust that his dream could come true so easily.

Sliding his free hand along her cheek, he lowered his head, nuzzling close enough to kiss her, overwhelmed by desire.

She stiffened in his arms, then leaned back her head and closed her eyes. Silent and still, she seemed to wait. Tipping his head, he kissed her mouth gently, felt his soul whirl.

Her lips softened beneath his, and her fingers clutched at his coat lapel. He felt her sway against him, felt a moment of surrender in her. He drew a breath, slid his hand around to the back of her waist, and let the kiss deepen.

A force poured through him, relief, joy, shaking him out of the torpor of years of grief and sorrow. He had found her. She was real. One desperate loss in his life had been restored to him, and it felt like a miracle.

Her hand slid upward to cup his jaw, and her breath warmed his mouth. He sensed true hunger in her that matched his own, and he felt her need, as deep and sincere as his. He wanted to hold her, cherish her, heal her reluctance and anger somehow.

She moaned a breathy protest and seemed to wake from the same heated fog that held him captive. Pushing at his chest, she stepped back. Then her hand lashed upward to crack across his cheek, sharp as a whip.

"What the devil—" He grabbed at her arm, but she snatched it away, whirled, and hurried down the sandy slope, breaking into a run as she headed toward the croft house.

Dougal watched her, palm nursing his stinging cheek. After a moment, he realized that the bright kaleidoscope overhead had faded once again to the dark, starry sky.

The wind blew fast enough to clear his thoughts like mist in the sun. She was no illusion, and now the events of that night took on a different meaning. He had ruined the girl, shamed her. No matter that she had gone willingly, passionately, wildly, into his arms. She had been a virgin that night.

Small wonder she hated him now that he had returned after seven years' silence.

Why had she been out there on that wicked night? He intended to find out, and he intended to explain himself to her, whether or not she wanted to hear it. He owed her a sincere apology.

He owed her far more than that, he told himself.

Watching the moving sea, he called himself every sort of bastard. Margaret MacNeill deserved more than apologies. He had been a heartless cad, though he had believed himself dreaming, or—God forgive him—enchanted. Morally, socially, and ethically, he was obligated to marry the girl.

That prospect gave him greater pause than any risk he had ever faced.

Chapter Four

"He is still there." Thora opened the door to peer out.

"Grandmother, please, he will see you!" Meg said.

"And what harm if he sees me feeding the chickens?" Thora asked reasonably, and opened the door to go outside.

Elga, Norrie's mother, chuckled as she sat on a stool by the hearth. Fergus's small daughter, Anna, sat on her lap, and the old woman fed the little girl spoonfuls of porridge from a bowl. Anna gazed up at the old woman with wide blue eyes. "The kelpie's come back for you," Mother Elga told Meg. "I told you he would."

Casting a sour glance at her great-grandmother, Meg crossed the room to shut the door and glanced outside. Dawn shone pink and blue-gray over sea and island, and Dougal Stewart still stood on the machair above Camus nan Fraoch, facing the sea.

She remembered another dawn, another pastel sky, when he had waited on a sea rock for a boat to fetch him while Meg had watched. She had kept that secret for seven years.

Now, her senses whirling again from his kisses, she

no longer wondered if he was the same man she had met on Sgeir Caran. She knew.

She sagged her forehead against the door for a moment. The night of Iain's conception had been desperate, joyful, wild. She had discovered the promises of happiness and security in his arms, and she had relished the feeling of his hard, slick body pressed against her own. She burned everywhere for him.

Placing a hand over her face, her mouth, she turned away. She wished she had never met him—but for her darling Iain. For years she had seethed and ached at the memories of that night, wondering what she would do if she ever saw him again, learned who he was.

Now that the chance was hers, she had succumbed to the same inexorable magic that had pulled her to him before. She had surrendered, and she was furious about it.

It would not happen again. Dougal Stewart had probably fulfilled a gleeful wager at her expense. In doing so, he had dishonored an ancient and secret tradition.

"Margaret, the bannocks," Mother Elga said.

She turned. "Oh!" she exclaimed, seeing smoke rising from the iron griddle by the fire. Hastening there, she removed the burned oatcakes from the heat to a plate.

"Your mind is elsewhere." Elga watched her, the towheaded baby in her lap. Tiny, wizened, and bent like a blackthorn stick, Elga nodded as she handed the spoon to Anna, who attempted to feed herself. Elga pointed a finger at Meg. "You are thinking of the kelpie."

"Not at all." Meg placed bacon slices onto a pan to cook them over the fire. Although she had purchased an iron stove for Thora, her grandmother still did her cooking in the traditional ways over the hearth fire, while the shiny cookstove in the corner provided a convenient shelf for stacking dishes.

"He has come back for you, disguised as a lighthouse man."

"He always was the lighthouse man, Mother Elga, and not the *each-uisge*."

Elga snorted. "So you want to think."

Meg sighed, cheeks blushing like fire, mouth pinched. She flipped the bacon too quickly and it spattered.

"Uisht," Elga said disdainfully. "You have forgotten how to cook, fine spoiled lady that you are now in your great castle!"

"I have not forgotten. But I do not cook or do chores in Edinburgh, only when I am here." She smiled at her great-grandmother. "And this is supposed to be my holiday!"

Elga was not in a humorous mood. "The *each-uisge* is real. You do not believe, even though you met him yourself and fell under his magic!"

"I fell under no one's magic, least of all his," she said as she turned the sizzling bacon. Remembering his recent, searing kiss, her knees felt weak all over again.

The door opened and Thora breezed back inside, her graying hair frizzled, brown skirt and apron untidy on her plush hips, her usual mild expression showing a faint and perpetual bewilderment, which Meg sometimes thought was real.

"He's still out there on the machair, watching the sea." Thora went to the hearth, took a steaming kettle from over the fire, and poured hot water into a teapot to steep.

"He longs to go back to his home under the waves," Elga said. "A kelpie does not like to wear his human guise for very long." She looked hard at Meg. "He wants to return to the water, and he's here to take you with him. He's the one. I know this."

"Ridiculous," Meg said. "He is just a man. A stubborn, infuriating man who came to our private island without invitation and refuses to leave. He's no kelpie." Meg transferred the bacon to three plates and spread the hot bannocks with butter after scraping off their charred surfaces.

"Then why were you kissing him up on the hill?" Thora asked. Meg did not answer.

"He may look human," Elga countered, "and he may be doing work on that rock, but we know what he wants. The kelpie and his ilk have long ruled that reef, and our island is under their protection. They accept the gift of a bride now and then to fulfill the old bargain, and well you know it, girl. Where's my tea?" Elga demanded.

"Here, Mother," Thora said, splashing the tea in her haste to serve it.

Meg placed the breakfast plates on the table and sat down while Thora poured tea into mugs and added sugar and cream for herself and Elga, leaving Meg's plain and fragrant, as she preferred it.

Anna spooned porridge into her mouth with fascination, and Meg glanced over her shoulder to the sleeping room beyond the main room, where Iain still lay asleep in his box bed. Norrie and Fergus had already gone down to the beach to start the day's fishing, and Fergus had mentioned that he might join Stewart's work crew for some extra money.

None of them needed extra money; none of them needed to work at all. Meg had offered to take care of all of them for the rest of their lives. While they accepted some things from her, the men would not allow her to pay for everything.

They had even refused to move into Clachan Mor, with its large and comfortable rooms. The croft house had ample room, they all insisted, and Norrie and Fergus had pointed out that it was closer to Innish Harbor. The house consisted of three spacious buildings attached under one roof, used separately for living, cooking, and sleeping quarters, with a byre for cows, goats, and chickens attached at the back. When Meg had inherited her fortune, she had insisted that the house be refurbished and enlarged and had added new furnishings. She had purchased Norrie a new boat and more fishing nets and had supplied her other kin and tenants with whatever they needed. For the last few years, though, the islanders rarely asked anything of her.

"Did you tell Mr. Stewart"—Thora pronounced it *Stoo-ahr*—"that you wanted him to leave Caransay?"

"I did, but it did no good. He'll stay, and his crew with him," Meg answered.

"Eich-uisge," Elga said. "Water horses, the lot of them." She nibbled on bacon. "Especially that leader. He is a prince of the sea. He prances about in the waves by night."

"I was just outside. He was not prancing," Meg said.

"Why do you think he chose to build his tower on the great rock? It has belonged to the water horses since the time of the mists, when the first *each-uisge* came out of the sea and took the form of a beautiful man and then fought Fhionn MacCumhaill. He made a bargain with Fhionn that he would keep the rock and let the people have the island, but he must have a bride from Caransay every one hundred years."

"They are only men," Meg said. "They are not water horses."

"So you say now that you are a fine lady with bags of coin, a castle, and servants," Elga said. "Years ago, when your heart was pure and your life was a simple one, you knew better."

"Did you tell him all the truth about you?" Thora asked.

"That she became his bride seven years ago?" Elga asked.

"He knows that, I think," Thora said. "I was at the harbor yesterday when he first saw our Margaret. He knows who she is. I saw it in his eyes when he looked at her."

Again Meg felt her cheeks grow hot. "He knows nothing."

Elga covered the baby's ears. "Does he suspect about his son?" she whispered loudly.

"Hush!" Meg glanced at the closed door of the sleeping room, where Iain still dozed. "He knows nothing, I tell you. He does not even know that I am Lady Strathlin."

"Good," Thora said. "Keep that from him while you are here on the island."

"I intend to tell him," Meg said stiffly. "It was just not the right time for it."

"You are keeping something from us," Elga said. "But I look into the fire and I know. He is the one."

"The kelpie? Or the engineer who has made my life miserable?" Meg asked. What she must keep from them was the hurtful truth of the trick the man had played on her that night long ago.

"Whoever he is," Elga said, "he's meant for you."

Meg sipped her scalding-hot tea and did not reply.

"*Uisht,* Mother," Thora said. "It is bad luck to talk so much of the kelpie."

"Why? He's come back for his bride," Elga insisted. "He's part of our family now."

"Oh, stop," Meg said, and groaned.

"He looks like a working man, but he is a prince of the deep, building a tower on his rock for his bride," Elga said.

Meg sighed and leaned her chin on her fist. Through the window, the early sky lightened to blue.

Since childhood, she had loved and respected her great-grandmother, and had listened to Elga's endless stories of ancient heroes, gods, and goddesses, and had given credence to Elga's divinations. The island's oldest inhabitant, Elga was also its mystic, its bard, its veritable queen. Revered by all, she was indulged as she became more eccentric and stubborn with age. Defiantly clinging to the old ways, she believed in legend and superstition, practicing spells and charms that she insisted had power. Elga lived in a medieval world, with a medieval mind, while the rest of the world had moved on, yet she was content in her ways and certain that they were right.

Meg felt very removed from the world of her childhood at times. Her years on the mainland had changed her irrevocably. She had matured into a practical woman with social status and financial power. Raised in the modern world and the world of tradition, she understood both. But time rolled slow in some parts of the Highlands and Islands, and Caransay was one of those places where tradition, routine, and simplicity reigned.

Meg owned Caransay's lease and had done much to improve living standards and add security to island life, but Elga would always live by the old ways, as would Thora. Norrie's wife was meek and kind, and so Mother Elga ruled the household and subsequently the beliefs in it.

Meg had not only outgrown the old ways, she had been deeply hurt by them when she had complied.

"Oh, mark me, he is the one," Elga said. "You made a bargain and a binding promise with the *each-uisge,* girl, and you had his child. Now the time has come when you must pay for your agreement."

"I have paid," Meg said quietly. She turned away, feeling the burden of that truth more than her grandmothers could suspect.

"It was our bargain, as much as hers," Thora said. "She did it for us, and everyone on this island has benefited. We have our homes and our livelihood safe. We have all that we could ever want, thanks to her generosity."

"That fortune of gold and riches came to her

through the kelpie," Elga said. "Just as much as that sweet child did."

"The inheritance came to me through my maternal grandfather's will."

"And never would have come to you at all if his first two heirs had lived," Elga said. "The old man died and left his fortune to his only granddaughter, an island girl. No one expected it. All this happened within a few weeks of your marriage to the kelpie. He made that magic happen."

"You make it sound like he arranged all that," Meg said. "There is no kelpie magic. And he is not my husband!"

"You did not resist him that night, girl, and we all know that," Elga said.

Feeling herself blush furiously, Meg sipped her tea.

"Once a woman is loved by the kelpie, he will haunt her heart forever," Elga said. "And none of us can argue what happened out there. We have Iain to prove it."

"Mr. Stewart is not my husband," Meg said through her teeth.

"He is the kelpie, and one night with him made you into a bride," Thora said. "Such marriages are still made in Scotland. It is an old custom."

"Go to him," Elga said. "More riches await you, and untold happiness. I've seen it in the fire for you. I've seen it in the water. This is a marriage that—"

"Enough," Meg burst out. She could not bear the thought of a marriage, even an inadvertent one, with so low a cad as the man who had tricked her that night. "I've heard enough talk of magic and kelpies. He is just a man, I tell you."

What a fool she had been, but she would spare her grandmothers the truth of how his mates came to fetch him after a night of mischief. "I'm going up to the Great House," she said. "I have correspondence to review, and Mrs. Berry is going to write some letters for me. Send Iain up there after he wakes and has his breakfast. He is to have lessons with Mrs. Berry in reading and mathematics today. And please tell him that if the weather is good and the waves are not too high, I will take him to the beach to play."

"We will come, too," Thora said. "Mrs. Berry is a nice woman. And small Anna loves to play in the sand."

"Small Anna likes to eat sand," Mother Elga grumbled. "But we will go, too."

"Good," Meg said, glad to be rid of the topic of kelpies. She grabbed her shawl and went to the door, and as she stepped out, she heard Elga murmuring to Thora.

"You know the kelpie has come back for his bride," Elga insisted. "We must have a great ceilidh to celebrate when she decides to accept the truth."

"He's so very handsome," Thora said. "She will see it soon enough. What woman could resist a man like that?"

Sighing, Meg went out into the pale morning. Dougal Stewart had gone, and the sun was bright over the sea.

His shelter was snug and cozy, the walls plastered thick to cut the wind and muffle the sound of rain. Barely ten paces in any direction, the single room was nicely warmed on cool nights by a coal brazier and not too hot during the days when the sun beat on the thick thatch roof. Small windows let in sea breezes—and sometimes rain and blown sand, unless Dougal remembered to close the shutters tight before he went out for the day.

The only luxury of the quaint place was that he had it to himself. Furnished with a canvas hammock, a cupboard, a wooden chair, and a table large enough for maps, charts, and a lamentable amount of correspondence, it could hold little more. He disliked writing letters and reports, but he made himself sit down twice a week to do it. As resident engineer, he was also required to keep a daily log of progress, crammed with figures and his notes and observations. The Stevenson firm and the lighthouse commissioners expected to be kept abreast of all events, problems, and successes.

The wind howled, and the evening skies were dark with rain. He was weary and sore from another long day out on Sgeir Caran, drilling through solid rock in the beating sunshine, relieved only by the refreshing sea spray from the waves that reached high enough to splash them. He particularly enjoyed watching seals cavort on the rocks, and a few dolphins had entertained everyone at lunchtime. After they returned to Caransay and had supper, the men rested and relaxed, but Dougal still had work to do. In another one of the huts, he knew that Alan Clarke and Evan Mackenzie worked on similar reports and analyzed maps and drawings.

Having finished his own report for the commissioners, he penned a long note to David Stevenson, who had recommended him for the job on Sgeir Caran after Dougal had assisted the brilliant designer and engineer with the lighthouse on Muckle Flugga, a nearly impossible challenge in an inhospitable environment. On Sgeir Caran, Dougal now faced some of the same problems of design and safety. With his worthy, experienced crew, he was certain that together they would build a fine lighthouse.

He sealed the envelope, then reached into a wooden box where he kept his correspondence to lift out another letter. This one was from Lady Strathlin—or more correctly, her Edinburgh solicitors. Opening it, he reread the letter and its curious postscript, which he had scanned earlier, setting it aside until he decided how best to reply.

You shall not build on Caransay without Lady Strathlin's permission, sir. Despite your parliamen-

tary order, we will see this enterprise stopped. Your structures will indeed come down, if not by Nature, then by legal writ.

Dougal sat back, pursing his mouth as he considered the threat. The new barracks were stout and strong; all ten houses held sound in the land edging Innish Harbor, protected by the high headlands. They would not blow out to sea as easily as the houses his men had constructed on Guga, the small isle beside Caransay, had done. Each shelter housed several men, with hammocks, furnishings, and plenty of large kegs of rainwater. There was scarcely room to move about inside the shared quarters, but the structures would stand in a high wind.

The letter, like the others, was written in the controlled script of some anonymous clerk or secretary. Regardless of their protests, he had built structures on Caransay, and he intended to remain until the lighthouse was done. Somehow he would convince the baroness and her lawyers of his determination and the worth of the project, and he hoped they would cease their threats.

Turning the page over, he read the curious postscript. Apparently it had been written by the baroness herself—the first direct contact he'd had from her in all these months.

Mr. Stewart, the birds who frequent Sgeir Caran may desert the rock if a lighthouse is placed there. A magnificent pair of golden eagles makes their home there each year. At any time of year there are gannets, puffins, and shearwaters—even the little storm petrels that are rarely seen and that make their homes on the undersides of rocky protrusions. The gannets in particular are hunted cruelly in other places. They are bludgeoned to death in a ritual called "the hunting of the Guga." But on

Sgeir Caran, they are safe and protected by ancient tradition. The golden eagles are, of course, most beautiful, most spectacular, and to be revered and protected.

For the sake of all these birds, I ask you recommend to the commission another location for the lighthouse. I understand the urgent need for a light to aid seafarers, and I applaud the courage of the men who would build it.

I beg you, sir, to erect your tower elsewhere.

Yours most sincerely,
Lady Strathlin
Strathlin Castle

Intrigued by this new action in their little war of words and missives, Dougal read it yet again. So far, each letter seemed to be either a counter or an offensive move, as in a chess game. Always surprised, never disappointed in what came next, he had secretly enjoyed their correspondence, wondering what the baroness and her lawyers would do next. He was certainly not intimidated by their little paper battle of wills.

The baroness provided an unexpected challenge. He found the tone of her lawyers' letters mildly amusing, and he inferred from them a good deal of spirit, passion, and determination in the baroness, hidden behind the screen of her solicitors' words. He had heard of her acts of charity and generosity, as well, and her preference for privacy, though he knew little else about her.

Sometimes he wondered if the baroness were a formidable old woman with a strong will and a generous heart. Or he wondered, instead, if she were a magnificent creature of mysterious beauty and perhaps tragic circumstances. Whatever she was, he thought she also took some pleasure in their game of wills. At times he anticipated her next move, but at other times she surprised him. She could be commanding, witty, haughty, or plaintive when she spoke through her minions. He had developed a grudging respect and an increasing curiosity about the baroness. He definitely did not care for her lawyers.

Her handwriting was not the tentative, wobbly hand of an elderly lady, but rather flowed in a petite and feminine way, with a touch of confidence, a hint of artistry. At first glance, given the handwriting and content, he thought the note had been written by a well-educated and sensitive young lady, rather than by a woman who was more than likely a tough old bird herself.

He laughed outright. The baroness must have asked someone younger, a companion or a niece, perhaps, to write it. His Aunt Lillian rarely wrote her own notes these days, dictating letters to his sisters, who lived with her.

The poignant touch of the little handwritten note had been meant to cajole and soften him. He would not relent. Nor was he overly concerned about the birds, who would be safe and would undoubtedly adapt to the changes on their rock—as the baroness obviously could not do herself.

Composing his reply, he smoothed a fresh piece of foolscap and dipped a pen in ink.

To the Right Honorable Lady Strathlin
Madam,

I am dismayed that your solicitors have not better informed you. Even as I write this, I am installed in comfortable quarters on the Isle of Caransay, with Sgeir Caran in view through my window. I saw a most spectacular sunset this evening, and the northern lights graced the sky last night. The weather currently is glorious.

The wind howled strong enough to rattle the door, and a gust of rain pattered on the shutters. Dougal shifted on the stiff wooden chair and squinted in the flickering lamplight.

I appreciate your concern regarding the wildlife on the rock. Let me assure you that it is not our intention to disturb Nature, or to significantly alter the appearance of the island.

I have not yet seen any golden eagles, madam. When I do I will give them your regards.

Smiling with relish, he signed the note, sealed the envelope, and dropped it in the mail pouch to give to Norrie MacNeill for posting at Tobermory the next day.

Chapter Five

"Madam," the housekeeper said, opening the door to the drawing room, "is something required?"

"Ah, Mrs. Hendry," Meg said, looking up from the writing table where she sat. A minute or so earlier, she had tugged at the bellpull, knowing that the housekeeper appreciated its use whenever Meg stayed at Clachan Mor. Although Meg preferred less formality on Caransay and spent much of her time with her grandparents and her son, Mrs. Hendry, who lived on the Isle of Mull when Meg was not at Clachan Mor, insisted on maintaining a household befitting a wealthy baroness. In her somewhat grim fashion, the woman seemed to enjoy it, so Meg indulged her.

"Please inform Mrs. Berry that I will shortly be ready to go down to the beach with her and Master Iain," Meg said. Mrs. Berry had long retired from schoolroom duties, but she enjoyed teaching Iain whenever she visited Caransay with Meg.

"Very good, madam." Mrs. Hendry's pursed lips and angular face were unsoftened by her luxurious silver hair and her lace cap. She closed the door, and Meg turned her attention back to the letters on her desk.

She wrote a quick note to Mr. Charles Worth in Paris, thanking him for his offer to send an assistant to Edinburgh to fit her gown for the September soiree. Mr. Worth was eccentric and exacting, but his creations were so elegant and lovely that Meg traveled to Paris every year to be fitted for a complete wardrobe at his shop on the Rue de la Paix. Angela Shaw, who understood haute couture far better than Meg ever could, had insisted on it. Meg had been delighted with each gown and garment from Worth's shop, and the new gown promised to be exquisite, judging by the sketches and fabric swatches he had sent her.

The next note was from Guy Hamilton, who reported that the Northern Lighthouse Commission had notified the law firm of Hamilton and Shaw that Mr. Dougal Stewart did indeed have governmental authority to proceed with the lighthouse on Sgeir Caran. Stewart was free to use his discretion to see the job done. With apologies, Guy stated that they were looking into a remedy to the problem and reminded Meg that she might encounter the resident engineer on the Isle of Caransay.

Too late, she thought. That damage was done.

She answered Guy and sealed it, adding it to the envelopes that Norrie would post when he sailed to Mull. He sometimes complained, with good humor, that the leather bag was too heavy for an old man whenever Meg was visiting the island.

Then she penned a quick note to Sir Frederick Matheson, who had written to express his very great desire to visit her at Caransay, since he owned the neighboring island of Guga. *Please do not feel that you need to come here for my sake, sir,* she wrote, *for my weeks here are peaceful but rather dull, and you would not be entertained.* She tucked the finished note into an envelope and looked through the other letters.

She felt oddly disappointed to find nothing from Dougal Stewart. He had not yet replied to the last letter the law firm had sent, to which she had added a note in her own hand pleading for the welfare of the birds on the sea rock and begging him to reconsider his plans.

Now she knew why he had not answered. He had been too busy building his barracks and drilling holes in Sgeir Caran. Through the open casement behind her, she could see the sea rock where the men worked with their sledges and drills.

She was tempted to sail out there, announce herself as the baroness, and demand a halt to the construction. But she had made an impulsive decision when she had first seen Stewart, and she was trapped by it. He believed she was an islander—and he knew that he had shared a night of loving with her years ago.

Not so easy, now, to tell him the whole truth.

If her past encounter with him became known, she risked genuine ruin. Even worse, her deepest, most carefully guarded secret might be revealed. She had enemies in business among kin on her grandfather's side who would relish the thought of her complete ruin. Sir Frederick Matheson might adore her to an uncomfortable degree, but others might not.

And if Dougal Stewart ever learned the truth, he would have enough fuel for any enemy's fire. He might be charming, but he was capable of reprehensible behavior. She could not trust him, and she was determined to protect her secrets.

Her stomach twisted with dread, for she knew that one day the truth would come out in some form. For now she would bide her time and keep her silence.

She turned to look out the open window. Clachan Mor was situated on a high rise at the north end of the island, and she could see the whole of the long strip of land. Its white beaches, rocky hills, and the softly colored machair were surrounded by vast blue skies and endless ocean. From here, she could view both coasts of the island. Scotland's coast and other islands were blue shapes to one side, and to the other, Sgeir Caran was a dark dot in the western sea.

Sighing out, she leaned her head in her hands. She must send Stewart away before he learned the truth.

The door of the drawing room opened, startling her. Iain burst in, fresh and smiling, and ran to her over the flowered carpet. His hair, shaped to a bowl and in need of cutting again, fell over his eyes. Meg smiled and brushed back the thick, golden-sheened hair to see his beautiful eyes, large and sea green. His father's eyes.

Her heart bounded, turned deep each time she saw him, with both joy and longing. Her love for this child nearly overpowered her at times, and she wondered how she had ever found the strength to give him away on the day of his birth, into the care of her cousin Fergus and his kind wife. Meg had never intended to leave him motherless. And most islanders believed that Anna and Fergus had taken the boy for fostering from unnamed relatives off the island.

"Berry says we can go to the beach!" Iain said in Gaelic.

"English, dear," Meg reminded him.

He nodded. "I did my lessons and read in English to Berry, who says I did good—well."

"That's excellent, Iain," Meg answered, looking up to smile at the buxom lady who entered the room after the child. "Mrs. Berry and I will certainly take you to the beach. It is a lovely day for it. Grandmother Thora and Mother Elga will be there, too. They promised to meet us there with small Anna."

"Master Iain did verra well today," Mrs. Berry said. "He's speaking nicely, and he's reading a little. His maths need work, and his handwriting, but that will come. He made a fine drawing of a sea monster. So fantastic, it frightened me out of me shoes!" Mrs.

Berry folded her hands over her ample stomach, which was encased in her usual black gown, her blue eyes crinkled in a deep smile. Iain giggled.

Elspeth Berry had been Meg's governess in the winter months, year after year, when she had stayed in her grandfather's castle as a young girl. Her impish smile, easy laugh, and practical, kind manner had endeared her to Meg from the very first. Mrs. Berry was a widow, and distantly related to Meg's deceased mother—whose father had left Meg the bulk of his staggering fortune.

With wealth and friends and loving family, with so much happiness in her life, she had dark secrets to balance the blend. They tugged deep at her heart, so that she never felt truly happy, never truly secure. Very few people knew she had given birth out of wedlock, and no one—outside of her grandparents—knew about the man she had met on Sgeir Caran.

She had hoped to keep those secrets safe forever.

"Good lad," Meg told Iain. "Bring a bucket to the beach so you can collect winkles and shells. If you find me some pretty ones, I will draw them in my little notebook. Berry would probably like to splash in the water, too. The day is perfect for it." Meg smiled at Mrs. Berry.

"Ma leddy, I'd like that. I'll fetch my bathing costume. And you, ma dear leddy, must remember your straw hat and your almond cream this time. We canna have you returning to Edinburgh looking like the nut-brown maiden! Your soiree is only weeks away!" She pronounced it *surree,* revealing her Lowland roots.

"You're right, of course, Mrs. Berry. Iain, will you run and ask Mrs. Hendry to pack us some things for the beach? A luncheon basket would be nice." As she spoke, he bolted toward the door.

"Walk, Master Iain," Berry said. "The leddy didna mean run!"

He slowed, hand on the doorknob. "I will ask Mrs.

Hendry to make us some cheese sand-witches." He glanced at Berry, who nodded approval. "Come, Berry. Hurry!"

"Och, aye, sir." Mrs. Berry bustled after him.

Alone again, Meg leaned her elbows on the desk and covered her face in her hands. For years, she had kept the secret of Iain's birth closer than any other. Only those present at the croft house on Camus nan Fraoch on the night of his birth knew she was Iain's mother.

Early on, Angela Shaw and Mrs. Berry had guessed that their new charge, the young baroness, was with child. They knew the child had been born on the island and given away, but they had never asked about the father, for Meg had let them believe that he was a fisherman she had known in the Isles before she inherited Lord Strathlin's estate. She trusted Angela and Mrs. Berry with her life, knowing they would keep her secret safe.

But she could never trust Dougal Robertson Stewart.

Gasping, she squeezed her eyes shut against tears. She could not risk losing Iain. If Dougal knew, he could expose their brief love affair and claim his child. No one would doubt his paternity, once they saw the man and boy together.

Stewart could destroy her life if he wanted. She could not live without her son—and yet she did, day after day, with a loneliness and heart-wrenching longing that she had become accustomed to over the years.

Beware, Elga had told her from the first day that Meg had whispered that she carried a child. *Beware. One day the* each-uisge *will come back to Caransay for his son and his bride, and he will take them with him to the bottom of the sea.*

The kelpie, Meg thought, was less a threat than the man.

* * *

Dougal sailed back to the island from the rock at midmorning, having left Alan Clarke and others laying black powder charges for the next stage in clearing the foundation pit. Intending to return before the fuses were lit that afternoon, Dougal had returned to the island to fetch some plans.

He had promised the baroness that the landscape would not significantly change, and he would keep his word. The beauty of the island and the Caran Reef meant as much to him as it did to her, though she did not know it. For him, every stone of the lighthouse would be dedicated in his heart to those who had been taken by the reef. He looked forward to the day he could set in place a ray of light to sweep the waters and protect those who sailed through these seas.

With a little time to spare before he was needed on Sgeir Caran, he walked across the center of the island toward Clachan Mor. Caransay was not large, seven miles long in all, three wide at its widest point. The Great House, as the inhabitants called the baroness's holiday home, was on the eastern side of the island, but it was only two miles from Innish Harbor over the machair and a line of low hills. The weather was glorious after a night of rain, with sunshine and white, puffy clouds in a summer-blue sky and brisk, fresh winds. From anywhere on Caransay he could hear the steady soothing rush of the waves and the constant call of seabirds.

No wonder the baroness cared so much about this place and its wildlife, he thought, glancing at the gulls wheeling overhead. The island had strong, simple beauty in its black rocks and white beaches, its flowery machair and heathery hills surrounded by blue sky and frothy waves. He felt a peacefulness here, a perfect balance of elements in sea and air and sunshine, in earth and rock. As much a part of the wonder of the isle were its earnest, handsome people and their fascinating legends. He would never disturb such beauty and serenity, though the baroness thought otherwise.

Hands in his pockets as he walked, he noticed Clachan Mor not far away, gray stone framed against a heathery hill. A small bay and beach separated the distance. Whenever the baroness came to the island, he planned to call upon her there. It seemed a better, more direct solution than endless letters.

Strolling behind a line of sand dunes, he heard women's voices raised in chatter and laughter. Curious, for most of the islanders kept to the westernmost beaches and bays, he walked to the top of a nearby dune and saw four women with two children.

Golden in the sunshine, Margaret MacNeill sat on a blanket on sand, legs curled under her brown skirt, a straw hat on her head rather than the provincial shawl. She held a book in her hand. Nearby, he saw Norrie MacNeill's wife and his mother, the elder holding a chubby baby, the other talking to a small blond boy.

A fourth woman waded in the water and called to the others, laughing. A black straw hat hid the wader's head, and she hiked up the black skirt of her elaborate swimming costume to edge deeper into the surf.

Wondering if he should step forward or politely retreat, Dougal paused. The boy turned and saw him, waving. Dougal waved back, recognizing the bold fellow who had climbed the headland the other day. As he stood there, the child ran toward him, and the three MacNeill women turned. Margaret stood quickly. Thinking she meant to come forward and speak with him, he crossed the beach toward her, to where dry sand met damp.

A breeze fluttered her hair, flattened her skirt against her, revealing her beautiful shape, slender legs, small abdomen, firm breasts. Feeling a lusty pang run through him, Dougal frowned. He knew far too much about this woman, and he found her far too distracting.

Watching her, honey bright and lovely as she came toward him, he could not deny how very much he wanted her physically. Desire shook him like a quaking of spirit each time he saw her. Remembering shared kisses and a stinging slap, he reminded himself not to give in to his impulses around her, to keep his self-control. Wanting to earn her confidence and trust, he intended to apologize whenever a certain rather awkward matter could be openly addressed—and he intended to discover the truth about that night.

She turned away from him deliberately and walked to the water's edge. He understood her rejection clearly, but he was not about to give up, though no doubt she thought him a complete and heartless cad—he had behaved like one, and more than once. Caution and respect would suit far better than airing his feelings, he told himself.

The little fair-haired boy, dressed in short dark trousers and a shirt of plain linen, padded barefoot over the sands toward him. "Hello! Are you Mr. Stooar?" he called.

"Stewart. Aye, lad. And who might you be, young sir?"

"I am Iain MacNeill." He puffed out his chest and pointed to himself. "Fergus MacNeill is my foster father, and he is a fisherman. Did you come here to go swimming or to catch a fish?" His English seemed good for such a small Hebridean. Dougal was no expert with children, knowing few of them personally, but he judged this one to be five or six years old, a fine, healthy child, with golden hair, a freckled nose, and wide greenish eyes. Dougal knew the boy was a fearless little creature, for he was surely the one Margaret had plucked from the rock when he had followed the older children upward.

Dougal bent to shake the boy's hand. "Pleased to meet you, Master MacNeill. I came out to find Clachan Mor, hoping to see the lady who lives there."

"I know her! She is my cousin. She owns all of this isle." He spread his arms wide to show the extent of her holdings. "She is not there now, though!"

So the baroness was related to some of the islanders. Many of them referred to each other as cousin, he had learned, though it did not always indicate a blood relationship. Often it meant simply a loyal bond. "Soon enough she will come back to Clachan Mor," Dougal said.

"But she's here," Iain said. He gestured vaguely behind him with his closed fist. Then he opened his fingers to reveal a periwinkle. "I found a shell. See?"

"It's quite nice. The lady is here?" Dougal asked in surprise, glancing toward the water where the boy indicated. Margaret MacNeill splashed barefoot in the surf, her back turned to him. The wife and the mother of Norrie MacNeill were close by, and the fourth lady, the wader, had gone too far out for Dougal to see her clearly.

Surely that was the baroness. "Is she in the water?"

"In the water, aye," Iain answered. "I have other winkles, too. I found them this morning. Come see. I have a whole bucket of them. Crabs, as well. Some of them are alive," he added, nodding.

"I'd love to see them. Is she the lady with the big hat, out in the water?"

Iain glanced around. "Oh, you mean Berry."

"Baroness?" Dougal stood as Iain's name was called. Norrie's wife, Thora, hurried forward and took the child by the shoulder. The older lady, Mother Elga, was with her.

"Come, Iain. Do not bother the man," Thora said. "Greetings, Mr. Stooar."

"Good day, Mrs. MacNeill. And Mrs. MacNeill." He nodded to them. The older one, tiny, wrinkled, swathed in a plaid shawl, gave him an intense and frank stare.

"Mr. Stooar," Elga said, her voice strong but tremulous, "left your rock, did you?"

"Er . . . aye. Fine day for a stroll," he said pleasantly, feeling uneasy under her regard.

"It is that," Thora said. "Come, Iain. I'll take you down to the water, like I used to do for Grandfather Norrie." She bent so that Iain could clamber onto her back. Then she straightened, hefting the child and grabbing his legs.

Dougal smiled. "Bringing the fisherman out to the boat?" He had seen the curious way that some of the fishermen's wives carried their husbands out to their boats so that they would not wet their trousers at the outset of a long workday. He had no doubt of Thora's strength, for she was built wide and powerful, but he wanted to laugh at the thought of her toting lanky Norrie into the water so that he would not wet his boots and legs on his way to a day's fishing.

Thora held the child securely, and Iain wrapped his arms around her neck. "I see you know our island traditions," she told Dougal. Mother Elga came close and peered up at him.

"Some of them. Young Iain will be a fine fisherman someday," Dougal said. The boy nodded vigorously.

"He could be, but she wants him to be an educated lad. She's hired tutors for him, and he's still so very small. He takes lessons at Clachan Mor when she visits here."

"You mean his cousin the baroness?" Dougal glanced toward the water. The mysterious lady sank down in calm water up to her chin, the wide black straw hat shading her face.

Closer to shore, Margaret strolled, lifting her skirt hem to her calves, splashing. She seemed to deliberately avoid him.

He could hardly blame her, but he was determined to find a chance to speak to her.

"The baroness says she will hire a tutor for his wee sister, Anna, too, when she is older," Thora said. She carried Iain, and Dougal walked beside her. Mother Elga followed, the plump fair-haired baby on her hip. "And I say, why so much education for them? They will not want to stay on the island when they are older. She should know about that. It's a good life on Caransay now that the baroness has made us all secure from the clearings. We can make a good living on fishing and lobster and collecting kelp and seabirds' eggs. We have little to worry about nowadays, other than the weather, which can be wicked at times."

"Wicked," Mother Elga repeated. "Have you ever been out in a storm, Mr. Stooar?"

"Aye, many times," he answered.

"Huh," Elga said.

"It must be a good life to live so near the water," he said. "I would very much enjoy it myself. It truly is a paradise here."

"So you like Caransay," Elga said. "And you like the ocean."

"Aye, very much," he said. "When I was a child, I swam like a fish. I loved the sea."

"Ahh," Mother Elga intoned, as if that were significant. She shifted the baby on her hip.

Dougal held out his arms. "Would you like me to carry the lad, or the little one?"

"We would not," Thora said hastily, exchanging glances with her mother-in-law.

"You shall not have our babies!" Mother Elga glared at him.

Dougal blinked. Had he offended them? Was there some island taboo against men holding children? He did not think so, as he had seen enough fathers watching after their own. Although the women seemed to speak adequate English, perhaps they had misunderstood him.

Thora set the boy down at the edge of the water. "Go with Margaret MacNeill," she said sternly. "Go on, now, and no arguing." She shooed him away.

Out in the mild waves, the other lady's head, capped in its straw hat, seemed to bob on the surface like a buoy. "I wonder if the baroness would give me a little of her time," Dougal said.

"You cannot disturb her," Thora said. "She is a very proper lady and she would not like to be approached while in her bathing costume."

"No, not now," Mother Elga repeated in her bizarre echo. She stepped closer, studying his face, then poked at his arm with an extended finger. Dougal eyed the old woman uneasily.

"Perhaps I can call on her later at Clachan Mor," he told Thora.

"Oh, not at Clachan Mor. She does not like visitors. You must leave the lady be, sir."

"Leave her be," Elga intoned. "Go back to your rock, water man. She will summon you when she is ready. We will talk to her." She examined him in her odd way as she spoke, walking around him, then scrutinizing his feet.

He turned while she circled him. "Ah, er, thank you. Perhaps you would be so good as to obtain an invitation for me to call," Dougal suggested. "Tell the lady that I am not the ogre she believes me to be."

Elga asked a question in Gaelic, and Thora answered her. Elga grinned. "Kelpie," she said, pointing to him. "Not ogre."

He was convinced that she was more than a little daft.

"We will do our best, sir," Thora said. "We shall see."

"Thank you." He wondered if they intended to help him, or help Baroness Strathlin avoid him.

Along the shore, Margaret began to walk back toward her blanket. Behind her, the woman in the water, apparently having soaked long enough, surged toward the beach, emerging from the water like a small black whale.

"Odd," Dougal mused. "I did not picture her quite so . . . corpulent."

"Turn away your eyes, sir," Elga said. "She is not wanting a man to see her now."

"Of course," he said, turning.

"Oh, she's coming this way," Thora muttered, hastening off.

When Dougal turned again, Thora had snatched up a linen towel from the sand and tossed it over the shoulders of the dripping woman in the black bathing costume. They walked down the beach together, pausing to talk to Margaret, who was seated again on the sand.

He saw that Margaret had taken up her little book, and Iain now played near her among some rocks that formed a small tidal pool. Pausing to speak with Thora and the baroness, she shook her head, then nodded, with a glance in his direction.

"Good day, Mother Elga," he said, giving the old woman a polite bow. "How nice to chat with you." He reached out to touch the fair, soft hair of the sturdy baby, who had been sucking its thumb, wide-eyed and quiet, while the adults had talked. He thought it might be a girl but was not sure. Dougal cooed and was pleased when the child laughed, showing four tiny teeth.

Elga backed away as if he meant to snatch the baby. The MacNeill women were overprotective of their children, he thought.

"Good day to you, water man," the old woman barked.

Impulsively, he winked at the baby, who giggled with delight. Dougal chuckled. Having had scant interaction with small souls, he was surprised to find the baby and the little boy so appealing. He winked again, but stopped when Mother Elga scowled at him.

Nodding farewell, he turned and headed across the sands toward the machair. Glancing in Margaret's direction, he saw that she still spoke with the baroness, but she paused to look past the lady toward him.

He had thought it best to leave her be, but the look she gave him was plaintive, so full of vulnerable longing, that he impulsively began to walk toward her.

Chapter Six

"Oh ma leddy," Mrs. Berry protested, "Please, I canna let the mon think I am Lady Strathlin!"

"He already thinks so, thanks to my grandmothers," Meg said, glancing after Thora, who had hastily retreated after delivering her news and now crossed the beach to join Mother Elga. The two older women bustled with small Anna to the other side of the little bay, obviously aware that their granddaughter would be upset with them for putting her and Mrs. Berry in such an awkward spot.

"Just let it be for now, Mrs. Berry," Meg went on. "I will correct Mr. Stewart later, in my own time and in my own way."

"Well . . . fine, but I canna talk to the mon when I'm in my swimming costume!"

"No one expects you to speak to him, Mrs. Berry. I will tell him that you value your privacy." Meg glanced over Mrs. Berry's shoulder at Dougal Stewart, who walked toward them, nodding politely to Thora on his way. "Oh! Here he comes—"

"Oh, verra well. I'll just go back in the water for a bit." Lifting the stiff skirt of her black bathing tunic, which she wore over knickerbockers and high laced slippers, Mrs. Berry walked down to the surf's edge. Meg had to smile, noting that the governess's posture was suitably haughty as she eased herself into the waves and stretched out to paddle along, the black straw hat hiding her face.

As Dougal Stewart walked closer, Meg turned and steeled herself. Would she ever be able to look at him without feeling a deep ache of longing, without recalling tenderness and power and love, as well as betrayal? She ought to tell the man firmly to just go away, and be done with it, she thought, scowling.

Watching him, she realized again how much the father resembled the son, despite their different hair color. They had in common their green eyes, firm chins, impish smiles, and Iain's nose would have the slender arch of his father's in years to come. Later, too, Iain would likely develop his father's build, with long, strongly muscled legs, a long torso and wide shoulders on a lean, athletic frame. The man had behaved in a vile manner with her, but he was beautiful to look upon. At least their son would inherit that.

Iain called to her from his perch inside the rocky tidal pool. He held up another shell for her to see, and she picked up her leather-covered book and walked over to him, bare heels sinking in damp sand.

"Oh, that one is lovely, Iain," she said, as he dropped a broken conch into a bucket. Together they bent to study some tiny, nearly transparent fish in the water. Lifting her skirts, Meg stepped into the water with him, and laughed with her son as the little fish tickled past their ankles.

"Cousin Meg, you must draw those in your book," Iain said.

"I will," she said. She drew the brown leather volume from the deep side pocket of her skirt and set it on a shelf of rock.

"Hello, Mr. Stooar!" Iain said. Meg turned, heart slamming.

"Good day, sir," she said stiffly.

"Miss MacNeill, good day to you." Today he wore a dark gray suit with a blue brocade vest and a black neckcloth. He carried a bowler hat and looked as if he had come calling. He smiled down at Iain. "Did you collect these shells yourself?"

"Aye, look!" Iain set his wooden bucket on a rock. Dougal leaned forward, holding out his hand while Iain lifted a few slimy snails and plopped them into the man's palm. Stewart admired them and put them back. Then Iain handed him a few tiny crabs, and he and Iain laughed to see one of those endeavoring to escape.

"Oh, I think this fellow deserves a chance," Dougal said, and he set the crab down near the water. "Go on, wee mon, back to your family." Inspired, Iain set the rest of his tiny captured crabs free. He and Dougal bent close to watch them scuttle away.

Dougal rinsed his hand in the water, splashing near Meg's bare toes, for she still stood in the shallow pool. Aware that he stared at her feet, she dropped the hem of her skirt so quickly that it soaked in the water.

Why bother to be self-conscious now? she thought. The man had seen her entirely nude. She had no physical secrets from him, at least. Looking up into the clarity of his gray-green eyes, she suddenly knew that he recalled every detail of that night, and she felt her skin heat in a fierce blush. Ducking her face under the shade of her straw hat, she stepped back onto the rocks and sat, covering her limbs and feet with her brown skirt and petticoat, as best she could.

"Is that why you came over to this side of the island, sir?" she asked coolly. "To rescue crabs and snails?"

"Well, I'm glad to be of service to someone. At least the snails and crabs on Caransay will think kindly of me."

She gave him a sour look.

"Actually, I just came out for a stroll on such a

bonny day," he said. He bent to pick up a shell, which he offered to Iain.

"Oh? Doing more puzzles in your head?" She tipped a brow at him, wanting to remain cool, but just the sight of him with Iain made her heart beat faster. He wiped some sand from his hands, then brushed a little sand from Iain's hands, too.

That made her heart melt. Not wanting to surrender in any way to this man, she frowned.

"I was pleased to discover that Lady Strathlin has come back to Caransay," he said, looking up at her. "She must have arrived in the last few days, while I've been busy on the rock."

"Mmm," she said, with studied disinterest, as she pressed some of the water out of the sopping hem of her skirt.

"Now that she is at Clachan Mor, perhaps she will allow me to call upon her soon." He glanced toward the water, where Mrs. Berry paddled contentedly in the gentle waves, only her hat and the occasional dark balloon of her swimming costume visible. "I seem to have found her at a most inconvenient time."

Iain giggled. "You have found her! Hasn't he, Cousin Meg?"

She glanced down. "Iain, the hole you dug over there is filling fast with water. You had better go save it."

Iain started off, turned. "May I wade in the water, Meg?"

"Yes, but do not go in higher than your knees," she said. He nodded and ran off. Though she knew that Mrs. Berry and her grandmothers would all keep an eye out for him, she turned to watch him herself.

"Meg?" Dougal asked. Hearing her name so soft upon his lips, she shivered. "I like it. It suits you—honest and beautiful."

Honest. She felt her cheeks burn with shame, knowing she could tell him the truth given the right words and enough courage. She was not like Dougal Stewart, who was boldhearted and brave and seemed to have a craving for risk. He was right to say that she was honest by nature, for she had always been that—until life and society had trapped her in a corner, forcing her to hide the secret of her son and her single night of loving.

Lies, she thought—how she hated them, hated herself for allowing them to rule part of her life, hated the way they made her feel, hollow and vulnerable and sad. She wanted to tell Dougal Stewart the truth. But once she did, she must tell him all of it. And she had to trust him first.

Not yet, she thought, glancing at him. Not yet. She could not risk losing Iain.

"My mother gave me an English name," she said, glad for something to say, for he watched her curiously, the wind ruffling his rich brown hair, his eyes keen and knowing. "She called me Margaret and Meg, rather than a Gaelic name. She was from the mainland, you see, though she lived here on Caransay with my father, who was Norrie and Thora's son. My parents died before I was twelve."

"I'm sorry," he murmured. "It is hard to lose both at once."

"Not together. My mother died of a sickness when I was eleven. I think it was a broken heart, for my father had died the year before—out there," she murmured, looking out to sea. "A storm took him."

"On the reef?" he asked.

She nodded. Her eyes stung with tears, not from sand or wind, but poignant memories. "My mother was lovely. Very kind, with the natural elegance of a lady," she said. "Her father was . . . He had some wealth and status on the mainland, yet his daughter went on holiday in the Hebrides and fell in love with a simple fisherman and married him without her father's consent. He was furious about that, from what I hear." She gave a hollow laugh. "He accepted it later."

"Your father must have been a remarkable man to win her," Dougal remarked quietly.

"He had such goodness in him," she said. "A big heart and much humor, and when he sang, as he loved to do, it was pure magic to hear him. He was handsome, too," she said, smiling. "Now that I am grown, I know why she fell in love with him so easily. But he died out there, taking in his lobsters. Went out on a bright morning, singing and laughing, and never came back. My mother never recovered from it." She shook her head. "His nephew, my cousin Fergus MacNeill, is very like him."

"And Iain?" he asked.

She turned to stare at him in surprise. "Iain?"

"Fergus's son. Is he like him, too?"

"Iain . . . is Fergus's foster son, though related to my father. Iain is blond, like . . . my father was." A breeze fluttered a strand of hair over her eyes. She reached up to sweep the wayward strands back just as Dougal did. Their fingers touched. His hand lingered on hers for a moment.

"Very blond, like you. Golden as sunlight, your hair."

Oh God, she thought, as her knees turned to fluid and deep longing spun in her belly. His touch had a kind of magic that stirred through her and would not let go. She should never let him touch her, she told herself, and stepped backward.

"That is very familiar, sir," she said primly. "We are not on those terms."

"We were once," he murmured. She turned her profile to him and stood silently, heart pounding, willing him not to say any more. "Forgive me, Miss MacNeill," he said quietly.

She was not ready to forgive him for either great

or minor offenses. First she had to trust him, and she could not do that. But she was beginning to like him far more than she would have guessed. She said nothing, watching Iain splash in the wavelets.

"Well," Dougal said after a moment, "I suppose I should be going. An introduction to Lady Strathlin would be awkward just now. Please tell her that I shall call upon her another time. We have much to discuss."

"Yes," Meg said.

"I had some hours free today, but the work on Sgeir Caran will require my presence much of the time," he said. "Perhaps next week I can call at Clachan Mor, if she is still here."

"If she will meet with you," Meg said.

"Perhaps you could speak on my behalf, Miss MacNeill."

"Why should I do that?" she asked sharply, glancing at him.

He smiled, his eyes crinkling. In sunlight, his irises were green and gold, framed by dark lashes. "You do not need to, of course," he said gently, "if you do not care to."

"Well, then," she said ineffectually, and lifted her chin.

"At least tell her that I look forward to meeting her in more appropriate circumstances."

"She will not be what you expect, Mr. Stewart."

"I am certain." He watched her, a little smile on his lips.

She narrowed her eyes, wondering how much he knew or could guess. He had realized quickly that she was the girl he had met on the rock. How long before he discerned the rest? She suddenly felt very vulnerable in his presence.

"Please tell Lady Strathlin," he said, "that I extend an invitation to her to come out to Sgeir Caran. I would like to show her the work we are doing there. Perhaps if she visited the site and had her questions answered, she would better understand the need for the project."

Meg frowned. "I'm sure your invitation will be appreciated."

"If you would care to visit the rock, as well," he said, "I would be more than glad of it."

The thought of standing on that rock with Dougal Stewart, even in the company of others, made her breath catch, her heart surge. She did not know if she could face it. "I will consider it, Mr. Stewart," she finally answered.

"Good." He smiled at her, and the mischievous curve in his upper lip dissolved something deep inside of her, one more barrier of resentment. He had an unconscious magic, this man, a naturalness, an ease of humor and intelligence that she found deeply intriguing. The slightest touch, the smallest smile cast spells over her.

His smile was like Iain's, too. If Iain grew up to be the image of Dougal Stewart, she realized, someone would eventually notice that. Even twenty years from now, what would she say?

Frowning, she turned away to busy herself gathering Iain's bucket and shells. Her notebook lay on the rock and she grabbed it, but her hands were full. The book fell at Dougal's feet, fluttering open to reveal pages dense with sketches and notes.

He stooped to pick it up. "Is this yours?"

She was so flustered that she blurted an explanation. "I keep a journal of the flora and fauna on the island. I enjoy drawing the shells and the fish, the flowers, the birds, and all things native to this island."

"May I see?" She nodded, and he flipped through the pages, examining her careful drawings, pausing now and then to admire a particular study of a bird or a shell, or to scan her brief descriptive passages.

"Fascinating," he commented. "You are both scientist and artist, Miss MacNeill. These are vivid, lovely drawings, and your text is equally interesting. And each drawing is labeled in English, Gaelic, and Latin. A remarkable amount of work."

"I have been doing it for years. I'd like the details to be correct, so I take time to look up the names of the plants and wildlife and so on in dictionaries."

"You must have a thorough library on . . . Mull, is it?"

"No, my grandfather collected a wonderful library at—" She stopped, realizing that she had said too much in her enthusiasm.

He lifted a brow. "Norrie MacNeill has a library?"

"My maternal grandfather had a respectable collection. I inherited . . . some of his things."

"I see." He flipped through more pages. "Gannets, gulls, puffins, curlews, shearwaters, storm petrels . . . ah, and the golden eagles on Sgeir Caran . . . I had no idea there were so many forms of birdlife on this island, let alone shells, starfish, crabs, and seaweed. Several varieties of kelp, I see, are all labeled here."

"The kelp is quite important on this island. It is gathered and dried for potash and then exported to the mainland and elsewhere. It's very useful in manufacturing glass."

"And gives the islanders a solid income. I have some investments in the kelp industry, and in herring, too—silver darlings make money for islanders as well as investors." He turned pages. "The heather in the hills . . . and the flowers on the machair. Ah, here we are—yarrow, daisy, buttercup, wild irises," he said. "And more, all here. Quite nicely done."

"Thank you. I have another journal like this one," she said, "filled with drawings and notations. This one is nearly finished, too. As you can see, there are only a handful of pages left in the volume."

"And every page is impressive. Will you begin another?"

"I thought to begin a more detailed study of the birds."

"Ah." He looked at her curiously, eyes narrowing.

"The wildlife and plant life are precious to us here, Mr. Stewart. Caransay is singularly beautiful and idyllic. It is one reason we do not want the lighthouse so close to here."

"Lady Strathlin agrees with you. No doubt she approves of your wildlife journals."

"No doubt." Meg gave him a sidelong glance, realizing he had read her latest letter, in which she had penned a fervent plea for the fate of the birds on Sgeir Caran.

Looking toward Iain, glad for an excuse to change the subject, she saw him splashing and jumping in the surf. She shaded her eyes with her hand. "Iain! Do not go too far out!"

"He's fine. He's an adventuresome lad, that one."

"Too adventuresome. He is likely to go diving or climbing without a thought for safety."

He smiled. "You sound more like his mother than a cousin." He glanced about. "Is the mother here? I have not seen her."

His simple question struck her to the heart. "Fergus MacNeill's wife died with the birth of the little one, Anna, there with Mother Elga. Iain is permanently fostered with Fergus, but now he . . . he has no mother." She walked over damp sand through a thin wash of water. Dougal went with her, his boots sinking prints beside hers.

"Very sad. Perhaps Fergus will take another wife to care for his children."

"Someday he will," she said. "For now, he lives with my grandparents."

They walked side by side. Seagulls dipped and fluttered overhead, and the soothing sounds of the ocean filled the air. Although she wanted to be on her guard, Meg felt surprisingly relaxed in his presence. She could have strolled along the beach forever, surrounded by peace, in company with him.

"I was a bit of a daredevil child, like Iain," Dougal

mused, watching as the boy splashed in the shallows. "My mother reined me in tightly, as you do him, to keep me from getting into trouble or hurting myself."

"You are still a daredevil to put up lighthouses in such dangerous locations. And you dare to confront baronesses and parliament, too, to get what you want. What does your mother think of that?"

He chuckled, and she loved the deep, easy rumble of it, though she did not want to like anything about this man. His expression, when she glanced at him, faded to sadness. "My mother would be proud, I hope, if she knew. She passed away when I was thirteen, at the same time as my father. They never saw my work with the lighthouses and never heard about my . . . escapades." He walked, hands in pockets, head down, the breeze fingering through his hair.

"Oh, I am sorry. I did not know."

"Of course you didn't. As for confronting baronesses and parliament—I admit I have given the baroness a bit of trouble."

"You are notorious on Caransay for that, Mr. Stewart."

"So I gather. I know you would like to see me leave here, and I'm sure others feel the same. But I warn you, Miss MacNeill. I will not be ousted or dissuaded from my goal. I have one quality, you see, that is both a flaw and a virtue."

"What is that, sir?"

He stopped and looked at her. "Once I decide upon something, I never give up. Never." The green of his eyes turned hard as glass. "I suggest you explain that to your baroness. And remember it yourself, Miss MacNeill, for it applies to you as well."

"Me? How so?" Her voice wavered.

He leaned down a little. "Shall I tell you now, in full view of the other ladies, or shall we wait a bit?"

Heart slamming, she gazed up at him. "We shall wait."

"Very well." He looked down at her leather journal, which he still carried. "This is admirable, Miss MacNeill. I hope you will consider publishing it one day."

"I doubt anyone would be interested in my journals."

"On the contrary, it is a unique and lovely thing. Scotland is very popular with tourists as well as the literati lately. I think you would do well to publish these."

"It is only a hobby. I never—" She stopped, wanting to be honest with him in one area, at least. She had dreamed of publishing her journals someday, but she did not think them worthy enough, even if she published them anonymously and at her own expense.

"Well," she began, "I have imagined my journals as a lovely set of books." She half laughed. "In green leather bindings with a flower design tooled on the front and gold lettering on the spines."

" '*A Hebridean Journal,* by M. MacNeill,' each volume would say," he suggested.

She shrugged. "A silly dream."

He touched her arm and looked into her eyes, sending a thrill all through her. "It is a very precious dream, Meg MacNeill. Hold on to it. Never give it up." His voice was deep and sincere.

"But I am neither a writer nor an artist. I just like to record the beautiful things on my—on the island. It is enough."

"Someday," he said, handing the book to her, "I hope you discover your dream."

She took the journal, her fingers brushing his. "Thank you," she said. "I have never spoken much to anyone about my journals before. I appreciate your . . . encouragement."

He smiled. She loved to see that warm play of mischief and affection in him. No one would have thought him capable of cruel tricks.

"I had an uncle who wrote books—poetry, mostly," he said. "Very romantic, lofty stuff, full of legends and tragedy, with much beating of breasts and so forth. Perhaps you have heard of him. Sir Hugh MacBride."

"The queen's own Highland bard! He was your uncle? I have read everything he wrote. How marvelous to have such genius in your family, Mr. Stewart."

He looked at her quizzically. "Your Hebridean education stretched to romantic poetry?"

"My island education was more than adequate, thank you. We were taught English and other subjects in the village school. We had maths, reading, writing—and yes, even poetry."

"I did not mean to offend, Miss MacNeill."

"In addition, from the time I was a small girl, I spent every winter on the mainland at my grandfather's house—my mother's father. He hired tutors for me. More poetry, languages, sciences, and far more mathematics than I cared to learn. I had deportment and music and drawing lessons, too, and a tutor who encouraged me to keep journals."

"Busy winters," he remarked.

"Very," she said. "I cannot say I looked forward to those months each year. I am not the fishwife you may think me, Mr. Stewart," she ended crisply.

He seemed amused. "Once again, I ask your forgiveness."

She heard the undercurrent in that and did not reply.

"I, too, had a tutor," he said. "But I loved mathematics and physics. The rest of it was deadly, though I enjoyed poetry readings at Dundrennan House—my uncle's estate. I often went there with my three sisters to visit our same-age cousins."

"Three sisters!"

"Does that surprise you?" He chuckled. "My cousins Aedan and Neill and I got into more than enough scrapes to make up for the femininity that surrounded us." He grinned. "I was scarcely out of skirts when we began scheming to avoid the girls and make towers and fortresses for ourselves. We made them out of my uncle's books." He grinned. "That did not meet with much approval."

A laugh bubbled up within her, and she let it go. "And you are still making towers."

He grinned down at her. "I suppose I am," he said, then sobered. "And neither you nor the baroness will be able to stop this project, Miss MacNeill. We are on Caransay for the duration."

"None of us want to see the island disturbed, even if we have no choice about the lighthouse. You were working on Guga before—I wish you would stay there, sir, and leave this island be. Find another sea rock, while you are about it. Sgeir Caran is not the place for your lighthouse."

"No other place suits."

"Commissioners and engineers have given no thought to traditions and legends or to the people of this island."

"Shall we allow legends to hold back progress, Miss MacNeill? Shall we allow more people to drown on that reef in deference to tradition?" He raised his voice, pointed toward the water. She saw the rare, hot spark of his temper, but he turned away, turning back a moment later after mastering his outburst. He was visibly tense with anger. "Tell your baroness that the lighthouse will go up and the barracks will stay, and if she wishes to further discuss the matter with me, it must be in person. No more letters. I have had enough of her lawyers and her tricks."

"Tricks!" Meg leaned forward, as did he. "How dare you speak of—"

"Come here." He took her arm, hard and insistent, a fire of awareness exploding through her when he touched her. Leading her toward the incline of a rocky hill, he pulled her through tough, flowering heather plants. She glanced back to be sure that her grandmothers were watching Iain, and she saw that he had already left the water and was once again digging in the sand.

At the top of the hill, the view of the western side of the island was expansive and beautiful. Dougal pointed toward the islet of Guga at the northern end of the island.

"Look there, Miss MacNeill. What do you see?"

"Guga," she said obstinately. "With the scars of your quarry work still raw upon her."

"I will grant you that. What else?"

She looked. "Nothing else."

"Precisely. Our barracks are gone."

"Oh!" She remembered that one of his letters had detailed losing those shelters to storms.

"We built some huts there. Gone now, as you can see. They were taken down by a gale for the second time—we put them up twice."

"Perhaps you should have taken that for a sign."

"I told you I do not give up, Miss MacNeill," he said curtly. "Guga is an inhospitable place, little more than a rock. We set up tents and lived on Mull after that. My men were miserable with the weather and the daily sea journeys. When Lady Strathlin and her lawyers ignored my pleas, I told the commission that we must find a secure site on Caransay for our quarters or the work would be seriously delayed."

"You could have stopped," she said.

He leaned toward her. "Never. This lighthouse goes up."

"And be damned to all. Is that what you think, sir?" She had never used such language, yet he did not blink over it. She felt a strange thrill speaking so boldly to him.

"Something like that," he said.

"Then why bother to meet with the baroness at all? You want no one's permission but your own for what you do."

"I want her cooperation—especially since we must quarry more stone, and it must come from Caransay."

"What! You cannot quarry on Caransay!"

"Frankly, Miss MacNeill, I can if I want, according to the writ. But I would like the baroness's approval. The rock in these hills is better quality than that from Guga. It's good gray granite, with few flaws."

"Mr. Stewart," she said, head lifted high, "the baroness will never approve that."

"The quarry would bring more work to the men of this island."

"They do not need the work. The baroness helps the people on this island. We do not want to see Caransay ravaged or defaced."

"I always make certain that my crews preserve the integrity of the landscape, wherever we work."

"Caransay has been undisturbed over the centuries."

"Given the poor state of things in the Highlands and the Isles, modernization is not an evil force, Miss MacNeill."

"When improvement threatens to destroy centuries of custom and eons of Nature's fine work, there is a great deal wrong with it. I suggest you make your quarters here temporary, sir, for you will not be on Caransay much longer."

"You are a fitting mouthpiece for your baroness."

"I must get back to watch Iain." She whirled and walked down the slope, and he came with her.

"Hey, Master Iain," he called, as the boy ran toward them.

"Did you see me in the water?" Iain asked. "I am learning how to swim!" He puffed his chest proudly.

"We did," Dougal answered. "When next we meet, young sir, I shall teach you how to swim the foam myself, as they say in the old songs. How would that be?"

"No!" Meg said quickly, touching Iain's shoulder. "No."

Dougal frowned at her. "He would benefit from that skill, living so close to the sea."

Fear rushed through her, a sense of warning, like the deep toll of a bell. "It's not necessary for you to teach him. Good day, Mr. Stewart. Come, Iain. We must get back." She took the boy's hand and urged him along with her.

"Mr. Stooar," Iain said, turning, "I will see you again!"

"You will, sir," Dougal said cordially.

Meg swept Iain along with her toward Thora and Elga, who waited. She glanced over her shoulder, but Dougal had already gone. Oddly, she felt his absence like a tug upon her heart.

It was unwise to surrender to his charm, she told herself. She must stay away from Dougal Stewart and see that he left the island.

I never give up, he had told her.

Well, neither would she.

Chapter Seven

Birds fluttered up from the sea rock like ashes on the wind. A flare, a noisy bellow, a plume of smoke, and then debris erupted from the massive rock. Falling rocks churned the water below, the ripples spreading out to bounce a dozen boats.

Cheers and applause rose from those watching inside the fishing boats. Norrie, hollering with the rest, lifted a hand in salute, then grabbed at the oars. Thora, Mother Elga, and Iain, riding with him all clapped and laughed, along with the others.

Meg sat silent in the bobbing bow, unable to enjoy the spectacle as they did. She had spent time and funds trying to prevent this very thing from happening. Sgeir Caran would never be the same. The blastings would forever alter the rock and the integrity of its ancient soul.

Most of all, she was concerned about the wildlife and bird colonies on Sgeir Caran. Watching more birds drift upwards from the rock like a spiral of dark smoke, she frowned.

Another sky-high eruption was greeted by yelling and clapping from those in the boats scattered over the water. Some of the islanders had watched the construction explosions on the rock for much of the morning. Neglecting lobster pots, nets, and chores, they were thrilled by the gigantic plumes of smoke and fire flaring into the bright sky. A little while earlier, Dougal Stewart had sent men out in a rowboat to ask the spectators to keep their boats well back for reasons of safety. The people had complied, declaring the view still marvelous.

Meg had witnessed pyrotechnics in Edinburgh, London, and Paris, and she understood that the islanders found these explosions to be novel and entertaining. Witnessing this with them, she felt only sadness. For her, the glorious beauty of nature far outstripped fireworks and explosions produced by man. Nothing could compare to the grandeur of the aurora borealis or the awesome sight of storms and lightning.

After a lull came another flare and an enormous plume of smoke, and wild cheers rose from the audience. Watching, Meg wished the rock could stay unchanged forever, a sanctum sanctorum for birds and seals, a monument to ancient traditions and legends. Sgeir Caran was a place of mystery and power, and it had a personal, treasured significance for her privately.

Nothing in life remained the same, and too often wonderful dreams fled with the dawn. She had learned that lesson well.

Soft, gentle rain fell on his hat and the shoulders of his gray coat as Dougal mounted the low slate steps of the entrance to Clachan Mor, lifted his hand, and knocked. As much as he hated wearing a hat, he had donned his bowler out of politeness. He adjusted its brim as he waited. Damn—he had forgotten his gloves, he realized. He shoved one hand in his pocket.

After a few moments the door opened to frame a tall, thin woman wearing a black dress, a white apron, and a lacy cap. She stared down her narrow nose at him with dramatic effect, for she not only stood a step above him, she seemed as tall as he was—and he bested six feet without boots.

Gaunt and solemn, she was a harsh harridan, despite the soft beauty of the silvery hair beneath her little cap. Her eyes were steely gray, and her gaze raked him up and down so that he felt like an unkempt little boy. All the governesses and dominies he had ever had glared at him through this woman's cold stare.

He smiled. "Good day. Is Lady Strathlin at home?"

He expected the formidable creature to shut the door in his face. "Who is calling?" Her intonation was stiff and studied, without a trace of Scots or the accent of a native Gael.

"Mr. Dougal Stewart, resident engineer on the Caran lighthouse, come to see Lady Strathlin."

She continued to stare at him, hard and unforgiving. No doubt she knew all about his dispute with the baroness, he thought, as did the rest of the islanders.

Glimpsing movement in the shadowed hall behind her, he looked past her into the entrance hall. He saw the gleam of polished wood, the glint of brass and crystal, the muted tones of Turkish carpets and brocaded furniture. Through a half-open door off the hallway, he could see a wall lined with books. The pocket door slid quickly shut.

"Lady Strathlin is not at home at present, sir," the woman said. "Your card?"

Card. Damn again. He had forgotten to carry one with him. Cards were rarely required while quarrying stone or setting black powder charges. He was lucky to have the jacket and hat. Patting his coat, he took out a small memorandum book and the stub of pencil and scribbled his name and address: *Dougal Robertson Stewart, Kinnaird Castle, Strathclyde, currently of Innish Bay, Caransay.* He tore out the sheet and handed it to the housekeeper.

She took the little page gingerly, as if it were the

tail of a rodent, and stepped back. "Lady Strathlin will be informed that you called. Good day, sir." The door closed with a solid click.

Dougal stood on the step in the drizzling rain. Too late, he realized that Lady Strathlin would probably consider a note scribbled in pencil to be the height of crudity and bad manners and dismiss his visit altogether.

Sighing, he walked away.

As Norrie rowed closer to Sgeir Caran, Meg saw that a quay existed where none had before. The broad ledge had been created by the blastings of a few days earlier. She looked up at the towering height of the rock and saw that crude steps had been cut beside the natural slope that had previously served as access to the top.

Alan Clarke, the foreman, stood waiting for them on the quay. He caught the rope that Meg tossed, looping it through an iron ring in the stone before turning to assist her out of the boat. His grip was strong and sure, and he was built like a golden bull, his eyes vivid blue beneath a shock of thick blond hair. She recalled how pleasant he was whenever she exchanged greetings with him on Caransay. Glancing up, she did not see Dougal Stewart among the men standing near the edge of the rock.

"Hello, Miss MacNeill, and welcome," Alan Clarke said lightly. "And Mr. MacNeill! Mr. Stewart said you might come out to see our progress." He led them toward the steps. "After the explosions, it's a bit of a mess on the roof, I'm afraid. Step carefully." Walking on the outer side of the rough steps, he ushered them carefully upward.

Attaining the high, flat plateau, Meg glanced around in dismay. The remote, isolated sea rock was a scene of chaos. A huge crater dominated the center area, and broken rock and dressed stones were stacked around its edges. Clusters of men worked with tools and clunky pieces of equipment. Workbenches, tarpaulins, ropes, kegs, wooden crates, and slabs of stone seemed scattered or leaning wherever she looked. Two smiths had set up a forge to one side, hammering iron rods over bright orange flames. Crane arms attached to a steam engine projected over the outermost edge of the sea rock, and ropes and platforms dangled down into the water.

A few men turned the cranks of two enormous spools, reeling heavy ropes and hoses down to the men working on the cliff below, while others operated what looked like gigantic bellows. Nearby, a few men peered over the side and called back orders.

The combined noise of shouts, hammering, and machinery was loud and incessant, while the steady shushing of waves and the delicate cries of the birds added a peaceful, familiar background tapestry to the harsher modern sounds.

Meg turned slowly, overwhelmed. The wind whipped at her skirts, and she drew her plaid shawl more snugly around her shoulders. Despite the warm, sunny weather, the breeze on top of the rock cut as chilly as it always had.

"We made a quay so that we could bring barges and tenders as close as possible," Alan Clarke said, explaining the features of the work site. "We're constantly loading and unloading equipment and materials, and now that we have the foundation pit for the lighthouse ready, we've been transporting the dressed stones that were quarried on Guga."

She nodded, watching masons work with sledges and chisels, their strokes refining the huge stones so that they would fit together to form the base of the tower. Several stones had been lowered into place and packed with mortar. The pit dug into the plateau was huge—eighty feet around at least and almost two feet deep, Alan explained.

"The cranes are used to haul the stones and other materials up to this level," Clarke said, pointing to some of the machinery. "Most of the stones weigh several tons apiece. We cannot bring horses and oxen out here, of course, though we use them on the island to transport the stones from the quarry, so we have to rely on cranes, pulleys, and roller bars. It took a week just to get all the equipment and supplies moved up here and secured in place. See there? We've built a wee shelter to house our things."

The "wee shelter" was a tall structure set at the far end of Sgeir Caran, where the rock rose upward in a natural tower. It resembled a giant spider, its metal walls and roof set high on riveted pylons drilled into stone. "Mr. Stewart was concerned about waves and wind destroying our work, so we built it to survive the weather. We store materials in it, and there's room for hammocks and a cookstove, so men can stay the night if the weather turns bad."

"Ach," Norrie said. "A good storm will sweep your house away like matchsticks."

"I hope not. Those spikes are driven deep into the rock."

"Where is Mr. Stewart?" Meg asked.

Clarke turned to look toward the edge, where the men cranked the arm of the huge spool. "He'll be up in a moment."

Hearing shouts and hammering from somewhere out of sight, Meg assumed that Dougal was working there. She knew from his letters to the baroness that he never hesitated to roll up his sleeves and work alongside his men. While that increased her grudging respect for him and his dedication to his project, she still wished the lighthouse could be built elsewhere.

Looking around, she sighed. Even if the work crews were to leave tomorrow, Sgeir Caran would never be the same. At the far end of the rock, the high, natural stack-rock tower was unchanged, providing a dramatic background for the future lighthouse and a lee against the winds. Beyond it, hidden in the crevices on the north face of the rock, lay the shallow cave where she and Dougal had once found shelter and solace.

Her heartbeat quickened. Though she had come to Sgeir Caran many times since then to sketch the wildlife, she felt a secret thrill—and an undercurrent of regret—each time she saw the cave where her life had changed so irrevocably. Now she dreaded the moment when she would face Dougal Stewart here.

Alan Clarke went to the cliff edge, where an iron railing had been installed and where the men worked noisy cranks and pumps to guide the stout ropes and hoses that snaked over the edge. He picked up a hose fitted with a funnel end, shouted into it, listened to a reply, and called something to the men on the machinery. They worked furiously to reel the ropes and hoses onto the spools.

He beckoned Meg and Norrie toward the iron railing. "Careful now, Miss MacNeill. Mr. Stewart will be cross with me if his bonny visitor falls into the water."

She saw with surprise that the ropes and hoses dropped far down into the sea. As the men steadily winched the ropes and hoses, the water began to bubble.

"Ah, here he comes," Clarke said, as a platform surged out of the sea, swaying on ropes.

A monstrous creature rode the planks, pale, saturated, and swollen. Its head was a sphere, its paws and feet enormous. Water gushed from the beast and poured off the platform as the ropes drew it toward the roof of the rock. Beside Meg, Norrie exclaimed in astonishment.

Meg had seen divers in engraved illustrations, but never in actuality. "Is that Mr. Stewart?" she asked.

"Oh, aye," Alan Clarke said. "He went doon the deep to look at the base of the rock."

"Huh," Norrie said. "Mother was right. There's your kelpie."

Meg blinked at her grandfather, who grinned and turned back to watch the diver.

As the platform rose higher, Meg glimpsed Dougal Stewart's face behind the small porthole windows set in the brass-and-copper helmet at front and sides. Three valves, attached to the hoses, snaked toward the bellows that she now realized pumped air into the helmet. The third hose ended in the funnel that Alan had used as a speaking tube.

Diving was common, she knew, in salvage and bridge and dock construction. Matheson Bank had financed such ventures on Scotland's east coast, but she had never thought that divers might also be necessary for a lighthouse project.

The platform drew level with the cliff, and men grabbed the ropes to swing it inward to safety. Some held it steady while others took Dougal by the arms and supported him as he walked. His steps were slow and cumbersome, and Meg realized that the diving suit, helmet, boots, and weighted belt were an enormous burden. He lowered to sit on a stone bench, and his assistants unscrewed the helmet while another man stooped to unbuckle his watertight gauntlets.

With helmet and gauntlets lifted away, Dougal reached up a bare hand to tousle his hair and rub his face. He coughed, accepted a drink of water from an offered ladle, and glanced up.

"Miss MacNeill," he murmured, "welcome to Sgeir Caran."

Meg felt her cheeks burn as she looked into his piercing green eyes. Seven years ago, he had also risen out of the sea. Heart pounding, she wondered crazily if Mother Elga had been right after all. "Mr. Stewart," she said calmly, "we decided to accept your invitation to see the progress on the lighthouse."

"Good. Hello, Mr. MacNeill. When I get free of this gear, Mr. Clarke and I will show you both around." He turned to Alan Clarke. "Evan?"

Clarke gestured toward the rim. "They've got him now."

Meg saw that the men had hoisted another platform down to bring up a second diver, who now emerged over the edge. His suit and gear were identical to Dougal's, and an array of tools lay beside his lead-covered feet. Men ran to his aid, supporting him while he stomped forward, dripping water, to sit near Dougal.

"Look there. Two kelpies," Norrie said. "Thora and my mother will want to hear about this! They worried that the construction would keep away the kelpies of Sgeir Caran. Now we can tell them that the creatures are still here." His eyes twinkled.

While the men laughed at Norrie's jest, Meg frowned.

When the second diver's brass helmet was lifted away, he sucked in breaths, rubbing his face as Dougal had done. His hair was black and curling, his eyes singularly beautiful—clear hazel framed in inky lashes under straight brows. He murmured to his assistants, exchanged nods with Dougal, and acknowledged Norrie and Meg with a polite inclination of his head. His gaze was calm and curious. "Madam," he murmured, "I am Evan Mackenzie. So pleased to meet you."

"Allow me to introduce our visitors," Dougal said. "Miss Margaret MacNeill and her grandfather, Norman MacNeill, of Camus nan Fraoch on Caransay. Evan Mackenzie of Glencarron."

"Mr. Mackenzie," Meg replied. He looked familiar, though she could not place him. As his quick smile transformed his serious countenance, he looked so astutely at Meg that she wondered if he knew her as Lady Strathlin.

Both divers were divested of their wide brass collars, weighted belts, and leaden boots, and then Dougal and Mackenzie stood to extend their arms in their dripping, oversized suits. Men worked around them like valets assisting knights in armor, opening buckles and hooks and then peeling away the upper part of the suits to their waists. They wore several layers of thick woolen underclothing beneath the suits, but even through those layers Meg could see their strong torsos contoured with muscle. Evan Mackenzie was even taller than Dougal, and he was an equally beautiful man. Meg caught her breath to see both of them.

Looking at Dougal, she felt a deep ripple, something indefinable and exhilarating, some secret chemistry that she could not deny to herself, though she could pretend she felt nothing whatsoever for him. She remembered, unwillingly, how he had first appeared to her on the rock years ago, when he had sat shivering and nude and she had given him her plaid.

"Forgive me," Dougal said, bowing to her, "for being improperly dressed."

Flustered—sometimes he seemed to know her thoughts unfailingly—she shook her head. "It's hardly improper here, where it's part of this world."

He smiled, his eyes crinkling. "Being 'doon the deep,' as Alan calls it, does create some extenuating circumstances."

With Dougal's permission, Norrie lifted a sleeve of the diving suit to examine it. "That's a hot and heavy thing to wear, isn't it? Needs a strong man to stand up in that gear. What keeps out the water when you're in the sea?"

"The suit is rubber sandwiched between layers of treated canvas," Dougal explained. "And very heavy. With lead boots and belt and the helmet and breast piece, it's a sorry thing to carry about on land. Underwater, it's not so bad, for there is a natural buoyancy in the water. All the weight helps sink a man and keep him down. Otherwise we'd float back to the surface too quickly, and suffer for it."

"When a man goes doon the deep, he must come up slowly or he could die," Alan Clarke explained.

"It sounds quite dangerous," Meg said.

Dougal shrugged. "Somewhat."

Alan snorted. " 'Tis a very dangerous thing, miss. 'Tis why Dougal Stewart likes it so well—he's known for recklessness, though when he dives he must go slow and careful. So in a way, this dangerous work keeps the lad in line. He canna misbehave as he might do elsewhere." He grinned at Dougal.

"Reckless, are you, sir?" Norrie asked.

"So they say," Dougal answered, and this time his gaze went directly to Meg, a flash of green fire. She returned it boldly.

"How deep can you go in that gear?" Norrie asked.

"A hundred and eighty feet without difficulty. I've been down nearly two hundred, though it's not generally done."

"A man shouldna go deeper than that and expect to live," Alan Clarke said.

Meg looked at him. "Do you dive, too, Mr. Clarke?"

"I leave that to the likes of Mr. Stewart and Mr. Mackenzie, who enjoy a bit of risk."

She glanced at Mackenzie. "You like it as well, then?"

He paused toweling his hair and smiled. "I suppose I do."

"Mackenzie has been doon the deep, and he's climbed mountains as high as he can go, too," Alan said. "He claims to prefer the heights."

"Well, it is drier up there," Mackenzie admitted, causing Dougal to laugh.

Norrie looked closely at the helmet, with its sealed window-glass openings and valves. "The air comes in here?"

"Aye. Pumped through the hoses," Dougal said. "Clean air flows in here, and foul air escapes here." He pointed to the valves. "The third valve is attached to a speaking tube, so we can communicate with the men on the surface."

"It takes a team for one man to go doon safely," Alan said.

"And the men on the pumps are the most important of all," Dougal said. "Our lives are quite literally in their hands."

"That's very true," Mackenzie said. He stood. "Dougal, I'll be in the office. I want to record what we saw down there. A few drawings will help us assess the condition of the rock."

Dougal nodded. "I'll show our guests around the site." He took Meg's elbow to guide her with him, speaking to Norrie and Alan while resting his hand on her arm. The subtle thrill of that slight touch made her catch her breath.

"Evan Mackenzie of Glencarron?" Meg asked, glancing at Dougal. "Isn't that property owned by the Earl of Kildonan?"

"Glencarron belongs to Mr. Mackenzie," Dougal answered quietly. "To be truthful, he is the earl's heir and a viscount himself, though he dislikes using his rightful title of Lord Glencarron. You've heard of his father, I take it."

"The man is notorious. He is much hated in the northern Highlands," she said. "He has a wretched reputation for cruelty in his methods to clear his people from his land in order to allow for sheep."

Dougal nodded. "Evan wants nothing to do with his father and refers to himself only by the family name and his own property. But I hear now that the earl is quite ill. If he passes away, he will leave the title of Lord Kildonan to an heir who does not care to inherit a single stick or coin from his father. Evan prefers his work in engineering. He designs bridges and docks, mostly on the east coast so far. A brilliant fellow, though he's the last to admit it. We attended university together, along with my cousin, Sir Aedan MacBride."

She nodded, having heard of MacBride's work in engineering along the byways of Scotland. Having financed some of the work herself, Meg knew more about Scottish bridge and road projects than Dougal Stewart could possibly imagine. "Mackenzie is an experienced diver as well," she said.

Dougal nodded and accepted a towel from Alan Clarke, wiping his brow and slinging the cloth around his neck. "Very competent, and an expert in the new science of geology. I asked him to come out here to advise me on the state of the foundation rock."

"Mr. Stewart is a master diver," Alan Clarke said. "There's none so skilled at it in all Scotland. 'Tis as if he were born to the sea. We can hardly keep him out of it, and though he's had his share of troubles in the water, he always goes back to it."

"Share of troubles?" Meg asked.

Dougal shrugged. "Shipwrecked, among other things. If you will excuse me, Miss MacNeill, I must change into dry clothing." He walked over the roof of the rock toward the strange iron barracks where Mackenzie had gone.

Shipwrecked. Meg narrowed her eyes, wondering if that was why Dougal Stewart was so adamant about building his lighthouse. Had he been involved in a wreck on the Caran Reef or perhaps lost someone to a tragedy?

He had assured her that they would talk, and she had dreaded it. Now she was impatient for the chance to learn more about him. So far, he had surprised her at every turn.

His behavior in the last few days did not reconcile with his prank seven years ago. Granted, she told herself, he must have changed in that time. She had changed, too, matured, and found a deep compassion for others and stronger respect for herself. And she could allow the possibility that what Dougal had done years ago, he might never do now.

But she could not forgive him so easily for the past.

Chapter Eight

Dougal noticed the relieved glance Meg gave him upon his return, as if she hoped for a rescue from Alan, who had begun an enthusiastic lecture on the mathematics of lighthouse design. Apparently the islanders had heard enough about the calculated strength of the tower's height and mass, factored to the pounds-per-square-inch impact of a gale-force wave.

"Miss MacNeill, are there some questions I can answer for you?" Dougal had already begun to think of her as Meg—the simple, forthright name suited her well.

The wry flicker in her aqua-blue eyes told him that her true questions were not about the lighthouse. She tilted her head and regarded him. "I admit I have sometimes wondered what it is really like at the bottom of the sea," she finally said.

That, at least, he could answer. "Magical, really. Quite a different realm—peaceful, beautiful, fantastic. When the light is clear from above, the colors are very bright, and it's easy to see the coral formations and waving fields of kelp. The various fish and sea creatures are astonishing, too." He described a few of them. "It's exceedingly cold, so we wear several layers under the air-inflated rubber suits. And it's noisier than you might imagine," he added, smiling, "with the sounds of the waves and the scrape of corals in the current, and stones and rocks and so forth knocking about."

"It sounds fascinating and quite challenging—for those who like risk."

"I'm convinced that anyone could do this, given the right equipment, proper instruction, and a good crew up top to see to things. It's quite enjoyable, really. On sunny days, if the water is calm, it's possible to see the clouds and the sky through the water. Sometimes the stars and the moon can be seen, too, if the hour is late enough."

"If the Otherworld exists," she said, "it must be as fantastic as the depths of the sea."

"It might indeed. I believe there is a legendary place called Land-Under-Waves, said to be very beautiful."

She nodded. "*Tir fo Thuinn.* Supposedly it lies somewhere in the deepest waters of the Hebrides. The inhabitants walk among us in human form, they say, so that we do not recognize them as sea fairies, selkies, kelpies, and the like."

"Interesting." He inclined his head, smiled at her.

"What were you doing under the waves?" the old man asked.

"Checking the rock bed to make sure the explosions did not damage it. A crack could appear or worsen once the weight of the stone tower is in place." Norrie nodded, then turned to ask Alan more about the explosions, which he had found fascinating.

Meg tilted her head. "Did you find anything?"

"Little enough underneath," he murmured, only for her to hear, "but a sea fairy was waiting on the rock when I came up." Meg blinked, and Dougal smiled, feeling warm toward her, affectionate, glad to know that she was real, after all. A strange coincidence of time and place had brought them together, and their desperate need for comfort had grown naturally to passion. But how the devil was he going to explain that he had mistaken her for a magical creature on what he thought was the last night of his life?

"Well," he said, picking up the thread of her question, "since the base of the rock is enormous, we have not yet finished our investigation. All looks stable so far, but I will not be satisfied until we have gone over every square inch."

"I wish I could go down there myself," Meg said.

"You, a wee lass!" Turning, Norrie chuckled.

"I am a strong swimmer, and I did a good deal of sea diving with my cousins when I was young," she said. "We used to dive down from this very rock, if you remember, Grandfather."

"That's a very different thing than going doon the deep in heavy gear," Alan Clarke pointed out. "I dinna think a lass could do it . . . or ever should do it."

"This one thinks all the world is open to her," Norrie said, adding with a wink, "as well she should."

Dougal found the exchange odd, seeing Meg scowl at her grandfather as if to hush him.

"I'd like to see what Mr. Stewart described," she insisted. "If I could go diving just once, I could later make some drawings of the coral, the fish, and so on, for my journal."

Realizing that she was sincere, Dougal nodded. "It might be possible," he said quietly. She nodded and smiled, quick and bright. "You'd need some courage for such a venture . . . but I imagine that you have it." He had seen her face a gale strong enough to tear apart the very rock beneath their feet.

"Miss MacNeill is a wee bit lass, and the weights are brutal," Alan said. "She couldna stand up in the suit."

"She would need help with that," Dougal agreed. "Once she entered the buoyancy of the water, she would be fine. Miss MacNeill looks delicate, but I suspect she is strong enough—and probably stubborn enough—to dive under the sea."

"Ach," Norrie drawled. "You have the right of it. She'll do whatever she minds to do, and in a quiet way. You'll never hear her fuss about it, but before you know it, she's managed to do the very thing you told her not to do."

"Aye, but a wee lass shouldna go diving," Alan said firmly.

Meg gave them a determined look. "I am simply saying that I would like to try it sometime."

"It might be possible someday," Dougal said, "though not practical or proper here on a construction site. Besides, there are creatures in the sea that would carry you off in a moment."

She looked at him sharply. "Oh? Kelpies?"

"I was thinking of basking sharks," he replied.

"Ach, a basker would not take her," Norrie said. "A kelpie, now—then she'd need to watch out. Especially on Sgeir Caran."

Dougal held Meg's gaze for a moment until she finally glanced away.

Eager to continue his tour, Alan led them along the plateau to look at the crater that had been leveled for the foundation. Over eighty feet wide and nearly two feet deep, the cavity was a bustling site. Men inside swept away debris, and masons wielded hammers and chisels to trim the huge blocks of gray granite, some of which had already been fitted into the circle. One was being lowered, as they watched, with ropes and pulleys.

"The walls," Alan said, "will be nearly nine feet thick at the base, greater than the rest of the tower, to sustain against waves and storms. The force of the strongest gale is calculated against the mass of stone blocks of this size, and the base will curve just so"—he demonstrated with a sweep of his hand—"to compensate for the impact of strong waves on the tower.

Each stone is trimmed within an eighth inch of Mr. Stewart's specifications. He carefully planned their shape so they will fit tight as a drum."

"It's based on the idea of a round medieval tower," Dougal explained. "The curved shape helps it resist storm force, just as arrows and cannon bounced off of round towers."

"How tall did you say it would be?" Norrie asked.

"One hundred and eight feet to the roof," Dougal replied. "Its beam will be visible for a distance of about eighteen miles on a clear night."

"You cannot measure fog and rain," Norrie pointed out.

"True," Dougal said. "So we make sure the light can be seen for several miles in the thickest soup, so that seafarers will be warned of dangerous rocks in the area. And a bell will also be installed to give warning in fog."

"How long before the light is working?" Norrie asked.

"Next summer, I hope, given good weather. Poor weather and fierce gales can delay us interminably."

"Ach, dirty weather will take down your tower altogether, lad," Norrie cautioned. "The storms on this reef are fierce."

"Aye," Dougal said gruffly. "I've seen storms on this rock." He did not look at Meg, but he felt her beside him like a flame.

"Many of us on Caransay think you cannot build your tower here at all. The sea will take it—like that." Norrie swept his hand like a cat's paw.

"That would make the baroness happy. But I am determined."

"And Dougal gets what he wants," Alan drawled.

"Does he, indeed?" Meg said, looking at him.

Dougal inclined his head toward her. "He does."

Her cheeks burned so pink that he wondered if it was windburn or sunburn, or the same turbulence of emotion that churned within him. But he reminded himself, the woman did not even like him, and with good reason. The challenge of earning her respect, the need for it, made him more determined than ever. He owed her a considerable debt, and he meant to pay it somehow.

This time, he thought, he would not shame her, as he had unwittingly done before. This time, he would woo her and win her. This time—

A feeling rang inside him like a bell, chiming deep. He knew, suddenly, what he wanted. Gazing at the bright, golden girl beside him, seeing her turn her exquisite aqua eyes up toward him, he knew.

In a secret place in his heart, he had loved her for years, believing she was only a dream. But she was real, made of flesh and blood and a tender heart. He felt a hardening of will and spirit. The intensity of the feeling quaked through him.

He had hurt her in the past, and now, in the present, his lighthouse threatened what she held dear. Certainly, he at least owed her an offer of marriage as recompense for his behavior years ago. He had always avoided such issues before, with other women, preferring the freedom and exhilirating danger of his work to domestic quietude.

Yet as he stood beside her in the damp, salty air, with the seabirds calling overhead and the diamond glint of the ocean in his eyes, he suddenly knew that he wanted to marry Margaret MacNeill.

Deeply wanted it, fiercely, as if the desire had been there all along, formed over years out of dreams and longing, waiting only for the revelation of her existence.

The wind was quiet, the sea mirror calm, yet he felt as if a gale had just knocked him to his knees.

Meg sat alone on the far side of the rock, making small sketches in her leather journal. Dougal and Alan had gone to tend to some work, and Norrie was talking with Fergus MacNeill and a few other Caransay men who had joined Dougal's crew. The need was great on Sgeir Caran not only for laborers, but for local men who knew the reef and the Isles and who understood the moods of the sea and the weather.

She sketched quickly, deftly, watching a pair of gannets return again and again to a nest perched on a ledge near the stack rock. The hushed washing of the water over the rocks below was a peaceful, lulling sound.

Turning the page, she began another sketch, but paused, glancing around, unable to ignore where she sat. The little cave they had shared was just beyond a cluster of rocks.

A shiver went through her, a deep longing, an ache so fierce it made her head spin. She moaned softly and sank her face into her hands.

"Meg?" He was there beside her suddenly, though she had not heard him approach. "Miss MacNeill—are you well? Is the sun too strong?"

She looked up. "I'm perfectly fine," she said tersely. "Is it time to go? Does my grandfather want me to come back?"

"Not yet. Norrie is having a fine time with his friends from Caransay. The men are taking luncheon now, and Norrie saw you come this way. We wondered if you might be hungry, and I offered to ask. Nothing fancy—just bannocks, cheese, and meat pies prepared by our cook back at the barracks on Caransay. But there's plenty to share."

She shook her head. "Thank you. I'm not really hungry."

"Well, then." He did not leave, but remained standing a little behind her. "I see you found some birds to draw in your journal, after all. They are not all gone, then."

"Yet," she said pointedly, and she closed the book,

tucking it and the pencil into her pocket. As she got to her feet, Dougal offered his hand in assistance.

Hesitating, she took it, aware of a thrill of comfort upon touching him. She released his fingers as soon as she stood.

"Mr. Stewart, let me show you something. Come this way."

Runnels of water over ages had worn an inclined pathway in the stone, and Meg took the slope upward, Dougal following, their steps careful on the damp rock.

To one side was the entrance of their little cave, and he glanced at it, tilting his head in question, clearly perplexed and a little startled. Silently Meg turned to face the sea.

She pointed below where they stood. On innumerable ledges and protrusions in the rock, hundreds of birds clustered. The closest birds to them were white with black markings.

"Gannets?" he asked.

She nodded. "They come here every year to nest. In spring, they gather by the thousands to raise their young and to seek shelter from storms. Shearwaters also nest on Sgeir Caran, and guillemots, and a few shags. Over there, see that one on its nest? The dark diamond-patterned feathering gleams in the sunlight. Sometimes we see the shy little petrels that skim close to the water. They make their nests beneath overhanging rocks—"

"Where they cannot be seen," he said quietly. "I know."

She flickered a glance at him. "Puffins nest here, too, though at the other end of the rock, where there is more consistent sunshine. This end lies in the shade of the stack rock. Seals sun themselves on the lowest slopes of the Sgeir Caran, there"—she pointed—"where the rock slopes toward the water. There is a little sandy beach they love." She gestured out toward the sea. "If we waited here long enough, we would see dolphins, perhaps a whale or some basking sharks. The dolphins and the sharks will not appear together—where there is one, you will not see the other. But either is quite a sight, a reward for the patient observer."

"Obviously you've spent a good deal of time observing here."

"I come here fairly often. Over the last few years, I have filled my journals with drawings and notations about the wildlife and the sea and birdlife on Caransay and Sgeir Caran." She faced the water, the wind fresh on her cheeks, ruffling her hair. "I come to study, but I love the peacefulness here, too."

"Miss MacNeill, I know the rock is a naturalist's paradise and a worthy habitat for many creatures. I can appreciate that, too, though you think I do not."

She slanted a sideways glance at him and waited.

"I assure you that we will not disturb any seabird or wildlife colonies. When we put up lighthouses elsewhere, the wildlife did not seem to be effected except during actual construction, when they shy away from the site. Does that suit you? Take that message back to Lady Strathlin, if you will, though I suspect neither of you will believe me or trust that I am sincere. Too many people have died on this reef. I cannot forget that."

"Nor can I, Mr. Stewart," she said stiffly. "But the construction will frighten away many of these creatures. Look up there," she siad, indicating the stack rock. "We call that Creig nan Iolair."

"Creig nan *yoolur,*" he repeated softly. He tipped back his head. "What does it mean?"

"Eagle Rock," she said.

"Aye, someone told me that eagles nest here."

She had told him, in a letter to which he had not yet replied. "They build aeries up there and have done so for many generations. We see golden eagles soaring around the rock sometimes, and for a few years, a pair of sea eagles has nested up there—the white-tailed *iolair mhar,* the rarest of the eagles in Scotland."

"And you are concerned that the lighthouse will keep the eagles away."

"Yes, the sea eagles in particular. Eagles are over-hunted, and every year there seem to be fewer of them—not only here in the Isles, but in the Highlands, too, so I hear. But they have always been safe on Sgeir Caran, and so they come back."

"They will continue to be safe," he said firmly. "We would never disturb their aeries or the nesting places of any seabirds here on Sgeir Caran."

"But you can do nothing about the noise and activity, the men, the boats going back and forth. Sgeir Caran has always been a peaceful sanctuary for the birds. It must stay that way."

"The construction is temporary. Once the lighthouse is up, the sea rock will be quiet again. There will be one or two keepers here with their families and some coming and going of boats, but no more than usual. Peace will return, I promise you."

"If they cannot nest here next season, they will not come back the year after that. Another improvement"—she uttered the word with contempt—"that is set to destroy a cherished tradition in these Isles."

Dougal shook his head. "Let me assure you—"

"You cannot!" she burst out. Her breath tightened as she glared at him. All thoughts of birds and lighthouses, the frustration of months of unpleasant letters, suddenly fell away as deep-set anger and the hurt and grieving of years overwhelmed her. "You cannot assure me of anything!"

She turned, meaning to stomp off, but his hand lashed out. He grabbed her arm and pulled her back. "Meg," he said gruffly, turning her swiftly, so that she came close to him, felt his heat, felt the subtle tug between his body and hers and the answering whirl in her belly.

She raised her hands to push him away. "Leave me be!"

His hands closed tight around her wrists. "Come here," he growled, yanking her toward him, holding her bent and resistant arms against his chest. He lowered his face toward hers, imprisoning her hands in his.

She half closed her eyes, tipping her head, expecting him to kiss her at any moment. Feeling the throb of need in her body, she wanted to be kissed just as much as she wanted to flee.

Instead he rested his brow on hers. "Meg MacNeill, hold now, and hear me out." His voice was a tender rumble. He leaned his cheek against her head and kept her hands pressed between them. Her knees went weak beneath her, and she closed her eyes, still expecting to fight, to struggle in defense of all the hurt, all the years of wondering, resenting, and longing.

"Let go," she gasped, a desperate half sob. "I do not want to talk to you any longer. You have nothing to say that I want to hear, and you cannot hold me against my will." She twisted her hands in his.

"It's only a precaution, should you feel tempted to slap me again," he said.

"Why? Are you going to kiss me?"

"If you want," he murmured, his face pressed to hers, his breath upon her lips. She longed for it, and did not want to, for his mouth hovered close to hers. His lips brushed the edge of her lip and traced over her cheek, an enticement rather than a kiss. Her legs felt so weak that she was glad for his support.

He drew back. "I only want to talk to you."

"We have nothing to say."

"You may have nothing to say to me. But I owe you an apology, and you are going to listen."

"Do not think to charm me again." She tried to

wrench out of his unrelenting grip. "If that is what you call it."

"Easy, love," he murmured. "First, let me apologize for that kiss when we were out on the machair."

"That hardly matters. And do not call me love." She crabbed her fingers on his shirt. His fingers were strong on hers, and his other hand, at the small of her back, pinned her against him.

"Be still and listen. Allow me the chance to speak before you claw me to bits."

"Seven years," she said between her teeth. "You come back after seven years—"

"And I found you, when I thought I'd never see you again."

"Found me?" She stared up at him. "Did you ever look?"

"My dear girl, I searched for you but did not believe it was possible to find you. Now that I have, you make clear that you have no desire to see me. Sometimes you seem so furious with me that I must fear for my life." His tone held a wry gentleness.

"Did you expect a happy reunion of lovers?" Meg wished, all at once, that she had a hand free with which to slap him—yet she wished, too, that he would pull her into his arms and kiss away the hurt, help her dissolve the bitterness she had carried for years. She wanted to be free of that anger and sadness, but did not know how to release it or if it was even possible after so long.

"No happy reunion," he said, "once I realized who you were and what I had done. I thought you did not remember me until we met on the machair and watched the northern lights. I hoped a kiss would remind you more clearly than an explanation."

"How could I have forgotten?" she snapped.

His grip eased on her hands, though he did not let go. "I do not know why you appeared that night, or quite what had happened—my memory of it is very dim."

"All but one part, I am certain," she said frostily.

"Aye, well. For you, too, I hope." He pursed his mouth. "The storm was fearsome, and the night was dark, and I was not sure what I saw or who you might be. I thought—" He paused. "You will think me a fool if I tell you what I thought that night, Meg MacNeill. Though you may already think me a fool."

"Just a brutal cad."

"Fair enough."

"Leave me be. And leave this rock and the island, too."

"I will stay until my work is done," he said firmly. "But I will leave you be, if that is what you want. First hear me out."

"You cannot convince me your behavior was justified."

"And what—whoa, stay with me until this is done!" He pulled her back gently but firmly when she jerked away. "This is not a pleasant encounter for either of us, but it must be got through. What, exactly, do you think I did then?"

"You took advantage of me, sir, and left me in a boorish and inconsiderate manner." She leaned forward, spoke hissing through her teeth, sharp and angry, fueled by years.

"Left you! My dear, you left me. I awoke to find you gone."

"I saw the boat," she said between her teeth. "I saw the men come to fetch you again, those who no doubt left you there. All of you—whoever the others were—schemed it together."

His brow tightened. "Just what," he said, "have you believed of me all these years?"

Meg searched his eyes, saw only sincere puzzlement, felt his free hand hold her snug and insistent at the small of her back. Their joined fists nestled against her breasts. He felt lean and hard against her. Deep within, she ached for him—but she would not give in to that.

"I believed what I saw that morning," she said. "Your friends came back to get you. They must have left you on the rock the night before, knowing that I would be here. The storm blew in and marooned us, so that your friends could not fetch you under cover of darkness. So I saw your departure at dawn. Norrie had already come to bring me back."

"Why on earth were you here that night? And I did not know that I would end up here myself." He shook his head as if confused. "Had you come out to Sgeir Caran to watch the birds, perhaps, and got caught in the storm?"

"I was here because my grandmothers sent me here for the night," she said, "and you know exactly why."

He shook his head again. "Tell me what you mean."

"Do not be insulting, sir." She heard someone call his name and realized it was Alan Clarke. Glancing up, she saw Clarke and Norrie standing on a rise in the rock, near the stack. "Go on. Go have your luncheon, and leave me be," she said.

He looked up, then glanced around. "They'll see us if we stand here. Come with me." Tugging on her arm, he led her under the dark arch of the narrow cave fronted by stones and pebbles. The sea swirled in little pools and eddies, green and frothy, hiding the sounds of their feet on the stones.

She held back at the entrance, but he drew her inside with him. Taking her by the shoulders, he turned her swiftly, so that her back was against the rock wall and her escape was blocked. His hands rested on her shoulders, and he stood close enough that his body brushed hers.

Warily, breathing quickly, she watched him, her heart pounding hard now that she was inside this place, with him. Outside, instead of a raging storm, she heard the soft whooshing cadence of the waves, and heard men's voices, then the crunch of stones as Alan and Norrie walked nearby.

Dougal pressed her into the deepest shadow in the corner of the confining cave, holding her tightly, one hand at her back.

"We must go," she insisted. "They will think we fell into the sea—"

"Stay," he whispered, and bent his head, his lips nuzzling her cheek. "Stay . . . There is something I must tell you."

His breath caressed her lips, and resistance dropped away from her like a lead weight. Her knees seemed to give, and she grabbed his hard arms, seeking support, even as she tilted her head in surrender. His mouth covered hers softly, and her heart seemed to shift, to turn and change, as his kiss began to fill the well of yearning that had been empty within her for so long.

Only for now, she told herself. *Just once more.*

Chapter Nine

He had not meant to kiss her, certainly not like this, his fingers deep in her hair, heart racing, fervent need flaring like a fuse. He wanted her, needed her, and had for years, had he only admitted the strength of it. Now he fought an overwhelming urge to make her his once more, in this place that had such a magical hold over him. He wanted to revel in her sheer existence and prove that he was neither madman nor dreamer—nor heartless, selfish fool.

He drew a breath, pulled back, struggled to find his reason again. But she moaned and sank against him, her lips giving, seeking. She filled his arms perfectly, her mouth willing on his, her fingers tender on his face and through his hair.

One kiss, then another, weaving a breathless, wild chain, and all the while he swore to himself that this one would be the last, that one the last. She was so willing and passionate in his arms like a reeling drunk, that he could not seem to stop.

He slid his hands down her back, shaped her hips, pressed her against him. Hardening like fire and stone together, he could not hide his need from her.

From the first time they had met, she had been his salvation, and he still felt that way, though he did not know why. He wanted to protect her, to rescue her, for to be of help, of use, made him feel alive with purpose. But this time he knew of no threat to her.

No storm whipped the sea to wildness. Outside, there was only warm sunshine and mild waves, bird-song, sweet breezes. And friends nearby, calling his name, calling hers.

That sound acted like a stinging slap. He stopped, pulled back, took her shoulders. All the while his breath heaved, body throbbed. Meg leaned back against the cave wall, eyes closed, chest rising, falling. Holding her by the shoulders, he felt her trembling.

"My God," he said raggedly. "You must think me a beast."

She opened her eyes, and tears shone there—her eyes were beautiful, he thought, delicate blue-green laced with gold, like sunshine glittering on the ocean. She raised shaking fingers to her mouth, then touched her finger to his lower lip.

"It was not just you who wanted this," she whispered, "then or now. Not just you."

They called his name again, crunched stones, came closer. His heart slammed. He wanted to stay here with her—there was so much to say. He wanted to erase what had hurt her, and begin again, if it were possible.

"Meg," he whispered, sliding his hands up to frame her face, tipping her head back. So earnest, so direct, that simple name, that earnest stare, and he sensed that her soul was clear and pure. But he saw hurt in her eyes, and wary mistrust. That, he surmised, was his doing.

"Listen to me," he said. "I am sorry, so very sorry—" He kissed her, murmuring while she moaned breathlessly against his mouth. "Forgive me. I did not mean to hurt you," he said, and he kissed her again. "I would never have let this time go by, had I known . . . where you were . . . I would have come for you—"

He kissed her all the while he spoke, tugged at her lips with his own, for she was like a drug to him. Touching her, kissing her, he knew he could do no more than that, or risk losing her trust again. "I would have made you my bride, if you wanted that with me, as I should have done then. . . . Forgive me. . . ." His mouth gentled over hers again, and she sighed, curved toward him, wrapped her arms around his neck.

Caught in a whirlwind of caress and impulse and feeling, he hardly knew what he voiced. All he said came from the heart, and once out, he did not regret it. He would have married her, indeed, he realized, if he had found her, and if she had wanted it.

She deepened the kiss herself this time, irresistibly, and he felt her breasts tightening against his chest, felt his body pulse hot against hers. He tasted the salt of her tears. He did not know if she would ever forgive him, but he knew that her heart had softened, opened a little toward him at last.

"I want to tell you why—what happened—" He heard Alan and Norrie call out again. He wished they would go away and leave them be in their hiding place.

"There is no time," she said, yet she stretched for another kiss.

He smoothed her hair away from her brow, her cheek. "I do not know if you can forgive me," he said. "I never meant to hurt you or shame you. If you thought so all this time, no apology will fix that. I will tell you how I came to be here, but I want to know what brought you here that night, too, and what has happened to you since then."

Something shuttered her eyes, and she drew back. "We must go." She turned away quickly, yanking away from his hold.

Stepping out into sunshine, she answered the men who walked along the rocky slope near the cave. By the time Dougal stepped blinking into the light, she was halfway up the slope with them.

"Dirty weather coming," Norrie remarked, glancing in the distance as he pulled on the oars to make their way home again late in the afternoon. Alan Clarke, seated behind him and wielding a second set of oars, murmured agreement.

Meg turned. Over the western sea, towering dark clouds promised rain and winds before long. Although the sun had been shining for much of the afternoon on Sgeir Caran, now the rowboat plowed through waters that had turned rough and opaque green, and the wind had turned chilly. Sitting alone in the bow as they sailed back to Caransay, Meg drew her plaid shawl closer around her shoulders. Dougal and Mackenzie sat on the cross bench between her and the rowers. They, too, examined the sky.

"I hope the crew has the sense to leave the rock and cross now, rather than later," Dougal said. "I do not want them there if a large storm hits that rock." He looked grimly at Meg. Knowing what he meant, she glanced away.

"There's the crew, not too far behind us now," Alan remarked a moment later. "We could race them to the harbor."

"No racing," Dougal said curtly, and though Alan grinned, Meg wondered at Stewart's sudden irritableness.

Waves slapped the sides of the boat, and she reached to brush droplets from her skirt. As she did, she saw a huge fin thrusting through the water, gliding between their boat and the harbor.

"A basking shark!" she said, pointing. Dougal turned with Evan Mackenzie, and Norrie and Alan craned their heads. Then she noticed other sharks skimming below the surface of the water, four or five in all, their bodies easily as long as the boat.

"Ach, baskers are not much to worry about," Norrie said. "They have huge maws and tails as tall as my granddaughter, but no teeth to speak of. They eat plankton, not people." He winked at Meg. "Although they've been known to carry off a man now and then, if they're feeling testy."

"They do not usually come this close to the harbor," Meg said, glancing at the massive headland that contained Innish Harbor just ahead. "Oh, they are magnificent!"

"Ugly creatures," Alan muttered.

Reaching into the deep pocket of her skirt, Meg drew out her leather notebook and the pencil she carried with it. She opened to a blank page and began to sketch the nearest basking shark, though the bouncing ride sometimes jerked the pencil's path.

"Look there," Mackenzie murmured as the boat bumped over the agitated waves. "That lad's a bit small to be up there by himself, isn't he?"

"Iain! What the devil is he doing there?" Dougal asked.

Meg turned to see her son standing on the crest of the headland, waving his arms in excitement as he saw their boat coming toward the harbor. "Iain!" she said. "He loves to climb up there with the older children. But where is Thora? She would never let him go so high."

"Thora's on the beach," Norrie observed calmly. "She's going after him now. No need to fret."

Meg nodded, seeing Thora begin to labor up the rock. The climb was not difficult, but it was steep, and though Thora was strong, she was not a young woman. Iain jumped about, waving wildly, enjoying his freedom while it lasted.

Raising her arm, Meg motioned him back. "Iain!"

she called, but her voice blew into the wind. "Get down from there!"

He leaped, skipped, flapped his arms and called out to them. Thora was nearly there, her skirts blowing, while she beckoned at him impatiently. Instead of obeying, the child ran a few steps away from her, stepping out on a crusty protrusion on the headland. Meg gasped and half stood in the boat.

Dougal placed a hand on her arm. "He'll be fine," he said. "She's nearly there."

Thora reached out for him, and Iain stumbled. He fell backwards into air, plummeting over the edge toward the sea, his small form pale against the massive dark headland.

Meg screamed, throwing aside her plaid shawl. In the same instant, Dougal stood too, and the boat rocked violently. He pushed Meg back as he ripped out of his coat.

"Stay here," he growled, and slipped over the boat's rim in a slick dive.

Mackenzie took her arm. "Easy, Miss MacNeill. Dougal will get the boy."

At Norrie's swift order, Alan lunged to grab the rudder, and together they turned the boat toward the headland. Mackenzie took the rudder then, and Alan joined Norrie to oar the boat swiftly through the rolling waves.

Ahead of them, Dougal cut through the water with strong, even arm strokes. Meg lunged toward the side, watching Iain's arm and head bobbing in the water. She cried out in agony, fearing Dougal would never reach the boy in time, although the man tore through the water.

When her son's head disappeared under the waves, she set her foot on the rim of the boat, ready to plunge into a dive herself, for she was a competent swimmer.

Mackenzie's hands went around her waist to tug

her back. "Stay here," he said firmly. "Dougal will get him."

Hearing shouts, she saw that a few men had launched a boat into the surf from the harbor beach, while a gathering crowd stood watching on the sand. From the direction of Sgeir Caran, a boat carrying some workmen began to gain on them once the men realized what had happened.

She turned her attention back to Dougal and Iain and saw the shark fins sliding toward the commotion made by the swimmer and the floundering boy.

"Oh, God—Iain!" Meg screamed. She stood again, unable to merely sit and watch. Mackenzie kept a steadying hand on her arm, keeping her from throwing herself into the water, as she might have done without his detaining hand.

Dimly she heard her grandfather growl an order to Alan. The foreman grabbed a coiled rope from the bottom of the boat, and as they drew nearer, he positioned himself to toss it toward Dougal.

The boy bobbed on the surface again, arms flailing, and went under within moments. Meg gasped, seeing that Dougal was nearly there, arrowing forward relentlessly. She pressed a fisted hand to her mouth and intoned a prayer under her breath.

The basking sharks were there, too, a circling menace. One sliced through the water between Dougal and Iain, its fin creating a wake. Dougal plunged on, passing over the animal's tail, probably brushed by it. Struggling, Iain managed to stay afloat, arms thrashing.

As Norrie's boat drew closer, Mackenzie slipped out of his own coat, ready to dive into the water himself if need be. They were within yards of the swimmers now, and through high, slopping waves, Meg saw that Dougal was only strokes away from Iain.

One of the sharks turned, opening its gigantic mouth, a monster streaming steadily toward the swimmers. Dougal rolled onto his back and shoved at it with his foot. The basking shark flipped its tail, raised a deep wake, and dove downward.

Dougal lunged forward and caught Iain to him. Seeing the small arms close around the man's neck, Meg sobbed out, slumping against Mackenzie in relief. Alan snaked the rope outward and Dougal snatched it with one hand.

Their boat cut a swath between the remaining sharks, and the fins turned toward the sea, sinking and disappearing. Cheers sounded from the other boats and from the shore.

Treading water, Dougal and Iain held the rope while Alan hauled them closer, faces pressed cheek to cheek. Behind them, Meg turned to see the boat carrying Dougal's crew approaching rapidly, while someone shouted from the other fishing boat that had rushed toward them from Innish Harbor. Lifting a hand, Mackenzie signaled that all was well.

Once Dougal hooked his arm over the rim of the boat, Alan lifted the dripping boy into the safety of his arms and Meg surged toward them, reaching out to gather Iain into her embrace.

The boat rocked with the effort as Dougal clambered aboard with Mackenzie's help.

Saturated and smelling of brine, Iain threw his arms around Meg, shivering. She wrapped him in her plaid, then simply held him, closing her eyes, feeling his sturdy weight in her arms, kissing his soft, wet curls. Turning, she looked at Dougal.

He sat on the crossbench, Mackenzie's coat tossed over his shoulders. Sinking down beside him, cradling Iain, Meg began to rub the boy's back and limbs to bring warmth to him. She looked at Dougal, close enough that her shoulder pressed his.

"Thank you," she said, her voice breaking, tears starting in her eyes. He nodded, shivering with cold himself, and reached out to ruffle the boy's hair. Then he placed his arm around Meg's shoulders as naturally as if he always had done it. She leaned against him, feeling warmth spring between them. With his other hand, Dougal massaged Iain's legs, talking quietly to him.

Norrie left the oars, found a plaid blanket in a basket, and draped it over Dougal's shoulders. He tucked the rest across Meg and Iain, then stooped to murmur to his great-grandson in Gaelic. He patted the boy's cheek and looked up, his eyes vivid blue.

"Dougal Stewart," Norrie said, "we are in your debt forever. I've seen brave deeds many times in my life, but never anything like that." He stepped away to take the oars and pull for home.

Under the plaid, Meg leaned upon Dougal. With his arm snug around her, they were wrapped together with Iain in a warm cocoon.

No one knew, she thought, what that close circle meant to her—father, mother, and child huddled together in a moment of gratitude and love.

"Dougal," she whispered, and he bent his head a little to hear her. "Thank you. I can never thank you enough—" Tears threatened, and she dipped her head to Iain's, her throat tightening, her heart too full for words.

"No need for thanks, Miss MacNeill," he said, while he rubbed Iain's legs. "And you, what a brave lad you were!"

As father and son regarded each other, neither knowing the other, Meg saw how alike their green eyes were, how similar their beautiful profiles. The sight felt like a lightning strike through her heart, a hole that brimmed with joy and sadness both.

Unable to hold back tears, she let them stream and leaned impulsively to kiss Dougal's cheek. His beard was raspy under her lips, his skin damp, tasting of salt. She closed her eyes, savoring her gratitude and his closeness.

Eyes crinkling in a smile, he looked at her. Secret

and rare, that smile, more in eyes than on lips, thrilling her deeply. Reaching up, he brushed at her tears.

"Hey, lass," he murmured. "Don't cry. He's safe."

Gazing at him, she suddenly knew that she loved him, deeply, profoundly. No matter who he was, what he had done in the past, what conflict she might have with him otherwise, she loved him in that perfect moment and in the secret spaces of her heart. The peace of that filled her, overflowed. She wept again, sniffling, filled with happiness as well as a keen, private despair.

Dougal pulled the blanket higher on her shoulders. "You're shivering, and so is Iain. We must get you both home."

She nodded and hugged Iain again. Glancing up, she saw Mackenzie watching them. He had given up his coat to Dougal, whose coat was trampled somewhere underfoot, and now sat in shirtsleeves and vest while he operated the rudder to help Norrie guide the boat toward the harbor beach.

"I owe you thanks, too, Mr. Mackenzie," she said.

"It's Evan."

"Evan," she acknowledged. "Meg. And thank you."

"You owe me nothing, Meg. I only kept you from hurtling into the water. The lass would have gone in after you, Dougal," he said. "She was determined to rescue both of you herself."

"I could have used help with that shark," Dougal drawled.

Iain looked up from his nest of blankets. "Mr. Stooar punched the shark! He made it go away! I thought it would eat me."

"You're too tough for a shark to bother with you," Dougal said. "And actually, I kicked it."

"Incredible," Alan said. Norrie nodded agreement.

"Not so incredible," Dougal said. "Baskers are placid, after all, as Norrie said. I simply gave it a shove with my foot, and it decided it wanted nothing to do with me."

"He's the *each-uisge,*" Iain said. "Mother Elga said so. That's why he could punch the shark and make it go away!"

"I'm the what?" Dougal looked at Meg, puzzled.

She shook her head briefly and touched Iain's head. "Look, dear—I think everyone on the island is there to welcome you!"

The prow entered the shallows, and cheers rose up from the fishermen and their families waiting on the beach. Thora splashed into the surf and ran toward them, tears streaming down her cheeks.

Chapter Ten

Sitting on the sand, Meg laughed while Iain danced a circle around her, shuffling sand as he showed her how he would cavort at the ceilidh, the celebration to be held later in the week in honor of his rescue three days ago. Amid their chiming laughter, she did not hear the man approach. She turned as Iain stopped, and the visitor spoke.

"My dear Lady Strathlin," he murmured, "how pleasant to find you here, and so obviously enjoying your holiday!"

She whirled, getting to her feet as he stretched out a long, black-clad arm to assist her. "Sir Frederick! Whatever are you doing here?"

He smiled and bowed, a cane in one gloved hand, his top hat secure on his head. Tall and solidly built, Sir Frederick was neatly dressed in a black frock coat and matching waistcoat, a blue neckcloth, checked trousers, and well-made boots. Hardly a speck of sand clung to him—and would not dare, Meg thought.

He was a striking man, not handsome but bold and proud in appearance, with a long hawklike nose and refined features. Nearly three decades older than Meg, he was graying in the whiskers and throughout his dark, oil-slicked hair.

Rarely did she feel at ease gazing into his eyes, for their brown was so dark and flat that they were oddly unreadable to her. Shrewd eyes, observant and sometimes cunning, but more likely that was only a reflection of his pragmatic sense, she thought. She had learned to trust him in financial and social matters, and he had gained her deepest sympathy after the unexpected death of his wife a year earlier, when his suffering had been genuine.

"Little man," Sir Frederick addressed Iain sternly, "go and play." With a startled look at Meg, Iain ran off.

The man turned back to Meg, his eyes glinting with interest as he took in her appearance. "My dear Margaret, how very quaint you look today. If this is how you dress when you are on holiday, I wish I had thought to join you before this. Playing the provincial shepherdess, are you? Allow me to be King Cophetua to your beggar maid." He bowed, tipping his hat.

She brushed her hands self-consciously over her plain skirt and dug her bare feet a little into the sand to hide them. "What are you doing here on Caransay, Sir Frederick?"

"Mr. MacNeill brought me over from Tobermory," he answered. She glanced down the quiet beach toward the harbor, where some fishermen worked on boats and nets, their wives helping them. A boat approached from Sgeir Caran, she saw, with a few men inside, perhaps returning during their luncheon break. Norrie stood on the beach, watching the sea. She turned back to Frederick.

"I did not know you were in the Isles," she said.

"I came at your invitation and your insistence, my dear."

"My invitation? But I asked you not to—" She realized that he would not yet have received her reply.

Perhaps he had taken the silence as acquiescence. "Well," she went on, "now that you are here, I am sure you will enjoy our little island."

He looked around, gloved hands folded on his cane. He was stiff and proper, and wholly out of context standing on the beach. "A pretty place, and I'm sure it is very relaxing. I thought you would appreciate some intelligent company here, with so little to do but watch the sea and . . . play in the sand." He glanced toward Iain, who was digging a hole with a sizeable shell. "I do hope you are taking care of your skin, my dear. My mother always says that fine, pale skin is a woman's best asset. You are a little golden from the sun, and I do not think it suits you."

She remembered her hat, which hung behind her on a ribbon, and she put it on. "Mrs. Berry has been ensuring that I wear the almond cream your mother sent to me. It was very kind of her to send it along. Will you . . . be staying?" She hoped not. Sir Frederick belonged in Edinburgh's intellectual salons, not on a Hebridean beach. "I will ask the housekeeper at Clachan Mor to make up a room for you."

"Oh, no," he said. "I came out only for the day. Mr. MacNeill assures me that his nephew will take me back to the Isle of Mull soon. I wanted a chance to speak with you. My mother is waiting for me to return, you see. I left her at the resort at Tighnabruaich. The spa is not far from Oban and the crossover point to the Isles, so I thought to take the day to visit you while she spent the day relaxing."

"How kind of you to think of me." She wished he had stayed on the mainland, sipping tea with his mother, an opinionated harridan who enjoyed gossiping.

"Walk with me, dear Lady Strathlin," he said. "Margaret. I hope you do not mind my familiarity. I think of us as such good friends, after all these years."

"Of course," she said, although lately she had become somewhat unsettled by his eager interest in her. Knowing that she must broach the subject of their supposed engagement, she wondered how to go about it without hurting his feelings.

He offered his arm, and she took it as they strolled. In her bare feet, she soon fell out of rhythm with his long stride.

Glancing down the beach, she saw the boat land, and several men disembarked, Dougal Stewart among them. She knew him well from a distance now, recognized every nuance of the easy, sure way that he moved. She would have recognized him even if she had not seen his face. His shoulders were broad in a white shirt and dark vest, and his gold-streaked brown hair gleamed in the sunlight. He shaded his eyes and turned to look down the beach.

For a moment, he stared at her, then lifted a hand in a brief, subtle salute before turning away to speak to Alan and Fergus, who were with him. Her heart leaped a little, unaccountably, at that small, private gesture.

"Did that man just wave at you?" Frederick asked.

"I do not think so," she answered.

"How long do you plan to stay on the isle, my dear?"

"I am not sure," she said. "Another week, perhaps longer. The weather has been mild, with very few storms. It's so peaceful here that I often find myself not eager to return to Edinburgh."

"You've had some excitement lately, from what Mr. MacNeill said. That was a quite a daring rescue," he went on. "The topic was on everyone's lips in Tobermory after Mr. MacNeill brought the news. Mr. Stewart is something of a daredevil, from what I hear. He performed another such rescue last year, apparently. Some men simply must act the hero." He sighed.

"He saved some men who were working on a bridge or a dock that collapsed, I think. That time, too, he happened to be there, and he had the courage and the skill to act. He was not the only hero the other day when he saved the boy. Others were ready to help, as well. We are all grateful to Mr. Stewart. If not for him, Iain might be gone."

"That little fellow over there?"

"Yes," she answered. "He is . . . my cousin's foster son. My family would have felt his loss very deeply." She felt Frederick's hand tense on hers. He stopped, turned to face her.

He was very tall, the black top hat making him seem even taller, so that he towered over her. His whiskers were fashionably trimmed in the long side-whiskers called Dundrearies. She did not find such hairy feathering attractive, preferring Dougal Stewart's simple habit of shaving every few days, so that his dark whiskers evenly shaded the planes of his face in a most becoming way.

"Sir Frederick," she said, "you did not truly come all this way simply to stroll with me on a beach."

"Ah, the lady is clever and perceptive," he said fondly. "Lady Strathlin—Margaret. I came to speak with you about a matter of tremendous importance. It simply could not wait for your return to Edinburgh."

"I, too, have something I wish to speak to you about."

He covered her hand with his own and brought it to his lips. "Shall I hope?" he whispered. "Shall I allow my heart to beat as it now wants to do, with the rhythm of adoration and deepest affection?"

"You can hardly control the beat of your heart, sir," she said curtly. When she tried to pull her hand away, his grip tightened and his lips touched her knuckles. Her skin seemed to crawl.

"Margaret, you know I lost my darling wife a year ago," he said. "My heart broke from abject loneliness. I felt certain I would never find a worthy helpmeet again. But my dear, you were there, like a lantern shining in my time of darkness, to offer me your generous friendship. My dear lady, you have come to mean a great deal to me in this past year, though we were excellent acquaintances before."

"I have always been grateful for your guidance, Sir Frederick. When my grandfather left his estate to me, I felt very . . . lost, confused, and overwhelmed. I needed good friends at that time myself. You gave me your advice as a member of the bank's board, and you and your wife were helpful in bringing me into new social circles. That made all the difference to me in the first years of my inheritance. I was only happy to return the favor when you were in need."

"So much in need," he said. "And fair Lady Strathlin came to my rescue. I am so very glad . . . Margaret, I cannot express to you how ecstatic I am . . . that you have consented to be my wife."

She stared up at him. "That I . . . Sir, I never—"

"Oh, Margaret, do not be coy," he said, smiling. "It does not suit. I am several years older than you, my dear, so allow me to guide you. Coyness simply does not become a woman of your stature and significance."

"Sir Frederick," she said, pulling back, "I have not consented to be your wife."

"Now the temper we see. *Tsk.* My dear, you do enjoy a game. Well, so do I." He continued to smile, so much that it gave her chills. "I asked you—twice, I believe—to marry me, and you agreed in a letter."

"Sir, if you read the letter, I refused you."

" 'My dear Sir Frederick,' you wrote, 'I am honored by your affection and would be equally honored to be your wife.' "

"I said that I would be honored to be your wife—"

"There, you see!"

"I would be honored to be your wife, *but,*" she ground out. "*But,* I fear it is not possible. Did you read the entire letter?"

"Come now. I know feminine wiles when I see them."

"I refused you then," she said. "And I refuse you now. I am sorry if you choose to be a little blind to that. I must ask you, please, not to tell others that we are engaged. It is not true."

"Not true yet," he said blithely.

"Not true and never will be true," she said.

"Not true yet," he said stubbornly. "Tell me something, my dear. That little boy over there . . ." He turned to look at Iain, who had piled up a little hill of sand and was kicking it into fine sprays. "Is he your son?"

She stared at him, all the blood leaving her face, leaving her cold. "My . . . what?"

"Your son," he said. "He looks like you. And I know you have a child."

"What? . . . Who told you such a thing?"

"Come walk with me." He tucked her hand in his elbow again. Stunned, she walked beside him, her heart slamming in fear.

"I met a man a few years ago," he said. "A very pleasant fellow, especially when he was in his cups. He is a doctor, and he told me, over some very fine whisky, that he had attended Lady Strathlin when she first inherited her fortune? A very nice fellow," he said, smiling. "But he had run into some problems with his finances, poor man. He said the lady fell ill, and he had attended her several times. Do you know what he told me, Margaret?" He stopped again and turned to look down at her, her hand imprisoned in his arm. She could feel the hard, stringy muscle beneath his coat.

"Wha—what did he say?" But she knew. She remembered the doctor that Angela Shaw had insisted on calling to visit her more than once when her stomach did not agree with her and she had felt faint almost daily for a while, in the first few months of the pregnancy she was trying valiantly to hide.

This doctor, an older man with greasy hair and a mild manner, had told her that she was suffering from a female condition that he could not name for modesty's sake. He had declared her overwrought by her new position and responsibilities. Advising her to take a long holiday among close family, perhaps for several months, until spring at least, he had looked at her pointedly before leaving.

She had known what he meant and what he knew. And she realized that some way or another, Sir Frederick had managed to coax the truth out of that doctor.

She faced him. "What did he say?" she repeated. "Tell me."

"He said that Lady Strathlin would have a child by now, a healthy child by all the looks of it, and would have had that child in the spring following the year she inherited her grandfather's fortune. In other words, when she accepted the role of the Baroness Strathlin, the lady was already with child. And never married, of course." He gazed down at her.

The pounding in her head was so fierce that she thought she might faint. She watched Iain play on the beach, watched, far in the distance, the harbor where a few men stood in a cluster and talked. She saw Dougal Stewart's head and shoulders above those he stood with, and she wanted to run to the safety and security of his arms.

But he was too far away to hear, too far away to help. And he must never learn about this conversation—never.

"Well, my dear?" he murmured. "You cannot deny it."

"That man was a drunken fool."

"And that spring," he said, his voice smooth and his grip so tight on her hand in the crook of his elbow that her fingers hurt, "a little boy was born and welcomed into the MacNeill family, fostered with a cousin of yours. This child's parentage is somewhat obscure, from what my sources say. But every year, several times a year, Margaret, you come back to Caransay and spend a great deal of time with that child. I believe you have arranged for his education with your former governess. You have not done that for any other child on this island, as far as I am aware. The harbormaster in Tobermory is a cheerful companion over beer and loves to gossip like a woman," he added. He stood watching Iain, his expression benign.

She wanted to slap him, shriek at him, shake him until the evil in him showed. But he only smiled in a smug and unbending way, waiting.

"He looks very much like you," he said. "So blond, with a winning smile. But I think his nose is not yours, nor is his chin yours. That must belong to his . . . father." He glanced down at her. "This news would be of great interest in certain circles, don't you agree, Margaret?"

"Who—you would not tell—" Oh, God, she had admitted it.

"Of course I would not tell. A man never betrays his wife in such a reprehensible fashion. Her secrets are his."

"Wife," she repeated dully.

"Now, he may wish to betray a mere friend, a woman who falsely represents herself as having good moral character and has inherited a position of some merit. It would be a service to others, I think, if her story were known to the public."

"What do you want, Frederick?" she said, resigned.

He bowed, kissed her hand again. "Autumn weddings are so very lovely, my dear baroness," he said, his use of her title faintly mocking. "Kiss me, Margaret." He leaned down.

Meg tipped her face up, but as he lowered his

mouth to hers, she turned her face to the side in revulsion.

"How can you deny me, my sweet Margaret," he murmured against her cheek, "when my heart beats only for you and my thoughts are only of you?" He took her hard by the shoulders, for he was a large, strong man, and kissed her soundly on the mouth. His lips were too soft, slightly sticky, his breath heavy.

Meg broke free. "I need time—to think."

"Of course. Until the soiree, then," he said, caressing her cheek with his gloved finger. "That night I will have my answer."

Leaning away from his touch, she whirled in silence to leave him standing in the sand. He did not follow, and she knew he would be leaving soon with Fergus, smug in his cruel victory. Trembling, she felt as if her whole world stirred beneath her feet, ready to collapse.

She could not bring herself to look back and see if Dougal Stewart still watched. Somehow she sensed him there, steady as sunshine on her shoulders and sharp as a crack of lightning.

Chapter Eleven

"Good to see you enjoying yourself, Mr. Stewart," Angus MacLeod said, raising his voice above the sound of Norrie MacNeill's fiddle. "After all, our ceilidh is to honor your brave deed in pulling wee Iain out of the waves."

Dougal nodded as the song drew to a rousing close amid wild clapping and shouts for more. "Thank you, Angus. The lobsters were excellent, by the way—our cook made a fine meal for all of us." The crofter fisherman, an old friend of Norrie's, had brought a bucket of lobsters to Dougal at the barracks two nights after Iain's rescue to express his personal thanks and admiration.

"There's more lobsters and fish from my catch for you and your crew, anytime." Called for by an acquaintance, he excused himself and turned away, leaving Dougal content to stand in the midst of the crowded main room of Norrie MacNeill's house.

Anywhere he turned, he was shoulder to shoulder with the inhabitants of Caransay and most of his work crew, as well. Seated in a chair beside the hearth, Norrie wielded the bow over a burnished fiddle, filling the room with his skilled music. For more than an hour,

Norrie's songs had varied from joyful rhythms that set the dancers spinning, to exquisitely evocative songs that captured the emotions and raised more than a few tears.

Norrie was accompanied by others, including Angus's son Callum MacLeod, who tapped out cadences on a worn bodhran, and Fergus MacNeill, who played fiddle with less deftness than Norrie but great verve. Fergus also sang, and Dougal remembered Meg's fond remark that Fergus reminded her of her deceased father.

As the evening grew later and the whisky flowed as freely as the music, Dougal had been surprised to see Evan Mackenzie take the lead in singing, his voice so rich and sure that people grew quiet when he sang. Evan seemed familiar with many old Gaelic songs, and when he sang a ballad in broad Scots, the islanders joined him in the refrain. Meg lifted her voice along with the others, and Dougal listened, closing his eyes to let the magic of her sweet voice flow through him.

The walls fairly shook with dancing and stomping feet. Voices rose in natural harmonies, and the house seemed to glow with laughter and chatter. Content to listen and watch much of the time, Dougal leaned a shoulder against the wall as Meg swirled past him in Alan's arms, cheeks flushed and eyes sparkling.

He was more than glad to see the delight in her face. Her mood had seemed somber despite the light hearts that surrounded them. He thought something troubled her.

Remembering the gentleman who had walked with her on the beach the other day, he frowned to himself. A quiet question to Norrie that day on the beach had revealed that the man was Sir Frederick Matheson, the owner of the Isle of Guga, who had come out for the day to visit Miss MacNeill.

Not surprised that the landowner might be enamored of a girl from Caransay, Dougal had noticed the evidence of her returned interest—her arm in Sir Frederick's as they strolled the sands and the fact that she had allowed the man to kiss her within sight of others. That sight, proof of a serious courting relationship, had struck him hard as a blow.

Dougal had gone back to the sea rock and his work, returning to Caransay to find Matheson gone, though he had expected Guga's owner to inspect the quarrying site and meet with him.

Just as well, he thought, that he had not met the man.

Now the dancers changed partners, and Meg whirled through some complex steps with Iain, their effort so comical that Dougal, watching, laughed outright. Meg caught his glance and smiled, and he felt a flood of affection tinged with longing.

Kissing her, hidden within their little cave, he had believed that she was attracted to him, that she cared—he was certain of it, damn it, he thought. If she already had a relationship with Matheson, he could not expect that his arrival after a seven year absence would make much difference outside of an impulse. He sighed, smile fading, and folded his arms.

Angus's daughter, Peigi, a handsome, buxom young woman with neatly braided brown hair, came toward him and gave him a cup of whisky brose, a strong, creamy blend of whisky, oats, honey, and spices. Although he had downed three already, he took the cup out of politeness. Peigi spoke in rapid Gaelic, and though he ventured a few words in reply, he ended with an apologetic shrug. She laughed, pointed toward the hearth where Norrie now tuned his fiddle, and shoved Dougal forward.

Anticipating another round of songs, he stood ready to listen as Norrie began a slow, poignant song. Meg came up to him then and tapped at his shoulder.

"Go on," she said. "Grandfather Norrie wants to see you."

"Unless you like caterwauling, do not expect me to sing a tune with him," he drawled. He noticed that Iain stood with her. "Having a fine time, lad?"

"Oh, aye! I know all the dances. Do you want to sec?"

"I saw you dancing with Meg MacNeill," Dougal answered. "It was very fine indeed." He looked at her, smiling a little, and saw a burst of pink in her cheeks. She glanced away quickly.

He watched her thoughtfully. Just speaking with her, just standing near her, felt so good. He wanted only to enjoy the evening in her company, but the memory of seeing her kiss another man hovered between them like a shadow.

"It's very late," she told Iain. "You should be going to bed soon. Where is Fergus MacNeill?" She turned.

"He's gone off with Peigi," Iain said, "and he does not care when I go to bed. Even small Anna is still awake. I want to stay up with the rest."

"This is the lad's celebration," Dougal said in his defense.

"It is," Iain agreed.

Meg shook her head. "He will be exhausted tomorrow when it's time for his lessons—"

"Lessons?" Dougal asked.

"Berry is teaching me English and reading and maths at the Great House," Iain said. "I'm doing good."

"The baroness is teaching him?" Dougal asked Meg, confused.

"Mrs. Berry," she answered, bewildering him further. "Oh, look, my grandfather is about to say something," she added quickly, as Iain began to talk. "Go on, now." She gave Dougal a small shove.

He stepped forward as Norrie waved him to the hearth, setting down his fiddle. The old man took up a glass of amber whisky and sipped it. Then he began to speak in Gaelic.

Unable to understand it all, Dougal was grateful when Meg leaned toward him to explain Norrie's words. Soon, though, Norrie began to speak in English.

"When Mr. Stewart first came to Caransay," he said, "we were not of a good mind toward him or his working men or their lighthouse. Some of us have not changed our minds about that." Dougal shot Meg a quick frown and saw her cheeks turn fiery.

"But we are of one mind that Mr. Stewart is a good and brave man," Norrie continued. "He rescued our wee Iain and plucked him safe from the sea. And then he drove off a shark, even if it was a basker," he added wryly. "I am thinking he is the equal of the great hero Fhionn MacCumhaill himself! He is as great as any kelpie or selkie in the sea, a man of true courage, capable of magical feats!" He grinned. "To Mr. Stewart—the Great Toast!" Norrie stepped up on a stool and raised his glass.

Everyone who held a glass or cup lifted it, then lowered it, held their drink out and pulled it in, all the while chanting in unison, first in Gaelic, then in English.

Up with it, up with it,
Down with it, down with it,
Over to you, and over to you,
Over to me, and over to me.
May all your days be good, my friend!
Drink it up!

They shouted the last line together, walls ringing, and drank. Norrie smashed his drained glass on the hearthstone, and a rousing cheer went up. Dougal, laughing and accepting handshakes and claps on the back, hoisted Iain to his shoulders. The little boy raised his hands to touch the roof beams, yelling happily.

"Aye, my wee friend. Celebrate," Dougal said, grinning. "All this is for you." As he held Iain's legs, he turned to see Meg. For a moment, her sparkling smile and the strange undercurrent of sadness in her eyes dimmed all else around him.

"Thank you, Mr. Stewart," she said, so quietly that he bent to hear her over the ruckus, "for saving our wee Iain."

"You are very welcome, my dear Miss MacNeill," he answered. Norrie spoke again, this time in Gaelic, and he turned. The crowd cheered once more, and glasses clinked in another salute. "What did he say?"

Meg blushed. "Oh, they're drinking a toast to me now."

" 'And here's to our Margaret,' " Angus translated, standing nearby, " 'the finest lady with the kindest heart in all the Western Isles. May she have all the happiness she deserves!' "

"That is quite a compliment," Dougal remarked.

"Grandfather has half a keg of whisky in him by now," Meg said. "When his fiddle begins to sound wild and beautiful and he calls for the Great Toast, the drink has opened his soul."

"Ah, they do say the more whisky in the fiddler, the better the fiddling," Angus remarked, grinning.

"Whisky or not, I agree with Norrie," Dougal said. "She's a fine lady, our Meg MacNeill." He leaned toward her, lowering his voice so that only she could hear. "If Mackenzie had let you go into the water, I know you would have saved the lad yourself. And fought off that shark, as well."

Her somber eyes were so beautiful that he ached. "I would never have let the sea have him," she said fiercely.

"Iain should learn how to swim. I've offered to teach him. Perhaps his father will allow that, if I talk to him."

"His father—" She drew a breath. "Fergus wants him to stay away from the water until he is older."

"Oh, now," Dougal said, teasing a little, bouncing the boy on his shoulders, "that would break the lad's heart. He's like me, I think. He's drawn to the sea. It's in his blood."

"Aye, in my blood!" Iain said giddily from his perch. He stretched his arms high and laughed as Dougal spun around once.

Meg stared up at them, still serious, and Dougal wondered again at her thoughts. "Well, his family tree is full of fishermen and seafarers," he said, feeling an urge to explain.

Instead of answering, she whirled and shouldered into the crowd. Hands resting on Iain's knees, Dougal watched her go. As Norrie started a slow, poignant fiddle tune, Dougal slid the boy to the ground and fetched him a cup of the fruit brose that Thora had prepared with cream, oats, and wild strawberries.

Watching Meg from across the room, Dougal wondered what the devil he had said or done to upset her.

"Miss MacNeill," Alan Clarke said later, turning to Meg, who stood nearby. The most recent song had just ended, and Norrie bent to adjust an off-tune string, which gave a narrow whine. "I admit to being curious about something. Is that Lady Strathlin over there?" Alan indicated two women who chatted with Thora and some fishermen's wives while they served food and drinks.

Seeing Mrs. Berry and the housekeeper from Clachan Mor, Meg hesitated. She had dreaded a question like this ever since her grandmothers had told Dougal that Mrs. Berry was Lady Strathlin. Now Dougal Stewart also waited for her answer. The resident engineer turned with interest, hearing his foreman's question.

"Oh," she finally said. "The tall lady is the housekeeper, Mrs. Hendry, and the other is Mrs. . . . ah, Berry, who is Lady Strathlin's . . . former governess and is now her companion."

"Mrs. Hendry and I have met," Dougal said. "But I have not met Mrs. . . . Berry?" His tone sharpened.

Meg did not answer, looking carefully away from him. Though she had tried to stir up a better sense of joy for tonight's celebration, she harbored fear and guilt after her encounter with Sir Frederick a few days earlier.

"Everyone is here tonight but Lady Strathlin. Seems odd," Alan muttered. "Even such a high-and-mighty shrew as that one couldna fail to be moved by Iain's rescue."

"I assure you she was quite moved," Meg snapped.

"I'm sure she at least sent her respects to the family," Dougal suggested, as he stared thoughtfully at Mrs. Berry.

"I believe she did." Meg wanted to sink into the floor.

"I could swear," he said softly, "that Mrs. Berry was the lady who was pointed out to me on the beach as Lady Strathlin."

"Some women look alike," Meg said, "and some do not."

"Ah, true. So it seems that once more I have missed meeting the lady." Dougal looked at her over Alan's shoulder.

"It would seem so, Mr. Stewart," she replied. She dared to look at him. *I am your shrewish baroness, Mr. Stewart,* she thought boldly, watching him. *And I need you very much just now.*

He narrowed his eyes suddenly, as if he had understood her thoughts, and she flickered her eyes away, the risk too great.

"Och, she's probably here, guised as a fishwife while she observes the local peasantry in their habitat,"

Alan said. "The real Mother Elga is asleep in her bed, y'see, and that wee one there is Lady Strathlin, wearing auld Elga's plaidie." He grinned, and Dougal chuckled softly.

Scowling at both of them, Meg turned away, but Dougal leaned toward her. "Alan's joking. He means no harm," he murmured. The dark velvet of his voice shivered through her. "I'm almost certain the woman over there is your great-grandmother."

She pursed her mouth sourly at his jest and did not answer, while he gave her the subtle smile that he shared only with her—an impish curve to his lips, a green dazzle in his eyes that lingered after the smile vanished. He seemed more beautiful to her in that moment, more appealing, than she dared admit.

And Sir Frederick Matheson seemed even more dastardly for ruining her chances of true happiness.

She turned away to watch Iain dance between Peigi and Fergus, jumping and laughing. She remembered Dougal's sweet playfulness with Iain and his tender strength in rescuing a boy whom he did not even realize was his own son.

Sighing again, she touched her fingers to her mouth and realized that she was shaking slightly. She had hardly slept, had hardly spoken to anyone, pacing out long, solitary walks while she thought about Frederick's threats. His smooth, cruel words kept repeating in her mind. She would soon owe him an answer, and she faced an inevitable surrender.

Desperate, even hopeless, she felt as if her spirit beat its wings on cage bars. He had trapped her so smoothly, without lifting a hand. Somehow she had to resist the forced marriage and stop him from using his knowledge against her. She could not bear to live the rest of her life as Frederick's wife, living in fear that he would expose her youthful mistake and harm her son.

Nor could she bear the thought of living the rest of her life without Dougal. The other day, after mad kisses and breathless apologies, she had felt joyful just knowing that he had not played her falsely that night and that he cared for her. She had begun to hope that he could care for her as much as she did for him. For years, she had both hated and loved him, seeing his face in her son's, holding on to the dream of him while nursing the hurt.

As yet, she did not know his full explanation of that night; they had found no time for it. But the reasons did not matter as much as knowing and believing in his sincerity. Finally she could let that old hurt go, release it like water poured back into the sea. She was free of anguish at last.

Or so she had thought—until Sir Frederick had arrived.

Watching the dancers, listening to the music, she saw Fergus spin around with Peigi, both laughing brightly, without cares. Meg folded her arms tightly, feeling a piercing loneliness. She wanted to be in Dougal's arms again, felt the craving and the need like a weight in her soul. Tears pricked her eyes. She yearned to be alone with him, to tell him that she had forgiven him, that she loved him. She wanted to seek the wildness of her soul in his arms.

Would it be so wrong, she wondered, just once, to go to him and give of herself? Soon she would return to the mainland, to the other world, to Sir Frederick and a life of lies and fear. She would have to leave Dougal and Iain and all her newest hopes and dreams behind forever.

The dance ended, and she turned to see Dougal, his brow puckered thoughtfully, his eyes dark with concern. Tipping his head, he seemed to ask silently if all was well. She looked away. Despite her longing, she could not explain her heart to him.

The music began again, and several people separated into two lines to perform the Seann Triubhas, or Chantreuse, as she knew Lowlanders called the old dance still popular in the Isles.

Dougal moved toward her. "Miss MacNeill?"

"I . . . I would be delighted, Mr. Stewart," she said softly, glad for this chance to forget what troubled her for a little while, a chance to simply be near him and feel his touch.

They moved toward the dancers, some of whom shifted to offer them the lead positions. Facing Dougal, Meg curtsied as he bowed, and they stepped in natural harmony, folding into the center, gliding in unison on the rhythms of the music. With her hand on his lifted forearm, they reached the end of the line and separated again. Happiness bubbled briefly through her, rippling again as she faced him across the gap.

He smiled in the way that she had grown to adore, private and quick with twinkling eyes, as if his heart were hers alone.

Beyond this dance floor and this celebration, it could never be so. Here she was simply Meg, dancing carefree with handsome Dougal, and dreams were still possible. Out there, she was Lady Strathlin, with a desperate secret and a vile enemy—and Dougal, the man she loved, despised that lady.

"*Ach,* I should have sent the child to his bed," Fergus told Meg. "Look at him now. He cannot keep his eyes open, though he begged me to let him stay up the night." Tilting his head, he indicated Iain, half asleep on a bench, chin and arms leaned on the scrubbed pine surface of Thora's table. His eyelids drooped, flew open, then sagged again. "I'll take him to bed now."

"Fergus, I'll take him," Meg said, smiling as she looked at Iain. He had stubbornly lasted until this late hour, when guests were leaving, the lively music had ended, and the storytelling had begun with a smaller gathering. "They're waiting for you to join them with the stories and such. And . . . I'd like to tuck Iain into bed myself."

Time with Iain was precious to her, for she saw her son only a few weeks out of every year. Days ago, he had come close to death, and now another threat loomed, one only she knew about.

Fergus touched her arm. "A moment, Cousin. I want to ask you something." His golden-brown eyes seemed troubled.

Meg nodded. Her cousin had a good-hearted, earnest nature, and she had never regretted her decision to entrust her son to his care, even after Anna had died.

"I hear the lad is doing well with his schooling," he said.

"He's a bright lad, and Mrs. Berry is a fine tutor."

"I am thinking he will need much more learning, unless he becomes a fisherman, like me and so many of his kinsmen."

"He would do well to follow in the footsteps of you and Grandfather Norrie."

Fergus removed his cap and rubbed his head. "I am thinking he might do well in a mainland school."

She blinked, surprised by that. "Is that what you want for him, Fergus?"

"Well, I am thinking it is what you want for him." He kneaded his cap in his hands. "If you take him back to Edinburgh to live in your castle and your other fine houses, he can go to a real school. He can grow up to have all that a man dreams of."

If she took Iain back to Edinburgh, she ran a great risk of losing him entirely, now that Sir Frederick knew about him. Soon enough Dougal might learn the truth and take his son.

"I can think of no better place than Caransay for a boy to grow up," she said.

He smiled in shy agreement. "Margaret, I have not forgotten who gave birth to the lad. And though I love him with all my heart, he has no mother in my house now," he said sadly, glancing around to be sure they would not be heard. Most of the others sat by the fireside, creating a private corner for Meg and Fergus.

Meg leaned close, her hand on his arm. "On the day Iain was born, I trusted you and Anna with him. And though she is gone, I would trust you with him always. He loves you and small Anna. He would be heartbroken to leave you." Tears stung her eyes.

He nodded, looking down. "We nearly lost him the other day. So I am thinking you will want him to live with you now, in your great castle, where you can see him each day."

Her heart surged. "Is that what you want, Fergus?"

"I want him to be happy—and you to be happy, too."

"And for yourself?"

"I would miss him like my life," he said. "But it is good for a man to have an education. And the lad is smart. He read a story to me. Read it!" He smiled proudly. "I can sign my name and speak some English. But he can learn far more than I can ever teach him. What can I give him, but what I know about lobster fishing or the ways of the sea and the signs of the weather?"

"All that is just as important as a university education—even more so," she said fervently. "If, when he is older, he wants to go to school or to university, I will make it possible for him. For now, he is too young for anything but a tutor. He can learn from Mrs. Berry when we are on holiday here, and next year he can go to the village school. He should stay with you and the rest of his kin. Iain needs a family."

"But you are his—" He stopped, glanced around.

"He cannot learn the value of family by living with me in my cold and lonely castle, with only my servants and my advisers. And some of them are not very fond of children. Besides," she added, "where I live, he could not see the water each day."

Fergus nodded, still twisting his cap. "Now that is a sad thing. And yourself?" He looked at her. "Do you miss the sea?"

"Every day."

"And you miss Iain whenever you go back."

She gazed at Iain's golden head. "I miss him like my life," she whispered. "But he needs to be here." *He is safe here.*

"Someday there will come a time for you to take him. I have always known that," Fergus said.

"Someday," she agreed. "Not now."

Not for a very long time, she thought. In the outside world, Lady Strathlin would soon be forced to marry a banker and a minor baronet, a heartless man. In that household, she knew, her beloved little son would not be welcome.

Chapter Twelve

While several voices lifted in singing harmony around him, Dougal saw Meg and Fergus talking privately in a corner, their heads together, their discussion clearly serious. He wondered what troubled Meg that evening, for she had been preoccupied, even sad, in the midst of the revelry. He hoped she would at least confide in Fergus, who seemed a good friend to her.

Soon Fergus joined the others, and Meg led a sleepy Iain toward a connecting door. The boy sagged against her, and she bent to gather him into her arms. Dougal rose to offer his help.

"Let me take him for you, Miss MacNeill. He looks like a sack of grain. And you must be tired from such a long evening." He opened the door for her as he spoke.

She hesitated, then gave the boy up to him silently. Iain's head lolled on Dougal's shoulder, and small arms looped cozily around his neck. Meg led them through the door into a wing of the house. Camus nan Fraoch consisted of three croft houses joined together under one long thatched roof, each identical, only differing in their functions of main living area, kitchen and dining area, and what was called the sleeping room.

They entered a large room with low rafters, whitewashed walls, a stone floor, and two small windows. A hearth at one end blazed with a low peat fire. Through the shadows, Dougal looked around the sleeping room that the entire family shared with some privacy. Three curtained box beds lined the walls, and two small rooms were separated from the larger one by doors.

Meg shut the door, enclosing them in darkness and relative quiet. Being alone with her like this would have been shocking on the mainland. In the Isles, Dougal had seen more encouragement than suspicion when a young couple went off alone.

When Meg held aside a curtain to reveal a box bed, Dougal set Iain carefully inside. He stood back while she removed the boy's boots and knickers and tucked the linen sheets and woolen blankets over him. Sighing, Iain rolled over.

"Does he sleep alone in here?" Dougal asked. "Will he be frightened if he wakes later?" Thinking of the child's recent ordeal and the terrifying spectre of the shark in the water, he also remembered his own terrors and nightmares as a boy, when he would open his eyes in the darkness to realize that his parents were gone forever. Watching Iain, so small in the bed, those long-forgotten nights came rushing back to him. He glanced at Meg. "Should we stay here with him?"

She shook her head. "He will not be alone here. This is my bed at Camus nan Fraoch. I put him here for the night, though he has his own bed in the other room with Fergus, through that door, while Elga sleeps in the box bed over there. Small Anna's cradle stays near the door of the room that Thora and Norrie share, through there, so that we can all hear her if she stirs. Iain will not sleep alone for long."

He nodded, amazed at the close quarters, though

he knew this was a common—even spacious—arrangement for Hebridean homes.

While they spoke, a small black terrier padded toward them through the open door between the rooms, a dog that Dougal remembered had dozed near the fireside during the ceilidh. Tail wagging now, it jumped up and leaned its paws on Meg's skirt at the knee. She bent to pet it, then assisted the little dog in jumping onto the boy's bed.

"Iain has a good nursemaid," Meg said affectionately, ruffling the dog's head. "That's fine, then, Falla. Just for tonight you may sleep with him. Thora does not like any of their three dogs to sleep on the beds," Meg added, "but Falla can guard Iain for now." The dog curled beside the sleeping child, and Meg closed the curtain.

Standing in the darkness beside her, Dougal felt overtaken by a lush blend of contentment and passion that rushed from heart to groin, smooth and fiery as whisky and cream. He flexed his hand, wanting to touch her, hold her, more—so much more he dared not think of that. Reaching out in the shadows, he took her elbow and turned her toward him.

"Meg," he murmured, amazed that his heart could pound so hard over touching her arm or saying her name. Fascination and physical excitement built in him, as if each time was the first time he touched her.

The curve of her cheek was a warm glow in the light of the peat fire, her hair a halo of rich, rippled gold. She waited, silent, expectant, watching him.

He sought for something to say, not yet ready to go back into the crowded room when he could be alone here with her. "The ceilidh has been a grand celebration. I am very grateful for it."

"We wanted to celebrate Iain's safety and show our thanks for what you did, Mr. Stewart."

"Dougal," he corrected, and he reached up to brush back her hair where it fell softly along her cheek. She watched him, did not protest. "Any man could have done what I did."

"Iain was in grave danger, and what you did took strength and courage. The people of Caransay will talk of it for generations." She smiled at him in the darkness. "Even now, while you stand here with me, they are in the next room spinning a tale about Dougal and the shark."

"I would rather stand here with you," he murmured.

"I—" Her eyes gleamed as if with quick tears, and she looked away. "I have had no chance to speak to you alone since that day. I wanted to tell you—I need to tell you . . . how much it meant to me." Her voice quavered.

He shook his head. "No need to thank me again, my lass."

"But if you had not . . . we might be . . . holding a wake tonight," she whispered, as her chin began to wobble.

"Come here," he murmured, taking her shoulders, pulling her toward him. Stiff at first, she melted against him and began to weep quietly. Dougal held her, circling his hand over her back, murmuring soothing noises, while she pressed her face into his shoulder in the darkness.

He sensed that she rarely leaned on anyone for support, or else had not done so for a very long time. Sighing into the fragrant cloud of her hair, he wrapped her close and felt her arms slip around his waist.

Holding her, Dougal felt good, needed, essential to her. The feeling was new to him. He had faced urgent and dangerous situations before, but saving Iain had brought him an unexpected reward in a sense of true belonging with the islanders, who gave him their respect and seemed ready to cast aside their resentment about the lighthouse.

Comforting Meg, he felt oddly as if he fulfilled more

than her momentary need. Holding her approached a destiny, somehow. He belonged here with her.

Most of his adult life, that sense of being needed had been lacking. While putting up lighthouses, he had faced danger in order to eliminate risk for others. His own family had been devastated by a tragedy that he could now help prevent in the future. He was proud to be able to give others safety and security. His skills were needed—but he had never felt necessary to someone for himself alone. He had not even realized it until now, with Meg leaning her head on his chest and weeping.

What if she had needed him all these years—as he had wanted and desired her in dreams and imaginings—yet he had been only a hurtful memory for her? Closing his eyes in anguish, he told himself he should have searched more thoroughly for her. He hoped his apology had not come too late.

Unless he made a difference for someone, for her, he might always feel unsettled and at odds with life, always running toward danger in order to prove himself somehow. Rescuing Iain had opened floodgates of gratitude and goodwill such as he had never felt before, crowned by this moment with Meg in his arms.

Love brimmed in him and spilled over as he held her, and he felt a moment of magnificent, private surrender, as if part of him changed, subtly and surely. He wanted to ease what troubled her now—more than that, he wanted to be with her always.

"Hush, lass," he crooned. "Hush, my dear." Brushing his hand over her hair, he slid his fingers into the wealth of her hair. Meg leaned her head back to gaze up at him, her eyes luminous, awash in tears.

With deliberate gentleness, tipping her chin on his knuckle, he bent and kissed her, a sure brush of the lips, a slight, meaningful tug, another sweet brush. Then she pressed against him, urging them toward a deep meld of mouths and heartbeats. Cradling her face in his hand, he kissed her insistently, sinking his fingers into the golden richness of her hair. He kissed her breathless, until she clung to him and the room seemed to spin.

Through the half-closed door the music and light from the other room faded, but he still heard it and was dimly aware that they were not alone. He had to be alone with her, if only for a little while. Body and soul demanded it.

Tearing away from her, he took her hand, pulling her out of the room and through the outside door of the sleeping room. They stepped into the night, where the sky had finally darkened to starry indigo. He heard the rush of the sea.

Silently, swiftly, he drew her with him toward the bay. She moved beside him, making no sound as they crossed the reedy, kelp-littered sand of the little bay. Her hand felt fervent in his. He drew her down toward the sea, where the water washed, foaming, over the sand. He did not know why he wanted to take her there, but he followed his heart and pulled her along.

Wavelets rinsed over her bare toes, and she splashed a little as she walked beside him. He stopped suddenly, holding her hand, to work off his boots and toss them onto the drier sand, pulling his knitted socks off after them and tossing them, as well. The water felt cool and good over his feet. When Meg laughed, the sound made him feel even finer.

She hastened beside him, walking a little ahead of him, now pulling him along where earlier he had been tugging at her. He let her pull him over a hill and past the small headland that separated the larger bay from this small, private bit of beach in the shadow of the rock wall, with the moon-spangled water beyond.

She turned, walking backwards now, still holding his hand, and he followed her, feeling soft, dry sand beneath his feet. Then he tugged on her hand and pulled her into his arms. Under the moonlight, he touched his mouth to hers, feeling her body curve against him and her arms slide around his waist.

A keen burning slipped through him, and he kissed her in full freedom now, deep and wild and thoroughly, sliding a hand up her back, the other pulling her to him at hip and waist until her abdomen pressed hard against his rigidness. He groaned low and let his hands move upward.

She turned slightly, allowing his fingers to trace over the swell of her left breast, where she tightened like a pearl for him. He felt her small gasp in his mouth, and he touched her other breast, ruching that willing nipple, feeling her sag in his arms a little. She opened her mouth to him, teasing him with her tongue as he teased her breasts, her hands easing over his waist, moving down, then behind him, pulling him against her.

He could not get enough of her. She was like fire to him, like the burn of the whisky in his blood. He wanted her intensely, could not think past that urgency. His pounding heart and throbbing blood dimmed all reason.

Part of him, blood and soul, remembered the night they had shared, and he wanted that back again, not for its incredible physical satisfaction, but for the depth of the passion he had known only in her arms.

He proceeded with care, partaking slowly of the luxury of her, of this, though his heart slammed and his body urged him onward. He framed the deep curves at her waist, and he felt her hands move up his back, shaping, clutching at his shoulders. She gave a breathy moan and curved herself against him.

When he felt that hot, irresistible pulsing of spirit begin between them, when his body throbbed and demanded, he could no longer hold back, and he pulled her tightly against him.

Sinking with her in the sand, he dropped to his knees to face her as she kneeled also, and he pressed her to him in a deep kiss. Then she sank, and he went with her, stretching out with her on a soft cushion of white sand, rolling slightly, so that he lay beside her.

Gathering her to him, he traced his hands over her. Keenly aware of what he wanted, he hoped she wanted it, too. But he could not go on until he knew that she would be his entirely, without hesitation.

Cupping her face in his hand, he pulled his lips from hers and drew her into his embrace, placed his mouth at her ear. "I must know," he whispered, kissing her earlobe, "if you understand what we are about here, if you feel this, too, between us."

"I do feel it," she said, her lips brushing his neck, his jaw. "I know what we are about here." She stretched for his kiss.

"Meg," he said, dragging his lips from hers, determined to make certain all was clear between them, "I must know something. You walked with a fellow on the beach the other day. Norrie said it was Sir Frederick Matheson who came to see you. Tell me—if he means something to you." Voice low and ragged, he hated himself for asking. But he had to know.

"He is no one," she murmured, her mouth tracing over his. "No one at all to me."

He lay back, gathered her into his arms, held her. "You kissed him." Surprisingly, he felt only a little jealous; instead he felt a strange sense of knowing, of certainty that she was his and could belong to no other. He wanted to trust her loyal, caring heart and dared to hope that she shared his feelings.

"He kissed me," she corrected. "And it meant nothing to me. Do not think about it. And I will not think about it." She added in a low and oddly defiant voice, "Not now." She tilted her head to kiss him again.

He broke away. "Meg, my girl," he whispered, "I need to know what you want of me, of us, just now." This time he would ask—this time, he knew just what he wanted and why. Her, forever. He held still, heart driving hard in his chest, and waited.

She looped her arms around him and stayed so still that he thought, for a moment, she would simply pull away and end this. Fair enough, he thought, if that was what she needed to do.

Setting her cheek beside his, she sighed in his ear. "I want the dream," she murmured. "Just once, I want the dream that I am truly, deeply, utterly happy. Where I have all that I want and I am just who I want to be, with the man who has my heart in his keeping."

He sighed out low and traced his lips over hers, stirred so deep he could not speak. The dream, as she called it, was what he most desired himself. And she was the dream. He drew back, waited.

"For this one night," she went on in a soft voice, "though I know it cannot last, I want the beautiful dream that I have kept and treasured. After that—" She stopped, and he held her, feeling the thump of her heartbeat through her slim rib cage, beneath his hands.

"After that?" he whispered, easing his lips over her earlobe, teasing, tugging, as he waited.

She shook her head a little. "Then I will go back to the other world and do what must be done."

He nodded. But he intended to take her with him into that other world, as he moved from place to place, from city to remotest point. She was indeed the dream, had always been so for him. He dared hope, now, that he would be the dream for her, as well.

He rose over her then, propped on his hands while she lay back on the sand. The water rushed at their feet, and from far beyond, he could hear the faint strain of a fiddle and the sweet harmony of singing. He looked down at her.

"What do you dream?" he murmured.

She pulled him down toward her. "I have often

thought about what we had once before," she said, "that perfect knowing of one another, perfect caring for each other. And I dream that all the years in between never happened, that we have always been together. Just this once, I would like to feel that it is so."

He kissed her, then drew back. "It could be so. We could stay together forever." His feelings for her, he realized, had formed years ago and had not changed, staying deep and full, waiting dormant until he had found her. Now that he had begun to know her, with her kind heart for others and her sweet, honest purity, he knew that he loved her.

She shook her head gently, something he had not expected. "Just the dream," she said, sliding her fingers into his hair. "That is all I want tonight. Please," she whispered, and he heard a note of such plaintive force, such surprising desperation, that he felt himself run hot and deep with longing and desire. He wanted to give her joy, complete himself in the completion of her.

"Please—" she repeated, and he touched her mouth with his, took the word and turned it into a kiss. He traced his tongue over her lips and shifted lower, drifting kisses along her jaw, her long and beautiful throat, until he found the swell of her breast. He fingered gently at the buttons of her blouse and opened it, slipping his hand inside the warmth there, sliding beneath layered cotton and cambric. As he touched her incredible softness, she gasped, and his body tightened deep within, like a fist, and began to throb with a burgeoning need.

Dipping his head, he touched her nipple with his tongue, coaxed it to stiffen, heard her whimper as she slid her fingers through his hair, over his ear, and down, until she was tugging at his shirt, and he in turn slipped her blouse from her and fingered the delicate laces of her camisole.

Gasping, moaning softly, she undressed him quickly,

and he drew off her garments, one after the other, until they lay nude on a scattering of dark clothing and pale sand, hidden in the black shadow of the headland where no one could see them, where they had found a small private space to relish each other.

Feeling the gentle, cool evening wind on his skin, he drew her into his arms, her skin warm and delicious against his, and he traced his lips over her breasts, teasing her nipples to pearls, while she arched and breathed out in a cry. He traced his tongue over her breasts, between them, and downward over her abdomen, to where she was sweet, tender, and secret.

As she shivered under him, he teased her, stroked her, until she clutched at him and whimpered out her release. When she subsided, sighing like a wave, he could not control the powerful need much longer, his heart slamming, body and soul near to bursting. But he must not give her a child, not yet, though he wanted that, someday, with her. Even if he could not resist her—yet again—he would not knowingly compromise her well-being.

Through a haze, he reminded himself to be cautious, even as she pleaded with her writhing body and a low, throaty moan that sent a hot pulse through him. She moved in the soft sand beneath him, pulling him over her, and he gave a low groan, all fire and blaze and no longer himself.

As his body slipped into the glove of hers, she became his crucible and he hers, all fire and passion, all wind and sea and pounding heart. The storm tore through him, and somehow he found the strength to pull back, to spill himself into the warm sea that teased around them.

Breathless, he gathered her into his arms and rolled to his side to hold her. Moments later, he realized that she wept silently, hiding her face against his shoulder.

Chapter Thirteen

Moonlight on the whispering sea, the surf rinsing at her feet, and Dougal's arms around her would become memories to carry her through the rest of her life, Meg thought. Years from now, she would treasure this night and one other, and she would always remember him like this—her kelpie, so strong and beautiful, tender and kind, and hers alone.

Soon she must never see Dougal again. Once she resumed her existence as Lady Strathlin, she was sure that her future husband would not allow his wife—no matter her fortune or her desire—to return to Caransay alone, free, without threat.

She sucked in a quick breath against the pain of that and ducked her head against his chest.

"Love," Dougal said, "what is it?" He traced his fingers over her hair. They had dressed again and sat together on the sand, leaned against the rocky wall that still held the warmth of the day's sun, his arm wrapped over her shoulders. The water shushed and the moon sparkled over mild waves, and the exquisite joy of Norrie's fiddle sounded in the distance.

"Nothing. Just thoughts." She looked up, her cheek

resting on his shoulder, her palm quiet on his chest. "Dougal, what was it you began to tell me the other day, in the cave?"

She saw him smile a little. "We have a little time now before they come looking for us, I suppose."

"They will not come looking for us," she said. "Grandmother and Mother Elga would not let them bother us if they know that we left together."

"Why? Two unmarried young people out alone in the moonlight . . . There is no predicting what they will do." He smiled and kissed her hair.

"Mother Elga and Grandmother Thora want us to go out in the moonlight together," she said. "They have wanted it all along, ever since they met you."

"That I find hard to believe."

"Tell me your story, Dougal Stewart, and I will tell you mine, and then you will understand."

He looked askance at her for a moment, then shrugged. "Very well. Seven years ago, just before sunset one evening, I raced a rowboat against another fellow. Both of us were fairly drunk at the time, after a wake for a fine old man whose wife made some very good whisky—George MacDonald of Tobermory."

"We knew him. A good man, indeed. Why were you there?"

"I had been studying the Caran Reef, taking measurements of the rocks, calculating the wave force, and so on. We were sure, even then, that a lighthouse was needed somewhere along the reef. Several of us had been on Mull for weeks, so we were at the wake. We were damn fools that night, and when some of my men boasted of our daring, my friend and I had no choice but to prove them right. He got sick over the side, poor lad, but I kept going, seeing my chance to win. And I soon found myself going down the throat of a sudden squall that turned evil very quickly. I could not get away. A wave washed me overboard, and I took a blow to the head and nearly drowned. I was saved—" He stopped suddenly. "Well, you would find that too wild to believe."

"What saved you?"

"I suppose it was a wave, washing me onto the great rock of Sgeir Caran," he answered. "But for a moment, I thought that a pair of beautiful horses carried me over the water." He shook his head as if bewildered.

"Horses! You mean you saw . . . sea kelpies?"

He shrugged. "Imagined them, more like. But when I landed on the rock and saw you . . . well. Again my imagination was in full force. I had taken a blow to the head that night."

"Then you were shipwrecked on Sgeir Caran," she breathed.

He nodded, rubbing his fingers along her shoulder. "Aye. So you see, there were no schemes to have some fun with the young and innocent girl who sat waiting on the rock."

She nodded. "I am so sorry that I believed that of you. But . . . well, I saw the men fetch you in the morning."

"So you concluded that it was arranged. I understand."

"Who were they?"

"Alan Clarke and another fellow," he said. "I've known Alan for years. He was the one I raced against. When I did not come back and the storm blew in, they gave me up for lost. But Alan refused to accept that. He and the other fellow rowed out to look for me once the weather calmed. At dawn that day, they saw me standing on the sea rock. Alan, as you know, is a bull of a man and powerful at the oars. If he had not been sick that night, I would have lost that race. And then I never would have ended up on Sgeir Caran—or found you there."

"So we owe Mr. Clarke a debt."

He smiled. "We do."

"Dougal, do they—did you ever tell them—"

"About us?" As he spoke, he smoothed his fingers over the shell of her ear, and shivers cascaded through her. "I have never said a word of it to anyone. It was too precious a secret. And I thought—" He paused, half laughed, then shook his head.

"What?" she asked, looking up at him.

"You will think me mad," he said. "I thought you were not even real, that you were . . . a sea fairy. I was hazed with drink and from a knock to the head, as well. I believed that you were magical . . . or that I had imagined you."

She stared up at him. "You thought I was a sea fairy?"

"Aye, or a selkie, or some kind of magical sea creature. A kelpie perhaps, or a mermaid, come into human form." He shrugged. "I can offer you no better explanation than that. You were so beautiful, so gentle and kind, and it was a miracle to find you there in the midst of that wild a storm, and . . . What is it?"

Meg began to laugh from sheer relief and joy in the irony of the situation. "You thought I was a sea fairy," she said, "and I thought you were the great kelpie himself, the *each-uisge* of Sgeir Caran!"

He blinked at her. "The what? The kelpie legend that I've heard about?"

She nodded. "My grandmothers are convinced that I should be with you . . . well, forever."

Dougal tipped his head in bewilderment. "They think I am the kelpie of Sgeir Caran?"

She shrugged. "Thora is not so sure, but Elga is certain of it. You've more than proven it in her mind."

"How?"

"Norrie told her that you rose up out of the sea when we went out to the rock the day you were diving. And you wanted to take the children from her that day you met us on the beach. Stop laughing," she told him. "And you rescued Iain and sent the shark away."

"I seem to have misrepresented myself," he said, and chuckled.

"And my grandmothers think—" she paused.

"Come now. Tell me," he coaxed. "I have not told you anything less ridiculous than you could confess to me."

"They think you are already my husband," she blurted.

He leaned back, folded his arms. "Now this I must hear."

"Mother Elga and Grandmother Thora sent me out to the rock that night," she explained. "It is an old tradition on Caransay for a maiden to spend a night out there, once every hundred years, to wait for the great kelpie to arrive and make her his . . . well, bride. They told me I must submit to him, and gave me a whisky potion to ease my fears and make me . . . bold."

"Aye, well," he said, "you were bold enough."

She poked him playfully. "Our legend says that when the great kelpie of Sgeir Caran claims his bride, he will bestow good fortune on her and the people of Caransay. We needed good fortune then, for the previous leaseholder of the island was about to evict everyone and replace the tenants with sheep farmers and bring in English flocks. So I went to the rock to make the appeal to the . . . and there you were."

"And a lucky man, to be mistaken for the kelpie," he drawled, laughing as she pushed at him. "Your grandmothers never told you that the kelpie might be nearly drowned, did they?"

She giggled, and they settled together, his arm around her shoulders. "I was hazed, as you were, by the herbal potion my grandmothers had given me," she went on. "So I believed you were magical. And besides, you had no clothing. You did not look like a man washed up from a shipwreck." She plucked at his shirt.

"I took off my clothes to keep from sinking. I'd

rather wash up naked on some beach for all the islanders to see, than die clothed and decent for the fishes."

"I was lucky to find a beautiful naked man ready to do all my will, instead of a slimy, wretched sea monster ready to give me nightmares." She smiled as he laughed.

"Aye, you were lucky," he said, and he kissed her. "Did the kelpie bestow good fortune on you afterward? Or, now that he's back, are you waiting to find out?"

She smiled at his jest, but inside she trembled. The whole truth hovered on her lips, but there was too much she could not tell him, here and now, about Iain, herself, and now Frederick. Wanting desperately to tell him, she resisted, unable to spoil this magical night for both of them.

She shrugged. "We were not evicted, as it turned out."

"Lady Strathlin bought the island's lease? Very good luck, indeed. You had the blessing of the kelpie after all."

Gulping, she could only nod.

Growing quiet, he traced circles on her shoulder. "Girl," he murmured, "you are so good, so honest and pure in your character. And I am deeply sorry that you believed I was a wretched monster for so many years." He kissed the top of her head. "You have such integrity and strength."

She shook her head, torn by guilt. "I am not what you think."

"I never want you to feel ashamed of what we did that night or what we have done now. Listen to me. That night was very powerful. I do not believe what we did was wrong. We saved each other that night. And I will take the responsibility for it upon my shoulders. You were an innocent then, and to me you are innocent still, no matter what has happened between us." He touched her hair, kissed her brow.

She ducked her head against his chest.

"Meg MacNeill, look at me." He tilted her chin upward and kissed her mouth gently. "Meg, I want to marry you."

She gasped and felt tears begin to gather in her eyes. "Do not . . . feel that you have an obligation to me."

"I do have an obligation to you. But that is not why I am asking this. I want to marry you, if you will have me. Let me take care of you and your family."

She sat up, heart pounding, and shook her head. "I cannot—we cannot. It is not necessary for you to do this."

"Let me help you." He sat up with her, kept a hand on her back. "Life is hard in the Hebrides. I know that. I can help you and your family. I have . . . a respectable income."

"No," she said, getting to her feet. He stood with her. "Please, no."

"I thought—"

"I am grateful for the offer, but I . . . I cannot marry you."

He turned away, rubbed a hand over his face as if to summon patience, turned back. "Meg, I have wronged you. I have a conscience, woman. Allow me to make this up to you."

"I beg you, do not pity me or feel a sense of duty. I could not bear it," she finished, and whirled to walk past him.

He grabbed her arm, turned her back. "I did not ask you to marry me out of a sense of obligation, you darling wee fool. I love you."

Her heart bounded. A fierce ache of longing within her became deep remorse, then bitter pain at the irony. Here was all she had ever wanted—his heart, his love, his desire—and yet she was powerless to accept or to explain. She stared at him in anguished silence.

"I love you, Meg MacNeill," he murmured. "I want to be with you. I think I have loved you for seven years but did not know it until now. The night we met, you were my salvation. I owed you my life that night, and yet afterward I hurt you without knowing it."

"We saved each other that night," she said fervently. "There is nothing owed. You are forgiven, if that is what you seek."

"Listen to me," he said, his grip fierce on her arm. She felt caught as if by a spell. In the moonlight, his voice dropped to hoarseness blended with the sea. "You are not the only one with a dream."

She watched him through tears. "Mine cannot come true." The awful finality of that seemed to twist inside of her.

Suddenly he let go of her. "Aye, then," he said, and she heard a cold edge now in his voice. "Do what you will. I have made the offer, and it stands. I told you I never give up." He watched her. "And I have great patience."

Spinning on her heel, she half ran over the sand, her heart sinking with each step. She felt her heart and soul beating against the cage that had been locked around her by wealth and secrets.

The deepest hurt of all was that he had let her go, somehow. Yet she had given him no choice, no hope for their future.

She had never even told him that she loved him.

He saw blue sky and clouds through a depth of water as clear as crystal. Golden shadows rippled over the mountainous base of the rock as daylight streamed through the water currents. As he looked up, a pair of dolphins swam past overhead.

Good, Dougal thought. Where there were dolphins there would be no sharks, and he did not want to meet those fellows ever again. He turned, awkward in his gear and suit, and pointed upward.

Standing near him, Evan looked like a sea beast,

his tentaclelike hoses undulating. He raised a gauntleted hand to acknowledge the sight of the dolphins overhead and turned back to the undersea hill.

Dougal made his way over the rock with strange, slow clumsiness. Noises assailed him even through the brass-and-copper helmet, dominated by the sound of his own breathing as air whooshed in and out of the hoses and valves connected to his helmet. Every puff of air pumped down the length of nearly two hundred feet of hosing, smelling sharply of rubber, became his next breath. With each exhalation, he heard the click and suck of air drawn through the exit valve. Through the helmet, he heard the shushing waves and the sound of the wooden platform knocking against the rock, stirred by currents. The water was never still, never quiet, the sea too powerful here to be tranquil.

Dougal traced his gauntleted hands over recesses and protrusions, checking crevices as he searched for any signs of damage from the blastings on the rock. Sgeir Caran was massive under the surface, not overly high but as broad as any hill on Caransay, and too large for two men to walk around in one short diving session. As the blastings and construction continued, they regularly dove downward to make sure the rock remained intact.

"Dougal." Alan Clarke's voice came through the speaking tube, surprisingly clear through two hundred feet of hose.

"Aye," Dougal responded. "All is well here."

"Good. You've been down long enough. Another minute or so."

"Aye, then," Dougal said. He signaled Evan, who climbed onto the wooden platform and tugged three times on the ropes to alert the men above that he was ready to come up.

Dougal waited his turn, watching as Evan was hauled upward slowly. The platform stopped, then ascended a little farther. The crew members were always careful to bring up the divers in slow increments, halting frequently to allow their lungs to adapt to the changing depths.

Dougal brushed his gloved hand over the rock to examine a small horizontal niche, loosening a cloud of sand and debris. Something glinted in a soft spill of daylight, floating away. Dougal snatched at it, capturing it clumsily in his fingers.

Covered with an encrustation of coral, the tiny object winked golden in his palm. Thinking it was a coin, he scraped at it and discovered instead a bit of jewelry, though he could not tell quite what it was. He slipped it into the canvas bag attached to his belt.

The platform descended again, and he climbed onto it and tugged at the ropes. On the slow, careful journey upward, he made sure to breathe deeply and evenly to acclimatize himself to the shifts in pressure. Looking up, he saw clear, swirling water overhead, and then he surged into the air, craned upward by pulleys and ropes.

Leaving the solid cushion of water, he suddenly felt the crushing weight of the suit, helmet, lead boots, and weighted belt. Stepping off the platform to walk to the bench, he strained to bear the weight, breaking out in a hot sweat inside the suit, still breathing the last bit of air that had been pumped into the helmet, with its stale, rubbery smell.

Moments later, as his men unscrewed the brass-and-copper helmet and lifted it away, he felt cool air burst over his face and fill his lungs. His crew then efficiently removed his cumbersome gear, and he thanked them. Rising, he walked toward the iron barracks to change out of his diving suit and the layers of damp woolen undergarments.

Dressed once again in his customary dark suit and vest, he remembered the little gold piece he had found below. He fetched it from the canvas bag and took it to the doorway of the barracks to examine it in good light. He flecked the coral crust away with his fingernail and exposed a pretty bijou.

The piece was a pendant, with a translucent blue-green aquamarine set in a delicate frame of filigreed gold. The small chain attached to its loop was broken and crusted over, but the pendant itself would be lovely once it was cleaned. He scraped at it and turned it in his fingers.

Winking in the light, the luminous stone reminded him of Meg's beautiful eyes. He knew the pendant would be lovely hung around her neck, and he wanted to give it to her. But he hesitated, remembering her adamant, hurtful rejection of his declaration of love. Two days had passed since then, and even while he had been busy with his work, he had wondered if she would come to him—but she had not.

Expressing his heart to her had not been easy for him. She might want him to disappear from her life, but he did not intend to do that. Something troubled her, and he would not rest until he knew what it was. All was not done between him and Meg, he felt sure.

Frowning thoughtfully, he pocketed the little jewel and left the barracks. He felt the pendant between his fingers and suddenly decided that he might give it to her. If nothing else, perhaps she would accept it as a gesture of faith and loyalty—though for him it would be a gift of love.

Time might be the remedy Meg needed to decide if she loved him and could marry him. He had felt the keen edge of her silence when he had declared his feelings. Although he would have to accept it if she did not love him, every instinct he had—blood, bone, and soul—insisted that she shared his affection. Whatever else troubled her, he had the patience and the determination to wait it out—and the strength to share should she need it of him.

Once found, love was not a thing to give up easily, nor would he.

Chapter Fourteen

"I know the hour is late," Dougal said. A fine rain sparkled on his bowler hat and broad shoulders as he stood in the doorway of Norrie's house. "I've come for my mail. I heard that Norrie brought it in from Tobermory late today."

Having answered his knock, Meg now stared at him, her heart racing. A strong gust of wind blew past him, and she strained to keep the door from bursting out of her hold. Outside, she noticed a blustery sky with huge iron-gray clouds hovering over the sea.

"Dougal, come in!" Norrie stood as he saw the visitor. "I fetched the mail in Tobermory but have not yet given it out. Let the poor man in out of the rain, Margaret. We'll have a gale before long, by the look of that black sky out there," he added.

She moved back in silent invitation. Removing his hat, Dougal stepped inside, glancing soberly at her.

Not certain what to say, she just held her hand out for his hat, which he gave to her.

"Sit you down, Mr. Stooar," Thora said, angling a bench beside the stool where Norrie now sat. "It is a dirty night."

"Aye, it is indeed," Dougal agreed, standing beside

Meg. "Thank you, but I will not stay. I am sorry to disturb you, but I was out walking and saw the lamplight through the window. I thought to save Mr. MacNeill the trouble of delivering my mail."

"Sit you down," Mother Elga repeated, gesturing.

"I have work to do this evening, so I should be on my way soon," he answered. Meg, staying silent, was sure that he avoided looking at her.

Sensing his cool, shuttered mood, Meg wondered if he was still angry with her, or if he felt, as she did, a deep wrench of sadness. She had not seen him since the ceilidh, but now, standing so close to him in the dimly lit room, she felt the pull of him like a lodestone. The knowledge that she had hurt him still twisted like a knife.

"Ach, Mr. Stooar, stay. It is not good for a body to work all the time," Thora said. "Sit you down and have a dram with Norrie. The children are to bed, and we are just sitting here in the nice quiet, the four of us. And now you."

"Thora will get you a dram," Norrie said, "and Margaret will fetch the mail. The sack is there in the cupboard, girl."

Dougal acquiesced with a polite murmur and sat on the bench beside the fire, thanking Thora for the cup of whisky that she poured and handed him. Elga remained in her favorite seat, a chair tucked in a warm corner by the hearth, and smiled at him.

"Mr. Stooar," she said, "do you like the rains?"

"Aye, at times," he said. "Not when heavy storms interfere with our work on the rock, but a soft rain like this one can be rather peaceful."

"Ah," Elga said, nodding. "Like your home in the sea?"

He glanced quickly at Meg, who blinked wide-eyed at him, while Mother Elga smiled blithely. "As peaceful as the sea, Mother Elga," he said gently. "Thank you," he murmured to Meg when she handed him the bundle of letters. His fingers brushed hers when he took the envelopes. Startled by that warm contact, feeling the tug in her heart, she stepped back.

"Sit you down, Margaret," Elga said. "Ach, not here by me. Over there, next to Mr. Stooar," she urged, gesturing.

"Here," Thora said, insistently patting the bench beside Dougal, while she resumed her own seat near Norrie.

Reluctantly, Meg sat. The bench barely held two, so her skirts fell over Dougal's long, muscular thigh, warm beside hers, and her arm brushed his. The fresh, mingled scents of rain and wind and a hint of the flowery machair still clung to him. He seemed to radiate tangible strength and warmth, and her breath came faster, though she sat very still and silent.

While he chatted politely with her grandparents, she glanced at the letters he held in one hand. The topmost envelope, she saw immediately, was from her solicitors, Hamilton and Shaw. He slipped the letters into his pocket unread.

Dread plunged through her, for she knew that her advocates were attempting to stall, even completely disrupt, the work on the lighthouse, as she had asked them to do weeks earlier. Although the latest batch of mail held no new reports for her in that regard, she realized that her solicitor, Sir Edward Hamilton, had notified Dougal of the next move—whatever it might be.

"*Ach.* Now I am thinking that we need a lighthouse out there," Norrie was saying.

Meg straightened, looked at him. "But, Grandfather, you have always been against the lighthouse," she pointed out.

"In the beginning, I agreed with Lady Strathlin, who wants the isle kept private and the rock kept sacred," Norrie admitted. He pulled on his pipe and looked at Meg for a moment. Then he pointed toward the window and the bay beyond. "But now I am thinking the light would be a help out there and not much bother to us here on the island, but for the months it is being made. That wicked reef needs a light, and no question."

"The lighthouse could be placed anywhere along that reef," Meg said defensively. "It could be set farther south, where the treacherous rocks begin. Best to warn the ships at that point rather than here, two-thirds of the way along the reef."

"The light on Sgeir Caran would illuminate the whole length of the reef, Miss MacNeill. And the southernmost rocks are partially submerged in high tides," Dougal said quietly. "While lighthouses have been constructed under such conditions, it is not my preference."

"It is not his preference," Elga repeated precisely.

"Sgeir Caran is by far the best location," Dougal said.

"And that's the most important," Norrie said. "Besides, we are happy to have the resident engineer staying on Caransay." Meg could have sworn her grandfather winked. She scowled at him.

"Mr. Stooar is always welcome on Caransay," Elga said. "And so we like his lighthouse now, and him. Mr. Stooar rescued our wee Iain." Dougal nodded his thanks.

"A great many ships have gone down on that reef," Norrie said. "There is a tidal flow between some of those rocks that can spin a ship around and take it down in a few minutes' time. I've seen too many wrecks to ask you to set your light elsewhere."

"We do not want to see any more wrecks," Thora said.

"You've witnessed some yourself?" Dougal asked. The elderly people all nodded.

"We've all watched them," Norrie said. "And God save us, it is an awful thing to see. We tried to help the poor souls when we could, but there is little that men can do against the power of a great storm. We've saved too few souls over the years."

"You have rescued people from shipwrecks?" Dougal sat forward, looking at the old man sharply.

"*Ach,* myself and my brothers and my father before me. We did what we could whenever a ship foundered on the reef. My grandfather and great-grandfather and so on before them were wreckers, I am ashamed to say. They and their ilk wanted ships to break apart on the rocks, and would save no one."

"Wreckers still do their work in the Isles," Dougal said.

"Not on Caransay," Meg said. "It is not done here."

"Not anymore," Norrie agreed. "But it was done here long ago. Many relied on wreckage to bring goods into their homes and money into their pockets. Some even lured ships this way with lamps and fire signals. The wood that made that table and that cupboard there, came from ship timbers in my great-grandfather's time," he said. "But my father never wrecked, and neither did his sons. We could not bear to hear the screams. The noise is terrible when a ship goes down—the wailing, the prayers shouted up to God. It is an awful thing to hear, and so we try to help."

"I'm sure you did your best to save others," Dougal said.

"We sent out mortar lines when there were survivors to grab on to the ropes, and sometimes we rowed out as far as we dared, though the waves could have taken us as well. A few ships a year go down out there, sometimes more. We did what we could."

"Do you recall," Dougal said slowly, "a wreck from about eighteen years ago? A ship called the *Primrose* went down on the Caran Reef."

"*Primrose.*" Norrie frowned and sent a small puff of smoke out of his pipe. "I do recall that one. Many people were lost that night, though we rowed out. We heard from the inspectors who came to the island afterwards, that the ship was called the *Primrose*. It came from Glasgow and was sailing up to Skye with people on holiday."

"Aye," Dougal murmured. "That's the one."

"It was a sad thing, those people only sailing a little distance on holiday. A black storm blew out of the west that evening and took them down within minutes." He shook his head. "We did our best."

"I'm glad to hear it, Mr. MacNeill," Dougal said.

"Have you a particular interest in it, then?" Norrie asked. "Do you recall stories about it?"

"I was thirteen years old then, sir," Dougal said, and paused. "My parents were on that ship."

Meg glanced up in time to see a muscle bounce subtly in his cheek. She reached out impulsively and touched his forearm, without thought for the new, painful rift between them. She cared only about the pain he was feeling. He did not look at her, but allowed her hand to linger.

Sensing the deep, old hurt he carried, she understood it far too well. Her own father had drowned out on that reef. "Mr. Stewart," she murmured, "I am sorry. We did not know."

"Why should you?" he asked softly. "But thank you."

"Poor lad," Thora said. "We know what it is to lose someone in that way. We all do, here in this room. Our son, Margaret's father, was taken by the sea, too."

Dougal nodded, and although he did not look at Meg, he rested his hand over hers briefly. That silent gesture of compassion gave her a quick, bright hope that he still loved her. Her refusal of him had not destroyed that. She closed her eyes in relief. Though she was not free to marry him, she desperately needed to know that he cared for her, as she did for him, even if they had to part.

"It's a hard thing for a young lad to bear, Dougal Stewart," Norrie murmured. "I think this is why you build lighthouses—to save others from such a fate." He nodded his approval.

"Aye, sir," Dougal said quietly. "And that's why I want the Caran light to go up. It is especially important to me."

Meg caught her breath. Of course, she thought, Dougal would have a strong reason for wanting to build the lighthouse on that very spot. Now that she knew him as a man of heart and integrity, she realized that his private suffering had helped create the rich vein of compassion that was such a part of him. Further, she understood why he had been so stubborn and persistent.

She looked down at her hands, realizing that she had acted selfishly, had made assumptions, and had allowed solicitors to speak for the baroness. Far better, she thought, if she had taken the time to discover for herself why Dougal Stewart was so adamant and dedicated to his lighthouse project.

And the contents of the one letter in his pocket could very well destroy all of that. Pressing her lips together, she lowered her head, feeling heavy remorse. She should not have encouraged her solicitors in this matter.

"A lighthouse would not have saved our son," Norrie was saying. "He knew those rocks well. It was the strength of the squall that took him." He looked at Meg. "We will tell Lady Strathlin that there are noble reasons for putting that light just there and that Dougal Stewart has good reason to ask for her help."

"I doubt she would care," Dougal said.

Tears stung Meg's eyes. She opened her mouth to speak, finally done with holding back, done with the hurt and the ruse that she had hated. None of her lies had protected her. They had only caused more difficulties for her and for Dougal.

With this man, strong and deep and loving, there was no threat from which she needed protection. She had been wrong about the obstinate, odious Mr. Stewart, and she had hurt him deeply, with more hurt inevitable—and all at her hands.

"Mr. Stewart—" she began.

Norrie glanced at her and shook his head. "Not now, girl," he said in Gaelic. "Now is not the time to tell him."

She subsided, knowing he was right to stop her. If she told Dougal the truth now, he would hate her forever, but that could not be avoided. Once he learned about their son, he might well try to take him from her, which was within his rights as the child's father.

But she could not risk causing a threat to Dougal, too, from Sir Frederick. If Matheson discovered that the lighthouse engineer was the father of her child, he would do his best to ruin Dougal and his career. She was certain of it.

She bit her lip and sighed. First she must resolve her problem with Sir Frederick Matheson. Then, she thought, she could—and would—explain the truth with a great sense of relief, no matter what Dougal thought of her afterward.

"Thank you for telling me about the *Primrose,* Mr. MacNeill. I appreciate it more than I can say." Dougal set his emptied glass down. "And thank you for the hospitality, Mrs. MacNeill. I must go. The weather is poor, and I have some work to do yet."

He stood, although the elderly MacNeills protested with genuine warmth for him to stay. Smiling, he shook his head, and Norrie gestured for Meg to open the door for him.

She rose and went forward, opening the door without a word. Wind stirred the delicate golden strands of her hair, blew at her plain skirt. The sky beyond had grown darker, and in the little time that Dougal had been inside the house, the wind had grown colder and faster and the rain had increased.

"Dirty weather indeed," Norrie said from his place by the hearth. "It will blow hard tonight. Best get back to your wee house, Mr. Stewart."

"Aye. Good night, then." Dougal nodded toward the others, then looked at Meg. She watched him, a hand quiet on the edge of the door, her gaze wide-eyed and haunted.

He glanced around. The fire crackled in the hearth, the elders sat quietly, and the little black terrier slept peacefully at Norrie's feet. The scene inside the shadowed room was simple and cozy, and the amber glow of lamplight over Meg's hair and creamy skin was warm and lovely.

He did not want to leave, suddenly. The storm had nothing to do with it. The lure was the golden girl in the shadows, the welcome of hearth and home, the simplicity and honesty and goodness of this place and these people.

He hesitated, hand upon the door. The humble croft felt more like home to him than his aunt's grand manse in Strathclyde, although he dearly loved the kinfolk who had taken him and his sisters willingly into their home after the deaths of their parents on the Caran Reef. He would see them again soon, but he would not feel quite the sense of a true home that he felt so easily here.

"Good night, Mr. Stewart," Meg said. "You'd best take your hat." She lifted it from a peg and handed it to him.

"Miss MacNeill," he said quietly, formally, and reached into his pocket. "I nearly forgot. I also came here hoping to give you this." He handed her a small paper packet. "Open it," he urged, when she looked at him in surprise.

She peeled away the paper—he had used a small notebook page for the wrapping—and gasped to see the small pendant, its pale aquamarine polished and glittering in the golden setting. He had cleaned it and suspended it on thick black thread, having no suitable chain to replace the broken one.

"Oh! It's lovely," she said. "Where did you—why—"

"I found it in the sea, on the base of Sgeir Caran," he explained. "Evan Mackenzie and I went down in the deep the other day, and I found this caught in a crevice in the rock. We found some coins, too, Spanish by the look of them, and a silver spoon. They must have drifted on the tides and currents from the site of an old shipwreck and they became wedged in the rock. This, and the coins, were encrusted with coral, so they have been down there a long time. When I saw that it was a bonny wee thing, I . . . well, I thought of you. I apologize for the black thread. I had nothing else for it."

"It's beautiful," she said. "And I like it strung on simple black thread. I shall treasure it." She smiled and glanced up at him, and he saw tears glistening in her eyes. "The woman who owned this may have lost her life out there on the reef."

He nodded. "A very long time ago. It looks to be very old—perhaps it went down in a Spanish galleon out there. Though it is an old-fashioned thing, it might have some value. I thought you might like to have it." He shrugged, as if it meant little to him, when in fact, the dazzle of happiness in her eyes meant everything to him.

"Thank you, Mr. Stewart," she whispered. "I will . . . remember you always, when I wear this."

That hurt more than he could have imagined. He

gave no reaction, but kept his hand on the door, very near to hers. "Show it to Lady Strathlin," he said. "Remind her how many lives have been lost on the reef. Perhaps she ought to wear it herself, to keep the true meaning of that lighthouse clear in her mind."

Her eyes were wide and anxious, almost tortured, as she looked up at him. She did not answer, but reached up to tie the black thread behind her neck, suspending the pendant at her throat, over the simple neckline of her blouse. A small golden oval hung there, too, just below the pulse in her throat.

"I see you already have a necklace," he said.

"I wear this always," she said, her slim fingers graceful as they popped the tiny catch. Inside the two halves, he saw a miniature painted portrait of someone with golden curls perhaps herself as a child. She closed the locket quickly, but not before he glimpsed what was framed under glass in the other oval.

She carried a tiny braided circlet of red thread and human hair, golden and brown. The thread had been plucked from a plaid blanket. The sight struck him to the core.

He carried its twin, a plaited circlet inside the hidden compartment of his pocket watch. Instinctively he touched his watch pocket, tempted to show it to her and explain that he had carried it with him for seven years, ever since the dawn hour when she had placed it on his finger.

But he said nothing. Though he was determined not to give up on his love for her, he would not make a maudlin fool of himself by begging for her love. Enough, for now, to know that she still kept the ring, as he had.

"Well," he said, stepping back, giving her a cool smile, "I am glad you like the little jewel. Good night."

Thora rose to glance out the door. "You'd best stay

here, Mr. Stooar. On such a night as this, the storm will blow up so fast that soon you will not be able to stand up in it."

"I'll do. Good night." Dougal tapped his bowler on his head and stepped out into the battering force of the wind. Holding the hat's brim, he fought his way across the sandy, reedy yard toward the slope that led up to the machair.

"Mr. Stewart!" He heard Meg cry out. "Dougal, wait!"

He turned and saw her running out of the house, and stopped. The wind pushed at his back, nearly whipped the hat from his head. Rain slanted over his shoulders.

"Please—come back to the house and stay with us," she said, coming closer and stopping within arm's length. The reedy grass blew all around them, and the surf pounded loudly on the beach. "Norrie sent me. He said to tell you that it is looking more fierce. A man could get washed out to sea just walking home."

"I'll be fine," he said. "It's a wee storm. Go back inside. Go on, now. You'll be soaked."

She did not turn away. "You can be so obstinate, sir."

"And you, Miss MacNeill," he said bitterly, bowing. The next gust of wind beat at her skirts and blew her hair over her eyes. She brushed it back, held it while she watched him.

"I . . . wanted to thank you for the gift," she said.

"You did thank me." He wanted to pull her into his arms, kiss her wild in the rain. Instead he stood a safe distance away, water drizzling off the brim of his hat, his heart twisting for love of her.

"I wanted to give you something in return, to remember me by." She pulled a cloth-wrapped packet from her skirt pocket. "Please take it. But do not open it out here in the wet and the wind. Wait until later."

He accepted it, fitted its bulk safely into his pocket,

and tipped his hat. "Thank you, Miss MacNeill," he said. "I will be . . . glad to have something to remember you by." He kept his tone cool and neutral. "Are you leaving Caransay soon?"

"I am," she said. "In a few."

"Well, then. Perhaps our paths will cross someday."

She nodded, hands clasped in front of her, the rain slicking down her curls, wind billowing her skirt.

He felt a powerful urge to pull her into his arms and claim both her and her stubborn little heart. As he opened his mouth to tell her that whatever troubled her, no matter its nature, they would solve it together, she turned and ran.

Pride held him still, and he let her go. Turning, he made his way up and over the machair, hand on his pocket all the while, keeping her packet snug and dry.

As soon as he stepped inside his small hut and lit the lamp, then removed his wet hat and coat, he extracted the package. Unwrapping the square of linen, he found a leather-covered book tied with a ribbon.

Sitting down to turn the pages carefully, he saw that she had given him one of her journals. The book was the first one, he realized. Filled with pencil and ink studies, some washed with pale color, its pages were crammed with images of flowers, plants, shells, stones, birds, and wildlife. There were notations, too, in a careful script, for she had identified and written a brief commentary for every drawing.

He pored over the pages with great care, then closed it and wrapped it again in the ribbon and cloth. Resting his hand on it for a while, thinking, he turned to open his mail.

Outside, the rain began to pour in earnest. As he read his correspondence by lamplight and contemplated his answers, the wind shook the walls of his solid little hut, and he soon heard the waves crashing relentlessly onshore.

20 August 1857
To the Northern Lighthouse Commission
George Street
Edinburgh

Dear Sirs,

Recently we endured a storm of considerable force, with high winds, heavy rain, and breakers over six feet high. This confined us to our barracks on Caransay for two days. We emerged to find a world misted gray and littered with debris.

The work site on Sgeir Caran sustained some damage, including two work sheds and the smithy. The iron storage house, once riveted in the rock, now lists to one side. Missing are various tools, workbenches, and an anvil stone, all presumably blown into the sea.

Most astonishing of all, two stone blocks, weighing four tons each, were shifted off the rock by wind and wave, and now lie at the bottom of the sea. We hope to fetch all of these items up again with cranes and divers.

Funds are needed to repair and replace buildings and equipment. This will increase my original estimate of fifty thousand pounds by at least five percent. However, Lady Strathlin's advocates now inform me that some contributors who previously offered assistance will no longer extend it.

I plan to return to Edinburgh shortly. With the commission's approval, I hope to obtain promises from other contributors.

And I intend to pay a call on Lady Strathlin.

Yrs. respectfully,
Dougal Robertson Stewart
Innish Bay
Caransay

Chapter Fifteen

"So, you refuse to abandon this project," Sir Aedan MacBride said. "Good. I agree wholeheartedly, Dougal. That lighthouse must go up. The location is ideal, and the need is paramount." He leaned back in a leather-upholstered chair that matched the one Dougal occupied. The two men had retired after dinner to the smoking room on the top floor of Dundrennan House, Aedan's Strathclyde manse. "A shame Lady Strathlin cannot understand that."

Dougal nodded, appreciating his cousin's natural reserve and his ability to listen calmly, giving others time to sort things out for themselves. Lingering over glasses of port, Dougal had confided in Aedan, who was an engineer of highways and byways, his difficulties with the lighthouse as well as the baroness.

"Despite the latest maneuvers of Lady Strathlin and her mob of solicitors, I cannot, and will not, give up this cause." Dougal rolled the bowl of his glass between his palms, staring at the dark liquid sloshing inside. "I will build the thing myself, even fund it myself, though it would break me. I will set every damned stone with my own hands." He sat forward and rubbed a hand over his face, weary and frustrated yet feeling an almost overwhelming determination. "It has to go up."

Aedan regarded him steadily. "That persistence was a bit of a fault when you were younger," he said. "A more bullheaded lad there never was. But you've used it for the better by facing impossible odds and downright danger to build these lighthouses. The Caran light looks to be a magnificent structure, by the drawings and plans you showed me. The design is spare and elegant, combining aesthetics with practicality. It will outlast the ages. And it will go up. I have absolutely no doubt." He smiled. "I know you."

"Thank you. I hope you will make the journey to see it."

"I'd like that. How is Evan, by the way? Still trying to spit into the wind? The two of you must be a pair on that rock."

Dougal laughed. He and Aedan had attended Edinburgh University with Evan Mackenzie, so that Aedan knew the viscount as well as he knew Dougal. "Somewhat. He's subdued and keeps his own counsel since that awful incident last year."

"I am convinced that the bridge collapse was not his fault—though unfortunately not everyone agrees."

"Nor is he to blame for the faults of his father, the earl."

"Lord Kildonan is a discredit to the whole of Scotland. No wonder Evan rejects association with him."

"Nonetheless, he remains his father's only heir. One day our friend will be the Earl of Kildonan, which is the last thing he wants—or needs."

"An inherited black mark when his reputation has already suffered." Aedan shook his head.

Dougal stared at the tartan-patterned carpet beneath his boots. "Aedan," he said, "what do you know of Lady Strathlin?"

"Little enough, really. She inherited the biggest fortune in Scotland rather unexpectedly—the male heir and the next in line both died, and old Lord Strathlin shortly followed. Awful business, but I understand she's a credit to the title and a generous and charitable lady. Surprising that she has been so adamant in her attempts to prevent you from your work."

"It is surprising, in a way, and does not chime with what I've heard of her magnanimous nature. She bought the lease of that island years ago from the English lord who owned it, fired the factor, and secured the island in perpetuity for her tenants. She ensures that they will never have to worry about anything—but for the weather, I suppose," he added. "For all the trouble the woman has caused me, I give her credit for her treatment of the islanders."

"They say she supplied relief elsewhere in the Hebrides by sending food shipments and starting industries so that the people could better support themselves. My father spent much of his personal fortune on shiploads of grain and goods for Highlanders and Islesmen a dozen years ago, when the potato crops were blighted and so many Scots suffered. If Lady Strathlin has made a difference for those people, I heartily applaud her.

"Beautiful, as I recall, with an appealing quality, neither haughty nor vain. She is never without a veritable train of attendants and hangers-on, but I believe that is one of the pitfalls of such wealth. She did not seem to relish the attention. We did not converse—it was an introduction only."

"How intriguing," Dougal said thoughtfully. "I did not imagine her to be lovely, though I did not see her closely."

Aedan rose to his feet, and Dougal stood, too. "Shall we join the ladies in the drawing room for coffee?"

"Aye. Aunt Lill allowed her monkey to be at tea today, and I heard the wee beastie chattering in the hallway before dinner," Dougal said. "Does Thistle still keep late hours?"

Aedan grinned. "Are you asking if Miss Thistle will be taking coffee with us tonight?"

"Take coffee, toss cups, crack the china—whatever you will call it," Dougal drawled. Miss Thistle is always entertaining company."

"We are in luck. Amy is planning parlor games for tonight, and since she finds Thistle exceedingly tiresome, the beastie is banned from the drawing room. By way of warning, your sister is delighted to have another male available for charades."

"Please, not Amy in charge of charades!" Dougal groaned.

"We all must submit now and then," Aedan said, pinching back a smile.

"Have you not submitted yet, then?" Dougal asked. "I had the impression that my sister hoped to convince you that marriage to her, your fetching cousin, would be a safe and sensible route for you—considering your hesitations regarding marriage."

Aedan frowned, and Dougal saw the spark of humor diminish in his cousin's vivid blue eyes. "I am very fond of Amy, and she has been a great help to me in refurbishing this house according to my father's will." He gestured around the room, with its new tartan carpeting and chintz draperies. "But I am not sure that I love her in quite the way she wishes." He shrugged. "Still, I have not yet made up my mind what to do. I wish to marry someday, but . . . well, according to that black curse over my ancestors and myself, the lairds of Dundrennan can never fall in love. Unfortunately, I tested the rule and found it to have some truth." He still frowned.

"Someday," Dougal said quietly, "you will risk it again and find a way to break the spell that has haunted this place for centuries."

"I hope you are right," Aedan murmured, and he opened the door.

Dougal went with Aedan from the billiard room to the drawing room, where their aunt Lillian—Lady Balmossie—and Dougal's two youngest sisters waited. He could hear the monkey chittering as they opened the drawing-room door, and Aedan ducked out of sheer habit, as if to dodge some invisible flying object.

Dougal laughed and continued to smile as blond Amy, pretty and vivacious in yards of pink flounces, firmly shooed the tiny creature out of the room in the arms of a reluctant housemaid.

Glad to be home among his family, Dougal watched them, content and amused, and soon found himself wondering how Meg MacNeill would suit with them. Very well indeed, he decided. He could easily imagine her within these walls, chatting and laughing with his kinswomen and deep in some intellectual conversation with the laird of Dundrennan. Aedan would no doubt be very interested in Meg's journals. His father, Sir Hugh MacBride, had been a famous, prolific poet, and Sir Hugh's vast library was one of the treasures of Dundrennan House.

He knew that Meg would enjoy Lady Balmossie's blunt Lowland mannerisms, and he could even imagine her facing the truculent little monkey and winning a friend. Meg would fit in at Dundrennan as if she had always been part of the family.

But he had no real guarantee that the girl wanted to become part of his life. He did not even know when, or if, he would see her again.

He smiled while he watched his family, but inside his thoughts and emotions churned. Like Aedan MacBride, for whom love was a dark curse, Dougal still wanted a real, soul-deep love in his life. He had found it with Meg. Being with her would strengthen and improve him, help him to reach the height and breadth of potential. Loneliness had become a burden, and risk and danger seemed less satisfying than before. His meeting with a beautiful, mysterious girl on a wind-lashed rock had been a turning point in his life. He wanted to fulfill that destiny with her.

Soon he would return to Caransay, and if he could only see her again, he would woo her properly. He feared that his intensity and passion for her had only alarmed and confused her. No wonder she had distanced herself—though some instinct told him that her reasons went deeper.

But before he could return to Meg, he must face Lady Strathlin.

"Ah, here it is. . . . *Campanula rotundifolia,*" Meg murmured, spreading her fingers carefully on the thin page of the encyclopedia volume spread open on the library table in front of her. "The bluebell, or harebell, as it is known in Scotland." She copied the name and wrote some notations in ink beneath a finished study of a cluster of tiny blue flowers. Sanding the ink, she blew gently to dry it and sat back.

In Gaelic, the brog na cubhaig, *or cuckoo's shoe, is a pretty blue bellflower commonly seen on the machair that covers Caransay, as well as throughout Scotland. Fairies are said to make their hats from the flowers, and the tiny bells will ring out a warning to hares and rabbits at the approach of danger.*

"Working on your Caransay journal?" Angela Shaw entered the library after knocking on the door.

"Yes. I wanted to finish the pages that I did while on holiday," Meg said. She had arrived at Strathlin Castle a few days earlier, entering a whirlwind of demands on her time and attention. Craving the easier pace of life in the Isles, she found that working on her journals helped soothe and relax her in mind and soul. Re-creating Caransay's natural beauty also served as a remedy for the homesickness that she often felt so keenly after leaving Caransay.

This time she had left behind not only her little son, her island, and her family, but she had left Dougal, too. The tug on her heartstrings was deep and enduring.

In fact, she had not even seen him the day that Norrie had taken her and Mrs. Berry back to Tobermory to catch the steamer to the mainland. Dougal had been at the work site on Sgeir Caran. She remembered sailing past the great sea rock in Norrie's fishing boat, gazing up at its massive bulk, aware that Dougal stood somewhere on the rock—or he might have been under the sea in diving gear. Either way, she sailed past and out of his life without even a farewell.

Although it nearly broke her heart to go, she had not known how to say goodbye.

"Oh, harebells," Angela said, looking down at the open page. She smiled. "What a pretty drawing, and it captures them exactly. I remember how beautiful they looked spreading over the meadows on Caransay in spring and summer, like a soft, blue-purple mist."

Meg nodded, remembering it, too, and smiled sadly. She picked up her pencil to add some refining strokes to a drawing of wild oat grass and meadowsweet.

"Madam, I came to tell you that I had a letter from Mr. Charles Worth just before your return. He is sending a skilled dressmaker from his shop at the Rue de la Paix to fit your gown here. She will arrive next week. The coachman will fetch her at the train station in Edinburgh."

"Good. Ask him to bring her to the house on Charlotte Square, rather than out here to Strathlin," Meg answered, looking up. "Since I'll be wearing the gown at Number Twelve Charlotte Square the night of the concert and soiree, the seamstress should fit it there. Ask Mrs. Larrimore to prepare a room for her where she can stay and work in comfort."

Angela Shaw nodded. "I thought you might say that, so I sent a note to Mrs. Larrimore this morning to notify her. I can hardly wait to see this gown," she added, smiling. "Mr. Worth writes that he has outdone even himself with this creation."

Glad to see the joy in Angela's delicate oval face, Meg smiled. Her friend often appeared wan, but Meg attributed some of that to Angela's translucent ivory skin, pale blond hair, and light blue eyes. Together with Angela's preference for mourning colors, the contrast was striking. Today she wore a day gown in a black-on-black stripe trimmed in purple cording, and her black lace head covering hid the gleaming smoothness of her finely textured blond hair.

Although still in her twenties, Mrs. Shaw had been a widow for eight years. Newly bereaved and in need of employment, she had arrived at Strathlin Castle on the recommendation of Sir John Shaw, her deceased husband's uncle. Engaged to advise Meg in social matters just after Lord Strathlin's death, Angela had proven an invaluable aid and a loyal, gentle friend. Long after Meg had adjusted to her new life, Angela Shaw had stayed on as a lady's companion. Even years later, Angela had rarely spoken of her late husband. Meg knew only that they had been devoted young newlyweds and that shy, reserved Angela had loved him so deeply that she still wore mourning.

"The gown will be lovely," Meg said, "and you deserve some of the credit for that, Angel. Mr. Worth very much appreciated your suggestions for color and fabric." Meg continued to smile, though her delight in a beautiful gown and her anticipation of the event was now clouded by thoughts of Dougal. In fact, each time the party was mentioned to her—daily, and often—she dreaded the evening even more and felt a dull, deep ache in her stomach. She placed a hand to her snugly corseted waistline, beneath her day dress of blue plaid satin.

She wondered if Dougal would even attend her soiree on September first. Since her return to the mainland nearly ten days ago, she had not reviewed the final guest list as yet with Guy Hamilton and Angela Shaw, who had been busy with the arrangements.

"Angel, I was wondering if we have received answers to all of our invitations. For example, would you know if Mr. Dougal Stewart has accepted?" Meg asked the question casually, while she angled her open journal and used a soft pencil to refine some small studies of the flowers of the machair.

"Ah, the engineer?" Angela tilted her head, thinking, her slim fingers woven together. "I believe so, madam. Mr. Hamilton has the final list. But I can check that myself, if you are curious. A moment." She walked toward a secretary desk against the wall, opened it, and retrieved a packet of envelopes from a niche. Flipping through them, she turned with one in her hand. "Yes, it's here. Would you like to see it?" She came forward.

Meg's heart surged. "I . . . well, I suppose so." Her fingers shook as she accepted the cream stock envelope and took out the single reply card. *Dear Lady Strathlin, I am pleased to accept your invitation,* he had written, signing his name.

His familiar script, resolute and masculine, brought him back to her so sharply that she caught her breath. Looking at the envelope, she realized that it had been sent from Caransay.

He would hardly be pleased about accepting, she thought, once he discovered that Meg MacNeill was in fact the Baroness of Strathlin. *Oh, dear God,* she thought, with a spinning of dread in her stomach. *What have I done?*

She set the note aside. "Thank you, Angela."

A knock sounded on the door, and the little maid, Hester, looked in. "Mr. Hamilton, ma leddy," she announced, and Meg nodded as Guy entered. He had met with Meg earlier that day to go over preparations for the soiree. The event now dominated her household and seemed to loom in her future as inescapable as a tidal wave. She wished she had never agreed to it.

"Madam, the post has arrived. Ah, good afternoon, Mrs. Shaw," he added, his voice dropping to a murmur.

Meg was accustomed to seeing a bit of a flush on Guy Hamilton's cheeks whenever he was around the young widow, but she had not expected to see the pink color that brightened Angela Shaw's pale cheeks. Looking at her companion and her secretary with new interest, Meg felt intuitively certain, suddenly, that they had begun to feel mutual affection. She wondered if either of them knew. Both were reserved and private in character, each accustomed to guarding their feelings and thoughts carefully.

Perhaps falling in love herself had sharpened her awareness of it in others.

"Good day, Mr. Hamilton," Angela replied quietly, looking at him with what Meg was sure was a tiny, private smile. "Lady Strathlin inquired after the final guest list for the party."

"Aye," he said quickly, turning his attention to Meg. "It's done. I have it here." He set down the pile of mail and reached into his coat pocket, extracting a folded sheet, which he opened for her and smoothed out. "As you can see, nearly everyone has accepted. Our only refusals are from those who are traveling and thus unable to attend. Even Mr. Stewart will be there."

"Yes. Angela showed me his reply."

"Shall I have the targes and Jedburgh axes taken down from the walls and polished up?" Guy grinned.

"That is hardly amusing," Meg said primly, as she studied the list. *Dougal Robertson Stewart*. She forced herself to look at the entire list and comment on the guests. "It promises to be an interesting evening," she managed to say, stomach tightening.

"A private assembly hosted by Lady Strathlin herself, at her town home on Charlotte Square, following a concert by the most renowned songstress of our age," Guy said, looking at Angela, "and she thinks it will be *interesting*."

"If this Mr. Stewart comes, it will certainly be more than interesting," Angela said.

"Indeed," Guy agreed. "Baroness, I meant to ask if you met him while you were out in the Isles. You never mentioned him, so I assume you managed to avoid him."

"I . . . I did meet Mr. Stewart," she said curtly, and picked up her pencil to add some shading lines to a carefully drawn posy of harebells and buttercups.

"Did you leave the poor fellow and his lighthouse still standing?" Guy asked.

"Well, of course," Meg said tightly.

"So, you found it impossible to avoid the fellow after all," Guy said. "Did you discuss the lighthouse situation with him?"

"A little," Meg said. "Well, to be honest, I never quite told Mr. Stewart that I was Lady Strathlin."

"You what?" Guy looked at her incredulously.

"Whoever did he think you were?" Angela asked.

"He believed I was simply a girl from Caransay. I had reasons for keeping my identity a secret."

"Surely he knows now," Angela said.

Meg shook her head mutely, frowning over her drawing.

Guy huffed. "Dougal Stewart is neither a simple nor a stupid man. He will be furious when he finds out."

"I realize that," Meg said. "I know that the truth would have been best before I left Caransay. I planned to tell him, but I had no chance before I left the island. He will know the truth as soon as he sees me. I am not . . . sure what to do," she confessed.

"So that is why you seem preoccupied and distracted since your return," Angela said.

"In part," Meg admitted.

"Poor Mr. Stewart will be staggered when he realizes who you are," Angela said.

"Staggered? He will be furious," Guy said. Meg flinched. "He may never forgive her. Stewart has a great deal of stubborn pride and cast-iron integrity, I guarantee it."

"He is in Edinburgh now," Meg said. "Perhaps I should try to see him before the party. That might be best."

"Send a servant with a note asking him to call on Lady Strathlin," Angela suggested.

"Or send the man a written apology and explanation," Guy said. "He may decide then not to attend the soiree, or he may be forgiving and have a sense of humor about it."

"He deserves an apology in person," Angela said.

Knowing they were both disappointed in her, and equally disappointed in herself, Meg sighed. "I need to think about it," she said. "Was there anything of note in the mail?" she asked, eager to change the subject.

"Just the tickets for Miss Lind's Grand Full Dress Concert on the Monday evening of your soiree. And Mr. Worth sent his bill for the balance owed for the new gown," Guy said. "I meant to ask—would you like the amount paid by bank draft or deposited to an account? It is . . . well, a considerable sum."

"I believe Sir John deposited the first payment in Mr. Worth's London account, and we can do so again. No doubt you think it a huge sum to pay for a single gown." She saw his frown.

"That did cross my mind," Guy admitted, and then he shrugged. "But I will leave such choices to you, madam. I am merely willing to be dazzled. I'm sure every penny is well spent."

"You will be more than dazzled, I assure you," Angela Shaw said. "She will look divine."

"I am sure of it. And I am sure that milady's companion will look stunning, as well," he added quietly, gazing at Angela. A soft, sudden blush made her blue eyes sparkle.

Wishing to give them a private moment, Meg picked up her pencil to add some hatched shading to the sketch of the posy of flowers, tinted earlier with watercolor. She heard Guy and Angela murmuring quietly as she worked. After a few moments, hearing silence, she looked up to see them not gazing raptly at each other, as she expected, but at her.

"Madam," Guy said, frowning, "may we inquire what exactly happened when you were out in the Isles this last time?"

"I . . . Mrs. Berry and I had a lovely holiday," she said. "Nothing more. Why do you ask?"

"Mr. Hamilton and I wondered if something occurred of a more profound nature, madam," Angela said. "Ever since your return, you seem . . . changed."

"Profound?" Meg stared at them. She did not know what to say. Tempted to confide in them, she knew that she must keep her secrets to herself, to protect Dougal and Iain. Soon she would have to answer Sir Frederick, and it hung over her like a sword.

"You sigh overmuch, and look wistfully into the distance," Angela said. "You do not apply your attention to the matter at hand, to either your correspondence or your conversations. All of us are somewhat bewildered, madam, about what ails you. My guess is that there is no illness, but rather a preoccupation of thought and heart."

"Nothing troubles me, if that is what you think," Meg said.

"I think something troubles you very much, dear," Guy murmured. "Something consumes your every thought."

"We decided to mention this only in order to offer our help." Angela glanced at Guy. "As your very dear friends."

They were too perceptive, Meg thought, looking away. Through the window, blue hills spread into the misty distance. Far beyond, where she could not see but could still feel its presence, lay the sea and the island where her heart existed with Iain and the rest. A mile past that was the sea rock. She could almost feel the wind and the salt spray. She wondered if Dougal was still in the Hebrides, and she wondered, too, if he thought of her.

"I am just preoccupied by the plans for the party," she answered then. "I will feel relieved when the evening is finally over."

"Mrs. Berry," Angela said gently, "says it is not that. It is her impression that you are in love."

Meg ducked her head and took up her pencil again. "Mrs. Berry is a romantic and likes it overly much when people fall in love." She glanced pointedly at them, but their attention was fastened unwaveringly on her.

"Berry adores this Mr. Stewart and thinks he is not the least bit an ogre, but a brave and kind man who seemed quite taken with you," Angela said.

"Taken? Really?" Guy said, folding his arms. "The odious Mr. Stewart? Was he what you expected, madam?"

"Not at all," Meg said, her cheeks heating fiercely.

"Berry also mentioned that Sir Frederick Matheson came to Caransay," Guy said. "That must have been a surprise."

"There is no need to nudge me, either of you," Meg said bluntly. "I have nothing to tell you."

Guy shrugged and looked at Angela. "Well, I hope it was a pleasant enough meeting with Sir Frederick," he told Meg.

"He is always pleasant in manner," she said carefully. "And it was quite a surprise." *A shock,* she corrected silently.

"If ever he is not, I want to hear about it. I do not

trust the man," Guy said. "Mr. Stewart seems infinitely more trustworthy, in my opinion. Just keep cautious, dear Baroness, and remember that your friends are here to help you, should you ever need it."

Tears stinging, Meg ducked her head to apply her attention to her drawing, though the page blurred before her. "Thank you, Mr. Hamilton. I shall keep it in mind."

Chapter Sixteen

"Thank you for taking the time to meet with me, Mr. Logan." Seated in a wooden chair beside a wide, polished mahogany desk, Dougal reached into his pocket and pulled out a small linen-wrapped package. He laid it on the desk surface.

Samuel Logan, a heavyset gentleman with gray side-whiskers, a leonine head of dark hair, and a preference for tobacco, for his clothing reeked of it, nodded. "I always have time for a kinsman of Sir Hugh MacBride. Chambers Street Publishers was honored to produce the great poet's work." He gestured toward the bookcases that lined his walls, where Dougal noticed that his uncle's volumes of poetry and other writings were prominently displayed. "And we have published something of yours, as well."

Dougal laughed softly. "Nothing quite as memorable. A series of my articles about lighthouse design appeared in the *Edinburgh Review* a few years ago, and your firm published them in book form. *Principles of Pharological Design with Respect to the Forces of Nature* is hardly exciting reading."

"On the contrary, it must be fascinatin' stuff," Logan said. "We have respectable orders every autumn for *Pharological Design* from engineering classes at several universities in Scotland and England both. That must give you a wee income, eh?" He smiled, folded his hands. "What brings you here, sir? Have you another treatise on lighthouses for us to consider?"

"Actually, I did bring something, though I am not the author," Dougal said, sliding the package forward. "I hoped you might find it interesting. A dear friend who lives on a Hebridean isle wrote this little journal. Although I do not have your talent for judging the best in books, I think it worth a moment of your time."

Logan reached over an untidy pile of papers and a scattering of leather-bound books and picked up Meg's journal. Setting a pair of gold-wire glasses on his nose, he flipped through the book for a minute or so, nodding to himself thoughtfully as he turned the pages.

After a while, he looked up. "Did the author appoint you to be messenger, sir? Or is it authoress? I detect a distinctly feminine sensibility to this anonymous journal." He peered over his spectacles.

"It was my idea to bring it here. Miss MacNeill gave me her journal as a gift, but I believe she would not mind my showing it to you. In her modesty, she does not think her work worthy of publication. As you can see, it is not a personal diary, but rather a chronicle of nature on the Isle of Caransay."

"Aye. Fascinatin'." Logan slowly turned pages, murmuring. "Remarkable. Your friend is quite talented, sir." He continued to read, nodding. "Her drawings are skillful and pleasing, and very precise. Yet her descriptions are poetic. Exquisite thing, this wee book. It's as if we're peeking into a lady's diary while she shares her love for her home." He turned a few more pages. "She brings the island to life, and she seems very much a part of it . . . yet she remains mysterious throughout, giving no clue to her identity. Marvelous, actually. Unique."

"I agree. I hoped you might like it."

Logan paged through the book for a while, then glanced up. "Is this the completed work?"

"There is another one that she is finishing now. Both treat the flora and fauna, weather, the geological character of the island and its adjacent reef, and so on. She has a particular gift, I think, for capturing the beauty and variety of life on the island, and the moods of the sea and the seasons, all with these elegant, precise drawings. I can assure you that the other journal is equal in merit to this one. She plans a third journal as well."

"Might she allow me to see the other one?" Logan paused to exclaim his admiration for a sensitively rendered drawing of seals sunning themselves on Sgeir Caran.

"I believe so, sir. She has spent years on her journals for the pure joy of the work, but I think she also dreams of sharing them as books for others to enjoy."

"We may be able to arrange that for her. This is remarkable, really." Logan nodded. "There is a great deal of interest in the Highland culture just now. People are mad for Scotland, sir, for its history and its culture. Mad to tour the Highlands and purchase any souvenir that links them to Scotland. Some think we are wrong to perpetuate the romance of plaids and pipes and heather, when our country is so very different from that, but I say all this interest helps our economy and our reputation for romanticism and mystery. The queen herself writes Highland journals, did you know?"

"I had heard something of it."

"A Hebridean journal like this one, written and illustrated by a Scotswoman, would be highly popular. They would be beautiful volumes . . . aye, more than one." He tapped the desk with his fingers, thinking.

"Of course, we would send the drawings to the best engraver in the city for exact reproduction of the details. We could add hand-colored, tipped-in illustrations. Possibly we could also produce a smaller edition with line engravings at a lower cost."

"Perhaps," Dougal said, "they would look well as a set with green leather covers and a tooled design of flowers on the front. The gold lettering on the spines could read '*A Hebridean Journal,* by M. MacNeill.' "

Logan considered him for a moment. "I like that very much. I shall remember it." He nodded. "Aye, people would be mad to own such a lovely set of books. A naturalist's view of the Isles. Brilliant! Do you think your authoress would agree to allow us to publish them for her?"

Dougal smiled. "I believe she would, sir."

"Mr. Stewart, thank you for bringing this to me. How may I contact Miss MacNeill?"

"I met her through some of her kinfolk on Caransay. Since I'll be returning there soon, I'd be happy to deliver a letter to her through them."

"Good." Logan handed the journal back to Dougal, then took up a sheet of paper, dipped a pen, and began to write.

While Logan was occupied, Dougal flipped pages in the little book, pausing to glance at careful studies of seashells, their spirals touched lightly with washed color. Along the side of the page were some notes in Meg's small, rounded handwriting.

Periwinkles and large and small whelks found on the western Shore, Innish Bay. The whorls hold the soft, delicate colors of a dawn sky. Within the pink-shadowed spiral of the whelk, the sea sings its ancient song.

A shiver ran through him, deep and secret, as if Meg herself had whispered in his ear.

On other pages, Sgeir Caran emerged in clean lines and hatched shadowings, its shape unaltered by black powder blasts. Images of the rock filled three more pages, combined with studies of birds, including the eagles that nested on the rock.

Eagles mate for life, she had written beside a sketch of two birds in flight above the majestic rock, *and this pair has been together many years. Their loyalty is transcendent. To see them soar over the great sea rock in perfect unison is to realize the profound poetry of their devotion. Theirs is the pure love of two dedicated souls who, once joined, will never part.*

He closed the book quietly.

Logan sealed an envelope and handed it to Dougal. "I have taken the liberty of enclosing a cheque with my letter in the amount of one hundred pounds. I can offer the lady a little more once I have discussed the matter with my partners. Until then, I hope this will secure the privilege of publishing her journals. I assume that a sum of money would be welcome to her."

"Thank you, Mr. Logan. Very welcome, I imagine. And it is a generous gesture of faith."

"You may wish to act as her adviser, Mr. Stewart, since you have some experience in publishing yourself."

"Small experience, but I would be glad to be of assistance."

"If her journals become as popular as I expect, thousands of readers will soon know her name, and her bank account will benefit. Assure her of that." Logan smiled. "Please take the book and the cheque to her. I hope to meet with her soon."

Nodding, Dougal slid the envelope and the little book into his pocket. "I am sure the lady will be pleased."

Logan looked at him keenly. "But you do not know for certain, do you, sir."

"I admit I took something of a risk in coming here."

"You are a loyal friend, sir. Convince the young lady that this is her golden opportunity. I hope her own dreams are the equal of your dreams for her."

Dougal stood. "Believe me, sir. I hope so, too."

"Certainly, Mrs. Larrimore, if you think we will need extra staff for the soiree, please hire them," Meg said. She stood in the drawing room with Angela Shaw and Mrs. Larrimore, the housekeeper of Number Twelve Charlotte Square.

"You'll find willing maids of service at Matheson House," Angela suggested. "It is newly established, and there are several young women there eager for work."

"Huh," Mrs. Larrimore said dubiously. "*Them* lassies."

"They are well-bred young women caught by unfortunate circumstance," Meg said. "Many of them desire honest work. You can hire a few to act as kitchen maids and upstairs maids for the evening, at least. We will need some ladies' maids, as well."

"Well. I suppose I could inquire," the housekeeper said.

"Excellent. Now, we shall have music and a little dancing for our private assembly," Meg said. "The drawing room will be large enough if some of this furniture is removed to the upstairs rooms. The carpet should be rolled and placed elsewhere, too."

"The musicians can set themselves in that corner, near the garden doors," Mrs. Larrimore said, pointing to a roomy area beside the wide glassed doors leading to a small conservatory. "And we'll set conservatory plants about in pots."

"That will be lovely," Meg said. "Our own roses in the conservatory are still plentiful. We could use some of them. Mrs. Shaw, are the other flowers ordered?"

"Yes, madam. Yellow and ivory roses, mixed with other flowers for variety and color. They will be set about the room, and the buffet table will hold an arrangement of a tower of sugared fruits, very pretty. I personally made some tiny nightingales of silk and paper in the Japanese method to set among the flower arrangements, in honor of Miss Lind, since she is called the Swedish Nightingale."

"Splendid idea, and I'm sure very lovely. You have a delicate hand for craftwork." Meg turned to look around the room. "We'll use this room for music and dancing and the dining room for the supper buffet, with the doors left open for mingling. We'll need to designate two upstairs rooms for dressing rooms, one for the ladies and one for the gentlemen."

"Aye, madam," the housekeeper agreed. "I've told the maids to ready the blue bedroom and the upstairs sitting room. The rooms will be comfortably heated and well lit, and there will be plenty of soap and water, towels, combs, brushes, pins, and so forth set out for the guests."

"Excellent. And it will be a nice touch to provide rose water, lavender water, and some almond-rose cream for the ladies to use. And, of course, add salts and cologne as well."

"Aye, I'll see to all of it. And I'll order the grooms to lessen the fires in the grates toward evening. With so many guests, the fires will make the place too warm. We don't want anyone fainting!"

"A good thought. And we'll need two maids to take the cloaks and hats and store them for the evening in one of the bedrooms."

"Aye. A wee slip of paper pinned to each cloak with the owner's name on it will prevent a kerfuffle later."

"Good. I'll leave the rest of the details to you, Mrs. Larrimore. We'll be coming in that evening from the concert at the Music Hall, and most of the guests will be arriving from there, too. All must be in readiness by eight o'clock, I think. Oh, and I'd like a lady's maid exclusively for Miss Lind, as well, who will arrive later than the rest, of course."

"Katie will do. She's a good lass. What of the menu, madam?"

"I would not change a thing," Meg said, and she looked at Angela. "Mrs. Shaw, what is your opinion?"

"I like Mrs. Larrimore's suggestions to provide fruit ices and lemonade earlier, with a light buffet supper served at midnight," Angela answered.

Meg nodded agreement. "It will be a very late evening, but the concert from seven to nine dictates that it must be so."

"Very good, then," Mrs. Larrimore said. "I'd best get back to work, madam and Mrs. Shaw. Cook will start baking long before dawn on that day, and there will be a great deal to do—meats to roast for chilled slices later, dishes and punches to prepare, extra ice to be ordered and stored. And of course, the whole house cleaned and polished, top to bottom. It will all be done, though. Do not fret a bit about it. Oh, and the dressmaker from Paris will be here this afternoon."

"Thank you, Mrs. Larrimore." Meg smiled as the housekeeper bobbed her head and left the room.

"It promises to be a lovely event," Angela said.

"This is not a large house for such a party," Meg replied, glancing around. "I . . . oh, I suppose I am nervous, Angela."

"Strathlin Castle offers more room, but this house is more convenient for most of the guests, who can return easily to their homes afterwards. And it will be convenient for Miss Lind, as well, since she plans to travel the next day. I believe she has a concert in Perth the following evening."

Meg nodded distractedly. "None of that makes me nervous," she said. "I know that you and Mrs. Larrimore, and all the others, will work together to make this a wonderful party. It is . . . well, it is something else entirely."

Angela tilted her head sympathetically. "Can I help?"

"I'm afraid I must puzzle it out on my own." She thought of Dougal walking the machair of Caransay deep in the night, puzzling out his theorems as well as his feelings for her.

Seeing Angela's keen glance, Meg smiled brightly. "You are always such a help. We call you Angel for a reason," she said, tucking her arm in her friend's. "We had best hurry. We're expected at the opening of the new exhibit at the National Museum of Antiquities at one o'clock. They are displaying some recently discovered Celtic treasures, which I hear are quite stunning. It promises to be very interesting."

"Yes, I'm looking forward to it. The museum directors are delighted that you are free to attend, madam, as you and Matheson Bank are among the museum's chief contributors. They may ask you to say a few words."

"And I shall decline. I suspect the directors hope to flatter me so that I will sponsor their new museum building, on which they plan to break ground next year. But I will sponsor it regardless, and even more enthusiastically if they allow me anonymity today."

Angela smiled. "Some members of the bank's board plan to attend the exhibit's opening, as well. I know that Sir John Shaw and Sir Frederick Matheson are both invited."

The rhythm of Meg's step faltered slightly as she walked arm in arm with Angela. "How nice," she said, "to escape from the concerns of the party for a little while."

"Lady Strathlin, it is simply a joy to see you again," Sir Frederick said, as he stepped out from behind a stone column. The museum's spacious and bright foyer, where the exhibit had been arranged in long glass cases, was very crowded, filled with ladies and gentlemen attending the opening. Beams of warm sunlight poured over golden stone, green ferns, and the cheerful colors of the ladies' dresses, capes, and bonnets.

"Sir Frederick," Meg said, looking at him from under the brim of her dark blue bonnet, "what are you doing here?"

He doffed his top hat politely, although her greeting had been far from polite. "Why, the same thing you are doing, my dear, enjoying the exhibit," he said. "Although I'm glad to have a moment to speak with you. Have you thought about my proposal?"

She stared up at him. In the shadow of the huge column and lost in the noise of the echoing room, their conversation would be private. But she had no desire to speak to him, and she stepped away from the column, looking around for Angela Shaw or any other acquaintance who stood nearby.

Until Frederick's appearance, Meg had been lost in a pleasant reverie as she strolled past the glass cases, admiring the gold and silver and enameled artifacts displayed on velvet. The fascinating examples of brilliant Celtic craftsmanship and ingenuity captivated her, so that she had not noticed the tall, solidly built man in the black suit who now stood gazing down at her.

"I've given your suggestion some thought," she said carefully. "But I am not ready to speak to you about it. Certainly not here," she added in a near hiss, glancing around.

"Of course not, my dear," Matheson said. "I wanted to remind you."

"How could I possibly forget? Ah, Mrs. Shaw, there you are!" She called a little more loudly than she had intended. Hearing her, Angela turned and glided forward, her wide black bombazine skirt and half cape and her purple-and-black bonnet creating a somber note in the bright, sunny foyer.

"My dear Margaret, I look forward to hearing your answer on the night of your soiree," Frederick said. As Angela drew near them, he took her gloved hand cordially. "Mrs. Shaw, how delightful to see you again, and looking so well." Then he turned to Meg, who still watched him, her heart slamming. "I so look forward to your soiree, Lady Strathlin. We are to attend in grand full dress following Miss Lind's concert, I take it?"

"Yes," she said. "The details of dress and time are on your invitation card."

"Indeed. Oh, my dear ladies, please accept my apology. I must run. I have an appointment with Mr. Stewart this afternoon. I believe you know him, madam."

Smothering a gasp, Meg nodded. "Mr. Dougal Stewart? Yes."

"He and I have some business matters to discuss, now that he finds himself in a state of near ruin. I understand that he is coming to your private assembly. That should prove an interesting highlight for an evening." He smiled.

"Near . . . ruin?" Meg stared up at him.

"Well, of course, thanks to you and your solicitors. Had you not heard? I suppose your advocates work independently for your benefit, sparing you the details."

"I—they—well, no, I hadn't been told as yet." Meg realized that Angela was watching her with a slight frown. Puzzled herself, Meg wondered in a growing panic what her solicitors had done.

Frederick tipped the brim of his hat again. "It's true, they have triumphed over Mr. Stewart. Poor fellow. We shall talk further, my dearest Margaret," he said, taking her hand and bowing. "Mrs. Shaw." He turned away to stride through the crowd.

Meg watched his long black form as it cut a path through the bright dresses. She looked silently at Angela.

"I absolutely despise that oily snake," Angela murmured. Meg blinked, surprised by such a strong statement from her quiet, demure friend. "I hope you are not actually considering marrying him. He tells everyone that you are head over heels in love with him and about to announce it to the world."

"I'm not," Meg said. "Head over heels, that is."

"Good. I could not imagine it." Angela took Meg's arm. "My dear, have you seen the beautiful jewelry on display? You must come look. And I've found Mr. Hamilton—he was able to attend after all, when he thought he might be detained. We've just met the antiquarian who discovered many of these artifacts herself. She is lovely and delightful. Her name is Mrs. Christina Blackburn."

"I had heard her name before, but I have not yet met her."

"Then let it be my privilege to introduce you. Her family are the rather famous Blackburns—most of them are artists, although she is not."

"Yes. Her father and brother are both brilliant painters. I own a seascape by John Blackburn the elder," Meg said.

Angela nodded. "Her late husband was an artist as well, a cousin of the same name. There was a scandal a few years ago, but . . . well, it does not do to mention these things. She is the lovely brunette standing over there beside the tall man with the blond hair. That is Dr. Connor MacBain."

"Oh!" Meg said. "I know his excellent reputation, although we have never met." She remembered that Dougal had once mentioned that a cousin of his was the wife of Dr. MacBain of Calton Hill in Edinburgh. Her heart beat faster. "Is there—anyone else with them?"

"Are you thinking of Mr. Stewart?"

Always, Meg thought, but she did not dare say it.

"Dr. MacBain's wife told me that Mr. Stewart is her cousin. A most interesting coincidence!" Angela nodded.

"Is he here?" Meg asked urgently, glancing around. "Did he accompany his relations to the opening?"

"No. Apparently Mr. Stewart had a previous appointment today. Mrs. MacBain said that he rode up on the train a few days ago. He is staying with them on Calton Hill."

Dougal was in Edinburgh already. Somehow she had irrationally expected him to simply appear for her soiree. Of course he would be here now. She might see him at any time, through a number of social connections.

Even knowing he was not in the museum, she glanced frantically around, looking for those broad shoulders, that glint of brown, sun-gilded hair. She wanted desperately to see him again, but she felt a sense of unshakable dread fill her at the same time.

She had to tell him the truth. She could not wait until the night of her soiree. If Dougal met with Frederick, there was no predicting what he might learn. Fear struck her with such force that she did not follow what Angela was saying.

"Dr. MacBain also said that Mr. Stewart has lost funding for his lighthouse. And there is a rumor that he will be personally ruined over this fiasco."

Meg turned. "Is that what Sir Frederick meant? Oh no! My soliciting firm informed me that they would find some way to delay his work, but I have not met with Sir Edward since my return. I understood that the plan was as yet only a plan. Oh no," she murmured anxiously.

"I thought you were a force behind the decision to revoke his funding, madam. Were you privy to any attempt to discredit him?"

"Never! Oh, never! I was told that delaying the funding was the only way to keep the work crews and construction off the island and the reef. I was never told it might damage his personal reputation."

"Well, it appears to have done just that," Angela said sternly. "Dr. MacBain fears that Mr. Stewart's project cannot recover from serious financial damage, and his name will be dragged down with it. Your solicitors have more than achieved their goal. That lighthouse may never go up, and the engineer may be ruined as well."

Feeling a sickening ache of remorse, Meg strolled beside Angela, showing only outwardly calm. Inside she quaked.

She could no longer bear the weight of her secrets, for they would soon cost her everything. Now, because of her, Dougal stood to lose the lighthouse that meant so much to him, and his reputation, which meant even more.

She had to see him, and soon.

"Angela," she said, making an impulsive decision, "there is something I must do later this evening, after supper. I will need your help."

Chapter Seventeen

"Sir Frederick? I am Dougal Stewart." Inside the dim, smoky interior of Brodie's Tavern on the High Street, Dougal found Matheson easily, although he had met the man only once. In the crowded public room, several groups of gentlemen were meeting for luncheon, engaged in conversation and eating. At one table a man sat alone, a black top hat beside him and a brass-headed cane leaned against the high-backed bench.

Matheson was a tall man wearing a black suit and a vest of wine-colored brocade. He rose to his feet cordially, his gold watch chain swinging as he offered his hand to Dougal.

"Mr. Stewart! Thank you for meeting me here. Please sit down. I hoped you might join me for luncheon, so I ordered two plates of mutton stew in anticipation of your arrival. Beer, as well. The beer is particularly good in this place."

"Thank you." Dougal sat and briefly studied the man across from him. Matheson was a pleasant-looking man, in his mid-fifties or so, a man of obvious means judging by his expensive accessories and well-cut clothing. His graying hair was combed smooth, his long sideburns and mustache stylishly clipped, and his eyes were a very dark brown, unusually shrewd and piercing.

"I posted a letter to you recently while I was in the Isles, sir," Dougal said. He glanced up, smiling his thanks as a serving girl set down steaming plates of thick stew, two glasses of beer sloshing full, and a plate of bread rolls. "Once I arrived in Edinburgh, I was glad to learn of your desire to meet with me. A good idea, sir, to leave a message at the office of the Northern Lighthouse Commission."

"You are not an easy man to find." Matheson sipped some beer and patted his mustache with a cloth napkin.

"I understand that you were recently on Caransay, sir. Had I known, I would have taken time to show you around our quarry site on Guga and to show you the lighthouse site itself."

"Another time will do for that. I was there only for a quick visit to a good friend on the island. Generally I dislike traveling out there from Edinburgh. The journey is too deuced complicated, requiring different vehicles over land and sea. I prefer my life smoothed by convenience." He grinned amiably and gave his attention to eating.

"I understand. No doubt, however, you are curious about the state of your property out there."

"By now you've dug a right-size hole in it, I'll wager."

"We've quarried some excellent gray granite from your isle, sir. The stones have been transported to Sgeir Caran. Recently, we laid most of the foundation for the lighthouse."

"Ah. I am interested to see the progress of that remarkable erection. I plan to travel there again soon. I take a great deal of interest in that lighthouse."

Matheson sipped the stew and curled his lip slightly. "The meat is of good quality, but the vegetables are somewhat plebeian."

Dougal ate in silence for a moment, having no quarrel with the quality of the food. "Might I say, we appreciated your permission to work on Guga, and The Commission is grateful for your offer of a donation to the lighthouse fund."

"And so we come to the reason for this meeting."

"I wondered what you wanted of me, sir," Dougal said cautiously.

"I understand that you have come upon hard times with your project, sir, and more particularly with your charming enemy."

"If you mean Lady Strathlin, I cannot attest to her charm, though I am more convinced of her hard nature."

"I can assure you," Matheson said, "she is quite winsome."

Dougal frowned, not so certain of that. "Be that as it may, I know that the lady's advocates are a conniving bunch, whether or not she is part of it."

"Are you aware that she ordered her lawyers to stop you from setting foot on her island or putting up the light at any cost?"

"Ah. Now, that I had not heard in particular."

"What is the current state of your project, sir?"

"As of yesterday," Dougal said, "we've lost more than half our willing contributors. They were informed by Matheson Bank that the Caran lighthouse was a poor investment, destined to cost twice its estimate and destined to fail due to impossible conditions and faulty engineering."

"Ah, yes. I believe they were informed that if the Stevensons had supervised it, rather than entrusting the project to Dougal Stewart, this would not have been handled so incompetently."

Dougal fisted a hand and knocked the table in angry

but controlled frustration. "I have personally visited as many contributors as I could. Previously they had no quarrel with me, but they are unaccountably distrustful of me now. I am baffled."

"The bank said their funds would not be dispersed to you on suspicion of fraudulence. The lawyers claim that you plan to abscond with the funds and make off for the Continent."

"What!" Dougal leaned forward. "That is preposterous. How do you know, sir? Were you approached, as well? Are we meeting now," he asked suspiciously, "so that you can withdraw your offer?"

"I am a member of the bank board, which is how I know their dastardly scheme," Matheson said. "And you and I are meeting so that I may double my offer to you."

"Double it? That's exceedingly generous. But why do this?"

Sir Frederick leaned forward. "Because, sir, I am one of the few who wants you to build that lighthouse there."

"Lady Strathlin wants the island kept private. That is the crux of the problem. Are you willing to join that dispute?"

"Given time, I can end this dispute," Matheson answered bluntly. "The baroness will not prevail, nor will that island be private for long. Someday I will be making the decisions about Caransay, I assure you. Such a spectacularly lovely place could be an excellent resort to suit the very wealthy. Besides, Lady Strathlin has no need for a private island. She has too much freedom there," he added darkly.

Dougal sat back. "You own the Isle of Guga, adjacent to Caransay. Have you discussed your thoughts with Lady Strathlin?"

Matheson waved a hand. "Guga! That damned rock is useful only for birds and seals and for quarrying. I bought the lease because of its single virtue." Matheson sipped, then wiped his mouth again fastidiously. "It is nearest to Caransay."

"Why is that significant?"

"Lady Strathlin and I have property in common," Matheson said. "And affection in common, as well. We have become . . . very close. When she holidays on her island, she pines for the company of friends. Her island is a pretty place, but it is essentially a fishing village now, and she is accustomed to a sophisticated existence. It will take time to convince her, but I will."

The sleek confidence in the man's voice made Dougal wary. "Lady Strathlin apparently values the simple lifestyle of Caransay. She acts the recluse when she is there, and allows no one to interrupt her peace . . . not even to allow a lighthouse that would save hundreds of lives," he muttered.

Matheson chuckled. "I suppose she seems the hermit to those who do not know her well. The lady prefers my company, though." He lifted a hand in a modesty that smacked of falseness. "She could not bear for us to be separated while she was on Caransay, so I indulged her for the day. What fools these mortals be, eh?"

"Indeed," Dougal murmured, convinced that Matheson was ten times a fool. There was something cunning about the man. He could not imagine that Matheson cared so very much about setting up a resort for the wealthy on Caransay. He suspected something else but could not discern what it might be.

"Did you say you have not yet met the lady?" Matheson asked.

"Never formally. I saw her on Caransay, but only at a distance. It was not a moment to introduce myself, and she proved an elusive creature otherwise."

"Let me assure you that she is delectable and charming."

"Ah." Remembering the portly woman bobbing in the water like a seal, he frowned. Matheson had the focus of affection, he told himself. Perhaps the lady was lovely in the face and charming to friends. But she used her influence to strike hard at supposed enemies like himself.

"Lady Strathlin has a refreshing character," Matheson went on, "with a certain . . . coyness that is intriguing to a man of a hearty masculine appetite. I am sure you take my meaning, sir." He smiled, lifted his beer glass in salute, and drank.

You are a pig, sir, and most certainly a fortune hunter, Dougal thought. Although Matheson seemed at first to be a well-bred gentleman, Dougal was fast realizing that he was smug, self-centered, and quite possibly dangerous.

Some instinct told him not to trust the man's generous offer of help with the lighthouse. He narrowed his eyes thoughtfully.

"There is no question that Lady Strathlin has all the wealth and status a man could possibly desire in a woman," he said.

Something flashed in Matheson's dark eyes. "Do you take me for a Don Juan, sir? I give no thought to her wealth. Her kind heart and beauty are what matter to me. She is my goddess. I worship her, even when she goes around like a barefoot fishwife."

Dougal blinked. "Barefoot?"

"She adopts their quaint style when on holiday," Matheson said. He raised his glass and drank, then wiped his lips. "Surprising you never met her, sir. She moves about quite freely on the island, and everyone knows her there. She is quite the little naturalist, as well."

"She managed to avoid me, but then, we are not fond of each other." Dougal pushed his bowl of stew, half finished, away.

"It is possible she finds your contest of wills disturbing to her delicate sensibilities. That may explain why she turned over your argument to her advocates."

"Perhaps. I bow to your greater appreciation of the lady."

"I will speak to her on your behalf. As I said, I have an interest in putting the lighthouse through. When we are married, I hope to have a better influence with her. She can be quite stubborn in a delightful way."

Dougal frowned. "Married?"

"It is premature of me to speak openly, but a happy heart loosens the tongue. I have asked the lady to marry me, and her coquetry gives me hope that she means to accept."

Dougal stared at him. "Her coquetry . . . Sir, forgive my confusion. We *are* speaking of Lady Strathlin, of Strathlin Castle and Charlotte Square in Edinburgh?" *A lady fond of swimming in large hats, fond of her privacy, and very fond of sinking lighthouse engineers,* he felt tempted to add.

"Yes. Margaret—Lady Strathlin." Matheson nodded. "I would accept your congratulations now, but it is more seemly to wait until my darling makes the announcement herself. Therefore, I must ask you to say nothing of this to anyone."

Dougal felt a cold sensation seeping through him. *Beautiful. Charming. Winsome. A naturalist. Barefoot.* "Margaret . . . Lady Strathlin," he repeated softly.

"On the island she goes by the name of Margaret MacNeill. Perhaps you did meet her, after all."

Dear God, what a supreme fool he had been.

Dreary rain and the voluminous folds of a dark blue cloak wrapped Meg in shadows inside the hired coach as it rolled through the streets of Edinburgh. Swaying with the vehicle and listening to the steady clop of horse hooves, she glanced at Angela Shaw, seated across from her. Then she peered again through the window at the rain-washed street.

"The driver is slowing," Angela said. "We are nearly there. Oh dear, was a hired coach truly necessary? If we should be seen this way, your reputation would be ruined, madam. And I'm just not certain this is safe."

"I'm here to protect you, ladies," Guy Hamilton said. He sat in the shadows across from Meg and beside Angela, one booted foot propped on his knee. His expression was grim and dubious, but he had agreed to accompany them—had insisted on it when he had accidentally discovered Meg and Angela trying to slip away from the Charlotte Square address for an evening rendezvous.

"One of my own carriages might be recognized," Meg said. "And I simply must speak with Dougal in private."

"Dougal, is it? So you do hold some affection for him. My intuition told me so," Angela said. "I saw it in your eyes, in your wistful expression and your blush whenever he was mentioned. Obviously something wonderful happened on the Isle of Caransay," she added in a soft murmur, her eyes sparkling.

Meg looked out at the glinting rain. "Yes—wonderful, but unexpected. And I have made a thorough mess of it. I want to try to fix it now, if it can be fixed at all."

"Dougal Stewart?" Guy muttered. "It's incredible, really."

"Meg, I hoped such a blessing would come into your life someday," Angela said. "Does Mr. Stewart return your affection?"

"He returned it to Meg MacNeill, but . . . I am not certain that he will share it with Lady Strathlin."

"If it is true love, your name and fortune will make no difference," Angela said. "Love finds a way, so it is said."

"In this case," Guy said, "love's way may be littered with lawyers and bankers. It is indeed a thorough mess. The man has a great deal of pride, my lady. It will take more than a simple explanation to win his affection after he learns the truth."

"I do wish we'd left you at home," Angela said.

"You cannot do without me, dear Mrs. Shaw," he quipped.

"I have to confess the truth to him," Meg said. "I have to. I cannot live with this any longer. It was never my choice for it to continue like this and become so very complicated." She felt dizzy, staring into the darkness and rain, as if she poised on the brink of a cliff. She gripped the leather loop on the door.

"You surely must tell him in private, before he comes to the soiree and learns it in public," Guy agreed.

"I fear Sir Frederick may have already told him," Meg said.

"Matheson knows that Stewart thinks you are no more than a girl of the Isles?" Guy said.

Meg shrugged, for she was not sure.

"In all fairness, she *is* a girl of the Isles," Angela pointed out. "We should not forget that. Meg never truly lied to Mr. Stewart. She simply . . . omitted a few details."

"Thank you, Angela," Meg said.

Guy huffed. "I doubt Stewart will see it that way. What does Matheson know about all this?" he asked curtly.

"I wish I knew. He visited me on Caransay, and he saw that I wanted to be simply Meg MacNeill there. He could easily find out that Mr. Stewart never realized my identity. Sir Frederick might have told him already. They were to have a meeting today."

"Matheson will be too busy puffing his own feathers to waste time talking about anyone else," Guy remarked. "I wouldn't worry."

"I do worry. Guy, Angel, I must tell you. Everyone will know, sooner or later. I have . . . decided to marry Sir Frederick."

The silence, immediate and profound, did not last. "You what!" Guy exclaimed. while Angela gasped.

"I must. It's best for all concerned, I think."

"Best! It's plain foolish," Guy growled from the shadows.

"Why do this, dear? I do not understand," Angela said. "He was once a friend and supporter to you. I know that. But over time he has revealed himself to be a rather unsavory man. You cannot abide him. How can you accept him as a husband?"

"Because," Meg said, looking at Angela in the darkness. She could feel her heart pounding. "He knows about Iain."

"Oh, my God," Angela murmured.

"Who?" Guy asked.

"I will explain later," Meg said. Angela and Mrs. Berry, her closest confidantes, knew about Iain's existence, but Guy had never guessed. Now, for some reason, she felt ready to let Guy learn about it. She wanted to confide in her friends about Sir Frederick's evil threats, but she could not bring herself to explain Iain's existence to Guy directly. She leaned to look out the window. "We are nearly there."

"Who is Iain?" Guy asked. Angela waved her hand to hush him.

The coach slowed to a stop. "Calton Hill," the driver called. "Number Thirty-nine Calton Hill."

Meg felt the lurch as the driver climbed down. She looked at Angela and Guy. "Wait here. I will not be long. Once I tell Mr. Stewart the truth, he will not wish me to linger."

Angela reached out to squeeze Meg's gloved hand. "Courage," she whispered.

Glancing at her friend, Meg drew up the hood of her cloak and shifted to stand as the driver opened the door. Guy stepped out first, offering his hand in assistance to her.

"Tell me what is going on," he murmured.

"Angela will tell you. Go back and stay with her. Tell her that I want her to explain it all to you."

He nodded and walked her toward a stately stone house surrounded by an iron fence. Light warmed the wide bay windows of the first and second levels of the house. "Let me go in with you," Guy said. "Let me help you in this."

"I must do this myself. Go back to Angela. Do not leave her alone in the coach. Stay with her. Stay with her always, Guy," she added fervently.

"I intend to, if she will have me," he murmured.

"She will," she said. "Love finds a way. Even when hearts have been bitterly broken, they can heal."

He gazed down at her, then tipped his hat. "Sound advice, my lady," he said. He opened the gate for her and turned, leaving her standing in the darkness and mist.

She walked through the gate, her heart slamming, hands clenching inside her gloves. This was the house where Dougal was staying with family while he was in Edinburgh. She glanced at the brass address plaque and saw the name beneath the engraved number: *Doctor Connor MacBain.*

A doctor's household would be accustomed to unexpected visitors, and it was not yet late, although the rain made the darkness deeper. She would have to endure the awkwardness of asking to see a gentleman alone, but she would do whatever she must in order to see Dougal. She could not let him learn about her identity in public at her soiree. She owed it to him, out of respect and love, to explain it herself in private.

Drawing a deep breath, she strode up the walk and climbed the steps. Wide flower beds edged the foundation of the spacious stone house. Bay windows on the first and second levels were hung with golden drapes, warm with light.

Reaching up to the small black bonnet she wore under her cloak's hood, Meg drew a swath of black netting over her face. Then she drew a deep breath and picked up the door knocker.

Moments later, a woman in a dark dress and white apron appeared, then stepped back immediately to bring Meg into the foyer. "Are you here for the doctor, miss? He has guests and is not seeing patients at this hour, but if 'tis an emergency, Dr. MacBain is always available."

The house was cozily warm and smelled fragrant with cleanliness and baking spice. Toward one side of the house, she heard the rattle of dishes, and elsewhere, the harmony of male and female voices mingled in conversation and laughter.

Clutching the hasp of her cloak with a gloved hand, Meg felt a keen yearning to be part of the warmth and comfort that was so redolent in this place. But she was an outsider. She was suddenly very glad for the protection of her veil.

"I have not come to see Dr. MacBain. I was told that Mr. Dougal Stewart is staying here. I . . . I have an urgent message for him, if he is here."

"Mr. Stewart, aye. Who is calling?" The housekeeper produced a silver salver to accept Meg's card.

Reaching into her glove where she always slid a calling card or two out of habit, Meg paused, reluctant to produce one. The name Lady Strathlin would cause a stir. "Please tell Mr. Stewart that Miss MacNeill is here to see him."

To the left of the hallway, panel doors slid open and a lovely dark-haired young woman in a brown silk dress glided toward her. "Hello, miss. May the doctor be of assistance?" She smiled and held out her hand. "I am Mary Faire MacBain. My husband is here—Oh, there you are, sir." She smiled.

A blond man, wide shouldered and dressed in shirt-sleeves and a gray vest, appeared through the same doorway. "Who is it, my dear?" he asked, and then he saw Meg. He smiled and stood back to welcome her into the room.

"Miss, hello. I am Dr. MacBain. Please come in and tell us what we can do for you."

Everyone assumed that she was a patient in need. No one questioned her right to be here or acted as if proprieties were compromised. Meg felt grateful to them for their friendly acceptance, but she hesitated, feeling awkward and foolish.

"The young lady is here to see Mr. Stewart, sir," the housekeeper explained. "This is Miss MacNeill."

"Pleased to meet you, Miss MacNeill. But I'm afraid Mr. Stewart is not here. He has stepped out for a little while and did not say when he would be back. He has had a busy schedule of business appointments. Might I give him a message?"

Meg stared at them. "He is—not here?"

"Would you like to wait?" Mrs. MacBain asked. "We are about to have coffee. You are more than welcome to join us."

Through another set of half-open pocket doors, Meg saw a few others milling about engaged in conversation. If she waited here for Dougal, someone in the house might recognize Lady Strathlin.

"I—" Meg paused, looking back at the doctor and his wife. They regarded her kindly, with evident concern. The radiance of happiness and compassion shone in their handsome faces.

She would never have that, she thought, never. Not now.

"Miss," Mrs. MacBain said, "is there something we can do?"

Suddenly she felt lost, alone, and very unsure of herself. Wealth and social status meant nothing to her now. Dougal was not here, and she needed him very badly, needed his arms around her, needed the comfort of his voice, his calm wisdom and gentle humor, and the strength of his passion. She needed him to tell her that he understood. That he forgave her.

Not so long ago, he had asked for her forgiveness, had told her that he loved her and wanted to marry her—and she had not taken the chance then to tell him how much she loved him, had not taken the risk of explaining herself to him.

Now she was ready to do that, and he was not here. After the soiree, he might never be available to her again.

But she could not stay and wait for him, and she might have no chance to return.

"I—should not have come," she blurted. "Please accept my apology. I am sorry for disturbing your evening." Turning toward the door, she pulled it open and ran down the steps.

She picked up her skirts and fled down the path, her shoes tapping on stone. Passing through the gate, she ran toward the waiting coach. The driver seemed to understand. Without hesitation, he opened the door and swept her inside, then leaped onto the cab. The two horses launched forward.

"Did you speak to Mr. Stewart so quickly?" Angela asked.

Meg settled her skirts and collected herself, breathless for a moment, and looked at her friends. Angela and Guy sat close together on the opposite bench seat, both watching her.

She pulled off her gloves anxiously. "He was not there," she said. "He is out, and they do not know when he will be back—oh!"

Looking down at her gloves, she realized that the little cream card that identified her as Lady Strathlin was gone.

She glanced around, over her wide black crinolined skirt and down at the coach floor. Gone.

Peering out the coach window back toward the MacBain house, she saw Connor MacBain step outside the house, watching her coach disappear. He bent to pick up something from the ground and stood looking at it, then tucked it into his vest pocket.

Meg sat back with a soft groan and leaned her head against squabbed leather. "I did not say who I was, but I suspect the entire household will know soon. I dropped my calling card as I left."

"Oh dear!" Angela said. "Well, they will tell Mr. Stewart when he returns, and no doubt he will seek you out at the soiree for an explanation."

"If he comes at all," Meg said. *If I ever see him again.*

She looked at Guy and Angela, and saw by their somber gazes and the close way that they sat together that they had been deep in conversation while she was gone. And she could tell, simply by the way that Guy regarded her, that now he knew the secret of her son, the thing she had fought so long to protect.

She trusted Guy implicitly, but she realized that little by little her secrets would unravel and be told. The feeling was one of extreme vulnerability.

"So you know," she said quietly.

He nodded silently, then leaned forward and took her hand. "My dear baroness," he murmured. "You could have told me long ago. I might have been a help to you in this."

"A help," she said.

"You have taken a great deal onto your shoulders," he said. "But there are others around you, friends willing to share the burden. Willing to love the child, and you, without judgement."

Tears pricked her eyes. Meg nodded silently, gratefully, and leaned back, gazing out the window as the coach conveyed them back to Charlotte Square.

If Dougal knew, she wondered, would he feel the same way? He would be angry with her for keeping the secret, but she knew unequivocally that he was capable of real love and compassion. And he had a right to know his son, to love his son.

But she could not tell him. If she did, Matheson would find out somehow. The man had a way of ferreting out, and learning what was hidden. Some deep instinct told her that Matheson would become a dangerous threat to Dougal if he ever knew the true identity of Iain's father.

Although she had to tell Dougal that she was the baroness, she must continue to protect the secret of their child. In that way, she could keep both Iain and Dougal from imminent danger. Her continued silence, over the years, would ensure their safety.

She watched as the rain began a steady, pelting downpour.

Chapter Eighteen

"Now this," the seamstress said, as she knelt on the floor, arranging the overskirt of Meg's gown, "is why Monsieur Worth is so pleased with this gown—the tulle overskirt." She inserted another silver straight pin and fluffed out the silken netting until its soft veiling formed transparent clouds around the skirt of the gown.

"Oh! It's magical," Angela said as she walked around Meg in a wide circle. "Truly a masterpiece."

"I quite agree," Lenore Worth said. She was more than a mere seamstress, Meg had realized upon her arrival. Miss Worth was the couturier's niece, a capable young Englishwoman who worked with her uncle in his Paris shop. Arriving with the gown packed in a trunk amid layers of silk netting and lavender sachets, Miss Worth had a perceptive eye and a precise hand for sewing. Mere days after her arrival, the adjusted gown now fit like a glove and looked like a vision. The night of the soiree had finally arrived, and she would wear the gown at last.

Meg looked into the long, tilted mirror, which reflected back the shimmering gown. Of Lyons silk in a pale aqua, the low-cut bodice left her shoulders and upper breasts bared in a graceful sweeping line. A snug waist nipped her to an illusion of impossible slimness, and the wide skirt and graceful train poured fluidly over a lightweight crinoline that swayed in an airy, flexible bell. Over the simple but elegant gown, transparent silken netting in creamy white was caught with silver straight pins. The tulle fell in soft layers to give the impression of floating clouds. Sprinkled over the netting, snug bodice, and puffed elbow sleeves, tiny silver stars were embroidered in metallic thread.

Her hair, dressed by a maid following Miss Worth's suggestion, was pulled back gently to spill down her back in rippling golden waves, pinned with a few small pearls and a snood so delicate it was nearly invisible. Around her neck she wore only the gold and aquamarine pendant that Dougal had given her, threaded on a black silk cord, its extra length draped in sensuous loops beneath the mass of her hair and down her back. On her left wrist, over her white glove, she wore her golden locket as a bracelet, threaded on a black silk ribbon.

"Exquisite," Miss Worth said. "A perfect picture of grace and simplicity. The gown is divine, the jewelry is not overdone, and your hair is simply and beautifully arranged. Truly perfect."

Meg crossed the room to pick up her fan of carved ivory and cream silk, slipping its cord over her wrist, and came back.

"Heavenly," Angela said. "You float like a cloud when you move. It is a most splendid effect."

"Monsieur Worth meditated a very long time before designing this gown for you," Miss Worth said. "He was most inspired by the beautiful, unusual color of your eyes. He wanted to create something that suited your beauty and reflected your gentle nature."

"He could not have designed anything more gorgeous or more perfect for Lady Strathlin," Angela said. Meg saw her friend's wide blue eyes and smile reflected in the mirror.

"Mrs. Shaw, you would also look beautiful in a gown like this one," Miss Worth said. "Of course, your own gown is elegant tonight. That black watered silk trimmed with black velvet and the touch of pearls here and there, make a stunning contrast to your ivory complexion and pale blond hair. Yet I feel that Monsieur Worth could create something marvelous for a Nordic beauty like you, should you ever feel inclined."

"Oh, I could not—I could not afford it, truly," Angela said. "And I have worn second mourning for years."

"But you cannot think to wear it forever, as young and beautiful as you are," Miss Worth replied.

Meg looked at Angela in the mirror. "Whenever you are ready, Angela," she said, "we will ask Monsieur Worth to design for you. I would consider it a privilege to give that to you."

"Oh, Meg, thank you, but I could not—"

"You have birthdays like everyone else, and must accept gifts. And I'm sure Monsieur Worth can design something for you in mourning colors, if you'd like."

Angela sighed, then smiled, her light blue eyes brightening. "Someday I will come out of mourning and surprise you," she said. "I am finding it a dreary thing to have so little color in my life. Perhaps it does not . . . honor those who are gone."

"Life does go on, Angela," Meg said. Her friend nodded.

"Madam, allow me to just lift this one section," Miss Worth said. "It droops lower than the other side." She gathered her pincushion and knelt on the floor again.

While she stood still, Meg glanced in the mirror again. Unaccustomed to studying herself often, thinking herself only vaguely pleasing at best, she could hardly believe the transformation she saw.

But the sheer delight of a beautiful gown and the

joy of looking wonderful in it felt diminished by heartbreak and apprehension. She would see Dougal tonight, but all her yearning would come to nothing if he did not care to speak to her again.

If she could not gain his forgiveness, and she lost his love and respect through her foolishness, then all the glittering evenings and splendid gowns in the world would make no difference to her.

Besides, she reminded herself, even if Dougal loved her, and even though she loved him—she had decided to accept Sir Frederick's proposal so that Dougal and Iain could be safe. And tonight was the night she must give her answer. Tonight seemed like the hour of her own funeral, as if her life and all chance for happiness had ended.

But there were others she could not disappoint. She must carry on with a smile and proud demeanor for their sakes.

Drawing a deep breath, she waited as Miss Worth finished her work. Then she turned, aqua skirt and tulle cloud swinging gently. "Shall we go downstairs? Mr. Hamilton must be pacing impatiently with Mrs. Berry, waiting for us to come down for the concert. The carriage will be ready by now, and we are late."

Angela took up her fan and her shawl of black fringed lace. "Let him be impatient. I hope, when you come down the stairs, he falls to his knees in sheer astonishment. He will realize that waiting for you was well worth it."

"My dearest Angel," Meg said, as Miss Worth opened the door, "I rather think Mr. Hamilton is waiting for you."

Lamplight spilled golden over the lean planes of his freshly shaved jaw, flickered gleaming highlights throughout the waves of his hair. Gazing into the mirror, Dougal straightened the small bow of white silk wrapped just beneath his collar points and smoothed the lapels of his white brocade waistcoat, tugging at its buttoned front. He perfected the drape of the gold watch chain slung across his vest and pulled at his stiff cuffs.

His boots were polished, his coat and trousers immaculate, his skin lightly scented with a soap that mingled spices and vanilla. Sliding his long fingers into white kid gloves, he tugged at the long tails of his black dress coat.

He felt girded for battle.

Reflected in the amber sheen of the mirror, his eyes were cold and hard, green glass, the pupils mere pinpoints. A new leanness shadowed his cheeks, tiny lines etched the corners of his eyes, and his lips were pressed flat and humorless. Every fiber in his being had steeled to resolve and defiance.

He would face them all with the same gritty nerve and unflinching determination he had summoned to brave a gale, dive deep into the sea time after time, rescue men from a collapsing bridge, and shove away a monstrous shark to reach a small boy. None of the people he would see tonight, none of the havoc they had wreaked in his life of late—the lost funds, the rumors that undermined his sterling reputation—could be as terrifying as the physical dangers he had encountered.

Yet somehow those sniping, condemning people, with their damned opinions and judgements, their haughty criticisms and assumptions, seemed far more intimidating.

He had made this commitment and would not take the coward's route and stay away now. He would attend the concert with his cousin and her husband, and then he would walk into Lady Strathlin's fashionable home with all the dignity and backbone that he could muster.

Not only did he anticipate meeting some of those who had condemned him without reason, but he would also see the woman he loved, the woman he had asked to marry him.

There was little danger in that encounter. He felt sure that he could greet her, even converse a little, and move on through the evening, shielded by coldness. He had no more heart left to hurt, for it had gone numb inside him from anger and betrayal.

Easy enough to survive the evening in a cool and dignified manner, he thought, as he turned and headed for the door and his companions waiting belowstairs. How he would endure the rest of his life without her remained to be seen.

"Ma leddy, we will not acknowledge those who so rudely wish to catch your eye," Mrs. Berry said, leaning toward Meg from her chair beside her in the theater box. "Give your attention only to the performer, ignoring all else, once the concert begins."

"Of course I will, Berry." Meg watched the stage with its closed curtains of heavy velvet. Below, as the theater continued to fill with those attending the concert, she noticed several people turning to stare up at her and her companions in the box. Some were even ill-bred enough to point. "Concentrating on the performer will not be difficult this evening. Miss Lind is captivating."

"Staring up at a private theater box is so verra vulgar," Mrs. Berry complained. She turned away from some onlooker in irritation, snapping her blue feathered fan to hide her face.

Guy, dressed in black and white dinner attire, leaned toward them from his velvet-upholstered chair. He sat beside Angela, the two of them seated behind Meg and Mrs. Berry. "Lady Strathlin cannot help but attract attention. Nearly everyone in this theater is curious to see the elusive baroness. And with three such beautifully gowned, gorgeous ladies in this box,

I'm sure some of them are wondering just which one is Lady Strathlin."

"Well, true," Mrs. Berry conceded. She smoothed the skirt of her deep blue velvet gown and flounced her coiffed head, crystal earrings shivering. "Now remember, ma leddy, during the promenade at intermission, walk slowly and decorously, and dinna stop to converse, expecially with gentlemen. This isna the beach at Caransay."

"Oh? Did Lady Strathlin chat with a gentleman on the beach?" Guy asked. Meg turned to see his teasing smile. Mrs. Berry rounded eagerly toward Guy and Angela.

Lessons in decorum were no match for a chance to gossip a little, Meg thought, both amused and irritated.

"Indeed she did, wearing no more than a skirt and blouse, and barefoot, as well," Mrs. Berry whispered. "And I was in ma *bathing costume,*" she confided. "I was mortified!"

"Understandably. Who was the gentleman?" Angela asked.

"Mr. Stewart o' the lighthouses," Mrs. Berry replied. She folding her gloved hands one over the other, lips pursed. "He thought I was the great leddy herself, the baroness. Must be my manner o' deportment," she said, straightening her shoulders.

"No doubt," Guy murmured, smiling as Meg looked at him.

"This Mr. Stewart is a fine man, charming and handsome, though I havena spoken with him maself," Mrs. Berry went on. "Brave, too. He saved a small child from drowning in the sea. And fought off a shark to do it! Amazing heroics."

"Really? Quite impressive," Guy said.

"Madam, you never mentioned such excitement during your holiday," Angela said, leaning forward.

"Mr. Stewart did save a child from drowning, and very courageously," Meg said.

"Iain," Mrs. Berry said. "It was little Iain. You

know who *he* is, Mrs. Shaw." She looked pointedly at Angela, who gave an audible gasp. Guy Hamilton frowned thoughtfully.

Meg flapped her fan, rapid and silent. Mrs. Berry took the hint and sat back without further comment on the subject.

"I want to hear that story later. And think we should make it a point to congratulate Mr. Stewart on his brave deed," Angela said. "I, for one, look forward to meeting him, after all I've heard lately of him. It is a shame what Sir Edward and his cohorts have done to him. It's said they've nearly ruined him. And all over this dispute."

"Once," Guy began, "I might have said Mr. Stewart deserved it, for all his arrogance and aggression regarding the lighthouse. But I must agree with dear Mrs. Shaw—for all I've learned about him lately, he did not deserve this attack, which was unfairly done. Had I known what Uncle Edward was about, I would have done what I could to stop it." He glanced at Meg.

"Withoot fifty thousand pounds to spare," Mrs. Berry hissed, "no one can stop the poor man from losing his lighthouse."

Meg stayed silent, feeling utterly miserable. She looked out over the sea of heads and shoulders arrayed beneath them and listened as the crowd settled at last, quieting to a murmur.

He was here somewhere, she knew, in the theater. She sensed the inexorable pull of his presence so strongly that her heartbeat quickened as she looked around. She knew she should not glance around the theater but felt compelled to do so.

It was dark, though, and impossible to find one man in that vast and glittering crowd, no matter how well she knew the turn of that head, the set of those shoulders.

And if he did see her, she was certain he would turn away.

The orchestra tuned their instruments, the gaslights dimmed, and the voluminous draperies slowly parted. The stage was bare but for a pedestal holding an arrangement of flowers and a small table covered in a paisley cloth with a pitcher of water and a single glass upon it.

Silence deepened in the theater. Then a small woman walked out to the center of the stage, her brown hair pulled back simply, tucked with a small spray of pink roses. Her gown was cream colored, simple, lightly touched with lace. Jenny Lind looked like an innocent young girl, though Meg knew that she was easily in her mid-thirties. Clasping her hands in front of her, Miss Lind lifted her head and began to sing.

Her voice flowed outward, pure as crystal, a delicate trill like a lark in the morning. Listening, Meg felt her worries and fears ease a little under that magical sound.

During the promenade, the crush around Lady Strathlin and her party was deep and crowded in the wide foyer of the theater. From his vantage point across the hall, Dougal could scarcely see the baroness. He hardly cared to come any closer.

Still and silent, he waited out the intermission in the company of his hosts at the Calton Hill address, Connor MacBain and his wife, Mary Faire, Dougal's cousin. While the MacBains chatted with acquaintances, Dougal stood as cold and stiff as the jasper column beside him, although he nodded and murmured greetings now and again with unerring politeness.

Once he saw her clearly, when the sea of gowned ladies and black-clad gentlemen parted for a moment. Her back was turned to his direction, and an opera cloak of dark blue velvet covered her from shoulder to hem, but he knew the golden waves of her hair, had pushed his fingers through that mass himself. Now it was wound and pinned with gewgaws and a spray of feathers and roses.

Then she turned her head, and he saw the lovely profile that was so achingly familiar to him. His heart nearly stopped. She was uncommonly beautiful, and he loved her still, wanted her so intensely that it hurt.

Once he had told Meg that he would never give up on what he most desired in life. After what had assailed him since he had come to Edinburgh, he felt betrayed, even uncharacteristically defeated. Persistence, just now, was a challenge.

Yet his nature demanded that he continue through sheer will and determination. Despite setbacks, somehow the lighthouse would be constructed, even if, as he had told Aedan, he had to build it himself, stone by stone, and fund it out of his own pocket.

Watching her now, as the crowd closed around her again and her golden head was once more hidden from his sight, he decided that he must persist in one other matter as well. That new goal sat heavy and bitter in his heart.

He intended to forget Meg MacNeill, though it might take him all his life to accomplish it.

The carriage slowly edged forward in a long line of gigs, hansom cabs, and coaches approaching Charlotte Square. Dougal leaned sideways to peer ahead through the side window. He could see the baroness's town house a little distance ahead. The block of houses, made to look like a single palatial facade, had been designed by the celebrated Robert Adam. A magnificent and enormous building roofed several town homes as one, with a row of grand doorways.

Under the light of lanterns held high by grooms, footmen in dark livery assisted ladies out of vehicles, while gentlemen emerged clothed in stark black and white attire, in contrast to the garden colors worn by the women.

"I do hope we are nearly there," Mary Faire said. With gloved hands, she smoothed the wide flounces of her gown of pink silk. "The concert was marvelous—Miss Lind is astonishing to hear—but I am ready to move about after being seated for so long."

"We shall soon be dancing, Cousin," Dougal said, smiling fondly. He knew Mary Faire loved dancing and music, although she was otherwise a serious sort, a trained nurse who assisted her husband in his practice. He greatly appreciated the hospitality that Mary Faire and Connor freely extended to him whenever he came to Edinburgh, and he was glad that they had decided to attend the baroness's soiree this evening.

At least he would be certain of two friendly faces, although he knew that they did not plan to stay long at Lady Strathlin's soiree, having another invitation to honor as well that evening. Miss Lind's concert had engendered several parties.

"Patience, my dear," Connor answered, while glancing out the window as Dougal had done. "We'll be there in a few minutes."

The vehicle lurched forward again. Dougal flexed his gloved fingers, then rested them calmly on his thighs. He felt cold and detached, had felt so for days. Miss Lind's soothing, entrancing music had affected him briefly, but he did not want mellowing. As soon as he had glimpsed Lady Strathlin among the concertgoers, he had felt chilling anger seep through him again. He welcomed it, for that hard, brittle shield around his heart would see him through any encounters with her this evening.

"The crush of people at the theater and outside of it, was astonishing," Connor said. "I've hardly seen such a thing, but for a few years ago, when the Nightingale also came to Edinburgh. I wondered if we would even get inside the theater through the crowds waiting in the street."

"I believe the place was even more crowded because

Lady Strathlin had decided to attend," Mary Faire said. "There has been enough mystery around the baroness that people are curious for any chance to see her. They say she decided to give a soiree this evening because she is a great admirer of Miss Jenny Lind. Otherwise, I think we would hardly see her at all this season."

"With all the concert parties being held this evening, it seems Lady Strathlin is not the only one who admires Miss Lind," Connor said. "Though hers may be the only party that the singer actually attends."

"We were invited to three different parties, all held at the same time," Mary Faire explained to Dougal. "So we thought it best to attend two—Lady Strathlin's, of course, and one other, given by friends on Calton Hill, close to home."

"Ah. I've been meaning to ask," Dougal said, "if you know the baroness well."

"We met her once or twice at soirees and concerts," Connor answered. "And along with my associate, Dr. Lewes, I attended the wife of Sir Frederick Matheson, one of Lady Strathlin's banking associates. The woman had a chronic illness and became an increasing invalid until she died about a year ago. It was a very sad case. As I recall, Lady Strathlin insisted on paying all the medical bills. A very generous gesture."

Dougal frowned. "Indeed. I met recently with Sir Frederick, but I had no idea his wife had died. He never mentioned it." In fact, Dougal thought, he had mentioned that he shortly expected to become engaged to Lady Strathlin. "But I had the impression that he is not in dire need at all. Lady Strathlin's assistance in his expenses is . . . curious."

"She has a magnanimous nature for such a young woman," Mary Faire said. "She has modesty without arrogance."

"One might think so," Dougal said.

"After all, she inherited only six or seven years ago, when she was barely eighteen. The fortune had come to her somewhat earlier and was held in trust by the bank until she reached majority."

"Majority?" Dougal looked at her.

"Have you never heard of the Matheson Bank heiress?" she asked.

"I pay very little attention to the doings of society."

"True. You avoid parties and gossip like the plague, which is commendable in its own way," Mary Faire said. "And you're always out there on some rock or another."

"He quite literally seldom comes up for air, from what I understand of his work lately," Connor said, and he grinned.

"One does not hear much gossip under the ocean," Dougal drawled.

"I thought you were acquainted with Lady Strathlin and have carried on a regular correspondence with her," Mary Faire said.

"Aye, we thought you knew her," Connor added. "She came to the house to call on you and dropped her card—Lady Strathlin, it said, which was a surprise to me, for I did not recognize her."

"You have been introduced only once, and you do not have a good memory for faces," his wife said.

"She came to the house?" Dougal asked.

Connor nodded. "She seemed rather nervous and wanted to remain discreet—gave her name as Miss MacNeill. You came home so late that evening that I had no chance to tell you."

"I wonder what she wanted," Mary Faire said. "Lately her lawyers have turned on you in a most vile manner. I thought perhaps you two were . . . well, more devoted friends than that."

"The lady and I have corresponded, but it was through her lawyers for the most part and never . . . well, diverting." He twisted his mouth awry. "Essentially, I routinely asked permission to build on her island and she routinely refused through her soliciting firm, until the Lighthouse Commission finally authorized me to appeal to the government. I would not say that we are acquaintances, but more . . . adversaries." He felt the impact of that like a blow. And he wondered why she had come to Calton Hill—what had she wanted to say to him? "Tell me what you know about her."

"Her inheritance created quite a stir, from what I understand, although I was not in Edinburgh at the time," Mary Faire said. "She was originally from a simple Highland family, I believe . . . or was it the Isles . . . when her grandfather left her the greatest fortune in Scotland."

"Ah," Dougal said. "Her grandfather." He nodded once, remembering Meg's references to a grandfather on the mainland who had left her his library. Indeed, he thought bitterly. Quite a library it must have been.

"When did the initial inheritance occur, Connor dear?"

"Seven years ago, I believe," he answered his wife.

"It really is quite a romantic story," Mary Faire went on. "The amount was something like two million pounds, from a maternal grandfather. Apparently, his two sons had died without issue, and his only daughter had died years before, leaving behind a young daughter. The girl had visited her grandfather as a child, and he designated her his heir, to the shock and surprise of many, from what I understand. She was so young that a trust was required, as well as special tutors to train her to the position."

"She was born in the Isles," Dougal said. "When she acquired the inheritance, I suppose almost the first thing she did was purchase the lease to the island where she was raised."

"And thus began your difficulties," Connor told Dougal.

"It would seem so," he agreed.

"As a very young woman she took on not only an enormous fortune," Mary Faire continued, "but the formidable task of overseeing a bank. None of that could have been easy for one of her years, but she has done an admirable job of it, from what I hear. Lady Strathlin is well-known for her generosity, and she has been particularly helpful to Highlanders and Islesmen who suffered in the clearances."

"And closer to home as well. She has lately founded a home for unmarried mothers," Connor said. "It is apparently a particular sympathy of hers—these young women who find themselves in poor straits, with child and without husbands."

"She is not yet married herself," Mary Faire said, "yet she is a prize of such consequence that it is surprising she has not been caught before now."

"I'm sure her bankers and lawyers will have a say in her marriage. Someone of her position can afford to take her time. No doubt she has many suitors," Connor said.

"Aye," Dougal murmured. "No doubt."

That added to the blow of her betrayal. She had not told him who she was or that she intended to marry Sir Frederick Matheson. If it were true—instinct told him Matheson thought far too much of himself—then she was not the woman he thought he loved. She was neither the passionate creature he had met on the sea rock, nor the winsome, earnest girl with whom he had fallen so completely in love.

Who was she inside? What did she truly want? What scheme had the baroness concocted when she had led along the engineer whom her lawyers were setting up to ruin? Why would she come to see him anonymously at the house on Calton Hill? If she felt remorse and wanted his forgiveness, she would not have it of him.

He wanted to feed his anger and hurt. It sat cold within him, and he was not ready to give it up. If Meg had betrayed him as it appeared, all he had left was anger.

Chapter Nineteen

A vision of uncommon beauty waited in the drawing room, spun of aqua silk and netted clouds, sparkling with silver and pearls. As a steady stream of guests poured past Lady Strathlin, each person received her bright smile and the touch of her gloved hand in welcome. Dougal approached behind Connor and Mary Faire, watching Meg as he came forward.

As he waited, he glanced around at elegant furnishings and crystal chandeliers shining with gaslight, at oil paintings by old masters, and marble and bronze statuary. In a corner, musicians played violins and flutes, and through open doors in the hallway, he saw a long table draped in snowy linens and illumined by candlelight that gleamed on silver and over a variety of foods beautifully arranged on platters.

Everywhere he looked he saw luxury and privilege and the stamp of sophistication and graciousness. Nowhere did he see the Meg MacNeill he knew—yet she stood at the center of it all, impossibly beautiful in that tranquil, sparkling gown.

He ought to seethe in fury to see her as the baroness who had ruined him. He ought to reject her—he ought not to be here at all. Now, looking at her, within moments of greeting her himself, he knew why he had come, despite her betrayal.

He loved her. The simple strength of it, the warmth and certainty of it, flowed through him. He loved her and could never stop. He did not know why, after all that had passed, he still burned for her. Instead of feeling filled with joy and the discovery of love, he ached with the sadness of its loss.

Edging closer, he saw that her gown was the elusive shade of her eyes, the delicate blue-green of sunlight through water, the white veiling like the froth of a wave. She stopped his breath, stilled his heart, whirled him on the axis of his soul.

"Dr. and Mrs. Connor MacBain," the butler announced. "Mr. Dougal Robertson Stewart."

She looked up then, quickly, her eyes wide and startled, but that quickly melted into a smile as she greeted Connor and Mary Faire with murmurs and handclasps. Then Mary Faire glided past, and Dougal was a step away.

Meg tilted her head to smile at him tremulously, her eyes limpid and beseeching. If she meant to request his forgiveness, he had none to give her—not now, not yet, if ever.

She lifted her hand to his, and he took it, glove to glove, cool and cordial, and bowed; then he gazed at her. He knew the sweetness of those lips, the creaminess of her skin. He knew the silken feel of her hair. Now it was drawn back, scattered with pearls, revealing the perfect oval of her face, the slender line of her neck and shoulders. Her slender collarbones rose with the catching of her breath.

A single black cord encircled her throat. Suspended on it was the aquamarine and gold pendant he had given her, its gold a spark of warmth in the serene perfection of her ensemble. Seeing it there, he narrowed his eyes.

He wondered why she wore the pendant, for it had

little value. Surely she owned prettier jewels, although the little stone matched her gown and her eyes. Only he would know, only she, its meaning.

Then he understood. She felt what he did, that he was part of her and she was part of him, that their island paradise had existed for a little space in time. None of that would change, even if they were never together again.

He gave her a cool, polite smile, and felt torn asunder.

"Mr. Stewart," she said, "how very nice to see you again."

He looked at her keenly. He had expected to enact a new introduction, as if they had never met before, yet she greeted him like a friend.

"Lady Strathlin," he murmured. "Enchanted, madam."

She turned to an elderly lady and gentleman standing beside her. "This is Mr. Stewart. And these are the Lord Provost of Edinburgh and his wife, Lady Lawrie."

"Aye, we've met. Good evening, madam," Dougal said, taking the woman's gloved hand, then the Lord Provost's sure grip. "Sir. How do you do?"

"Mr. Stewart has been working near the Isle of Caransay, where I sometimes holiday," Meg said. "He will be modest about this, to be sure, but he is an exemplary hero."

"Really?" Lord Lawrie peered at him. "How is that?"

"During my last holiday in the Isles, I saw Mr. Stewart save the life of a small child who was drowning in the sea, and in the process, Mr. Stewart took on a fearsome shark," Meg explained. "It was the most courageous thing I have ever seen."

"Oh, Mr. Stewart, how amazing!" Lady Lawrie said.

"Madam, it was not so grand as Lady Strathlin implies," he said. "I merely kicked the shark and grabbed the boy."

"Oh, dear!" Lady Lawrie said, raising her fan and flapping it.

"You see how modest he is," Meg said, smiling.

Dougal glared down at her quickly to ask with a stern look just what she intended with this conversation. He would rather the deed not be discussed. "Madam," he said in a subtle warning tone.

Her touch was light on his arm as she guided him forward. "Lord Provost, I'm sure you can coax Mr. Stewart to give his account of it. Please excuse me, I must greet some guests."

She smiled up at Dougal with such brilliance that he felt bedazzled, and he very nearly forgave her. Very nearly. "Mr. Stewart, so wonderfully good of you to come tonight."

"Lady Strathlin," he said, as she turned to greet the couple behind him. As soon as he looked around, he was surrounded by several people eager to be introduced to him, anxious to hear the details of his encounter with the shark.

Swept from that group to another, he told the story twice in total, smiling as he refused, after that, to repeat it. The tale spread and became embellished, whispered and rumored from one guest to another. Dougal floated through the evening on smiles and congratulations and expressions of admiration. He endured one introduction after another, and his hand was clasped, his shoulder slapped, his arm hugged so often that he ached.

He danced with one woman after another, so many that their names and faces and flower-bright gowns blurred as he swirled and dipped and escorted them. He listened to gushing praise, smiled at shy or amorous glances, and turned down three coy invitations to stroll through the conservatory into the garden.

Late in the evening, he was introduced to Miss Jenny Lind, a slight and sweet woman. As he danced with her, he conceded, one last time, to tell the story about the rescue of the little boy, only because she was the guest of honor and begged him gently and charmingly to tell her what everyone was buzzing so about, and because he liked her fine, honest, trusting blue eyes.

As the night went on, one acquaintance after another, both new and old, told him that he was admired by Lady Strathlin in particular. She had made it clear to many that she thought him to be a courageous man of integrity; she thought his skills and abilities beyond measure and his work of great importance to the nation of Scotland. And it came back to him, too, that she regretted any inconvenience to Mr. Stewart and his project through the overzealous efforts of her solicitors.

Graciously and quietly, he accepted apologies from businessmen who murmured that they had been misinformed about him and that they would indeed be interested in contributing funds to his lighthouse project, if he still had need of it.

He even, at one point, was approached by Sir Edward Hamilton, a gaunt and gruff gentleman, and Sir John Shaw, a portly fellow with a pair of eyeglasses set awry on his large nose. Dougal had earlier noticed the men in an animated discussion with Lady Strathlin and her private secretary, a tall dark-haired young man named Guy Hamilton.

"Mr. Stewart," Sir Edward said, tapping him on the shoulder. Sir John stood beside him, clearing his throat repeatedly. "Might we have a word with you, sir?"

"Mr. Stewart, we may have misjudged you," Sir John said.

"Indeed?" Dougal murmured.

"While the lighthouse remains a matter of debate and negotiation and should not be discussed here,"

Sir Edward began, while Sir John harrumphed, "it might have been hasty of us . . . of our associates . . . to imply that you might be unprincipled."

"Mr. Stewart, we hope for peace between our parties," Sir John said. "Lady Strathlin desires it, as well."

Dougal shook their hands solemnly, wondering if the lady desired it for herself or for her advocates.

Not once, throughout that long, lively, and surprising evening, did he speak again to Lady Strathlin. Not once did he dance with her or murmur to her or hold her in his arms and whirl her about the floor in time to the music. Not once did he touch her or kiss her hand or have the chance to thank her.

Now and again, he caught her gaze across the room, those luminous eyes hauntingly somber in the midst of gaiety. Once, as their glances touched, he gave her a subtle nod that he hoped she would interpret as his acknowledgement of gratitude. She paused in her conversation with Miss Lind to angle her head in silent answer with majesty and grace. His heart stirred and his longing for her grew intense, searing through him like a living flame.

He turned away. While his appreciation was profound for the magic she had worked that evening, his pride was great. He loved her and could never doubt it, but he would not let it show.

Late in the evening, when most of the guests had gone, including Miss Jenny Lind and her husband, a soft-spoken Englishman, Meg turned to see a cluster of businessmen still surrounding Dougal Stewart, murmuring closely and privately, holding wineglasses that had been filled and drained repeatedly all evening. Dougal himself stood listening, no glass in his hand. He nodded intently, his hands shoved in his pockets and his coat draped back, one shoulder leaned against a doorframe, one polished boot crossed over the other.

He looked weary, she thought, for she saw the sag

in his shoulders and the subtle drawing down of his mouth. As she watched him, he glanced up, and the magical shock of gazes touching, gentle as hands might do, sent a thrill through her. But he looked away quickly, as he had done all evening.

Sighing, she turned and saw that the conservatory door was open. Angela and Guy strolled in the shadows, she realized, deep in conversation, dark and blond heads leaned together. Angela's hand was wrapped around Guy's forearm. Seeing that intimacy and knowing the spellbinding effect of roses and darkness after a long evening of wine and good company, Meg smiled to herself.

"My lady."

She whirled. Frederick smiled down at her.

She had managed to avoid him all evening, with so many guests and so many interesting conversations, with dancing and music and supper all requiring her attention as hostess. He had been a dark and lurking presence, though at times she had almost succeeded in forgetting he was there at all.

But she could not forget that he expected an answer of her this evening. That much was evident in his dark eyes, which seemed hungry and eager.

"Might I have a word in private, madam?" he asked, and he placed a hand on her elbow. "We've not had a chance to talk as yet. I haven't even had the opportunity to tell you how truly ravishing you look in that gown."

"Thank you," she said, glancing around distractedly. Across the room, she saw Dougal listening to an elderly man rumble on about something. A sharp glance from the engineer seemed to register that she stood with Frederick. He frowned and turned his attention back to his gruff, gesturing companion.

"A walk in the garden on such a lovely night," Frederick said, "would be the perfect ending to a perfect evening."

"I must stay here to say farewell to my guests," she said.

"Madam, they have all departed but for a few gentlemen who cannot seem to stop talking business," he pointed out. "They will not even know you are gone. I ask your complete attention for a few minutes only. Indulge me, I beg you." He smiled and leaned toward her. The smell of wine on his breath was very strong.

"Perhaps tomorrow," she said, turning to step away.

"Margaret, dear—we can discuss our business here, I suppose, if you are so devoted to your company."

She exhaled, recognizing defeat. "Very well." Turning, lifting her skirt with subtle grace, she headed toward the conservatory door, which led out to the garden.

The conservatory was dark, hushed, and fragrant as she walked with Frederick just behind her, his hand on her elbow. Ahead, between an aisle of tall, dense ferns in huge pots, she saw Angela and Guy turn, their faces pale in the shadows. They murmured a polite greeting as Meg and Frederick walked past.

Reaching the garden entrance, Meg waited while Frederick opened the door, then passed through before him, entering a quiet moonlit world. Somewhere in the distance, she heard dogs faintly barking, and late-night vehicles rattled occasionally over cobbled streets, muffled by the peace of the enclosed garden.

She turned. "I know why you wish to speak to me."

"Do you? Excellent. Let us get straight to it, this wee question of the heart."

"It is hardly that," she said, "and you know it."

"Margaret, you wound me, for you have my lifelong devotion. Now, please do me the honor of marrying me." He captured her gloved hands, his fingers strong and overly warm on hers.

She could not look at him, glancing toward the back garden wall, with its neatly tiered flower beds and espaliered fruit trees. This was one of her homes, a place she loved very much. Yet now she would have to allow him here, tolerate his presence, pretend to others that she loved him.

She would have to allow him into her bed. His hands seemed even hotter over hers, tugging at her wrists.

"Well, Margaret?"

"I—I must have more time," she said. "It is too important a decision to make so quickly."

"You have had months to think about it, from my first mention of it," he said. "I gave you these last weeks and was promised a final answer tonight."

"I cannot, Frederick," she whispered.

"Cannot answer or cannot marry me?" he asked.

"Neither," she said. "I can do neither."

He drew her closer, so that the flexible cage of her skirt flattened against his legs. "You will," he said, bending down. "You know there is no choice for you. I will tell all the world. You will be ruined, lady. *Ruined.*" He snatched her hard by the shoulders.

"Please—stop!" She twisted against his cruel grip.

"But I wish to God I had been the one to ruin you first," he growled, and yanked her toward him so fast that her back ached with the snap. He planted his mouth on hers in a rich, wet, eager kiss, grinding his lips and teeth against hers.

Repulsed and angry, she gave a guttural cry and shoved against his chest, then shoved again, hard. He flew backward, stumbling to the ground, protesting with a loud cry.

Surely she was not that strong, she thought, dazed. Then she realized that Dougal stood over Frederick in the shadows. He had grabbed Frederick and had flung him away from her. Now he clearly meant to finish the task.

Leaning down, Dougal hauled Matheson up by grabbing the lapels of his white waistcoat. Shoving the man against the nearby glass-and-stone wall of the conservatory behind them, Dougal pinned him there. Fisting the cloth, he half lifted the man, though Matheson was slightly taller and a stone heavier.

"So you intend to ruin the lady?" Dougal demanded.

"No—I—that's not what I said," Matheson protested, clawing at Dougal's wrists.

"That's what I heard," Dougal growled. "And I'll tell you what I saw." He shook Matheson again, pressed him flatter against the wall, his arms digging into the banker's chest. "I came out to say farewell to my hostess," he went on, his voice rough edged with controlled rage, "and I heard you threaten her and saw you grab her." He slammed Frederick tighter against the wall as the man struggled to get free.

"Mr. Stewart—please—" Meg said.

Dougal paused. "Are you harmed, madam?" he asked, still glaring at Frederick.

"I'm fine," she said. She glanced up, saw the businessmen who had been with Dougal, saw Guy and Angela, Mrs. Larrimore and the butler, and beyond them a thick cluster of maids and grooms, all gaping. "I'm fine, truly. Please let Sir Frederick go."

"I expect he needs to apologize," Dougal growled.

"I need not apologize for asking the lady to marry me," Frederick said. "She was on the verge of saying aye when you interfered."

"Is it true, Lady Strathlin?" Dougal asked, barely audible.

"I—he did ask—"

"Is it true?" Dougal demanded. "Were you about to accept?"

She looked at Dougal, with his strong and fierce heart, and at Frederick, whose heart was cold and vicious. She loved one and loathed the other. And she had to protect them from each other.

"He asked." she whispered. "I am considering. He did me no harm. Let him go."

The next moment was so tense and brittle that Meg

thought her heart might burst from the strain of waiting, watching. Dougal kept his grip tight, his posture confining, while he looked down, clearly seething. He did not look at Meg.

"Mr. Stewart," Sir John Shaw said, walking toward them. "Sir Frederick has had a bit too much wine, I think. He meant no harm at all. He's a good lad, Mr. Stewart, and cares for the lass—for Lady Strathlin very much. If you please, sir."

Silently, Dougal let Matheson slide back to his feet, gradually eased his grip on his lapels, and slowly stepped away.

Tugging at his coat, Frederick glanced at the onlookers and then glared at Dougal. "You will regret this, sir."

"I believe you will be the one to regret it, should you ever threaten this lady again." He flickered his eyes toward Meg, seemed to satisfy himself that she was unharmed, and fastened his glare on Frederick again.

"Our business agreement, sir," Matheson growled, "is at an end. I withdraw my offer."

"So be it," Dougal said easily. "Do you wish to take leave of your hostess?" he asked in a stern and hinting tone.

"Madam," Frederick said, "we will continue our discussion at some other date. I am grateful and flattered that you desire so fervently to marry me—"

Meg gasped. "Sir, I did not—"

He held up a hand. "I understand if you feel embarrassed. Ladies should not indulge in more than a glass or two of wine. It sets their heads to reeling. Nevertheless, I am honored. But after this evening, I must reconsider my proposal, in light of your appalling misconduct."

"Sir, I have never misconducted myself!"

"No?" Frederick murmured. "Not even once, long ago?"

She gasped. Dougal stepped between them, indicating that Frederick should say no more. Meg prayed that Dougal did not guess Frederick's reference, and prayed equally that Matheson would never learn the identity of her little son's father.

"Good night. An excellent party, otherwise." Matheson gave a curt bow and turned. The crowd by the door parted, and he walked through, shouldering past Guy Hamilton.

Guy gave him a dull blow to the stomach with his elbow, enough to make Matheson grunt and turn toward him.

"I beg your pardon," Guy said. "Are you inviting me to spar with you, sir?"

Frederick muttered under his breath and left, storming through the conservatory and out the front door. Meg heard it slam even from where she stood in the darkened garden.

Dougal stood near her, watching as the remaining gentlemen took their leave of her. Dougal said hardly a word, nodding his thanks and farewells. She was grateful for his silent presence. Her limbs still shook so that she did not feel ready to walk back to the house as yet. Relieved to see the last few guests leave without ceremony, she was glad for now just to stand in the dark, quiet garden, in the moonlight, with Dougal.

She glanced at him when they were alone. "Dougal—"

He inclined his head. "Farewell, Lady Strathlin. Thank you for a wonderful evening. Apart from the last few minutes, it has been unexpectedly enjoyable."

"You're leaving?" she asked, her voice quaking.

The smile that played at his mouth was the small, private, fond smile that she had missed so very much. Seeing it made her heart surge, filled her with warmth, made her want to cry.

"I cannot stay," he said. "Madam." He bowed and turned, striding through the garden.

She picked up her gown to follow him. "Dougal, please."

He opened the door for her, and waited while she stepped into the shadowed conservatory. She could hear the chink and clatter as servants gathered the dishes and glasses inside the house, and Mrs. Larrimore directing the maids.

"Please," she said, and laid her hand on his arm. "Do not go. Not yet." She watched him in the darkness, the air around them heavy with the scent of roses and gardenias, with earth and stone. Heavy with promise and pledge, with need and forgiveness.

He looked down at her. "What do you want me to do, madam?" he asked, leaning closer in the shadows. "Stay with you?"

"Yes," she said breathlessly. "Yes."

Chapter Twenty

He growled something low as he pulled her back into darkness with him, behind the crowding ferns in pots, behind the glossy gardenia leaves and the drowsy, drunken scent of roses.

Her gown floated like clouds around her as he took her into his arms and kissed her, his mouth tender and hungry over hers. His hands were strong yet gentle on her bare shoulders.

She looped her arms around his neck, crying out softly in sheer, desperate relief, and gave herself into the kiss, opening her lips to him, his mouth insistent. Her tongue danced over his, slipped away, sought again. She leaned her head back and felt his mouth trail hot along her jaw, the length of her throat, his lips caressing the upper swell of her breasts, breath heating the space between her breasts, above the snug edge of her corset.

One hand snugged against her waist, pulling her hard against him, so that her skirt floated outward, its cage tipping backward like a ringing bell, the silken tulle crushing against his thighs. She pressed deep into his arms, torsos tightly meeting, and even through layers of silk and netting and cotton and the light, flexible cage of her crinoline, she could feel him against her, hot and hard and so blessedly familiar.

She sighed into his mouth with deep contentment and moaned breathily as his hand slid upward, rounded over her confined breasts, found the soft swell above the edge of her bodice. Her body pulsed and wanted to weep everywhere for him, for want of him. She wanted to tear away the layers of the exquisite gown and feel him like steel and fire against her.

"Oh, God," she whispered against his mouth, as his lips found hers again. Her knees were weak beneath crinoline and petticoats, and she clung to him, arms circling his neck, her fingers threading deep into his thick hair.

He smelled of spice and wine, of vanilla and strength and caring, and she loved him. God, she loved him. His hands were divine upon her, caressing, lightly teasing her so that she shivered and craved.

He framed her face in his palms and kissed her deeply, once more, then tore himself away, breaths coming hard.

"Lady Strathlin," he rasped out, "I must go."

She grabbed his coat sleeve. "Stay with me. I beg you, do not leave. Dougal, please," she ended in a whisper.

He stopped suddenly, cold as stone. "What are you asking of me?" he murmured, looking down. "Is it for a night? Or forever?"

"Forever," she whispered. "Oh, God, forever. You know that."

"Forever," he said, his tone cold, bitter. "That requires trust, and honesty, and commitment. And it would hardly do for you to marry someone else. I wonder if you can manage that."

"Dougal, please, let me explain."

"Or is this another game that the baroness finds amusing? Forever becomes a day or two, until the game is no longer interesting? Bare feet were pleasant last month; this month it is precious gowns. Is that it?" His tone sliced through her.

"No, it is nothing like that."

"And now and then, there is the engineer to provide entertainment." He stepped away.

She moved after him. "I know I made a terrible mistake with you, but I intended no hurt."

"Madam," he said, "do not make a fool of the man who loves you. He feels foolish enough already." He paused. "I think we are done." He turned.

"No, please," she whispered, her voice, her heart, breaking.

"I apologize for any inconvenience to your person or to your lovely gown. Good night." He inclined his head and stepped through the ferns, fronds brushing his black-clad shoulders.

She glided with him. "Listen to me."

"Lady Strathlin," he murmured, so softly she hardly heard, "you are so beautiful in that gown—a magical, alluring siren. I will never forget the sight of you tonight." Then he turned.

She pushed through the ferns after him, her gown brushing along a shelf of potted green plants. "Will you not hear my explanation? I listened to you," she said firmly, as he strode away. "I gave you the chance. And I forgave you—all of it."

He stopped then, standing in the aisle between the roses and the gardenias. Meg caught up to him in a few steps. His broad back was turned to her, blocking her passage.

"Why did you do it?" he asked woodenly. "Why did you keep the truth from me about who you were?"

"When I saw you on the island, I realized that you were . . . that we had met before."

"On the sea rock."

"Yes. For years, I had . . . hated you, I think, yet I had also loved you. Loved the memory of you. Do you understand?"

"Aye," he said gruffly. "You loved the dream of me, as I loved the dream of you. Go on."

"So I thought you were the horrid man who had used me cruelly on the rock, and I did not want . . . anyone to know. And I did not want you to use me again . . . like that."

"I never did." He leaned down. *"Never."*

"I know that now. Not then."

"Yet once you realized that I was not the ogre you thought me to be . . . you still kept the truth from me."

"What could I do? You despised the baroness. You did not trust me . . . as Lady Strathlin. If you learned who I was, you would not . . . I feared you would not . . . love me," she said, and she began to cry in great, gulping sobs, salt tears and the scent of roses and his broad, black, turned figure, cold and unrelenting.

"I always loved you," he murmured without moving.

"And I love you," she whispered, starting to sob again, aching for the feel of his arms. "Oh, dear God. I do love you."

He did not answer, stood so long she reached out to touch his arm. He sucked in a breath.

"If I were to accept that," he said carefully, "and I were to ask you again to marry me, what would you say?"

She caught her breath. She realized that she must tell him about their son, before anything else transpired.

And then she remembered that Sir Frederick knew about Iain.

Even if she did marry Dougal, even though Iain was their son, Sir Frederick knew of his illegitimate birth. He would spread that word. He would find proof in the records of the island kirk, even though the minister had promised secrecy. Frederick would see that the baroness was thoroughly ruined.

And the damage would affect Dougal as well.

"I must answer you . . . later," she said in a small voice. "Let me think on it. I beg you."

"Too much in the balance, is there, madam?" he asked. He glanced down at her over his shoulder. "We cannot let an untitled gentleman come too close to the accounts, can we? Or is it that you have already promised yourself to Sir Frederick? Perhaps you did not want to be saved from your wee garden interlude. I should not have interfered."

Murmuring protest, she reached out to him, but he walked away. With a fast, angry stride, he left the conservatory and crossed through the drawing room to the front door, where she heard the butler inform him that a hansom cab was ready and waiting to take him home.

Meg stood in the darkness for a long time. She thought she would never inhale the fragrance of roses and gardenias again without feeling her heart break.

Perhaps he should not have come.

Hat in hand, Dougal stood in the front entryway of Strathlin Castle after being admitted inside by a surly butler who had hastened off to deliver the message to Lady Strathlin. Several days had passed since the soiree on Charlotte Square, days when Dougal determined he should never see Meg MacNeill—Lady Strathlin—again. But he had one matter to attend to before he could try to endure that painful sentence.

Yet each time he had picked up her leather journal and the publisher's cheque to send them to her, his hand stayed. Finally he had decided to bring it and leave it for her. But the old butler had tottered off before Dougal could voice his intentions.

Now he turned slowly, gazing at red mahogany paneling on walls that soared to ornately carved ceiling beams at an impossible height; crystal chandeliers in full gas flare, though it was yet daylight; polished carved furnishings set on plush Turkish carpets; and a march of stately portraits that lined the upper gallery above the grand staircase that divided the front hall.

And that, he told himself, was just the foyer. Strathlin Castle was a luxurious and stately home in grand Scottish baronial style, quite possibly the work of David Burn—he had a good understanding of architectural style and appreciation for its details, which had helped him attain a certain elegance in his own lighthouse designs.

Turning, strolling, sitting for a moment on a tapestried bench and standing again, he contemplated a grouping of oil paintings of lush seascapes filled with wild, frothing waves and atmospheric light. He paced a path on a thick Oriental carpet and wiggled his hat in his hand.

Although he admired elegant simplicity and particularly liked homes that were plush and cozy as well as aesthetically beautiful, he realized that he could never give Meg MacNeill the sort of home she was accustomed to having. His engineer's salary would never support a place like this, nor would the respectable nest egg that he had inherited at a young age, which included his own manse. He visited Kinnaird House too seldom in his wandering, hectic life, and left its primary upkeep to his elder sister, Ellen, and her husband, Patrick.

Perhaps, he told himself, he ought to leave now, walk down to the stables and fetch the horse he had hired for the long ride from Edinburgh. He had no real reason to stay.

"Mr. Stewart?"

He turned. A lovely young woman came toward him, slim and pale blond with vivid blue eyes, dressed in a high-necked black gown that subdued her delicate summery coloring. She smiled.

"I am Mrs. Shaw, Lady Strathlin's companion," she said, extending her hand. "We met at Lady Strathlin's soiree."

"Aye, of course. I remember. How nice to see you again."

"May I be of some service to you, sir? MacFie said you did not wish to disturb Lady Strathlin, but you had a message for her."

"Aye." He reached into his pocket and pulled out a linen-wrapped packet, the cloth and its ribbon a little rumpled from much handling. "I came only to give Lady Strathlin this." He pulled an envelope from his other pocket and added, "And this." He handed both to Mrs. Shaw. "If you could see that she gets these, I will be on my way."

"Thank you, Mr. Stewart. But Lady Strathlin is at home and would be happy to see you."

Though it might be a social victory to be welcomed by the lady, he had no desire to see her. He could not trust himself to maintain the cool distance that he needed when he was near her.

He could have sent the package with a note, but something had urged him to bring it here, some desire to see where she spent much of her time, so that he would better understand her.

But he did not want to see her again.

"Thank you, Mrs. Shaw," he said, inclining his head. "Actually, I am quite rushed today. Please see that Lady Strathlin gets the package, and give her my best regards." He tipped his hat again.

"Very well, Mr. Stewart, if you are certain," Mrs. Shaw said quietly. He saw a flash of sympathy in her pretty eyes, and gentle friendship. In other circumstances, in other worlds perhaps, he would have liked her very much and would have welcomed her as a friend. He would have learned more about Meg from her, for he was sure that the two young women were devoted friends.

"Aye, I'm sure, madam." He smiled and turned away, expecting the ubiquitous butler to materialize and open the paneled door.

Instead, he heard a rustling of skirts, and a graceful figure emerged from the shadows behind a tall potted palm. She came forward from a downstairs doorway that adjoined the foyer.

"Mr. Stewart," Meg said, resting her hands on the full skirt of her blue-and-green plaid satin dress, which buttoned primly to a white lace collar that matched her white half sleeves. The effect was elegant and modest, even to the demure wings of golden hair piled into a black net. She regarded him calmly.

"Lady Strathlin," he said. "I did not mean to disturb you, madam. I came only to return something to you."

Mrs. Shaw stepped forward and handed the linen-wrapped package to Meg, who nodded silent thanks. "Mr. Stewart," Meg said, "we cannot talk here. Please come this way." She turned.

"I'll see that you're not disturbed, madam," Mrs. Shaw said from somewhere in the shadows of the hallway.

Dougal did not want to talk, but he had no polite choice other than to follow. Leading him behind the potted palm, down a hallway and through an open doorway, Meg ushered him into a library and closed the door behind them.

Books lined the walls from floor to ceiling, a vast array of leather spines organized on oak-and-brass shelves. The room was bright and warm, filled with sunshine from tall windows draped in golden brocade, the floors covered in thick rugs patterned in blue, gold, and rose tones. Noticing the painting over the mantelpiece, he knew that Meg had chosen it, for the seascape was recognizably Innish Harbor on Caransay, commissioned, no doubt, of some renowned painter. Altogether a beautiful room, he thought, that reflected its owner perhaps more than she knew.

"You told me once that your grandfather had left you his library," he said. "You never said it was on this scale."

"If I had, you would not have spoken to me afterward."

"I am speaking to you now," he pointed out.

She looked down at the cloth-wrapped package in her hand and untied the ribbon, peeking at her leather journal. "There was no need to return this to me. I meant for you to have it."

"Open the envelope," he directed.

She broke the waxen seal and extracted a piece of paper, reading the contents. "A . . . cheque?"

He nodded soberly. Ever since he had learned about her fortune, he had been unsure how she would react to what he had done and to the publisher's modest sum. "I met with Mr. Samuel Logan at Chambers Street Publishers. He is an acquaintance of mine, so I took the liberty of showing him your journal. He was entranced and found it remarkable and unique. He'd very much like to publish your work, if that's agreeable to you. He'd like to call it *A Hebridean Journal,* by—"

"By M. MacNeill," she breathed, reading the letter as he spoke. "I—I do not know what to say."

He shrugged. "Do what you will with the offer. At the time, I did not realize . . . your circumstances." He glanced around the elegant library. "The money will mean little to you, I'm sure, but at the time, I thought . . . well, I thought you might be pleased." He twisted his deuced hat like an embarrassed schoolboy and felt an urge to flee. Until now, he had not thought about Lady Strathlin's reaction to the publishing offer. He had imagined only Meg MacNeill's delight.

"I am very pleased. Thank you, Mr. Stewart," she said softly, and she unwrapped the bulky leather journal, laying it on the gleaming surface of a nearby table and setting the bank draft beside it. She sniffled, and then Dougal realized that tears were slipping down her cheeks.

"Here," he said awkwardly. "I did not mean to offend. If you do not care to bother with this, I will send back the cheque."

She shook her head with a little watery sob. "No, I am . . . so very touched," she said, the last word wobbling. "I never thought that my little journals had much worth other than as a hobby. I had always dreamed about it, but did not believe . . . but you did believe in me . . . and my work," she said, her voice rising and cracking with tears, "and you took the time to show them to someone. You cared about it," she added. "Truly cared."

"Of course I did," he said. God, he wished she would not sob so. It made him want only to pull her into his arms and hold her. And he could not allow himself to feel that way. "There is no need to cry about it. I . . . know it is a silly wee sum."

Her face crumpled at that, and she sniffled loudly, tears streaming fresh. She touched the cheque with slim fingertips. Dougal wanted to reach out to her so desperately that he bunched the brim of his hat in one hand.

"But it is the first silly wee sum I have ever been given for myself," she said, gulping tears.

"All this—" he said, waving his hat.

"All this was inherited," she said. "I never wanted it, never thought to have it. All this was never meant to be mine, but for circumstance. The two heirs died. I was left. I had to leave my home in the Isles to live here, and for years it did not feel like home to me at all."

"Yet it is all yours, and it is an awesome responsibility."

She nodded, sniffling again, and extracted a handkerchief from her sleeve. "I suppose it is," she said. "But I have so many advisers, bankers, accountants, and such a large household staff at each of my homes, that I do not feel the responsibility as keenly as you might think."

"How many homes do you have?" he asked.

"Four. This castle, the Charlotte Square town house, the manse on Caransay, and a modest house near Inverness, as well."

He watched her without answering. He could well imagine that none of the houses were modest.

She touched the journal. "But the silly wee sum is a wonderful thing, and I thank you for it, very deeply."

"You are welcome, madam," he said stiffly. "Well. I must go. I'm on the afternoon train from Edinburgh to Glasgow."

Her eyes grew wide. "You're leaving Edinburgh?"

"Going back to Caransay and Sgeir Caran. I've been gone far too long. The work has continued in my absence, but some matters cannot proceed until I return."

"What of the—the damage from that storm just before we left? There were repairs to be made. I suppose you have heard from Mr. Clarke and Mr. Mackenzie?"

"Aye. They've seen to it all while I've been gone. But certain things have been delayed . . . through lack of funds. I hope that is sorted out now, but it remains to be seen." He bowed a little, aching inside. "Farewell, then, Lady Strathlin."

She twisted her handkerchief in her hands, and her eyes brimmed again with tears. "Just that? Just farewell?"

"There is little else to say." He watched her, wary of his emotions, fighting to keep temper and desire in check. "Your life here has no room for such as me. I am well aware of that. You have your obligations. So, aye, it is just that. Farewell." He turned and walked toward the door, though his heart fell to his feet, and every instinct in him told him to stay.

"No," she said firmly. "No."

He stopped, did not look back. "I will not be ordered, Lady Strathlin. I have my own life, my own obligations."

"What is it you want?" she asked, her voice breaking. "What would keep you here?"

He closed his eyes, paused. "Nothing you have, my lady. Nothing you own."

"I am not offering you money, if that is what you think. Though if you ever need it, it is yours. Only tell me what you want." A plaintive whisper, those words, filled with need and sorrow. They pulled at him. "Dougal, please."

"Meg MacNeill," he said softly. "I want her. Need her."

She did not answer for a long moment. "But you have no use for Lady Strathlin."

"The baroness, I hear, is engaged to marry a banker." He thought he heard her whimper behind him. He could not look at her, glancing only at her books, her possessions, the evidence of her astonishing wealth. "So I think she could not keep me here."

"Why must you leave?" Her voice quivered.

Hurt, he wanted to say. *Pride.* But there were other reasons too, layered one upon the other. He did not turn, knowing that if he saw her, he would want only to pull her hard into his arms. All his pride, all his resistance, would wash away for the chance of one touch. He felt too much pain to allow that surrender.

"For freedom, I suppose," he murmured. "I like wanderlust too well, and risk. I like my pride as it is, I think. Good day, madam." He stepped toward the door.

As he reached out for the door handle, something struck him between the shoulder blades. He looked down.

A narrow leather boot lay on the floor, its side buttons loosened. Before he could look up, another boot hit him square in the hip. He whirled.

Chapter Twenty-one

She sat in a chair, having worked off her boots to fling them at him. Now she slid off her silk stockings, hastily rolling them down her legs, pushing up the embroidered hems of her knickers to get at the garters. The silk hosiery flew outward and floated down to the carpet.

"What the devil are you doing?"

Without answer, she stood and reached under the voluminous hem of her dress, tearing at the tapes of her crinoline. The cage dropped to her feet and she stepped out of it, still struggling with other hidden drawstrings. She wriggled out of a white flounced petticoat, another of cotton, a third of red flannel.

He strode toward her. "What the devil are you up to?"

"You want Meg MacNeill," she muttered, "and so you shall have her." Stepping out of the pool of cottons and laces, she then ripped off her embroidered half sleeves and tossed them outward. One of them flapped over his face. He tore it away.

Pulling at the black net that bound her hair, she tugged it free, scattering silver hairpins with it. She whipped her head from side to side, and her hair spilled out, gloriously wild and rippling with natural curl, full as a golden cloud.

"There," she said, lifting the limp hem of her skirt to reveal her bare feet, small toes deep in the plush of the blue-and-gold carpet. "There. Meg MacNeill."

He stared at her, heart pounding, head reeling with surprise and with a hope so fragile he hardly dared express it.

"I like my freedoms, too," she said, chest heaving. "I have lost them. I want them back." He heard a faint trace of the Gaelic in the rhythm of her speech, as if she had tossed aside her perfect English with her fancy clothing.

God, how he loved her. His heart overflowed with it.

"What else do you want?" he asked softly, coming closer.

"You," she said, watching him. "I want you."

He gave her a slow, quizzical smile. "And what of Frederick and your promise to marry him?"

"He is an odious bully. I will not let myself be afraid of him any longer." She paused. "*You* are not afraid of him."

He huffed to express the truth of that and walked carefully over what seemed an acreage of lace, silk, and cotton scattered at his feet. "I'm glad you're showing some sense, lass."

"I will need some help to break free of him, though." She lifted her head as he stopped a handbreadth away. "It will not be easy. I owe him loyalty for all his help to me in the past, but he has proven himself lately not a . . . pleasant man. Nor will you will be pleased with me, once I tell you the rest."

"So there's more," he murmured. "Miss MacNeill, you are never dull. You are more a challenge than any I have ever faced. Far simpler to charge into a storm or dive into the sea than to keep pace with you, with all your turnabouts."

He reached out and tipped up her chin, and with a thumb wiped the damp traces of tears from her cheeks. Her delicate nose and exquisite eyes were touched with pink.

She sniffled, tilted back her head. "You said you needed Meg MacNeill. I have found her for you."

"So you have," he murmured. "And the baroness, too. The lass tends to herself quite well, but the lady needs reassuring."

"But you do not care for the baroness."

"Did I say it? The bonnie lady is a fetching creature," he said, "and she has all my heart—but for the deepest part, which belongs to the bonnie lass." He bent down, slipping his hands along the fine-boned frame of her jaw.

Unable to help himself, he felt his anger dissolve under the magic of her winsomeness. Later, he thought, he would seek the rest of the truth, for he sensed there was far more she had not told him. Now, though, he felt trust and faith return full force. He wanted only to love her and leave the rest until its time. He lowered his head and kissed her.

Caught in the spell of his lips, Meg felt herself melting into his kiss, turning to flame as his fingers gentled over her throat and downward. She pulled in a quick breath as he found the swell of her breast, his hand lingering there, a warm cradle. Her knees turned buttery, and she grabbed his arm for support. He broke the kiss, drew back and dragged a fingertip over the shell buttons that closed her bodice.

"What about," he murmured, "your stays, madam? Will you dress again, now that you have made your point, or will you revel in a little more freedom?"

Freedom. She longed for it, had been caged too long as the baroness. He understood her need, shared it himself. Her fingers flew to the neck of her gown, slipping off the lace collar, working the long line of buttons. Dougal reached out, and his fingers worked the buttons slowly, his knuckles next to her skin, grazing over the swells of her breasts.

She tipped back her head, closed her eyes, sighed as he worked down to her waist and opened the bodice of her gown. He drew the separate blouse away from the skirt, exposing the corset cover, the bothersome stays, and the ruched chemise.

Silently he turned her to work the laces at the small of her back, drawing away the stiff whaleboned canvas. Then he spun her to face him, and she came willingly into his arms.

Her body felt free and sensuous, clothed now only in chemise and knickers, for Dougal quickly loosened the tapes of the satin skirt and let it fall to the floor. She looped her arms around his neck and leaned into him, reaching up to work off his coat and his waistcoat, while he kissed her so deeply that she faltered where she stood, moaned breathily.

He lowered her with him to the floor, down to the thick blue-and-gold carpet that reminded her of the beach at Caransay. They sank down behind a blue horsehair sofa, and Meg stretched out beside him, the silky thickness of the Aubusson carpet cushioning her back.

Kissing him, she sighed as his lips, the tip of his tongue, swept the shell of her ear. Her fingers were nimble at the buttons of his shirt, and she tugged the linen away, finally sliding her palms over the firm planes of his chest. Leaning forward, she touched her lips to his warm skin, its taste slightly salty. He streamed soft kisses along her jaw and down the arch of her throat until his lips touched her upper breast.

Gasping deeply, she threaded her fingers into his thick hair and writhed under his mouth, his deft fingers. The fine golden chain around her neck shifted, and she felt the slight weight of the gold locket against her throat, a reminder.

She must stop, she told herself hazily, stop this and

deny herself what she wanted so very much. What remained unsaid between them still burned in her. Honest, he had called her once. Earnest and pure.

She had to tell him. But his hands, his lips coaxed her to wait. Just one more kiss, once more to touch him like this, like that, as she explored his body with more boldness. Her fingers found him, shaped him, caressed, and he groaned against her lips. Slipping her hand under wool, under linen, she took him in her hands, warm velvet over heated steel, and he sucked in a breath.

And then she could not stop, not then, for he had found her, too, discovered the tender places that only he had touched, that honeyed slick for him. Tearing at his clothing, rolling and shifting with him on the silken carpet, she surged against him, moved with him like the sea, merging and seeking, soaring and arching, and then, through some sparkling natural magic, vanishing into him as he poured into her.

"This way," she whispered, tugging at his hand. Her skirt and crinoline, restored to her, rustled and swung gently against his trousered legs as he followed her into the room.

She took him into a small study off the spacious library, a cozy room with dark, gleaming wood paneling and a large mahogany desk, leather armchairs the color of sherry, carpets of red and gold. The walls were crammed with books from floor to ceiling. The fireplace was cold and dark now, but there was more than enough fire and spirit in the masculine elegance of the room.

"This was my grandfather's study," she said. "He preferred this small room to all the others, in all the houses he owned."

She went to a small japanned cabinet of black and gold and opened a door to take out a box of inlaid wood. The exotic smell of sandalwood wafted from it as she set it on the desk and opened it, removing two thick bundles of letters tied with white ribbon.

"When I first inherited and came to live at Strathlin," she said, "Mr. Hamilton and I were exploring this study looking for some important documents. I found this."

"To be stored there," Dougal said, "they must be from someone special."

"They are all from me," she said, "to him. I wrote to him for years. I visited him every winter for several weeks and spent most of that time with tutors. My grandfather was already a widower, and his sons were grown. My mother, his only daughter, would bring me here to visit."

He recalled what little she had said of her parents. "I thought Lord Strathlin did not approve of her marriage to her Hebridean fisherman."

"He did not, but she remained loyal and still came here to visit, bringing me with her. After she was gone, I came to Strathlin myself every winter until my grandfather died. And I wrote to him often."

She lifted a packet of letters, fanning the edges without opening the ribbons. "I told him about Caransay," she went on. "I described the island and the flowers on the machair, the shells on the beach, the birds and seals on Sgeir Caran. I told him about sailing and fishing with Grandfather Norrie and about how I played on the beaches and swam in the sea, climbed the hills and the headland. And I would make drawings for him, lots of drawings." She touched the bundle. "They are all here."

Dougal felt a sense of amazement, realizing the importance of that for her. "Your journals started with these letters," he said, "when you were a child."

She nodded. "He never wrote back to me. Except for a yearly invitation to come to Strathlin Castle for tutoring and for the fitting of a new wardrobe, he never wrote, never even mentioned the letters I sent. But I sent them, one after the other."

"He must have appreciated your loyalty," Dougal said. "He must have been glad to know you were fond of him."

She nodded. "Gruff as he was, I loved him. And I felt sorry for him," she added. "I thought he was lonely here. I did not realize how busy he was, building a shipping and banking empire. I was a child, and I scarcely knew about Matheson Bank then."

She walked around the great mahogany desk, fingers trailing. "He would sit here working, ignoring me when I stayed at the castle. When I was small, my mother would bring me in to talk to him, and I would tell him about our puppies on Caransay or show him my drawings. He would write or read, and I would chatter on. And then he would tell me to go."

She shrugged. "I thought he did not love me, that he tolerated me as an obligation, especially after my mother's death."

"But then he left everything to you. His sons were gone. There were no others in line for it?"

She shook her head. "Only cousins after us. And he designated me his heir—I did not even know about it. But when I came here to live, after his death, I discovered this box."

Dougal nodded. "He kept your letters."

"Every one I ever wrote. Every drawing I sent."

"He loved you very much. Perhaps he simply did not know how to express it at the time, and so he left you all he had."

She nodded as she put the letters back in the box and shut it away in the cabinet. "Nearly two million pounds, they told me, when the will was first read out, along with title and properties and ownership, though not authority, over the bank."

"Astonishing," he murmured.

"Incomprehensible to me. I did not want it. I railed against it, cried, refused at first. I wanted to stay on Caransay, for that was my home. But the will was ironclad. I had no choice, or the estate would go into the bank's control, and this beautiful house, all the others, would be locked to Lord Strathlin's descendants. I was to inherit it all, the title as well, which could be done easily enough in Scotland. I had so much to learn in the first years after the inheritance. Fortunately, Mrs. Shaw became my tutor and companion, as did Mrs. Berry, who had been my governess whenever I stayed here at Strathlin."

"Ah, Mrs. Berry. The lady who is fond of swimming." He grinned a little.

"And the bankers and solicitors were good men, well intentioned if not accustomed to dealing with young women outside their own families. They honored Lord Strathlin's wishes and brought me up to the task, holding my hands like a child that must learn to walk. Including," she added, looking up at him, "Sir Frederick."

Dougal nodded, frowning. "You mentioned that he has been helpful to you."

She nodded, faced the window, where clear afternoon light showed her deeply creased brow. "My grandmothers on Caransay believe that the inheritance came to me through . . . magic," she said. "From that night we spent together on the rock."

"Aye, magical indeed," he murmured. Then he realized that something greatly disquieted her, for her posture was taut and her eyes had darkened to a stormy blue-green.

"The legend," she said, "of the kelpie of Sgeir Caran who comes for his bride on the sea rock. He grants good fortune on his bride and on Caransay. . . ." She paused, turning to look at him, her eyes wide with that look of haunted emotion that he had seen when something troubled her greatly.

"What is it, love?" He reached out his hand to brush at her hair, which was loosely caught up in a black net after their lovemaking; a few wayward curling strands had slipped free. "It seems almost as if there is some truth to that legend."

She nodded. "I came by much good fortune after I spent the night on the sea rock, just as the legend says," she murmured.

"Even though the kelpie did not really appear to you," he said with a soft chuckle.

She did not smile, remaining so somber that it puzzled him. "My grandmothers believe it. And they . . . they have their reasons. Dougal, I need to show you something."

She slipped a finger under the high neck of her plaid bodice and drew out her small golden chain with its dangling locket. Wordlessly, she flipped the tiny catch and opened the twin oval frames.

He saw the ring made of threads and golden and brown hairs that she had woven that morning and beside it a tiny portrait, a towheaded infant whose sweet face reminded him of her. He thought it must be a picture of herself as a child, perhaps commissioned by her mother.

"Aye," he said, his voice roughened, low. "The ring. I know." He pulled out his pocket watch and opened the hidden compartment in it, a false backing lined with thin glass, then held it out to her. She gasped.

The glass circlet pressed his own woven ring, which she had made for him and slipped on his finger as he slept. "I've carried it with me everywhere," he said. "It was all I had of you, those years . . . and all the while, I was not sure you existed. I had this, which was real, but I wondered if it could be a bit of fairy thread, woven of magic."

"While I always knew that you *were* real. Too real," she said. "But my grandmothers thought you were the kelpie of the reef. They still believe it. They believe . . .

that we were married that night and that the ring proved it. And . . ." She paused, looked at him, her eyes lustrous and tormented.

"And what? What other proof could they have of it?" He almost smiled, but for her solemn mood.

"They say the kelpie of the sea rock bestows unusual good fortune if his bride pleases him greatly," she said, fingering the little open locket with its ring and its portrait, "and gives him a child."

He frowned, baffled. "But you—you did not—you are not—"

She gazed up at him. "I did."

He grabbed her by the shoulders. "What do you mean? What are you saying? A child came of that night? Our child?"

She nodded, her eyes swimming in new tears, some of them spilling free down her cheeks.

"For the love of God, woman," he said, nearly shaking her. "Tell me!"

"Iain," she whispered. "He's . . . Iain."

"My God," he breathed. "How could you not tell me that!" He nearly shouted, stepping away. Shoving a hand through his hair, he turned back to her, stunned. "Iain?"

She nodded, her lower lip wobbly. "I have kept the secret of it for years, and I knew I had to tell you, but I . . . I could not, until I trusted you and knew you would not try to take him away from me."

He stared hard at her, not certain how he felt—angry, elated, still shocked. "My God. I would never do that."

"I know that now. I did not know it then."

"Fair enough." He rubbed his brow, thinking. "Who knows about this?"

"Very few people. My grandparents on Caransay and Fergus, of course. And Mrs. Shaw and Mr. Hamilton." She paused. "And . . . and Sir Frederick knows."

Dougal felt a cold chill run through him. "Sir Frederick?"

She nodded. "Somehow he found out from a doctor who tended me in the early months. Frederick told me that he knew and that he would tell everyone that I had an illegitimate child being fostered with a family on Caransay. So I . . ."

"So you promised to marry him," he finished for her. "That supreme bastard," he muttered under his breath.

Meg squeezed her eyes shut against an onslaught of tears, and lowered her head. "Dougal, I am so sorry," she whispered. "I have made a mess of this . . . from the very . . . beginning."

"Hush." He crossed to her in two strides and pulled her into his arms. "Hush, my bonny," he murmured. "When I think of you alone with this—bearing a child, not knowing the father, I am angry at myself for allowing it to happen to you. But now that it is out, we can fix it easily enough."

"How—how is that?" she gulped.

"Well, I suppose I ought to marry you," he whispered against the soft crown of her head. "I do not see how it can be avoided."

She laughed, a watery burble. "But what about Frederick?"

He held her for a moment, considering. Then it came to him like a sunburst of pure thought, illuminating, exhilarating. "Why, Mrs. Stewart," he said, drawing back to look down at her, "we've been married for seven years."

Meg gaped at him. "We . . . Oh! The rings!" She nodded. "My grandmothers insist that there is an old custom of self-made marriage in Scotland."

"I've heard of it," he said. "I believe all a couple has to do is declare their love and exchange rings, and they are considered married without benefit of clergy or even witnesses."

"But we did not declare our love."

"Madam, I rather think we did." He dipped down to kiss her. "And Iain is the proof of it."

"You would be willing to tell Frederick this?"

"I would be delighted." He gathered her close. Then he gasped, remembering something. Meg pulled back to look up at him. "The train," he said. "I forgot. I have to get to the train." He let her go, took her hand to pull her toward the door.

"Dougal, surely you can miss the train, after all this," she said. "Take the next one."

"No," he said firmly, tugging her along. "I agreed to be back on Sgeir Caran tomorrow. There is a meeting assembling there of some lighthouse commissioners and a few investors."

"Stay the night," she said. "Take the morning train."

"I have to go." He stopped, looked down at her. "Sir Frederick Matheson is in that party."

"Dear God," she said. "Iain is on Caransay, and Frederick hates you and me just now!"

"Exactly what I was thinking," he muttered grimly as he pulled her with him through the library.

"I'm going with you," she insisted.

"No. Stay here. Let me take care of this."

"I'm going with you. Mr. Hamilton!" she called as they entered the hallway. "Mr. Hamilton! Mrs. Shaw!"

"No, Meg," Dougal said, spinning her to face him. "The fellow could be very dangerous. I will not allow you to go!"

"Allow me?" She stared up at him indignantly.

"I do not want you to go, madam," he amended, speaking through clenched teeth.

Guy Hamilton appeared in the foyer from a side door with Mrs. Shaw just behind him. "Madam, what is it?" he asked.

"I need a ticket for the Edinburgh to Glasgow train," she said. "And Angela, if you please, I need a satchel of clothing and a traveling cape and some things for a train journey. Oh, do hurry!" Mrs. Shaw nodded and grabbed her skirts, rushing up the steps, and Guy went at a half run into the library.

"Buy the ticket when we get to Waverley Station," Dougal grumbled. "And wear whatever your grandmother can lend you. We have no time—we must go."

"I do not handle the cash. Mr. Hamilton handles the cash."

"I will pay for the blasted ticket myself," Dougal said.

"And he makes all my travel arrangements. We'll need a carriage brought round, too," Meg called over her shoulder as Dougal pulled her toward the door.

"We can take your carriage from here, but I have already hired a carriage from Glasgow to Oban, and all the rest. You'll have to travel with me—as my wife, I suppose," he said.

"I suppose that would be fine." She glanced up at him.

"Good. Here comes Mrs. Shaw," he said, as the young woman ran down the steps with a tapestry satchel in one hand, something cotton and lacy spilling from it. Dougal rushed over, grabbed it from her while thanking her, and ran back to the door where Meg waited.

The butler appeared from the shadows to open the door for them, and Guy rushed out of the library with a wallet in his hand, which he pressed into Meg's hands. "I think this will be sufficient for the trip, madam," he said. "If you need more—"

"I will take care of her expenses," Dougal said. "Thank you, and good day."

Meg embraced Mrs. Shaw, who then draped a black half cape on Meg's shoulders and helped her fasten a little black bonnet on her head and pull on gray kid gloves.

"Madam, you will need an escort," Mrs. Shaw said. "I'll gather my things."

"I have an escort. Mr. Stewart . . . is my husband."

"He's what?" Hamilton and Mrs. Shaw stared at her. "When?"

"We're married," Meg said, her cheeks flushed, "and we've been so for a very long time." She looked up at Dougal, who smiled. "It was a well-kept secret."

"Very well kept," Hamilton said, frowning.

"We'll renew our vows with a ceremony," Dougal added, "just as soon as we return from the Isles."

"Farewell," Meg said, and Dougal pulled her out the front door while her assistants and her butler gaped after them.

As they hastened through the yard toward the stables, Dougal took her arm. "I'm glad you're going with me after all."

"I want to be there when you confront Sir Frederick about the evil rumors he plans to spread."

"I'm referring to the hours of travel time we have ahead of us, when you will tell me all about the past seven years," he answered as they rushed along. "I want to know about Iain's birth. I want to hear everything—what he was like as an infant and as a smaller boy. What he said, what he did. I want to know what I've missed as our son was growing."

Meg slipped her arm around his waist, and he encircled her shoulders and hugged her to him.

"Now let's hurry," he said as the driver brought the carriage out of the coach house, "and find our son."

Chapter Twenty-two

"Out to the hard place, you say," Norrie said, "and you just coming in from Tobermory the now?" He worked the rudder as he spoke, with full sail unfurled on his fishing boat while a fast streaming wind moved them toward the Caran Reef.

"Aye, Norrie MacNeill, out to the hard place straightaway," Dougal answered. "I need to go to the sea rock immediately, but I want you to take Meg back to Caransay with you."

"I am going with you," Meg protested. She leaned toward him as she insisted, clutching her half cape at its buttoned collar. The journey to the Western Isles by train and carriage had taken so long that the day had grown dark, and she and Dougal had spent the night at the resort hotel in Tighnabruaich—as Mr. and Mrs. Stewart—and while the sweet joy of those hours with him lingered in her body and her heart, the urgency of traveling to the Isles as quickly as possible had not changed.

"You are not coming with me," Dougal said.

Norrie lifted a brow. "I am thinking that everyone is wanting to go out to the hard place today," he muttered.

Meg exchanged glances with Dougal. "Everyone?"

"Who else went out there?" Dougal asked sharply.

"A steamer came to Mull yesterday," he said, "with a group of men dressed all in black. They were wearing tall hats—like ravens, they looked, and ready to feast on your lighthouse, I am thinking."

"Quite possibly," Dougal said.

"They stayed the night in Tobermory and sailed out to the rock this morning. I saw them when I was there. The fellow who owns Guga was with them, the one who has come to see you, Margaret."

"Sir Frederick," Meg said quickly.

"He's the one. He said he saw you both on the mainland and that Dougal Stewart would know that he and the other gentlemen were going out to inspect the rock today. He said you might be along later, Mr. Stewart. A good thing I was still in Tobermory, fetching the mail from the mainland steamer, so that you did not have to hire a fisherman to take you over to the hard place," Norrie added pragmatically.

"I'll go with you out to the rock," Meg told Dougal firmly.

"You will not, Meg," he answered.

"Meg, is it?" Norrie asked mildly, hand resting on the rudder. He smiled a little. "If you're calling her Meg, you are now good friends, I am thinking." His blue eyes glinted.

"More than good friends, sir," Dougal said. "And she's not going out to the rock."

"I am," she said. "I must."

"Well, everyone wants to go to the rock. Wee Iain was a happy lad because Sir Frederick let him sail with them—"

Meg gasped. "Iain is with them?"

"What the devil!" Dougal growled.

"*Ach,* the young one came with me to Tobermory this morning, and he wanted to ride the steamer ship back again, since all the men were on it, so he and

Fergus went with them. Sir Frederick said it would be all right and that we could all trust him with the care of the lad."

"Thank God Fergus is with him, at least," Dougal murmured.

"I am going out to the rock with you," Meg said, and she looked at Dougal. "And no doubt of it."

"Aye, then," Dougal agreed, frowning, while Norrie grunted in amusement. Meg realized with relief that her grandfather did not suspect Frederick might scheme to harm anyone.

She reached over to clasp Dougal's hand, his answering grip strong on her gloved fingers. They rode in silence, the waves splashing against the sides of the boat as Norrie shifted the rudder to speed them through the currents.

She drew a deep and anxious breath. Ahead loomed the long, distinctive shape of Sgeir Caran. As they drew closer, she saw the dark shapes of men moving about on top of the rock, although she could not identify anyone from this distance.

Soon Norrie took up the oars to guide the boat slowly and carefully through the treacherous path of the reef as they approached Sgeir Caran from a southerly direction. He concentrated on his task, and no one spoke. Meg watched the powerful surges and eddies as the water sliced and swirled through the maze of upthrusting and submerged rocks, and she glanced anxiously at Dougal. He smiled, quick and somber, and squeezed her hand.

The black bulk of the rock soon loomed over them, blocking much of the daylight in its shadow. Norrie drew in beside the quay, boat rising and falling with the slop of the waves. Two men came down the steps to assist them, one of them Alan Clarke.

"Hullo!" Alan said heartily as he assisted them onto

the stone quay. "It's good to see you, Miss MacNeill! What a pleasant surprise." He turned to Dougal. "You're back just in time, sir."

"I know," Dougal said as they climbed the steps cut into the rock. Norrie came with them, as well, refusing mildly to turn back to Caransay; Meg realized that her grandfather's acute perception and natural curiosity had alerted him to the tension that she and Dougal felt. "I hear we have visitors."

"Oh, them," Alan said. "They want only to look at what we're doing. Thinking of contributing to the funds for this lighthouse and future projects, so it's a verra good thing."

"Indeed?" Dougal turned to look at Meg, who frowned.

"Though it's an inconvenience to have them here at such a time," Alan continued.

"Such a time?" Dougal asked. "I assume you've been working on the repairs following that gale just before I left."

"Aye, we've cleaned up a good bit o' the damage and repaired what we could. We've retrieved all but one of the stones that were swept into the water, and that one is roped and ready to bring up. But there is a problem with the rock beneath the water, sir," Alan said. "Evan Mackenzie went doon the deep to check the rock after our repairs—we were bringing up those dressed stones that fell, too—and he discovered a crack in the foundation stone."

"What!"

"Aye, sir. A sizeable fissure, from what he says. He'll be glad to see you're back, as will the rest of the men. Evan has been anxious to go doon to have a better look at it and to begin measures to shore it up. I hope you recovered some funding. We'll need it. Evan thinks we're going to need to build a sea wall."

Dougal swore and began to ask Alan further questions. As they reached the topmost surface of the rock, Meg felt the wind push over the plateau, whipping her cloak and skirt.

Evan Mackenzie called a greeting and hastened toward them, and Dougal ran to speak with him while Norrie, Alan, and other members of the work crew gathered around.

Meg turned and saw that a group of men in dark suits and hats, some with canes, all of them looking out of place on the sea rock, were strolling around the foundation cavity. Sir Frederick Matheson stood in the midst of the visitors. His gloved hand clasped Iain's as the boy walked beside him.

"Iain!" she called, running forward, skirts billowing. Seeing her, the boy broke free and ran to her. She caught him in her arms, dropping to her knees to embrace him, her heart pounding. Straightening, she looked up at the man who approached.

"Sir Frederick," she said coolly.

"Why, Lady Strathlin, what a fetching picture. And rather surprising to see you out here in such a wild place."

She touched Iain's shoulder. "Might I ask why you are here, sir?"

"I am interested in contributing funds to the lighthouse," he said. "I came out with some members of the Northern Lighthouse Commission, who wanted to see the progress on this rock."

"But, Sir Frederick," she said pointedly, "to my knowledge, you have no funds to contribute. You've been borrowing from me for the last three years. I must wonder why you are making promises to the lighthouse fund. Have you some other source of wealth?"

"Well, to be honest, madam, I expect to be married soon to a very wealthy baroness. Please don't tell me that you have changed your mind, Margaret. That would be so . . . unpleasant." As he smiled, he reached out to touch Iain's golden head.

She pulled the boy away from him, hiding Iain partly behind the fullness of her skirt and petticoats. "I have most definitely changed my mind," she said. "I will not marry you, Frederick. In fact, I cannot marry you, ever. It would be impossible."

He glowered down at her. "You gave me your promise."

"The lady is already married," Dougal said, striding toward them. "Good day, Sir Frederick." He tipped his hat.

"She's what?" Frederick barked out. "What a preposterous thing to say. And what would you know about it?"

"I am her husband," Dougal said, shifting his arm so that Meg could slip her hand in the crook of his elbow, a natural gesture of familiarity. She tilted her head prettily.

"And I am his wife," she said.

"That's impossible," Frederick muttered. "I left you only a few days ago! You scarcely know each other."

"We were married years ago," Dougal said, glancing down at Meg, "in a simple Hebridean ceremony. We were . . . estranged for a while. But we have happily resolved our differences."

"I refuse to believe that. If you think to save the lady from the embarrassment she has earned, sir, it will not suffice. I suppose you know whose child that is."

"Aye, we all know whose child that is," Norrie said, walking up to them. "Come here, lad," he said to Iain. "Fergus is over there looking for you. Run and see what he wants." Iain took off.

"Walk," Meg called without thinking. "He did not mean run!"

"That lad," Norrie said, looking at Frederick, "is

the child of my granddaughter and her husband, this fine fellow, Mr. Stewart, who was a visitor to our reef and our island several years ago. They were wed then, as they told you. I am thinking all of Caransay's residents will be ready to swear to that."

Meg looked at her grandfather, smiling through sudden tears. "Yes," she said, turning back. "All of them will swear it."

"Though we are waiting for another ceremony to renew those vows," Norrie said, looking hard at Meg and Dougal.

"Preposterous," Frederick said. He turned to the crowd gathering around them, made up of lighthouse commissioners and workmen, including Alan and Evan. "This is absurd!"

"It's true," Meg said. "I have known my husband for a long time. We met years ago on this very spot." Meg smiled at Dougal, her hand snugged in his arm.

"We could not tell anyone before this," Dougal said. "We kept it secret, for it was an awkward situation until we decided that we could carry on with our marriage."

"Congratulations, Lady Strathlin," Evan Mackenzie said.

"Lady Strathlin!" Alan Clarke exclaimed. Dougal leaned forward to murmur a fast explanation while Alan gaped at her.

Evan bowed to Meg, and she offered her hand. "Your husband is a fine man, and a lucky one, too," he said.

"Ah, thank you, Lord Glencarron," she said, as Evan kissed her gloved knuckles. "How very nice to see you again."

"And you, madam," he murmured. "Meg, I've known you from the first," he whispered, smiling, his lips close to her glove. "I saw you at a concert last year in Edinburgh, and I never forgot bonny Lady Strathlin."

"Thank you for keeping it to yourself," she said.

Evan released her hand. "Would I ruin my lady's holiday?" He smiled and turned to Dougal. "Whenever your marriage took place, sir, I can honestly say I am delighted. And the news of a secret marriage—and a secret child, am I to believe?—will simply delight everyone who hears it. I will certainly add my hearty approval of such a romantic circumstance to any who might care to hear my opinion." He fixed Matheson with a stare.

"Thank you," Meg breathed. "Thank you."

Evan then glanced at the black-clad, somber men who stood nearby. Most of them nodded, smiled, or murmured congratulations.

"Lord Glencarron?" Frederick demanded. "The son and heir of the Earl of Kildonan?"

"The very one, sir," Evan said. "And you are—?" Matheson sputtered while Meg introduced him. "You seem to be disappointed in the lady's marriage, Sir Frederick, though I have no doubt you are the sort of gentleman who can be gracious about it."

Matheson mumbled something, then turned on his heel and stalked off, accompanied by a few of the commissioners.

Evan turned to Dougal. "Are you ready, sir?"

"Aye," Dougal said, and he turned to Meg. "We're going down to look at the flaw in the rock."

"Now?" she said. "But the waves are picking up."

"Just for a few minutes," Dougal said. "I need to see it for myself, so that we can best decide what to do about it, if anything. I'll be right back, love," he said. "We can safely stay down for only ten minutes or so. You know that. Iain might find our diving venture quite interesting. If you'll send him along, we'll show him the gear as we're getting ready."

She nodded and watched him walk away with Evan. Frowning, she felt a heavy sense of dread in the pit of her stomach.

All seemed resolved with Frederick, who could not

threaten her again. His objections and arguments had been laid to rest.

There was nothing to worry about, she told herself.

As the wind whipped at her skirts, she looked out to sea and saw how choppy and opaque the waves had become. Far to the west, the sky was gray and heavy.

And then she knew the source of her unease.

Gauntleted hands careful on the curving slope of the rock, Dougal followed its contours. The water was neither as clear nor as still as he liked for the task, but he could see well enough to judge the dimension of the flaw.

Evan pointed to a particular area, and Dougal made his way there, his steps clumsy, a strange slow dance to the click and cadence of the air that rushed in and out of his helmet valves.

Nearby, the two platforms that had lowered the divers banged rhythmically against the side of the rocky underwater hill. Higher on the incline, the single dressed stone that had tumbled into the sea was trussed with heavy ropes, ready to be craned back to the surface. Seeing that, Dougal realized and appreciated how much work his crew had done in his absence.

Turning back to check the rock face, he soon saw the long black fissure. It split the rock from well above his head to the ocean floor, which varied in depth here, rolling like the hilly land above the water.

He walked up the slope with Evan, so that he stood not far beneath the surface. He could easily see the dark mass of the rock rising above the water, could see a boat or two on the surface while waves rushed overhead. The water was flowing much faster, he noticed. They could not stay down long.

From the canvas bag at his belt, he removed a measuring tape made of oiled cloth and stretched it over the crevice. Floating there, tugged by the underwater currents even in his heavy weighted suit, he managed to estimate the length of the crack, moving hand over hand along the rock. Reaching his arm deep into the fissure, he realized it was nearly as long as his arm. A few small fish drifted out of the crevice, and he waved them away.

Making his way toward Evan, he caught his attention with gestures. Floating, sinking, Mackenzie measured the rock with Dougal, then signaled that they should go up to the surface.

Dougal returned a wave. He had seen what he needed to see down here. The split in the rock was large enough to be of some concern, particularly considering the weight of the gigantic tower that would be erected on its surface.

"Dougal." Alan Clarke's voice came through the speaking tube, surprisingly clear through yards of tubing.

"Aye," Dougal answered. "All is well down here. Up there?"

"A storm is brewing in the west. It will not reach us for an hour or more, Norrie says, but the wind and waves are strong. Come up. We are preparing to return to Caransay."

In the few minutes that he and Evan had been underwater, the water had grown murky as light faded above the surface, and the water currents had become strong and noticeably colder.

"Aye, Alan," he answered. "We'll come up."

Dougal pointed upward, and Mackenzie motioned that he understood. They walked slowly toward the wooden platforms suspended on ropes and hovering nearby. Dougal stepped onto the wooden deck, tugged three times on one of the ropes to indicate his readiness, and held on.

Within a minute or so, he felt the platform being drawn upward through the water. Holding on to the ropes, he glanced down to see Evan stepping onto the second platform.

A strong wave washed through like a train, smashing Dougal's platform against the broad side of the sea rock, knocking so hard that he was nearly thrown from the wooden planks. He held on, bending his knees to keep his balance. Reaching out with one foot, he shoved the platform away from the rock, where it had wedged and slowly felt it rise again.

The crew who craned his platform upward, and Evan's as well, halted the divers' ascent often as a precaution. Feeling the deck stop again, Dougal clung to the ropes and took slow breaths, giving his lungs time to adapt. With a lurch, the platform began to move again.

Another wave cracked the planking against the rock. This time the impact spun him outward, and his boots slid off the wooden deck.

Scrabbling up the rocky slope, breathing as carefully as he could, he snatched the rope of the platform again and tried to step onto the shifting deck. Seeing Evan ascend slowly past him, Dougal gave him a reassuring gesture to show that all was well.

Well enough, he told himself, if he could get back on the platform. Propped precariously against the steep incline of the hillside, with a wealth of water sweeping around it, the deck bucked like a horse. Moments later, Dougal managed to climb on and tug at the rope again, signaling to be lifted upward.

A horrible sound grew to a loud rumble, and the world shuddered all around him. He glanced up to see the trussed granite block break loose from its moorings and begin to slide down the rocky slope. Dougal swung his weight to yank the platform out of the way, but as the stone grazed past, it caught the platform ropes and ripped the deck away from him.

Four tons of granite scraped to a halt, bumping past Dougal's shoulder and knee in a near miss. Silt and debris clouded the water to midnight darkness, and Dougal could feel the barrier of the immense stone just in front of him. The monster had missed him by inches. Breathing a sigh of shaky relief, he pushed upward to float past it.

But he could not move. His lead boot was caught by its thick toe ridge just under the corner of the granite block.

Chapter Twenty-three

The wind grew stronger, blowing Meg's cape, flapping the ribbons of her bonnet. The western sky condensed and thickened into a dark, boiling mass.

"That storm will blow over this way before nightfall, I am thinking," Norrie said, standing beside her.

She nodded, unable to shake her deep sense of fear. "Oh, thank God, they're coming up now," she said, seeing the commotion at the rim of the cliffside, where the diving platforms had been lowered. With Norrie, she ran to the iron railing embedded near the edge and looked down.

A diver burst out of the water, clinging to his platform ropes, and the men hauled him upward. The man gestured insistently as Alan and others unscrewed the bolts that secured his helmet to the wide brass collar that covered his shoulders.

Meg saw Evan's head emerge, saw him gasp in a breath. "Dougal," he said. "He's caught! The block broke loose."

"Oh, my God!" Meg rushed forward. "Dougal—is he harmed?"

"I did not see. I cannot say," Evan told her.

Alan ran to the speaking tube and set the funnel to

his mouth. "Dougal! Dougal, are you there!" He pressed it to his ear for a reply, then nodded, waving to the others to show that he heard something. "His foot is caught, he says," Alan told them. "He's not harmed, but he cannot get free."

"His hoses?" Evan snapped.

"Open and fine so far, though pressed between the incline and the stone block," Alan replied, after asking.

Mackenzie grabbed his helmet from the man who held it. "I'm going back down."

"If you do that, man, you're risking your life," Alan said. "Your lungs cannot take the up and down of the pressures. Let someone else go down."

"Who else is there to do it?" Evan growled. "No one else is trained to use this equipment but Dougal, me, and you, Alan. And we all know you've acquired a dread of the water since that storm that nearly swept you and Dougal away years ago."

Alan stared hard at him. "I'll go doon the deep," he said.

"I'm suited up," Evan said, and he put the helmet back on, gesturing his hands for the crew men to screw it into place. Within seconds, he was ready and waiting on the platform, which was quickly lowered back into the water.

Alan called orders to the men on the air pumps and hose cranks. "Give Dougal as much slack as you can, and keep the airflow steady," he reminded them, though they were capable men and were already doing what was needed. "Aye, that's it." He stood murmuring into the funnel, then listened to Dougal's answer.

Meg paced back and forth, watching while the platform surged down into the water. She whirled, skirt billowing, and came face-to-face with Sir Frederick. He grabbed her by the elbow.

"What do you want?" she snapped. "Let me go."

"Come away from the edge," he said. "It isn't safe."

"Leave me be," she said and broke loose to begin pacing again.

"I want to help," he said.

"I find that hard to believe," she replied. "Just stay back and let them do what must be done."

"I am not so heartless as you think," Frederick said. "It disturbs me that I was wrong about you and that in my desperate love for you, I acted poorly."

"Poorly!" she gasped. "And I would hardly call that love."

"I regret my behavior. I admit I thought ill of Stewart, and now he's in difficulty. I want to help."

Pacing, she turned and stopped to stare mistrustfully at him. Norrie came to join her, staring equally at Frederick.

"If you've had a change of heart, go see if you can help with the cranks or the pulleying," he said, "and leave my granddaughter be."

Frederick turned and ran to offer his services, taking off his coat to lend a hand on the crank arm of one of the giant spools that held the hoses and ropes, and Norrie turned away to help the men who were guiding the ropes and hoses that spilled over the side of the rock into the water.

Seeing that Alan was speaking to Dougal through the funnel and hose, Meg ran there. "Let me talk to him," she said, and Alan handed her the funnel.

She held the metal cone to her mouth. "Dougal," she said. "Dougal!" Then she moved the cup to her ear for the reply.

"Meg?" His voice sounded strange, so far below, touched with a tinny sound. The funnel smelled of the rubber hosing.

"Dougal! Oh, God," she said, gasping out. Alan put a hand on her shoulder to caution her, and she drew a breath, calmed herself to sound calmer for him. "Are you harmed?"

"I'm fine," the voice answered. "My lead boot is

caught by its edge. Evan is here. We will work it free, my love."

"My love," she echoed. "I'm here."

"Good. Don't worry. Give the funnel to Alan, lass."

She handed the speaking tube back to Alan and waited while he spoke with Dougal and they discussed what must be done with ropes and the great steel crane that was even now being wheeled into place to haul the giant stone away from the trapped man.

A gust of wind tore over the face of the rock, whipping her skirts and cape, threatening to take her bonnet from her. She withstood it, an arm to her hat, an arm to her chest, and looked to the west, where the sky roiled, lead colored and foreboding. Far out to sea, she could see the breakers rising, white with froth, peaking and rushing toward the reef. Droplets of rain spattered her, cold and stinging.

She remembered, suddenly, vividly, standing on top of this very rock while she endured heavy winds and lashing rains. But she'd had Dougal with her then, Dougal's arms around her, his body and his courage shielding her.

Alan spoke into the funnel again and looked toward the crews who worked furiously on the machinery, ropes, and hoses behind him. "They canna move the stone between the two of them," he called. "We'll need more hands on the ropes up here to haul that stone up and free Dougal!" The crew rushed to man more of the ropes and intensify the effort to raise the stone.

Meg turned to Alan. "How can two men move that stone at all down there?" she asked. "I don't understand. Can we not just lift it up using the ropes and cranes?"

"It's not as casy as that," he said grimly. "The stone has to be trussed with ropes for lifting. But Evan and Dougal can shift the stone just enough to free Dougal's foot."

"But it weighs tons!"

"On land it does," he said. "Down there, 'tis a different matter, the weight of things. That stone can be shifted with the strength of two or three men." He stripped off his coat as he spoke and unbuttoned his vest. "I beg your pardon, Miss MacNeill—er, Lady Strathlin. I'm going down there to help." He pulled off his boots and tossed them aside, so that he stood in shirtsleeves and stockinged feet. His thick ash-blond hair ruffled in the wind, and his linen shirt blew flat against his broad chest and heavily muscled arms.

"But Alan," she said, "you are . . . bothered by the water."

"My friend is in danger," he said firmly, and he turned to inform the men that he was diving in to help. "Dougal says he's but forty or fifty feet down," he told them.

"You have no gear," Meg said.

"Och, a man can go down that far without gear, just holding his breath. But he canna stay down, like the lads with the hoses. I'll do what I can, then come up for air." He handed the funnel to Meg. "Talk to him. He will want to hear your voice. And pray for us all, lass." He winked at her and turned away.

Pausing on the cliff edge, beaten by winds and dappled by the rains, Alan fisted his hands for a moment. Then he dove cleanly over the side, and Meg saw him cut through the water.

"Dougal," she said into the funnel, "Alan is coming down."

"What the devil—aye. Fool!" Dougal replied.

"He says he can help you push the stone," she told him.

"Aye," Dougal replied. Then there was silence.

"Dougal?"

"Meg—my love . . . Air . . ."

"Dougal, what is it?"

Silence. Meg caught her breath, fisted her hand to her mouth, looked down over the side. Bubbles rose where the various hoses and ropes entered the water, and she thought she saw shadows moving far below, but the surface of the water was increasingly agitated. "Dougal?"

She turned, saw Frederick and the other men busy on the cranks and pulleys and hoses, saw Fergus with Iain close at his side, watching from a distance, saw Norrie hurrying toward her.

"He's not answering me," she said, and Norrie took the funnel from her.

"Dougal Stewart," he said, and he put it to his ear. "Dougal!"

Meg looked down at the greenish, slopping surface of the water, roiling with peaks and waves, and thought about Dougal far below, and her heart wanted to burst. He had to be saved. She could not bear to stand on the rock and wait, listening to the urgent silence while he lingered far below, in trouble.

She could not bear to live without him now.

Though she knew that he had friends to help him, she wanted to do what Alan had done, tear off her clothing and dive down to be with him, to help him. He had saved Iain and so many others. He had saved her in countless ways, from the first moment she had met him—saved her, body and soul.

Tearing off her bonnet, she set it aside, hardly caring when it skittered over the edge into the water. She was already working the buttons of her cape and bending to undo the loops and buttons that fastened her ankle boots.

"What are you doing?" Norrie asked, then lifted the funnel again. "Dougal Stewart, answer me!" he called.

Below, Alan burst out of the water, gasping, treading in the waves. "The hoses!" he called up to the men on the edge. "Dougal's hoses are caught! I need a lever to move the stone!" One of the men climbed downward and extended a long iron rod. Alan snatched for it, then dove down with it.

Meg lifted her skirts and reached beneath to undo the tapes of her petticoats. Without a crinoline, four petticoats provided fashionable fullness, and she wished desperately that she had worn the simple garments common to Isleswomen. She tore at the buttons of her blouse.

"What in blazes are you doing?" Frederick called, his hands busy on a cranking handle. "Here, you cannot do that, madam!"

She ignored him, slipping out of her blouse, dropping her skirt to stand in chemise and knickers. "Get this thing off me," she said to Norrie, yanking at the laces of her stays.

"Madam!" Frederick said. Some of the other men protested.

"Turn away," she said over her shoulder as her grandfather gave the corset cords a yank, "though I'm sure you've all seen a lady in her knickers. But none of you seem inclined to ruin your fine suits—and these other men are all essential on the equipment. There is no one to spare. Fergus, keep Iain with you, or he'll fall in," she called, as Fergus ran toward her with Iain chasing behind him.

She had to do this. She could not bear to watch this any longer, knowing that she could help as well as any of the men, and better than some, with her smaller frame and nimble hands and her ability to swim and dive. Not all the men could help, she knew. Fergus, for all his fishing skills, did not swim well.

"Lady Strathlin!" one of the commissioners in black called.

"I'm going in," she announced to everyone who stared at her in dumb shock. She walked to the edge of the cliff.

"Dougal Stewart," Norrie said into the funnel, "if

you do not answer, I am thinking your lass is coming down there herself. Go find your kelpie, girl," he added to her.

The wind bit cold and cruel through the thin cotton layers of her garments. She stood in the open, looked down at the water below, bent her knees and poised her hands.

Eerie and murky, the strange watery world around him grew chilly and dim. He shivered, felt the deep cold entering his bones. The rubber suit, normally inflated with air to add buoyancy and warmth, had torn along the sleeve and now filled with water, growing heavy and exposing him to the cold brunt of the water. The valves in his helmet clicked and whooshed, the reassuring sound of air—and life—but the air seemed odd, thin, and he could not fill his lungs.

Nor did he have strength left to shove. Evan pushed beside him, and Alan Clarke had appeared not long ago to lend his power to the effort, setting his bullish shoulder to the block. Now they repeated the attempt, and he heard the scrape of the stone on the underwater hillside, felt his lead boot give way. He pulled it back, motioning sluggishly to show that it was free.

But he could not escape to the surface. Shifting the block from his foot had trapped his hoses, compressing the flow of air into his helmet. And the world was growing dimmer.

Alan surged upward for fresh air, came down again, carrying a long iron rod used for levering stones into place. He set its narrow tip against the base of the stone and directed Evan and Dougal to push again.

A strange buzzing began in his ears as he pushed. He tried to fill his lungs but could not. The airflow had diminished so much due to the compressed hose, that he was in serious jeopardy and could easily suffocate.

The stone shifted a little, and a burst of fresh air

came through. Dougal gasped it in, exhaled, heard the clicking valves. The stone shifted again, and the air valves quieted ominously.

He had to get free, had to, or die here, at the foot of the reef where his parents had died so long ago. He had faced risks, stared down enough danger in his life to realize that sooner or later the wheel of fortune would spin away from his control and he would lose.

But he did not want to die. He had far too much reason to live. The woman he adored, who held all of his heart in her gentle, whimsical keeping, waited for him on the sea rock, where their love, and their life together, had begun. Their beautiful young son waited with her, the child he had just discovered and could not lose so soon.

He would come back to them no matter what it took.

Gasping for another breath, he realized that the air was stale, that nothing fresh had come through the hose. He gestured to the other men, tried to show them that he was suffocating. But even then, there was little they could do. He realized he might die here even while his friends tried to save him.

He gazed up at the surface, where the water swirled fast, the waves so heavy now that the sea all around them was an obscure and dusky green.

Alan burst away and went upward again. Dougal pressed the last of his strength and weight into the unyielding stone, and the dimness grew alarming. He clutched at the valves, ready to tear out the hoses. Clutching at the helmet, he tried to unfasten the bolts. He would rather takc his chances without his gear than let his gear be the cause of his death.

He felt the stone shift again, and a trickle of air came in, enough to clear his head for a moment. Alan was back, and the men shoved once more at the entrapping granite block.

Growing dizzy, Dougal realized that the airflow had stopped yet again. His head pounded, and his vision grew shadowy.

He looked upward, and a vision emerged from above. A pale, graceful sea fairy undulated through the water toward him, her white garments veiling her beautiful form, her hair streaming out behind her. She lowered beside him like an angel, placed her hands on either side of his helmet, and looked at him.

God, how he loved her. He reached out for her, but she slipped away, turning, to take the bar from Alan's hands. Following their direction, she inserted the bar under the lip of the stone. As the men pushed, she pressed down on the lever.

The stone shifted, and this time, with the added help of the bar, it stayed up long enough for Dougal to snatch the air hose free. He looped it around his shoulder as he usually did, his movements slow and lethargic, and he moved as if in a dream.

Evan and Alan grabbed him by the arms and pulled him onto the platform, tugging at the ropes in a frantic signal. As the deck began to rise with the two divers, Alan Clarke let go of the ropes and took the sea fairy's hand. He pulled her upward with him as they surged toward the shining, swirling surface.

Moments later, Dougal burst through the water into freedom.

Meg stood shivering, draped in a blanket produced from somewhere, while men worked frantically to free Dougal's helmet. When it was lifted away at last, she saw his ashen face, but it was the most blessed sight she had ever beheld.

She waited while the men worked to loosen his gauntlets, weighted belt, and boots. Several others worked to free Evan of his gear. Alan, nearby, held the folds of another blanket around his shoulders. She waited, stepping forward in impatience, but Dougal's gaze lingered on hers, telling her that he was well, that he was safe.

He gave her a slow and secret smile, only hers, that only she understood. Meg came forward as they lifted away his brass collar and removed his heavy belt, and she sank to her knees beside him.

He extended his free arm to pull her close, his treated canvas suit stiff and wet against her, gushing seawater from a tear in the fabric. Slipping her arms around his neck, she did not care who saw or what they thought.

"Oh, God, Dougal," she whispered, pressing her face to his.

"Love," he said, "you came down there like a sea fairy. I thought I was dreaming—or dying. I thought you were not real."

"I am so real," she murmured into his ear, only for him, and snuffled then against his cheek while he laughed low and soft. His hand pressed on her back, strong and reassuring, and she felt his lips against her hair.

The wind blew a hard blast, bringing rain, and she lifted her head to look at the mass of clouds coming nearer.

"We'd best get into the boats," Norrie said. "Gentlemen, come this way, as many as can fit in my boat. Alan, can you take another boatload of men from this rock? Are you in shape for the rowing?"

"Aye. I'm fine," Alan said, and he began to run.

Meg separated from Dougal, standing beside him while he was still being divested of his boots. "Where's Iain?" she asked. "He should go with Norrie. Fergus—where—oh!"

She heard a shout at the same time as she saw Fergus running across the plateau of the rock. Then she saw why, and she screamed out and began to run as well.

Iain stood at the lower edge of the rock, where the

incline slid down to the water. He turned to look at them, and Meg ran toward him, her bare feet slapping on the wet rock while the wind beat hard against her, shoving her backward, but she pushed onward.

"Iain," she called, words torn in the wind. "Iain, come here," she urged. Rain pattered around her now. The winds were picking up, and the waves had begun to slosh hard against the rock, rising higher with each new current.

"I want to see the kelpie that comes here," he said. "I want to see him."

"Not today," she told him calmly. "Come here."

After a moment, the boy turned and began to walk toward her, and she let out a sigh of relief. Dougal appeared beside her, having scrambled out of his diving suit, still clad in layered shirts and leggings, with a blanket round his shoulders.

"Iain, lad," he called. "Come here. That's it. Stay away from the edge." He began to walk forward.

A gust of wind came through, and with it a heavy wave that knocked Iain to his knees. He fell, crying out, and scrambled to his feet. Then Meg saw the wave that arched behind and over him, and she screamed out. Together, she and Dougal surged toward their son, who was caught in a downward crash of water.

A new wave surged over him and sucked back, this time pulling Iain with it, so that the boy scrabbled with hands and arms covered in water. Meg screamed out, and Dougal lunged forward. More than one man dove for the boy, since there were others nearby, about to get into the boats.

Iain was sliding down the ramp of the rock when a blur went past all of them from a closer direction. A man sliddown the ramp and plunged into the water, snatching the boy from the water and tossing him back. Dougal caught him just as Meg tumbled down into the water with them.

Another wave arched and crashed, and the wind tore wildly. Now Meg saw that Frederick was the man who had surged after Iain. As he scrambled to get higher on the inclined, slippery rock, Meg stretched forward to grab his hands, but missed.

Shoving Iain into her arms, Dougal pushed them safely aside and lunged forward to snatch at Frederick. He grasped his wrists and hauled him onto the rock while the water, agitated and swollen by the coming storm, washed heavy over both of them.

Moments later, they crawled upward and came to their feet. Meg, breathing hard, clasped her son to her and looked at both men, her lover and her enemy. They were all bound to one another now by salvation, by acts of selfless caring—however unwilling the bond might be.

"Frederick," she whispered. "Thank you."

He stared at her, breath heaving. "Madam," he said coldly. He turned to Dougal. "Sir, I thank you. I will not forget it. Nor will I forget . . . the rest of it. But neither of you need fear anything from me. I swear it." He glowered at both of them, then turned and walked away.

With a little sob, Meg stepped into Dougal's arms, as exhausted as he was. Leaning into his embrace, she stood with him in silence, near to tears. Iain crowded between them, and Dougal smoothed his hand over the boy's hair, then dipped down to rest his brow against Meg's head, while the wind whipped and the rain stung.

She stood in his arms, surrounded by his strength, his deep and caring spirit, with their son safe between them. He brought a hand up and cradled her face, kissing her.

Returning it with deep fervor, with a sense of blessed relief and uncommon bliss, she felt her knees falter. A power welled up from inside of her, opening her heart, filling her to the brim with something so warm, so loving and safe, so enduring, that no storm could weaken or threaten it.

As the kiss ended, another began, and another, until she was laughing and tearful, and he chuckled. He pulled back and gave her that sweet, small, private smile that was theirs alone.

And suddenly, while she stood with him on the rock, draped in a blanket with him and with their son, enveloped in the warmth of love that could withstand any onslaught, the wind lessened, and the rain lightened.

Looking up at Dougal in the strange eldritch light of the passing storm, Meg realized, deeply and fully, how very fortunate she was, for the gift of the kelpie had blessed her beyond measure.

He looked down at her, smiling, as if he knew her thoughts. "Let's go home, Mrs. Stewart," he murmured. "We all need some rest. And we can all dream a few more dreams." He looked down, touched Iain's golden head. "They do seem to come true."

Epilogue

April, 1858

"All the way up?" Iain asked, as he and his parents stepped into the shadows in the high, narrow stairwell.

"Straight to the top," Dougal agreed, as he shut the door to the lighthouse behind them. Turning, he smiled at Meg and Iain. "The lighthouse keepers and the commissioners will be here soon, but I wanted to take you two up before the ceremony begins."

"I will be first!" Iain said, as he scrambled up the steps ahead of Meg and Dougal.

Turning to his bride of several months, Dougal held out his arm. "Mrs. Stewart? Are you sure you want to do this?" He knew that she much preferred her most recent title to that of Lady Strathlin, especially when they came to Caransay.

"Of course, but go ahead. You and Iain climb far faster than I can these days. I will take my time, I promise," Meg assured him, when Dougal hesitated, watching her. She placed a gloved hand on her expanding abdomen, hidden by the tented hem of her dark blue brocaded jacket.

"Come on!" Iain yelled down at them, hopping impatiently.

"Wait there, lad—and do not jump about, it makes your mother anxious," Dougal said. He bounded up the steps two at a time to meet Iain on the first landing of the long climb. Sweeping the boy onto his shoulders while Iain giggled, he turned again to be certain that Meg was having no difficulty.

She looked so beautiful, he mused, so graceful, every bit a baroness in her outfit designed by that English fellow in his Paris shop. A blue velvet bonnet was perched on her head, and her golden hair was twisted smooth beneath the drape of a short dark veil. Her rounded shape and full bosom only deepened his desire, his love, and his respect for her. Dougal liked best to see her hair gloriously loose and her clothing simple—as she herself preferred—but he was always proud of her when she adopted the elegant guise of Lady Strathlin.

Dougal wore the black suit he had worn to their small and quiet wedding, and Iain was dressed in a new outfit of brown velveteen, although the boy had protested loudly when Mrs. Berry had produced the thing. Meg had explained to him that everyone must look their best that day, for guests would arrive soon—a party of commissioners and investors would come over the water with Norrie and Fergus. Then the christening ceremony for the newly completed Caran Reef Lighthouse would begin.

Smiling up at Dougal, Meg waved him on. He climbed slowly, glancing back now and again. He knew that she was strong and healthy, and he was proud that she maintained a full schedule whenever they were at Strathlin Castle or the Edinburgh town house. Yet he felt a few anxious qualms about her welfare.

He had missed so much with Iain, and although he made up for that every day, he wanted to be part of the second child's life from the very beginning. He was determined to be available for Meg whenever she might need him, for he had failed at that years before. Recently he had turned down a chance to supervise a new lighthouse on a wild northern sea rock—there would be other opportunities for other light towers.

The birth was four months away, and already he was nervous as a cat. Thora tried to ease his fears, while Elga enjoyed teasing him a little. Both women told him that his apprehension was groundless, predicting that he and Meg would someday have a house full of strong and beautiful children.

"Let me open the door," Iain said, and Dougal set him down so that he could turn the gleaming brass knob in the oak door at the top of the stairs. While climbing, the boy had stopped a few times to open doors on the two levels below, peeking at bunks, kitchen, sitting room, and storage rooms.

Soon Meg joined them at the top, smiling, the faint flush in her cheeks brightening her beautiful aqua eyes, shining like the sea in sunlight. "It's not so very high," she said. "And I think the exercise is very good for me."

"Madam, you did well," he murmured, bowing while he waited for her to preceed him into the lantern house.

The walls of the compact, circular room were glassed all around above the wainscoting, giving an expansive view of sea and sky. The room was dominated by a huge, complex arrangement of glittering prismatic lenses in amber and clear glass.

"Oh!" Meg gasped. "What a beautiful lantern! I've never seen one of these so close." She took Iain's hand and walked with him around the perimeter of the huge light, which gleamed like a diamond, its hundreds of polished-glass surfaces cut like prisms, arranged in slightly angled rows to provide the most powerful illumination. The brass framework and fittings added even more brightness and beauty to the lens.

Pointing upward, Iain stood on his toes, trying to get a closer look. Dougal picked him up and held him high.

"Go ahead. You may touch it," he told Iain when the boy reached out. "The lamps are not burning yet. Oil lamps are used to light the lens," he explained, glancing at Meg. "They are lit at dusk and kept burning until dawn."

"This is what is called a Fresnel lens?" Meg asked.

"Aye, a Fresnel of the first order—there are seven levels of size and power. It was rather expensive to acquire a lantern as powerful as this one, but well worth it. Our investors will be pleased, I think. This lighthouse will be both enduring and functional, and it will protect this part of the coast for centuries." Dougal reached up to smooth his hand over one of the glazed, brilliant surfaces.

Meg went to the window and gazed out over the sea and sky. "How far can the light be seen?" she asked.

"We estimate eighteen miles on a clear night," Dougal said. "In deep fog, when the light may not cast far, there are bells set in a cupola in the roof. One of the keepers will ring out patterns to warn passing ships that there is a reef and a lighthouse nearby."

Meg nodded. "Fergus and Norrie will be quite busy."

"Aye. And I'm glad they were given this assignment. Those two are the perfect choice to be the keepers of the Caran Light. Of course, the Lighthouse Commission considered the excellent recommendations of the resident engineer and Lady Strathlin," Dougal added with a grin. "And The Commission prefers local men as lightkeepers, particularly seafarers, since they understand the moods of the sea and the changing weather peculiar to their own region."

"Grandmother Thora is pleased, too—I know she

worried about Norrie going out each day for the fishing, now that he's getting older. And with three men tending the light, Norrie will still have time to fetch the mail, which he insists on doing."

Dougal set Iain down, and they joined Meg at the window. In the pale, vast sky, gray clouds moved fast over the horizon. Far below the high tower, down at the base of the immense dark rock, the sea was choppy and greenish in the rising wind.

"There! A boat, I see it!" Iain cried, pointing.

"Very observant, lad," Dougal said, peering toward the south. "You'll be a help to your grandfather and to Fergus MacNeill whenever you come to Caransay with us." He ruffled the boy's golden curls. Before their marriage, he and Meg had gently explained to Iain the truth about his parentage—as much as the child could understand at barely six and a half years old.

Iain had accepted the news easily, something Meg had attributed to his young age. Deeply grateful to have gained Iain's affection so readily, Dougal was sure that the boy's trusting heart had been shaped by the generous lessons of love and acceptance taught within the MacNeill family. He knew that he, himself, had learned from them as well.

"That must be Grandfather Norrie with our guests," Meg said, looking down at the boat coming over the water.

"Aye. My dear, I hope you do not object, but I believe Sir Frederick is among them. One of the commissioners mentioned the invitation in his last letter."

"If so, then he is welcome." She touched Iain's shoulder as she spoke. "We will always be in his debt. I sent word through my solicitors that his selfless deed more than paid the monetary debt that he owed . . . the baroness, and that she would not accept repayment of the funds."

"That quality of generosity," he said softly, "is one of the virtues I love best about the baroness."

"She learned the importance of generosity and forgiveness, too, in her struggles with that odious resident engineer," she said, wrinkling her nose.

He chuckled. "There are several men in the boat," he said, watching as the little craft approached the rock. "One of them will be the experienced lightkeeper assigned by the commissioners to train Norrie and Fergus. We prefer three keepers for each light, so that two may stay on duty while the third rests."

Meg nodded and stood silently for a few moments, flattening one gloved hand against the pristine glass. She did not watch her grandfather's boat, but gazed out to sea. Dougal touched her slim shoulder.

"Your thoughts, my love?" he asked quietly.

"I am thinking," she said, "that I was wrong, and that the resident engineer was right."

He looked down at her curiously. "What do you mean?"

"I am thinking," she went on, "that this light is a beautiful monument indeed, a lantern upon a finer future. It stands here in honor of all the lives lost in those waters—my father and your parents among them. With luck, no more lives will be lost because of this great, dark reef, and the future will indeed be brighter for all of us."

Dougal slipped his arm around his wife's shoulders and pulled her close. He dipped his head to kiss her temple softly beneath the tilted brim of her hat. For a moment he could not speak, for his throat tightened.

"I wish," he whispered, "that my parents could have known you. They would surely love you as much as I do."

She smiled silently, and he saw tears glaze her eyes.

"Look!" Iain said, pointing out to sea.

"Aye, the boat," Dougal said. "Thank the Lord

they're so close to the quay at the base of the rock. The winds are picking up. We'll have a storm before long."

"I hope we can finish the ceremony before it sweeps in," Meg said. "Although I would not mind being stranded with you again on this rock, Mr. Stewart"—she smiled up at him so fetchingly that he felt desire spin inside of him—"I do not relish the thought of spending the day in the sitting room of the lighthouse entertaining a group of lighthouse commissioners." She slipped her arm around his waist.

"They would enjoy it, though, for it would give them time to solicit even more funds from Lady Strathlin." He grinned. "Don't fret. The ceremony will not take long—simply the cutting of a ribbon and the sharing of some whisky. No whisky for you two," he added. "Mrs. Berry sent a fruit brose for you both to drink."

"Look there!" Iain said again. "Do you see them?"

"See who, dear?" Meg asked.

"The water horses! Far out on the water. The *eich-uisge,* all of them, are coming this way."

"What?" Meg gazed in the direction that her son pointed.

"What are you seeing?" Dougal asked.

"The white horses, there, in the foam," Iain said excitedly.

Dougal narrowed his eyes. Suddenly he saw, as he had seen once before, the beautiful, prancing shapes of a legion of horses, their hooves pounding forward, their manes spilling down, then rising again as their proud heads and chests were lifted. He watched, entranced.

"Oh!" Meg said. "Those arc wave curls. The white foam on the highest waves sometimes looks like—"

"He's right, my love," Dougal said. "I see them, too. Look there, where the light pours through the waves as they crest."

"Ah, I do see them," she murmured, smiling.

"Must be a hundred, all racing for the rock!" Iain laughed with delight. Dougal scooped him up to give the child a higher vantage point.

"They've come to give their blessing to the lighthouse today," Dougal said. "And you saw them first, my lad."

"He's got the magic of seeing the water horses. And why shouldn't he?" Meg asked with a smile. "He's the son of the most wonderful *each-uisge* of them all."

Dougal chuckled softly and drew them close, his son and his wife and the small one she carried, tucked them in his arms and closed his eyes in silent gratitude. A wave of love poured through him, magical, powerful, wholly real. When Meg tilted her head toward him, he kissed her mouth tenderly.

"We'd better go downstairs now, my dear baroness," he murmured. "We've guests to welcome to the Caran Light."

Author's Note

Scottish legends often tell of kelpies, the water creatures who inhabit rivers, lochs, and oceans. Most common were river and freshwater kelpies who took the form of dark horses or great bulls—these were unpleasant beasties who could drag an innocent human to a drowning death. Sea kelpies appear in the oldest Celtic tales, and are the most ancient form of these supernatural water creatures.

The *each-uisge*, or water horse (*eich-uisge* is the plural form) could appear as either a beautiful white horse—sometimes seen dancing and racing in the strongest waves—or that of a handsome man, often with green eyes. In the guise of a man, the kelpie would find a maiden to bear him a child, and later he would return for his offspring and take he or she with him under the waves, never to be seen again. Tradition claimed that if a maiden gazed upon the kelpie in dawn's light, she would be haunted by her love for him forever.

In *Taming the Heiress,* I wanted to write a romantic and passionate story that would blend Celtic myth with the "modern" setting of Victorian Scotland, when the dynamic tension between tradition and improvement was high. The integrity of the Gaelic culture had been compromised in the eighteenth and nineteenth centuries by English rule, modern advancements, and the devastation of the Highland clearances. However, many dedicated Scotsmen and Scotswomen worked to protect and preserve the ancient and beautiful Gaelic language, legends, music, and customs, and kept them from being lost in an English stew.

Just before and throughout the Victorian age, engineering feats transformed Scotland and opened the remote and beautiful Highlands to the world. Increasing national pride, Queen Victoria's love of the Highlands, and an appetite for adventure fed the burgeoning tourist industry, although the Scots sometimes greeted the wave of visitors with mixed reaction.

Other elements of Victorian life and advancement intrigued me while I researched this story. Diving was used routinely by engineers whose works involved bodies of water. In fact, Robert Louis Stevenson, himself an engineer, wrote of his own experiences while diving to examine the submerged foundation of a lighthouse. The magnificent lighthouses that ring Scotland owe their existence primarily to several generations of the Stevenson family, and I am indebted myself to Bella Bathurst for her brilliant study of those men and their works in her book, *The Lighthouse Stevensons* (HarperCollins, New York, 1999).

I hope you loved Meg and Dougal's story in *Taming the Heiress*. Please look for the other two volumes in my Victorian Scottish trilogy from NAL Signet, featuring characters from this book. *Waking the Princess*—the story of Aedan MacBride's quest to break the ancient curse that prevents him from ever knowing true love—will be out in September, 2003. Then Evan Mackenzie—the newly inherited Earl of Kildonan—returns to the Highland mountains of his childhood to face a private demon and meet a Highland angel in

Kissing the Countess, to be released in November, 2003.

I love to hear from readers, and the best way to contact me is through my website at www.susanking.net. I wish all of you happy reading—and enduring happiness.

If you liked the first book in
Susan King's trilogy, then return to
the Scottish Highlands in

Waking the Princess

Coming from Signet in September 2003

Turn the page for a special preview. . . .

The pool of candlelight revealed stone steps curving around a slim central pillar. Christina Blackburn drew up her skirts with one hand, balanced the brass dish in the other, and descended. The housekeeper had assured her, upon Christina's arrival at Dundrennan House, that she was free to take the old steps down to the library if she preferred to work late at night during her stay.

The narrow, wedge-shaped steps fanned steeply downward, and she moved carefully in the darkness. Since her room was on the third level, she guessed that the library must be on the second or even the first level, but she saw no door as yet. Moments later, she heard a squeak, and felt, over her foot, the breezy passage of a mouse.

Gasping, she jerked, and her thin sole skidded on smooth, worn stone. She reached out for the wall, losing her grip on the candle dish, and recovered her footing, but the brass dish clattered away, extinguishing. Blackness engulfed her.

Muttering under her breath, she turned to inch back up the steps. Hampered by her skirts, the darkness, and the steep, oddly shaped stairs, she missed her footing again and fell hard to one knee. Gathering her skirts, she stepped upward, but tilted and then tumbled helplessly into the inky pit behind her.

Half sliding down the steps, bumping and turning, her shoulder and head knocked painfully against the wall, and her hip struck the edge of a step. Somehow she managed to slow her descent, and soon collapsed in a breathless heap on a stone platform which felt blessedly large and squarish in shape.

Groaning, she sat up a little, then winced, for her back and shoulder ached, and her head spun wickedly. She leaned against the wall and touched her head with a shaking hand.

A latch clicked, a light bloomed golden, and a man emerged from a doorway. Exclaiming softly, he crouched and reached for her. Strong, gentle hands took her shoulders.

"My dear girl," he murmured. "Are you hurt?"

Woozy uncertain, she wondered if she had been knocked cold and now dreamed, for she looked into the face of a warrior angel, strong and dark and powerful. She felt his arms harden around her, and saw the halo around him.

Various small pains told her that she was awake, and a further glance proved that he was only a man after all. Lamplight haloed him, glossed his black hair, poured gold over his shoulders. His arm tightened around her, and she leaned gratefully into his strength for a moment.

Sapphire eyes, straight jet brows, and a thick wave of raven black hair made her catch her breath. He was handsome enough to startle, with the strong, beautiful bones of a pure Celt, a touch of thunder in his snapping eyes and frowning brow.

"Are you hurt?" he asked again.

"I'm fine. I fell." She winced again, and tried to sit up.

"Stay still," he ordered. "What the devil were you

doing in this old stairwell? Don't move. Take a breath."

"I'm fine." She shifted awkwardly, feeling a sharp pain in her shoulder, and began to sit up. "I should go back to my room— Oh," she said, as her head swam. "Oh, my. Perhaps I should sit here a little longer." She leaned against the warm, powerful curve of his arm.

"Just rest for a moment," he said. "Stay still."

Without a doubt, Aedan MacBride thought, she was the girl in the painting. He had wondered, from the moment he had seen her, upon her arrival, if she was the one. How odd that the National Museum, in sending an antiquarian to examine the ancient find on his property, should unwittingly send the model for a rather delicious, and somewhat scandalous, painting in his possession.

Indeed, her face was identical, though she seemed smaller and more fragile in person. Fascinated, Aedan studied her. If she had not modeled for that image, then she had a sensual, beautiful twin.

Behind spectacles framed in blue steel, her eyes were wide and beautiful. He had long wondered at their color: silky hazel, ringed in black lashes. Her overall appearance was demure and modest, not at all like the tantalizing, earthy goddess of the picture. But her graceful features, her lush lips, the long curve of her throat all matched the painting.

She sighed, shifted her head to lean back against his upper arm. A pulse beat under the creamy skin of her throat. Her lovely face, her swanlike neck, and her auburn hair spilling from its pins, she was the living image of the painting.

A little imagination brought to mind the exquisite details of breasts tipped pink beneath translucent fabric, the gentle swell of a bared hip, the long, smooth length of a thigh.

More than simple lust blazed through him in that instant. He felt a desperate, burning need to hold her, to save her, to love her. Leaning forward, for one wild moment he nearly kissed her.

Then he jerked back, saving himself from acting a damned fool. The urge still rushed through him, fervent and hot. Never had he felt such a shivering heat, like a deep force pulling at him. He actually trembled in its aftermath.

He cleared his throat. "Miss Blackburn," he said.

Her eyes opened. "It's Mrs. Blackburn. Christina Blackburn. How do you know me?"

Christina. Somehow that crystalline, graceful sound suited her perfectly. "I know everyone else in my house, but not you. Therefore, you must be the lady sent by the museum. Welcome to Dundrennan, Mrs. Blackburn," he drawled. "I am Sir Aedan MacBride, Laird of Dundrennan."

She blinked slowly. "Sir Aedan . . . oh!" She tried to sit up.

"Relax." He grasped her shoulder to keep her still. "I do not think you are quite ready for stair climbing."

"Perhaps not." She squinted up at him, narrowing her eyes in the lamplight that spilled from the open doorway behind him.

Her little spectacles were missing, he realized. Seeing the delicate steel frames within easy reach, he plucked them up and handed them to her.

She perched them crookedly on her nose, and looked at him again. "Thank you. Forgive me, Sir Aedan. I wanted to go to the library this way—Mrs. Gunn said it would be all right—but I fell. I do apologize."

"Not at all. Had I known, I would have ordered the sconces lit in the stairwell. Generally only I use this stair. Can you stand, Mrs. Blackburn?" He rose, keeping hold of her arm.

She began to lift to her feet, then faltered, wincing.

"You're in no condition to go up or down, my lass," he murmured, and bent to scoop her up into his arms. She felt slender and fit beneath layers of clothing, and he picked her up effortlessly.

"Really, sir, I'm fine," she protested.

He shifted her against his chest, and she circled an arm around his shoulders. "That was a nasty fall, Mrs. Blackburn. Come inside. I want to be sure you're uninjured before you go wandering anywhere else tonight."

Mortified, Christina rode silently in his arms as he carried her over the threshold into a small, lamplit room. Her head ached, as did her shoulder and hip, and she was grateful for the reassuring strength of his arms.

His face was close to hers, his scent a pleasant mix of spice, wine, shirt starch, and subtle, earthy masculinity. Dressed in a white collarless shirt and a dark vest and trousers, the hardness of his torso pressed against her softer curves. She could feel the heat of her own blush, unseen in the dimness.

The room was similar in shape and function to her own little sitting room, although it contained one armchair and a desk. An oil lamp on the desk surface revealed an untidy pile of papers and open books. The fireplace housed a cozy peat fire. Sir Aedan MacBride set her in the leather armchair, her back to the hearth.

"Really, I am fine. I must go, sir." She rose, and pain sliced through her hip and shoulder. Sir Aedan guided her down with a firm hand on her shoulder.

"Not so fine as she claims," he said, kneeling beside the chair. "Tell me where it hurts, Mrs. Blackburn." His earnest concern, his nearness, thrilled her unaccountably. He was a stranger to her, and yet he seemed familiar somehow, his manner relaxed, confident, and engaging, all at once.

"I really must go—"

"Sit." He detained her with a gentle hand.

"But this is . . . your private sitting room." Through a second door, she saw a bedroom with a canopied bed, its covers folded back, pillows plumped. A dark dressing robe lay on the bed. "This is very improper," she protested.

"It's more improper to send you away limping," he said. "No one need know about this but us, madam." His voice was low, his glance penetrating.

She subsided in the chair, and he dropped to his haunches to look up at her. Firelight flowed over him, and his eyes were dark blue and sparkling.

"Mrs. Blackburn, please tell me where you are hurt."

She relented, shrugged. "My . . . left shoulder."

His hand slid up her arm, his fingers tracing over her shoulder, pressing lightly. Something elemental tumbled inside of her, and all she could do, when he asked what she felt, was nod dumbly or shake her head in silence. Withdrawing along her arm, he took her hand to move her fingers one by one.

A wonderful feeling surged through her, and her hurts lessened wherever he touched her. She dared not look at him, feeling her cheeks heat like fire, but she watched the grace of his hands upon her.

"Nothing seems broken. Where else does it hurt, madam?"

"My . . . head," she whispered. "And my . . ." She could hardly tell him that her hip and bottom felt bruised, though her ankle also felt strained. "My . . . ankle."

"I have a sister and female cousins. I've tended to twisted ankles before, without scandal, I assure you." He smiled.

She extended one foot, and he pushed her skirts above her ankle. Sliding his fingers over her foot, he flexed it gently. Shivers cascaded all through her.

"Those slippers," he murmured, "are not suited to a medieval staircase."

"So I learned," she answered, setting her foot down.

"Your head hurts, too?" he asked. She nodded, and he leaned toward her to spread his fingers in a cap over her head, probing. She nearly groaned with the sweet pleasure of it. When his arm brushed over her blouse, her breasts tingled, tightened.

"Oh,'" she breathed.

"Does something else hurt?" He glanced at her.

"Oh, no," she murmured.

"There is a bump on your head, but all seems well, though I am no doctor. No doubt you'll feel some bruising for a few days." He rested his hand on her shoulder.

Even the simplest of his touches stirred a craving in her, a ready rush of desire. She had not felt like that in a long time.

The warmth of his fingertips, the rhythm of his breath upon her cheek as he bent toward her, the clean, male smell of him—all of it seemed to tap a wellspring of need in her. Sucking in a breath, she leaned away. Feeling no threat from him, she knew the wariness came from her lonely, aching, foolish heart.

She moved as if to stand. "I must go now. Thank you, sir."

"Stay. I do not want you climbing those stairs just yet." Willingly, she sank into the chair again, glad for an excuse to remain, to feel his delightful, relaxing touch again.

"You'll need to rest tomorrow, and use soothing packs on those aches, I think," he said.

"I cannot rest tomorrow. I came here to work, and I must go to the hillside in the morning to look at the excavation site for the museum. Truly, I'm fine, Sir Aedan." She stood slowly, and he rose beside her.

"Stubborn lass." He frowned. "You might have broken your neck on the stairs in the dark, in those cumbersome skirts and little slippers. What was so important that you took the stairs alone, and at this hour?"

"I could not sleep. I have a habit of studying and writing late at night, and I wanted to look up some local history and geography before I went out to the hill tomorrow. I'm sorry to have troubled you, sir. Thank you—very much." She stepped past him, wincing and stiff, feeling a little embarrassed, and a strong sense of surprising regret. After tonight, she would be merely his guest from the museum, and he would be the properly distant host. They could never again touch so freely.

Turning toward the door, she stopped, and gasped.

The painting hung over the fireplace. She had not noticed it until now. Heart pounding, she walked toward the hearth and gazed up at her own image.

She had forgotten what a masterpiece it was, exquisitely rendered, a passion of luminous color and sensuous shape, poignant and powerful. Lamplight and shadows heightened its astonishing dark grace.

"Dear God," she whispered.

He stood behind her. "You haven't changed."

Her heart pounded. So he knew that she had posed for it—he had already plumbed the secret that she had tired to hide for seven years. Slowly, she turned to stare at up at him.